Runn

Praise fo

'Sidesplittingly comical an ....gly tragic . . . A brilliant debut' *Cosmopolitan*

'Hugely funny. You often hear about books which combine humour and pathos, but very rarely do they live up to the billing; this one does . . . Maxted writes beautifully not only about death, but about regrets over what might have been, while at the same time writing a social comedy about current social movers with some seriously sharp dialogue' *Express*

'Witty and clever . . . Like Bridget Jones, it refuses to gloss over life's ordinary squalor; unlike Bridget, however, its heroine's traumas are serious, giving it an edge which makes her predecessor's worries laughably small. It's compelling, humane and worryingly funny, and better written than many more "literary" novels.' *Evening Standard*

'Readable, often poignant and always funny . . . Revealing a touch for comic timing and versatility, she paints scenes of hilarious pitfalls, biting sarcasm and heart-wrenching pathos. While comparison between this work and [Helen] Fielding's is unavoidable, Maxted's laugh-out-loud debut novel will come out ahead.' *Publishers Weekly*

'Maxted is a gifted comic writer and she manages to extract humour from even the most unpromising situations . . . had this reviewer laughing out loud' *The Times*

Anna Maxted is thirty-one. She lives in London with her cats, Disco and Natascha, and her husband, Phil. She read English at Cambridge, and is a freelance journalist. Her first novel, *Getting Over It*, was published by Arrow to great acclaim and was a bestseller in Britain and America.

Also by Anna Maxted

Getting Over It

Running in Heels

Anna Maxted

ARROW

Published by Arrow Books in 2001

1 3 5 7 9 10 8 6 4 2

Copyright © Anna Maxted 2001

Anna Maxted has asserted her right under the Copyright, Designs and
Patents Act, 1988 to be identified as the author of this work

This novel is a work of fiction. Names and characters are the product
of the author's imagination and any resemblance to actual persons,
living or dead, is entirely coincidental

This book is sold subject to the condition that it shall not, by way of trade
or otherwise, be lent, resold, hired out, or otherwise circulated without the
publisher's prior consent in any form of binding or cover other than that in
which it is published and without a similar condition including this
condition being imposed on the subsequent purchaser

First published in the United Kingdom in 2001 by Arrow Books

Arrow Books Limited
20 Vauxhall Bridge Road, London, SW1V 2SA

Random House Australia (Pty) Limited
20 Alfred Street, Milsons Point, Sydney, New South Wales 2061, Australia

Random House New Zealand Limited
18 Poland Road, Glenfield
Auckland 10, New Zealand

Random House (Pty) Limited
Endulini, 5a Jubilee Road, Parktown 2193, South Africa

The Random House Group Limited Reg. No. 954009
www.randomhouse.co.uk

A CIP catalogue record for this book is available from the British Library

Papers used by Random House are natural, recyclable products made from
wood grown in sustainable forests. The manufacturing processes conform
to the environmental regulations of the country of origin

ISBN 0 09 941019 2

Typeset by SX Composing DTP, Rayleigh, Essex
Printed and bound in Germany by Elsnedruck, Berlin

For Phil Robinson, my hero.

Acknowledgements

Last time I was quite mean with my thank-yous so, be warned, I intend to compensate. I couldn't have written *Running In Heels* without the help of a lot of very kind, patient, generous people. So, huge thanks to: Phil, for your love, support, jokes and genius (sorry, but Cheryl and I are allowed to say that); Cheryl herself, for all matters relating to food; Mary, for withstanding yet another fictional nightmare mother; my best sister, Leonie, for dutifully reporting every 'He wears slippers, yes, but he's not from London' anecdote; Jonny Geller, occasional luncher and best agent in the world; Lynne Drew, for her brilliant editing and her willingness to attend pantomimes; Andy McKillop for his kindness and support; Mark McCallum for the lunches; the very clever Grainne Ashton; Ron Beard, who never gives up; Karen Gibbings, my aeroplane partner; Kate Parkin for general loveliness; Glenn O'Neill for the gorgeous cover; and all the talented people at Random House, without whose help this book would still be a vague notion in my head.

I had great fun (some might say, too much fun) researching *Running in Heels*, and I am enormously grateful to all the following people for their time and expertise: gorgeous Jim (I adore you); Anne Sacks, a wonderful loyal friend; Jo, the Queen of Hearts (you're so glamorous); Elizabeth Ferguson and Jane Devine, you were great; Jane Paris, so were you; John 'is this restaurant swanky?' Perry, to think that once I didn't like you; Paul Byrne, forgive the dyslexia; Steve from Contempo; Judith,

Ray, Wendi, Sophie, Martin, Pier, John Nathan (I made it all up, honest); Caz Mercer (for knowing everything); Jason Rackham (Tony couldn't have done it without you); Gina Short, in the nicest possible way Frannie owes you; Harry Selby, the fixer; Emma Beattie, for being inspirational – and letting me ride in the fire engine; the men on her watch (frankly, you'd set your own house on fire); Steve Vassell, you hero; Maurizio of Amici Deli, any mistakes are mine; Uncle Ken: Phil and I think you're great; Eleanor Bailey, my fellow mother at toddler group; Trevor Blount, Pilates guru; Anna Cheevley, you're mad; Sam Neville, for talking and talking; Frank Tallis, you clever man; Lucy, for knowing Italian; Deanne Jade, for her expertise; Elizabeth Davies of the National Osteoporosis Society, thank you.

Lastly, this is a book about friendship and – except for the slaps – a tribute to Leah Hardy, Alicia Drake-Reece, Jo Kessel, Sarah Maldese, Wendy Bristow, Sasha Slater, Laura Dubiner, Emma Dally, Anna Moore, and Caren Gestetner, all of whom helped me with *Getting Over It*, and much, much more.

Chapter 1

The bride is climbing a tree.

'Babs, that branch looks unsafe. Are you sure—?'

Crash. Splash.

'Oh well,' she says, squelching from the pond, a happy green and brown mud monster. 'At least I got the ball down.'

A *tut!* of wonder drags me from my thoughts and I realise that the bride is no longer twelve years old and soggy. She is all grown up and gorgeous, a Botticelli come to life. There is a swish of silk and a rustle of taffeta as my best friend halts and turns to face her groom. Her gaze is so intimate that I look away. A goose honks, or, possibly, my mother blows her nose. The vicar smiles crossly until there is quiet, then compares marriage to building a house.

I'm craning over the rows of prettily feathered hats, when my brother digs a sharp elbow into my ribs and says, 'There's nothing like a big bride. Always reminds me to lay off the cake.'

I blush. 'Please, Tony!' I whisper, 'Babs is Amazonian.'

My brother needs attention like other people need to breathe, but despite his ungracious presence this day is a perfect day for Babs. It is her own personal fairytale made real in a haze of confetti and lace. She looks radiant. And I know as I sit here, sighing and cooing with the rest of the crowd, that I'll never forget her wedding as long as I live. It is the beginning, and the end. The start of a marriage and the end of a beautiful relationship. Ours.

*

To say that Babs is my closest friend is like saying that Einstein was good at sums. Babs and I know each other like we know ourselves. We were blood sisters from the age of twelve (before my mother prised the razor out of Babs's hand). And if you've ever had a best friend, you'll know what I mean. If you've ever had a best friend, I don't need to tell you about making blackberry wine in the garden and being rushed to hospital, puking majestic purple all the way. Or about our secret language (which is lucky, because I'd have to kill you). Or when we touched tongues to freak ourselves out. Or about our Spanish holiday aged sixteen. Or when Babs dated the coolest, tallest, blondest guy in school and set me up with his wetter, shorter, prematurely balding friend. (He wasn't keen on me either.) Or when Babs thought she was pregnant and we bunked biology to beg the morning-after pill from her GP.

I don't need to tell you of the endless talk about details – the use of toothpaste to zap spots, the way some dads suddenly bolt to LA with their secretaries (adultery is rarely original), being fitted for a first bra in a shop where rude old ladies roar out your chest size, the odds on marrying Matt Dillon, wearing an orthodontic brace that Hannibal Lecter would reject as unflattering, mothers who collect you from parties with their nightie showing under their coat – so much talk, we talked ourselves into our twenties.

Even when our ambitions defined us, we couldn't bear to be apart. I chose a London college to be near Babs. We shared a flat, we shared lives. No man could hurt us like we could hurt each other. Blokes came and went – and feel free to take that literally. There were a few serious boyfriends, and a lot of jokers. We weren't too bothered. There was always next Saturday night and anyhow, we were in love with our careers. Babs and I had such a beautiful relationship, no man could better it.

And then she met Simon.

*

2

I watch him slip the ring on her finger and see his hand tremble. What do I know? Is this love, or a hangover? Dubious thoughts to be having in church, so I file them under 'envy', kiss and hug the happy couple, and when Tony mutters, 'I've counted seventeen strings of pearls,' I ignore him.

I squeeze through the perfumed crush of guests, to where the table plan is mounted on a large easel. I'm hoping to be sat next to at least one of Babs's Italian male relatives (her mother Jackie is from Palladio, a small town near Vicenza, and its entire population – seemingly composed of film stars – appears to be present). I scan the Ms until I see Miss Miller, Natalie. *Table 3*. There is a disappointing dearth of Cirellis and Barbieris on this table, but it's a nice distance from Mrs Miller, Sheila *(Table 14)*.

That's the trouble with close friendships formed in early adolescence. Your families see it as their divine right to muscle in and before you can say 'inter-parental surveillance,' the lot of them are as enmeshed as the jaws of a zip. Having been shadowed by my mother throughout the service, I'm pleased that we're dining apart. She'd have tried to cut up my poached salmon for me.

I jump as someone smacks me on the bottom.

'Fluff,' trills my mother. She gazes at me, licks her finger and rubs it around my cheek.

'Mum!' I feel like an extra in *Gorillas in the Mist*. 'What are you doing?'

'You've got red lipstick all over your face, dear,' she explains.

'Oh. Thanks.' (It would be cheeky to suggest that lipstick is preferable to spit.)

'So who've you been put with?' she demands, peering at the board.

'Tony—'

'Ah! He wears a tux beautifully!'

'Frannie—'

'Frances Crump! A dot of blusher would make all the

3

difference. She looks like a gypsy in that purple skirt. I don't know what Babs sees in her, yes, who else?'

'Er, some guy called Chris Pomeroy—'

'Sounds like a poodle, who else?'

'Andy—'

'The brother of the bride? The brother of the bride! What an honour! I must go and say hello, haven't seen him for years what with all that fiancée business, terrible shame, and leaving his job like that. Apparently he only got back last week, darling, you *must* remember to thank Jackie, a note *and* a telephone call I think would be appropriate, not tomorrow though, she'll be inundated, leave it till Monday, would Monday be best? Yes, I'm sure Monday would be best, the day after your daughter's wedding is always fraught, although saying that, what would *I* know—'

If you haven't already guessed, my mother has a habit of thinking aloud. Incessantly. I suspect it comes from living alone, but it's a quirk easier to understand than to tolerate. When the Master of Ceremonies orders the *ladies en gentlemen, boys en girls* to take their seats, I'm the first to obey.

The chairs are adorned with winter roses. White roses in January. I find mine before anyone else has even approached the table. I check the namecards on either side. Tony is on my left and poodle man is on my right. Frannie – in an error comparable to handing a pyromaniac a blow torch – has been placed next to Tony. I am studying the menu (which I already know by heart as Babs devoted as much time to it as a scribe on the Magna Carta), when the chair beside mine is yanked out and a man wearing a white jacket and a crumpled black shirt sags into it. I look up, smile doubtfully, and he nods, once.

Under cover of the menu, I watch Andy. He is leaning across the table listening to Frannie.

Tony's eyes gleam. 'All right, Anders!' he roars, slicing through Frannie's chat like a knife through lard. 'How you doing? Bit swish, this!'

Andy – who is irritatingly tanned – raises a hand and grins. 'Good to see you again, Tone,' he says. 'We'll catch up!' He winks at me, mouths 'Hello, Natalie,' then turns back to Frannie.

His memory may be selective, mine isn't. Twelve years ago, when Babs and I were fourteen, our older brothers were great friends. They had masses in common, for instance a pathological desire to make their sisters' lives wretched. Where do I start? When Babs and I took Silky Drawers, her family retriever, for a walk and Tony screeched in front of the neighbourhood, 'Anders, look! There's three dogs!' When my mother gave Andy a lift home and I sang in the car and Tony said afterwards, 'Anders found your singing very amusing.' When Andy released my budgie from its cage because it 'looked depressed' and it flew to the top of the curtains and Tony tried to coax it down with a broom and crushed its head.

And there was other stuff.

I smooth my napkin on to my lap. Tony has been distracted by the little disposable camera, placed in remarkably good faith on the table for guests to record their own celebrations. He unwraps it, and slides low in his seat until his hand brushes the floor like an orang-utan's. Then he casually tilts the lens so that it points up Frannie's skirt.

'Tony, no!' I whisper, trying not to giggle. 'Don't, please, you know what she's like, she'll prosecute!'

Tony's blue eyes crinkle and he cracks up laughing. He wriggles upright and punches me gently on the arm.

'I'm playing with you, floozie,' he grins. 'Your face though. Priceless.'

Tony (thirty this year) is like a hyperactive child – sugar and encouragement are bad for him. I bite my lip and squint at poodle man's namecard. Then I tap him lightly on the arm and say, 'Excuse me, Chris, could you possibly pass me the water?'

Chris, who is picking a cigarette to bits on the cream

5

tablecloth, slowly turns and looks at me and my heart does a double take. I wish I was either wittier or invisible. The man has a face like a fallen angel. Dark shaggy hair, designer stubble, sulky brown eyes, and a wide pouty mouth. My mother would describe him as in need of a Dettox bath. As for me, I'd join him in it. He looks down a fraction, at my chest then up again, glances lazily at my namecard, and drawls, 'Yes, *possibly* I could pass you the water.'

He retrieves the Perrier and pours.

'Thank you,' I mutter, cursing my mother for teaching me manners. Chris leans back in his chair and doesn't smile. I snatch up my glass but – I am still being ogled like a lab rat – feel unable to drink from it. I am about to take a sip when he leans towards me and says, 'You have a blow-job mouth.'

I nearly bite through the crystal. My brain paddles in thin air for a second, then from nowhere, I produce a reply. 'But what a shame you'll never know for sure.'

I scurry upstairs for a cigarette and try to compose myself. My hand shakes as I flick the lighter. You can't just *say* what you think. And what is a liability like Chris doing at Babs's wedding? You don't meet dark smouldering sex beasts at weddings (I *knew* I'd be cordoned off from the Italians). You meet balding Keiths who wear Next ties, work in marketing and laugh at their own jokes.

I suppose I have the groom to thank for my good fortune. Babs has a protective nature and if she'd devised the table plan I'd have been sat next to the vicar. I grin and lean over the balcony. Andy is still listening to Frannie. He raises a finger and gets up. I wonder where he's going. I glance at the top table and I see the bride bend towards the groom. His head is tipped back like a fire eater and he is gulping champagne from a large flute. She whispers in his ear. Instantly, Simon places his glass on the table and gives it a small push away from him. Wow. It must be love.

I close my eyes. Babs would still be single if it weren't for me. It was her idea to go clubbing ('Come on, Nat. It's a seventies night. I'm sick of the modern day, I need to dress up!'). But I approached Simon. Normally I don't approach men. I'd prefer to approach a grizzly bear: you have less chance of being rejected.

But this was different. I was trying to locate the beat in *Ain't No Stoppin' Us Now* and wishing I hadn't worn a poncho, when a lanky guy in brown flares and stacked heels clumped up. 'Where's Scooby?' I thought. But Shaggy looked through me as if I was wearing glasses (pink heart-shaped glasses, to be precise), placed a hand on Babs's lower back, and shouted something profound in her ear. I believe it was, 'Are you a model?'

Babs, who weighs eleven stone in her socks, tossed her hair and tee-heed daintily until her cartoon suitor relaxed. Then she stopped laughing – in that abrupt way that gang bosses do in films shortly before they execute a minion – and shrieked, 'Are you a moron?' A smarter man would have run for it. But Shaggy chuckled senselessly and roared, 'No, but seriously, what do you do?'

Babs bellowed, 'I eat men like you for breakfast.'

Shaggy smirked and yelled, 'I look forward to it.'

By now, I was feeling about as edgy as a goat in a voodoo doctor's waiting room. I slunk off, lit a cigarette to give my presence meaning, and watched Babs dance. Two smokes later, she staggered over.

'He's called Will,' she boomed. 'He's not such a dollop as he looks. Come and chat to his mates.'

Conscious that *I* was dressed in the theme of 'the decade that style forgot' while all the other women were glam-rock to the tips of their fake eyelashes, I declined.

'I'm wearing a red fright-wig,' I said. 'I look like Ronald McDonald. I might go home.'

Babs pouted. 'You're all right if I stay?' she asked.

I hesitated then nodded. 'Oh! yes. Yes.'

Babs beamed and said 'Brilliant.' Then she added

humbly, 'I don't know why he picked me with *you* about – he must be blind. Blind drunk, maybe.'

All very consoling. But as the girly rule 'I'm So Rubbish You're So Great' was, in fact, written by me, I didn't fall for it.

'Go and play,' I mumbled. 'I'll see you tomorrow.'

I shuffled off to the Ladies and, as I emerged, passed Babs on the way in. 'Will's at the bar getting me a vodka Redbull,' she said gleefully. 'Check out his beautiful arse!'

I dutifully scanned the bar for nice bottoms, but saw none. But I did see a huddle of guys, all crumpled with laughter, except one, who was shaking his head.

'You bastard, Will,' drawled the head-shaker, a tall bloke in a safari shirt and dark trousers. 'You're such a *heel*.'

Apart from the fact I'd never heard the term 'heel' applied to anything but a foot, I was intrigued. I crept closer.

'She'll find out, Will. She always does.'

'She won't. She's not back till tomorrow night. Look, I've bought some bird a drink, I've not shagged her!'

Got it. And, while I am the girl that geese say 'boo' to, I won't have Babs made a fool of. I poked Will in the back and said, 'I'd drink that drink myself if I were you.'

Will burst out laughing. 'Yeah? And why's that?'

'Because when I tell Babs what a sleaze you are she's going to pour it on your head.'

Will laughed again but head-shaker looked embarrassed. 'Who – er, who are you?'

I was wondering whether to repeat the Ronald McDonald line when a small worried voice said, 'Nat, what's going on? Where's Will?'

Head-shaker and I swung round to see Babs standing forlornly in front of us, and a large empty space where Will and his henchmen had been.

Head-shaker gazed at my friend. 'Barbara, isn't it?' he said softly. 'I'm terribly sorry, but Will had to go. I – er, well, to be honest he's a twit. His loss. Your friend and I were arguing about it. But I'm Simon, and if you don't mind, I'd love to buy you a drink.'

I grimaced but Simon looked through me as if I was wearing orange tie-dye trousers. Within seconds I was feeling like a goat again. This time I went home immediately.

That was five months ago, and now this! I look down on Babs in her frothy white dress and can barely believe it. I should have realised there was mischief afoot when she went missing for three days.

'Don't worry, though,' she purred when she finally bothered to call. 'I'll do your share of the washing-up rota next week!'

To which I retorted, 'Thank you, Barbara, and now if you'll excuse me I have to call the police to inform them the search for your body is now off.'

I wanted contrition but got instead, 'Good idea, because Si's been conducting his own investigation! Pah ha ha! It's been very in-depth!'

'It's very *English*, isn't it?' says a voice, making me jump.

Andy leans his arms on the balcony railing, and turns to me, smiling.

'It's lovely,' I reply, torn between loyalty to Babs and wanting to snub Andy.

'Mum didn't want to have hymns – Italian weddings don't have hymns – but Simon's parents wouldn't budge.'

'Your parents are very easy going,' I say. I hope this doesn't sound friendly.

'Unlike Simon's. I think Mum and Dad feel like Germany at the Treaty of Versailles.'

'That's a shame,' I reply. I have no idea what he's talking about.

'So, Nat,' he says. 'How about a dance later? To *Rule Britannia*, probably.'

'Well, I—'

'We should, we're practically brother and sister!'

'Thank you, but I already have one brother,' I say. 'And believe me, he's more than enough.' I return to our table.

Tony is chatting to a Keith over Frannie's abandoned chair. My brother and Frances Crump do not get on. She calls him an 'unreconstructed Neanderthal' while he refers to her as 'Forkhead' (meaning he'd like to stick a fork in her head). I glance at the top table and see Frannie crouching before Babs like a eunuch in front of Cleopatra. I swallow hard. I don't get on with Frannie either. Frannie is The Third Friend. She follows Babs around like a pimple on a bottom.

I smile helplessly at Chris who grins in a way that squeezes the air from my lungs.

'I can't be doing with weddings,' he drawls. His voice is soft and scratchy, honey on gravel. Its faint northern twang goes straight to my knees. He holds my gaze and adds, 'Normally.'

I smile and say, 'Me neither.'

Chris tips back in his chair. He seems to have ants in his pants. Meanwhile, Babs and Simon are smooching up for the first dance.

Chris murmurs, 'I'd ditch all this and go to Vegas.'

I giggle and say, 'Me too.'

Then we fall silent as Kenny And The Drum Kit Krew start up a terrible racket which is faintly recognisable as *You're Nobody Till Somebody Loves You*. This is a hardline wedding, I think, as everyone claps. My mother, I notice, applauds so furiously she looks like a Venus fly-catcher on speed.

'I'd go to Vegas,' says Chris again. He and I sit out *Lady In Red*, and *Come On Eileen*. I ask Chris why he's not wearing a tux like all the other men. His answer is to sniff twice, and cast a withering look at all the other men. Andy, I note, is dancing with Frannie.

'Vegas,' mutters Chris.

'As you said,' I say politely. He grinds his teeth and I'm

10

not sure if he has Alzheimer's. He then asks why I'm wearing a brown hat. My answer is that my mother over there making a spectacle of herself to *Agadoo* said I should, except I don't get that far because Chris grabs the hat from my head, drops it on to the violently-patterned carpet and – as I sit there frozen and speechless – unpins my butterfly clasp and rakes his hands through my hair, shaking it out so that it tumbles over my shoulders.

Then he leans closer and closer until we are nearly touching and I can almost taste his bittersweet breath.

'Natalie,' he murmurs, twirling a yellow curl around his finger. 'You should let your hair down more often.'

I am dazed and drooling at the delicious raw nerve of the man when a white moon face appears between us, forcing us apart, and Frannie sings, 'Nataleeee! Where's your boyfriend? Saul Bowcock!'

11

Chapter 2

I've known Babs for a long time. I know what makes Babs laugh – place names like Piddlehinton and Brown Willy. I know what makes her cry – anything, from news reports on starving children to the end of *Turner & Hooch* when Hooch dies but leaves behind a legacy of puppies. (She bawled, 'It's not the same!') I know she hates small teeth, and the texture of apricots. I know she gets a rash from underwired bras. I know she can beat Tony in an arm-wrestle. I know she has a tiny black spot above her left knee, from a childhood accident with a sharp pencil. I know her favourite words are 'hullaballoo' and 'pumpkin'. I know what Babs sounds like when she's having sex.

So you can imagine my pique when Babs re-introduced me to Simon a week after the seventies night fiasco and he said, 'So, ah, how do you know Barbara?' I could barely believe he'd made such a blunder. Like asking God, 'So, ah, how do you know Adam?'

'How do I *know* her!' I squeaked before lowering my pitch as bats were falling out of trees clutching their ears. 'I've known her for ages,' I choked eventually. 'We're very close friends.'

I was too stricken to say more but the question stormed round my head like a bully in a playground. How obsessed must Babs and Simon be that in seven solid days of crash-course intimacy, she hadn't mentioned me? I soon found out. Their enthralment was mutual and total. There was endless fondling in front of me. I wanted to roar, 'Stop it at once!' But they literally had eyes and ears for no one else.

When I spoke, or smiled, they barely saw or heard. I was excluded. It was offensive. It was like a thief shutting you out of your own home. I couldn't believe it. *My* boyfriend could have written a thesis on Babs within a fortnight of knowing me. But then maybe Saul Bowcock is less in love than Simon.

Maybe Saul is too sensible to be in love. We are driving – at a sensible speed – to my mother's solitary white house in Hendon to attend a celebratory dinner for Tony's latest promotion. (From Executive Marketing Manager to Vice-President of Marketing at Black Moon Records. Although, as my boss Matt observed, 'I'll bet there's a Vice-President of Teabags at Black Moon Records.')

Saul likes seeing my mother, as she clucks and fusses after him in the vain hope that he'll propose to me. 'Should we stop off and get Sheila some flowers?' he says, slowing as the traffic lights turn amber instead of speeding up like a normal person.

'Good idea,' I nod.

That's the trouble with Saul. He's considerate but he's also so screamingly *proper*. He is allergic to straying from his schedule. He thinks an impulse is a deodorant. I glance sideways at his face, and try to think kind thoughts. Saul is a nice man. Honest. Predictable. Safe. Affectionate. The only man I know who taps his girlfriend on the back and says, 'I need a cuddle.' 'A willy cuddle?' said Babs suspiciously, when I told her. No! A fully-clothed frisk-free *cuddle*. Saul isn't like other men. We met nine months ago at the chiropodist's and his chat-up line, I'm sorry to say, was 'You have such an intelligent face. What do you do for a living?'

As he was never going to get anywhere with any woman ever with hopeless patter like that – surely even the Pope has a sharper spiel – I didn't have the heart to snub him.

'I'm senior press officer for the Greater London Ballet Company,' I replied kindly. 'And you?'

'I'm an accountant,' he told me solemnly. 'But I do have a nice car.'

I wait in the green Lotus Elise while Saul hurries into Texaco to purchase a bunch of fiercely coloured blooms, and bite my nails. Or rather, bite the skin on my fingertips as I finished my nails last week. I am looking forward to dinner as I look forward to a cervical smear test. It's nearly a fortnight since Babs's wedding and I know my mother will want to dissect it and I don't have the energy to fight her off.

'I wonder what Sheila's cooking for supper,' says Saul as he bounces into the driver's seat. 'I'm famished!'

Barry Manilow singing *Copacabana* is audible from the driveway. In a powerful puff of Dune and fried onions, my mother appears, straightens my jumper, and crushes the air out of Saul in a pincer hug.

'Don't you look well! A crying shame you missed the wedding!' she exclaims, shaking her head so fiercely I'm surprised it doesn't come loose. 'But you managed to get all your work done?'

Saul gratefully breathes in upon his release, and says, 'Yes, thank you, Sheila.' My mother scuttles off to fetch him a glass of milk. Yes, a glass of milk. Saul is a strapping twenty-nine-year old but he drinks more milk than a parched baby elephant. Call me lactose intolerant but it's a trait I can't get along with. It's almost as odd as his habit of sleeping with a black jumper sleeve over his eyes. Which is like *The Mask of Zorro* without Antonio.

I follow my mother into the steamy kitchen while Saul collapses on the sofa and starts shelling pistachios. I can hear the crack-crack-cracking sound. I chew my fingers and look around. The shelf above the hob is jammed with books. On the left is *The F Plan Diet, The Hollywood Pineapple Diet, Beverly Hills Diet, Complete Scarsdale Medical Diet, Dr Tooshis High Fiber Diet, The Grapefruit Diet, Dr Atkin's New Diet Revolution, Reader's Digest*

Mind and Mood Foods, Rosemary Conley's Complete Hip and Thigh Diet, Carbohydrate Addicts Diet: The Lifelong Solution to Yo-Yo Dieting, The Food Combining Diet, Dieting with the Duchess, A Flat Stomach in 15 Days and (the altogether less efficient) *32 Days To a 32-Inch Waist.*

On the right is *The House & Garden Cookbook, Step-by-Step Cooking with Chocolate, Delia Smith's Winter Collection, Leith's Book of Desserts, Good Housekeeping Cookery Club, Evelyn Rose – Complete International Jewish Cookery, At Home with The Roux Brothers, The Dairy Book of Family Cooking, Mary Berry's Ultimate Cake Book, The Crank's Recipe Book, A Wok for All Seasons, A Table in Tuscany, A Little Book of Viennese Pastries, Amish Cooking, 365 Great Chocolate Desserts, The Naked Chef* and *The Artful Chicken.*

'What can I get you? When did you last comb your hair?' demands my mother as she tips a brick of Lurpak into a casserole dish. 'Orange juice? You look like something out of Black Sabbath.'

I reply, 'Water's fine. I'll brush it in a sec.' I watch as she pours a slick of sunflower oil on to the spitting butter. She's an expert on heavy metal but thinks cholesterol is a vitamin.

'Are you sure you need all that, Mum?'

My mother wipes her hands on her apron, 'And what do you know about cooking herby orange poussin?'

Fair point. 'Well, would you like me to make a salad?'

My mother hands me a glass of water, flaps at me with a Beefeater dishcloth and says, 'You'd only chop your finger off. You be a good girl and go and chat to Saul.'

As I trudge towards the lounge, the cloying stench of alpine breeze air freshener intensifies with every step (it's never occurred to my mother to open a window). Then someone presses his entire bodyweight on the poor little doorbell and keeps pressing. Drrrrrrrrrrrggggggggg!

Tony. My mother zooms past me in a blur and wrenches open the front door. 'Hello, my love,' she says in a

15

sympathetic tone, in honour of the exhausting trek he's made from Camden Town in his black BMW 5 series 2.0 520i four-door saloon. 'How are you? Here, let me take your coat. Hard day? What can I get you? Something to drink? I've got that champagne you like in the fridge and I'm doing your favourite desserts, lemon syllabub and chocolate cheesecake. I know it's naughty but we deserve a treat. I went to Weight Watchers yesterday so tonight I'm free!'

Tony kisses Mum and grins. 'Mother,' he sighs, 'you're a saint. I can hardly believe we're related.'

I smile with my mouth shut. Since the divorce Tony and I are hostage to my mother's needs. Except Tony plays the game better than I do. (In fact, he plays it so well you might suspect him of cheating.) Mum dyes her hair black, tends to wear yellow, and carries a handbag tucked under her arm like a machine gun. You don't want to upset her in the way that you don't want to upset a wasp. She lost her capacity for fun fourteen years ago when my father scribbled her a letter on his surgery notepaper that began, 'Dear Sheila, Sorry about this but I'd like to jump ship on our marriage . . .'

You'd think that such an event would dissuade her from chasing her offspring up the aisle. No, indeed. She read *Bridget Jones's Diary* and cried. I kiss Tony hello, and brace myself. Our bottoms brush our chairs and she's off, like a greyhound after a rabbit.

'So Barbara got her happy ending. I spoke to Jackie last week, and this morning, and yesterday – oof. Such a plush do. Altogether she felt it went very well. The groom, Simon, nice looking boy. You'd never think it, what with his mother's jaw and teeth. What a fright. And her dress. Cream. And with a figure like that. You just can't. It did nothing for her, nothing. I said to Jackie, you looked at *least* twenty years younger than her, at least. You were the belle of the ball, apart from Barbara, of course. She looked a picture, she really—'

'Mum,' says Tony, with a sly glance at me, 'She looked

like what she is. A fireman in a skirt.' Saul coughs into his watercress soup. I place my spoon at the side of my plate. Tony has not forgiven Babs for making him the victim of her party trick (in front of an audience, she flipped him over her shoulder and ran down the road with him, as if he were as light and inconsequential as a blow-up doll).

I say, 'Babs is a fire *fighter*, Tony. That's the correct term. And she did look nice. Tanned, tall—'

'Why aren't you eating?' interrupts my mother. (She's justly proud of her cooking and takes offence if you slow down during a meal to, for instance, breathe.)

'I *am* eating,' I cry, hoping to ward off an explosion. 'It's delicious.'

I wave my spoon in the air as evidence, as my mother says, 'I go to all this trouble and you sit there huffing at your soup like it's bilge water! I don't—'

'Sheila, you must be very proud of Tony,' suggests Saul. 'I forget. How many times have you been promoted in the last year, Tony?'

My brother shrugs and replies, 'Three.' Saul and my mother and I wobble our heads in unison.

'Amazing,' murmurs Saul. He coughs, curling his fingers into a tube to, I presume, catch the cough. 'You must be marvellous at what you do.'

My mother exclaims, eyes glazed, 'Oh, he *is*, Saul, he's such a credit to me, he's so talented!'

Saul smiles at her and says, 'And so are you, Sheila, this watercress soup is sensational. I don't suppose there's any m—'

'Of course there is!' booms my mother. 'My pleasure.'

'Are you sure?' replies Saul, ever the gentleman. 'I mean, Sheila, have *you* had en—'

'Me?' she exclaims, 'Don't be ridiculous! I'll heat it up for you.' She speeds to the kitchen at the pace of a cheetah in a rush and I slump in relief.

'Nice one, Saul mate,' murmurs Tony. 'Don't know when to stop, do I?'

17

Saul beams with pleasure and gratitude. I suspect it's the first time in his life he's been called 'mate'. Then again, there's something about my brother that bewitches people. He is without doubt an Alpha male. You want to please him. A smile from him is like a kiss bestowed by a film star.

I look at Saul, who grins back. 'I didn't realise you were so fond of watercress soup,' he says. 'I can make it for you if you like.' I suppress a whimper. Saul is to cooking what whirlwinds are to Kansas.

'That's sweet of you,' I reply, 'but I thought you were going on a health kick.' Saul's face drops.

'You what!' hoots Tony. 'You're not dieting are you? You big girl! You want to play a bit of sport, mate. *FIFA 2000*, something like that!'

Saul blushes. 'I'm, er, actually I'm not all that good on the football field—'

'It's a video game, Saulie,' I murmur, as my mother bustles in. She deposits a bowl of soup in front of my boyfriend with the reverence of a courtier presenting the crown jewels to the king, and instructs him: 'Eat!' We sit in brief silence while Saul eats.

'Didn't think much of the food at the wedding,' exclaims my mother, who has been itching to reintroduce her specialist subject for the last three minutes. 'Now if *I* were organising a wedding, not that I ever' – here, in deference to Saul, she catches herself – 'Well, if *I* were to organise a wedding I'd spend a lot less on the drink, it's not necessary for people to get so away with themselves, and a great deal more on ensuring the food was restaurant quality because – and naturally I didn't say anything to Jackie – but the asparagus were' – here, my mother's voice drops to a low hiss – 'tinned!' We digest the import of this grave news in silence. 'And the shame of it is,' continues my mother, 'that Jackie wanted to have food from the deli. But Simon's parents were paying and they insisted on using *their* caterers,' she adds, in the tone of one personally affronted by this slight.

I catch the scent of an approaching tailspin.

'But you liked the dancing, didn't you, Mum?' I say, in an encouraging tone. 'You're a bit of a Ginger Rogers when you get going.'

'Well, I hope not! She's so old she's dead!' retorts my mother.

'I reckon Mum had been at the Special Brew – you're a bit partial to a can of Special, aren't you, mother?' grins Tony.

'Anthony, stop it!' My mother's mouth is a stern line, but she is trying not to laugh. 'That was once, and a long time ago, and you gave it to me in a wine glass and said it was *Chateau de Sleepeengruff*. I wasn't to realise it was so potent! Anyway, as if they'd serve lager at a smart wedding like Jackie's. I mean, Barbara's!'

My mother adores being teased by her son, so all hail to my brother, the evening is resuscitated. That said, when Saul drops me in slow motion at my flat later on, I am too tired to invite him in for coffee (by which I mean a cup of Nescafé). Which is fortunate, since when I press the play button on my large grey dinosaur of an answer machine it whirrs and clicks and grumbles before drawling – in a dry breathy voice that makes my skin tingle – 'Hi, Natalie. I've been thinking about you . . . letting your hair down.'

19

Chapter 3

I've been suspicious of letting my hair down since Rapunzel let down hers and found a ruddy great bloke on a horse hanging off it. Let your hair down and before you know it you're wearing elastic waistbands, eating pizza in bed, and justifying the purchase of an £800 coat from Harvey Nicks on the thin premise that you haven't had children, a facelift, or a month's holiday on a large yacht in Monte Carlo, and have therefore saved yourself a vast sum and are technically economising.

Even so, I think of Chris and drool. After Frannie shattered the mood with all the grace of a demolition van, reality hit and I blushed. 'I'm sorry,' I blustered to Chris, 'I am seeing someone. I – er, you are lovely but I shouldn't be doing this. It's bad of me.'

But Chris seemed unruffled by Frannie's interruption. He stared at her and said, 'Why are you so white?' When she withdrew, speechless and bristling, Chris tutted. 'If there's one thing I can't stand,' he said, 'it's rudeness!' I hurriedly lit a cigarette and breathed in the nicotine like – well, like a drug. Chris added, 'It's *bad* of you? You don't know the meaning of bad.'

Aware that I was coming across like Mary Magdalene at a mixed sauna, I replied squeakily, 'Yes I do.'

'I'd like to show you,' said Chris.

'Actually, I –' I began.

'So do you have a number or is it classified?' he said.

'I didn't bring anything to write with,' I croaked.

'Well, princess, how about you scrawl it on my chest in

lipstick,' he replied. I smiled as he removed a slender pen from his jacket and handed it to me. Then he pulled a Rizla from its packet and gave me that too. Obediently, I scribbled down my home number. I'm sorry, but he was so pushy and, for the first five minutes of a relationship, I like that in a man.

'Don't use it,' I said, to salve my conscience.

I listen to his message again. My heart jumps like a cricket in a box. The man should come with a health warning and a free chastity belt. I won't call him though, it's not fair on Saul. Saul is so trusting. If only he was suspicious I'd feel justified. No. I *can't* call Chris. I mean, I really can't – I don't have his number. Then I press 1471 and I do.

I stare at the pale blue walls of my hallway until they blur. I wonder. I still can't call him. I won't. I'm with Saul Bowcock. We're in a sensible relationship (as Romeo said to Juliet). I can't cheat on him. It's not fair. I can't end it. I don't end relationships – it's too upsetting. I'm fond of Saul. Really. He's a sweetie. If only Babs were here I could bore her about it. She'd know what, or who, to do. I double-lock the front door and plod along the corridor to bed. Surely she's got to be back from Mauritius soon; it seems like she's been on honeymoon for the last decade.

The first thing I *used* to hear on walking into the office was, 'Your mission is to retake the building with minimal loss of life,' but not any more. Matt – my immediate boss – has been promoted to Head of Press and Marketing and now shuns computer games as 'underplaying the pressures of the real world'. This morning he is hunched in front of his screen and acknowledges my entrance with a silent wave. His basset hound, Paws (full name, Pas de Quatre), is slumped at his feet chewing at a pinkish rag.

'Dinner OK?' says Matt, still tapping.

'Not *too* terrible.' I'm touched that he's remembered. 'How's Stephen? Is he still in hospital?'

Matt swings round. 'No. He was discharged – mm, nice word – on Saturday.'

'How is he?'

'Crotchety, demanding, no change there. But the main thing is, I've escaped to the orifice, and you survived dinner. *Were* there lots of wedding questions?'

I nod. Matt rolls his eyes. 'The bride, wasn't she beautiful? That dress, wasn't it faaabulous? The groom, wasn't he a dish? Oh, I love a wedding, Natalie dear – Saul, such a pity you missed it! Am I warm?'

I giggle. 'You must have had me bugged.'

'Your life fascinates me. And I'm gagging to meet that wicked boy Simon.'

'I'll bet you are,' I say. A small sigh escapes me.

'Hey. Don't be miz. She'll come back. They didn't live together, did they? Oh lord. Six months of pooey pants on the floor and bristles in the bath and noisy wees and car rows and crusty socks stuffed down the side of the sofa and you'll see more of Babs than you did when she was single. And I should know.'

'Aw Matt, I *am* happy for her, bu—' I'm interrupted by a loud canine cough. Sounds like a basset hound choking on a dirty pink shredded rag – oh my God, it's a pointe shoe! 'Where did Paws get the shoe from?' I ask, glancing in horror at what Matt and I call the tat cupboard. I'd like to blame Belinda, our assistant (a woman whose mouth never quite shuts, even when she's not talking). Pity she's on holiday in Crete for two weeks.

'What shoe?' says Matt. I lurch to the cupboard and start raking through the rubble on the second shelf.

'It's the one signed by Julietta,' I groan. 'He's only gone and pinched the one signed by Julietta!' Julietta is our Principal Dancer. The Greater London Ballet Company has six, but Julietta is a principal principal. She has hair the shade of buttermilk (mine is tart-blonde compared to hers), moves like a wisp of heaven, and – as one critic put it – is 'womanly, without it spoiling her line'. She is intelligent, intense, and has a thing about people thinking ballet dancers are stupid. She terrifies me. The media love her, and once in a grovelling while we'll persuade her to sign a worn pink satin shoe which then serves as a competition prize – supposedly for some ten year old girl, but probably for a middle-aged male.

'The shoes are on the second shelf,' I say. 'Paws is the height of a toadstool. What did he do – stand on a chair?' By now, Matt is crouching beside Paws. He has thick black hair (Matt, I mean – Paws is brown and white) and five o'clock shadow at 11 a.m. When he smiles his face creases with laughter lines. He isn't smiling.

'You's a bad dog,' he says lovingly. 'Naughty naughty boy!' To me, he says, 'Did you lock the cupboard door on Friday before rushing off to the gym?'

I stop myself from pulling at my hair. 'I was sure I did. But anyway, how could he reach?'

Matt sighs. 'Paws has diddy little legs, Natalie, but he makes up for them with his impressively long torso.' A pause. 'What's got into you lately? Nat, for someone in a senior position you're doing a good impression of an airhead. You used to be so efficient. And now is not the time to be seen as dead wood. Lock the damn door in future.'

I flinch. Matt is more like a friend than a boss. It's horrible when he asserts his authority and dispels the illusion. *You used to be so efficient.* I flashback to Matt buying me an orchid after I got a willowy senior soloist a picture spread in *Hello*. And to Matt kowtowing and crying; 'We are not worthy!' after I cajoled the *Daily Mail* into doing an interview with our Artistic Director and – the surprise bonus – printing it. Suddenly, I'm furious at my mistake. Especially as Matt is correct: now is *not* the time to be seen to be slacking. The company has exceeded its budget (they went all out on *Giselle*, hiring a white horse and a pack of beagles to make the hunting party's arrival in the village more dramatic. Unfortunately, the

23

horse trod on a beagle and killed it, resulting in a lawsuit). The rumour is, a 'restructure' is imminent.

I blurt, 'I can't believe I was so stupid. What a thick, stupid, brainless prat.'

Matt holds up a hand and says, 'Easy on the sackcloth, dear. What's done is done. Wheedle Julietta into signing another shoe. Although it's not *my* idea of fun, other people's verrucas.' I think Matt takes pity on me because after a pause, he says cheerily, 'He's my dog. I'll ask her. Later. When I'm begging about the other stuff.'

'What other stuff?'

He drops a copy of *Hiya!* magazine on my desk. There, on its shiny toilet-paperish cover, nestling naked in a snowy heap of feathers, is Tatiana Popova, star of the Southern Royal Ballet – our main competitors who for their winter season are staging *Swan Lake*. Normally, the Southerners are so stuck up, you'd think their every swan had laid an egg. But here is Tatiana, getting into bed with a downmarket rag. That's *our* turf!

'The Southern have gone tabloid!' I gasp. 'How dare they! No wonder *Hiya!* didn't return our calls!'

'I'm seeing the boss in three minutes,' says Matt. 'To explain our counter-strategy.'

'What counter-strategy?'

'Exactly,' says Matt, drawing a finger across his neck. 'I bequeath you Paws,' he adds, marching to the door. 'One thing, though,' he calls from the corridor. 'The *Telegraph* is getting back to us *re* a possible shoot with Julietta. See what you think. The minute they call, see about getting it pencilled into the Ballet Schedule. I'll speak to the dancers, and then we'll go to work on the details. Guard the phones with your life!'

I salute in the direction of his voice, and when the phone rings I leap on it. From now on my standard of work will be so high, I'll make God look like a slacker. Resting on the seventh day indeed!

'Hellogreaterlondonballetcompanypressofficehowmayi helpyou?' I say breathlessly.

'Natalie? Germaine Greer is chairing a debate on Thursday at the Barbican,' declares Frannie through her permanently blocked nose. 'I have a spare ticket and I thought you might benefit.'

'Oh! Hello, Frannie. That's very kind of you. What a surprise!' I wince. That came out wrong. Or maybe not.

'Not at all. As I say, I thought you might benefit.'

I bite my lip. The problem I have with Frannie is that she refuses to be nice, even when she's being nice. 'What's it about? It's lovely of you to think of me.'

'*Is gender a continuing identity or a feature of personality?*'

'I don't know.'

'Oh Natalie, really. I'm not asking you, that's the title of the debate!'

'Right. Well. The thing is, Frannie, work is very busy this week and –'

'If you don't want to come, Natalie, that's your right and you can say so.'

'No, no, no, it's not that, I –'

'You don't want to come. Not a problem! By the way, I spoke to Babs last night.'

'What!' I gasp. Eventually I say, 'What, you called her at the Paradise Cove Hotel?'

'That would hardly have been appropriate. She and Simon flew home yesterday morning. Babs called *me*.'

'But, but –' I blurt. Then I stop. Cool as a cucumber, cool as a cucumber, I tell myself.

'But why hasn't she called *me*?' I bleat, cool as a boiled cucumber.

Frannie sighs happily. 'She can't call everyone,' she replies.

Having dealt her knockout blow, Frannie trips breezily on to other topics. But I am deaf with confusion and mute with pique. My nose is so out of joint I consider going

25

straight to casualty. Call *Frannie*! Call Frannie and not me? Babs always calls me! Even when we lived together we rang each other three times a day.

I wait until Frannie has said her piece (and it's a bloody big piece). Then I call Babs.

'Yeah?' says a sleepy voice.

'Babs!' I exclaim. 'It's me! Why haven't you rung? How was it? Did you have an amazing time? Was it hot? Are you outrageously brown?'

There is a brief silence then Babs says stickily, 'Oh hi, Nat, hello love. What time is it?'

I glance at the clock. 'It's, er, it's quarter to ten.'

Babs groans. 'I'll kill you! It's the middle of the night!'

I feel like I did aged six when I blundered in on my father naked. 'Oh no!' I squeak. 'Did I wake you up?'

'Forget it,' she yawns. 'My fault. I should have taken the phone off the hook.'

'It's just that I was excited about you being back. You, you rang Frannie, so I – I . . .'

There is no reply and I can make out a husky voice in the background saying, 'Who is it?'

And then I hear Babs reply distantly, 'Natalie Miller.'

Natalie *Miller*. How many other friends has she got named Natalie?

'Sorry, Nat,' says Babs, loud in my ear. 'Him indoors. What were you saying?'

'Not much,' I reply grumpily. 'I'd been expecting to hear from you, that's all.'

'Give us a chance! We only got in last night!'

'I know,' I say hurriedly. 'But –'

'Natalie,' begins Babs, 'you're worse than my mother. I *was* going to report back to you, the minute I woke up. The reason I rang Frannie last night was because she'd wanted to come round this afternoon, and frankly, I'm way too tired for that kind of excitement.'

I grin down the phone. 'Oh of course, Babs, I'm sorry. So . . . how was your honeymoon? Was it wonderful?'

'Mmm, yes, yes it was,' replies Babs, yawning. 'A-r-r-r-r! thank you.'

I decide that as she seems to be in an unshakeable trance, this isn't the time to ask her how the sex was. I say instead, 'Your wedding was gorgeous, Babs, really fantastic. Everyone had a lovely time.'

For the first time, there is real joy in her tone. 'Oh thank you! Did you think so? We thought so. It was wicked, Nat, I can't tell you how brilliant it was! Mad but brilliant. We can't wait to get the pictures back. It went so fast though, but really, it's true what they say, it was the best day of our lives!'

I giggle. I didn't realise that marriage confers royalty alongside its tax benefits. 'How do you know that when you haven't yet *had* the rest of your life?' I say teasingly.

'You're right,' says Babs. 'I should say, second best. The best day will be when I give birth to our first child.'

With great self-command, I don't faint. I whisper, 'You're not – are you pregnant?'

Babs giggles. 'Not yet,' she replies. 'We're still practising.' And then, 'So you loved the wedding then?'

'It was great,' I say warmly. 'Wonderful. It was nice to see Andy again. In f—'

'Arr! I know! I'm so happy he's back! He was pleased to see you too, he said he couldn't believe how much weight you'd lost –'

Bloody cheek. 'So what's he saying? That I was fat before?' I force a laugh. 'But Babs, guess what, there was something I wanted to tell you about the wedding. You know the guy I was sitting next to?'

'Er, we had a hundred and fifty guests. Remind me.'

'Chris! Chris Pomeroy?'

'Oh yes. Chris. He's an old mate of Si's.'

'Well . . .' I take a deep breath and tell her about Chris. When, eight minutes later, I stop talking, there is no response.

'Babs?' I say, 'You still there?'

27

'Oh Nat,' she murmurs. 'What about poor old Saul? He adores you.'

I don't know what to say. Finally, Babs speaks.

'Look, doll,' she says. 'Right now I've got a head like cotton wool. Let's talk when I'm more awake. I'll give you a shout later. You take care.'

I sit at my desk opening and shutting my mouth like a large wooden puppet and then I pull a small tear of paper out of my bag, smooth it defiantly in front of me, and dial the number scrawled on it. I replace the receiver just as Matt reappears.

'You look like a cat in a dairy,' he remarks. 'I assume the *Telegraph* is champing at the bit?'

'No, sorry,' I say. 'They didn't call. I'll give them a ring in a sec. But – I have a date. Tonight. With a drop-deader!'

'Naturally you don't mean Saul,' says Matt. 'Do tell.'

Matt, unlike Babs, is eager to encourage me on my way to sin. His mood is restored because our Director of Public Affairs decided he adored the *Telegraph* idea – an exclusive pic of Julietta in Verona, for their Valentine's Day issue – to trumpet our spring season performance of *Romeo and Juliet*.

Matt extends my lunch hour so that I can shop for a new me. And when I roll in disguised as a bag lady he volunteers to sort the retail wheat from the retail chaff. It's a poor harvest. For instance: 'Those boots are going back, you look like you're standing in a pair of buckets. Oh lord, you'd fit both my aunts in that top. A skirt from Laura Ashley? How old are you, Natalia, forty-five?...' I wouldn't mind but Matt is the worst dressed gay man I've ever met in my life (all his creative energy is spent on Paws). He sighs, and clips the pampered one to his Gucci lead. Then he marches me to Whistles, and orders me into a clingy pink shirt. I feel like a large sea worm and try to sneak a baggy cardigan past him but he confiscates it. Like all my friends, Matt gets a kick out of spending my money, and within forty minutes has cajoled me into buying a tapering cream corduroy skirt, and a pair of tall brown snakeskin boots. It's like being fitted for a first bra all over again except this time I'm paying for it. His last words are, 'I trust you're wearing decent knickers.'

When Chris shows up at 6.45 I am a new, if poorer, woman. And I'm ready to rock.

Chapter 4

I won't watch TV alone. When *Brookside* is on I have to have someone else in the room, or I feel like a loser. There are exceptions, obviously. *Buffy the Vampire Slayer* is allowed. But not *Roswell High,* it tries too hard. *Martial Law* is borderline. *Wheel of Fortune* is so utterly sad that you might as well shun society altogether and live in a caravan with a chemical loo. I suppose I'm not very good at being alone. But the truth is, I felt alone long before Babs left the flat to get married: she was so busy practising her new signature and obsessing about whether the brides-maids should wear roses or ribbons in their hair, that Radio Two was better company. Not that I'm saying I'm lonely, bu—

'Princess,' says Chris, interrupting. I stop talking so fast my mouth shuts with a clack.

'Sorry,' I slur, wobbling my glass at him. 'One sniff of the barmaid's apron and I start babbling.' As I say this, I moan inwardly. *One sniff of the barmaid's apron!* When I'm nervous I start talking like a granny in a BBC sitcom circa 1973. And Chris is so deeply darkly sexy that my intellect is melting. I am so square and he is so carelessly cool, that the harder I try to match him, the more I blurt out ninety-degree blunders like 'pertaining to'. I may be possessed by a demonic bureaucrat.

'Princess,' says Chris again. We are sitting in a cold sleek bar in EC1 and he is stroking the inside of my wrist. 'You're like an icicle scared of melting.'

An icicle scared of her boyfriend walking past. I glance

furtively at the huge pane of red glass that divides us from the street.

'You know what you remind me of?' he adds, leaning close. I shake my head. Chris taps his ash on to the granite floor and declares, 'An urban fox. You're so . . . watchful. And wild at heart.'

I know this is a compliment but as the only urban fox I've ever seen was an orange creature so obese from foraging through bins that it wheezed, it takes me a while to look pleased. I bend over the mean stub of a candle on our grey Formica table, light a cigarette, then say, 'Oh, thank you . . . Er, you never told me what you do.'

Chris swigs his White Russian. 'I manage a band,' he says, gazing at me with sleepy brown eyes. He grins and adds, 'I'm a servant to rock.'

As such a preposterous claim could only be made in jest, even by Ozzy Osbourne, I expel a puff of air through my nose in amusement and – it snuffs the candle! 'Sorry,' I say, hastily relighting the candle with a match. 'On non-fox days I moonlight as the Big Bad Wolf.'

Chris laughs, and I feel ridiculously gratified. I feel I could live on the sound of that laugh. I scrabble to think of something else to amuse him.

Silence.

I soon realise that Chris is blissfully unfettered by the normal constraints of polite conversation (the necessity to talk). So I say, 'How do you know Simon?' Chris looks mystified, so I add, 'the groom.'

'Uh, Simon was one of those geezers who was, like, around. Can't say I think he's done the right thing. He's an all right bloke, Simon, but he's twenty-five, he's still a kid. You're big mates with his missus.'

I think this may be a question. 'Yes. Babs. She's lovely. It's weird, her being married. I know it sounds awful but I feel like I've been robbed. Did I tell you she's a fire fighter?'

Chris grins. 'Do you reckon she carried him over the threshold then?'

I giggle. 'So what's the name of your band?' I say, in a rush of confidence. 'Should I know them?'

'Blue Veined Fiend,' he replies proudly, like a new mother revealing the name of her firstborn. He rummages in his pocket and pulls out a crumpled flyer. 'You will know them. They're going to be massive. They've got the vibe.'

'They sound great,' I say, knowing that Tony would spit on them. ('You can always judge a band by its name. If they don't have the inspiration to give themselves a good moniker, what else can they do?') 'Which label are they signed with?'

Chris replies, 'I'm on the brink of a mega deal.'

I glance at the flyer. The Fiends' last gig was at the Red Eye, near the Caledonian Road. To put it kindly, this is the music industry's equivalent of Off Broadway.

'That's brilliant,' I say carefully. 'Have they played anywhere else?'

'The Orange,' says Chris. (Off Broadway, turn left, over the roundabout . . .)

I don't repeat what I know from Tony: an unsigned band should not continually play gigs up town because 'the A&Rses will only go and see them once'. (Tony is not a fan of A&R men as he has to – and I paraphrase – 'work their rubbish'.)

I say, 'I'm sure the Prodigy will be their support band in no time.'

Chris smiles, sunshine after rain. 'I'll play you their demo,' he says, his sandpaper voice dark with passion. 'You'll love it.'

I beam. Suddenly I feel more hip. (Last week, Saul and I queued with a frankly aggressive swarm of pensioners to hear the BBC Concert Orchestra play Bach at the Hippodrome in Golders Green.)

'I like you, Chris,' I blurt. 'You're fun. It's like' – I can feel the champagne bubbles popping in my head, deleting braincells as they go – 'it's so nice to be sitting in this bar, you know, talking, and, I mean, look around, I bet, I bet not one of these people is marr—'

Chris stops me by pulling me to him and kissing me. He tastes illicit and delicious. Lip to lip he murmurs, 'A little less conversation, a little more action, please.' And the fact that I know Elvis said it first doesn't make it any less appealing. I am weak with desire. I stand up and let Chris take me home.

Radio Four harangues me awake at 7.45 a.m. and it takes me a second to realise why I feel like a slug on Mogadon. I gingerly approach my conscience to see if I feel guilty and – quite rightly – it slaps me round the face. I bite my lip. What time did he leave? I wriggle under the duvet and dream of last night. Kissing in the taxi like rampant teenagers (though as a real teenager I was more dormant than rampant), tumbling into my baby blue flat, then realising that beneath my retro skirt and saucy boots lurked a timeless contraceptive: knee highs.

'Wait!' I screeched, peeling Chris off me. 'I'll be back, I'm just going to' – I racked my brain for a cute excuse – 'the toilet.' I ran into the bathroom, and when I ran out eight minutes later (after a futile attempt to erase the pop-sock marks) Chris seemed manic with excitement. I was wondering whether to explain that I hadn't actually *been* on the toilet all this time, when he yanked me to him and ripped off my clingy pink shirt! A bold maneouvre that would have been all well and good had we been Hollywood film stars, getting it on in our latest block-buster, where all our designer items came courtesy of the wardrobe department. I was so horrified, I nearly protested. My new shirt, sacrified for the sake of two seconds' showing off!

I'll never be a rock chick, I thought, staring at the scatter of pink buttons on the floor. The first time Saul kissed me, he asked respectfully, 'May I have a kiss?' Chris didn't ask. He kissed like a demon sucking out my soul. His stubble rubbed my chin but – as other body parts rubbed more pressingly – I didn't care.

'You're getting a cold,' I said, kissing his nose.

'And you're getting hot,' he purred. 'Come here and be corrupted.'

I shuffled towards him.

'Lie down,' he whispered. 'I want to eat you.'

I blushed and couldn't say it back. I tried not to think like a nanny (now, boys and girls, have you washed your privates?) and let him push me on to the kitchen table. At first I was as relaxed as a lobster in a pot. I kept slamming my knees shut and squeaking. It didn't help that Saul rang at this point and left a message. ('Nat, the Royal Shakespeare are staging *Coriolanus*, I thought we might book tickets, the mid-range seats are fairly reasonable.')

Chris paused from his toil and muttered, 'How do you stand the pace?'

I covered my eyes and cursed Saul for tarring me with his mid-range brush. Saul never goes down on me – I vetoed it and he's too polite to protest. Chris wasn't.

'Come on, darlin',' he said in the creamy voice one might use to coax a small kitten down from a tree. 'Just relax, it's going to be beautiful.'

And, to my surprise, it was. I felt like a piano being played by a genius. What can I say? It's like admitting to a criminal record or collecting stamps. The sordid truth is that I've tried to love sex but we've never clicked. It's always been a gauche tangle of arms and legs and 'excuse me's'. Probably my fault for shaking off my virginity with a man who exclaimed, 'You've got hairs on your bottom!' But then maybe I'd have been a disappointment even with a bum like an apricot.

Babs couldn't understand it. She bought me a vibrator and a filthy book entitled *The Joy of Selfloving – Sex for One*. 'You can't wait for a bloke to make it happen,' she scolded. 'You might as well hang round Tesco's waiting for

34

the Messiah. You need to know how to make it happen yourself.'

But the harder I tried the worse I got, until my knickers froze if I overheard the word 'coffee'. The one time I successfully thawed, the guy pinkly jiggled out of the room in a huff and bawled from the corridor, 'It's like trying to get blood from a stone!' After that I preferred to fake it. (I screamed and screamed and raked my nails down their backs.) And now, from nowhere: Chris Pomeroy, purveyor of the big bang. It was so unexpectedly glorious, my eyes watered.

'You didn't look like a girl who was getting any,' Chris murmured later as we shared a cigarette. 'You're built for it, princess, you've been wasted.'

I scruffed up my hair so it hid my face but he smoothed it back.

Then he added, 'I'm going to have to love you and leave you, gorgeous girl – things to see, people to do.'

I felt a flutter of panic, but he said he'd call me. Minutes later I was as deeply asleep as if I'd been hit on the head with a bin lid.

I grin at the clock – it's 9.20 a.m. Guilt about Saul briefly squeezes my insides but thick lust stifles it. I've never felt this sort of longing before. The sex is not enough, I want to infuse myself with Chris, wallow in Chris. And a small mean part of me feels triumph – *you* can't do this any more Barbara, you're stuck with the same man, the same thrills, but I am free – Hang on a minute: *9.20?* – shit! I ping out of bed, run to the wardrobe, and drag out clothes, I'll be late for work, I am never late for work, never, I can't be, I won't, Chris Chris Chris what have you done to me, I race to the tube. Do I look different? I have a creepy suspicion that people are staring. I race from the tube, and hurl myself into the office at 10.15, panting like Paws after the trek from his food bowl to the sofa. It's deserted.

There's a message on my voicemail from Matt, saying he'll be out all day in meetings, but the Chief Exec has

OK'd the *Telegraph* press trip to Verona (we're paying), so 'Thunderbirds are go.' I grin. Matt's happy absence surely marks the rebirth of my reputation. I compose a treacly letter to the Italian State Tourist Board press office outlining our plan. I also spend an inordinate amount of company time dribbling and sighing over Chris. I am loath to use the phone for work purposes in case he calls.

I am dawdling between the words 'magnificent' and 'majestic' (schmoozing is a precision art) when the door creaks open and a pale child with black pigtails and a petulant mouth peeps around it.

'Melissandra,' I say, snapping to attention. 'How *are* you?'

Mel glides in, her gossamer form muffled by leggings and tights, a thick jumper, and a mysterious wraparound item, possibly a skirt or shawl.

'I'm tho-tho,' she says, gazing at me through lowered lashes.

'Oh dear!' I say. 'Why's that, can I help?'

Mel frowns, and replies, 'Pothibly.'

I smile encouragement. Mel might look like Pippi Longstocking but she is twenty-nine-years old. She is a good dancer but, allegedly, not as good as she thinks she is. Matt's verdict on seeing her as Clara in *The Nutcracker* was, 'A bit glacial for me,' and the critics agreed. 'Melissandra Pritchard,' they wrote, 'is technically perfect but parched of passion: the Gwyneth Paltrow of ballet.' The company consensus is, she adds nothing of herself to a role (confirmed when a ballet mistress begged Mel to 'interpret' the movement, and she snapped, 'I'm a dancer, not a choreographer!'). But she is beautiful. She looks as fragile as spun glass.

'Would you like some water?' I say gently.

'No thanks,' lisps Mel prettily, bending low over my desk and lifting one leg up and up and up until it is vertical. 'Did you hurt your face?' she adds.

'My faith?' I splutter. 'Oh my *face*' – please, I think,

36

don't hold back! The eye bags must be worse than I thought – 'Um, no, I just didn't have a chance to do my make-up yet.'

Mel shoots me an odd look. She says, 'I've got some cover-up stick.' I try not to show offence.

'It's so sweet of you,' I reply. 'But I'll be fine. More importantly, tell me what I can do to help *you*.'

Mel extends a slender arm and tugs gently at her raised foot (which is currently hovering above her head). This impossible maneouvre requires no effort at all. I gaze at her and wish I could do that. Unfortunately I am as pliant as a dry twig. I'll go to the gym tonight.

'I am upset,' announces Mel, lowering her leg, and pulling anxiously at her red pigtail ribbon. 'I respect Julietta, I think she's a sweet dancer, I won't have a word said against her . . .' – I brace myself for the torrent of slander that always follows this phrase – '. . .but it's not fair that she hogs all the publicity, she's always in the paper, every day there's a massive picture of her showing off her nice swayback legs – which I must say are so hyper-extended they're practically deformed! – and I can't see how she ever has time to rehearse – she seems to spend all her time talking to journalists! I'm a principal too, why can't they interview *me*?'

Mel's lower lip wobbles. I feel a rush of pity.

'Don't be upset, Mel,' I urge. 'I'll sort something out for you,' I add rashly.

Mel claps her hands and – to my surprise – flings her arms around me. It's like being hugged by a bag of nails. 'Do you promise?' she cries. 'Thank you so, so much!' She pauses, then says, 'I know! Why don't we go for a coffee and talk about it? You could sit in on rehearsal on Friday then we could go out. Out of the building! I don't know anywhere around here but I'm sure you do! It would be fun, oh please say yes!'

I'm shallow enough to be chuffed at the chance to chitchat with a star. I am also mesmerised by her eyes, so huge and blue and doleful, how could I refuse? I agree and watch her skip out. She sings Tori Amos' *Cornflake Girl* all the way down the corridor.

I grin and realise my chin hurts. A spot. Great: my first orgasm and I get a rash. I force myself not to touch it or look – this place is made of mirrors and frankly I'm sick of the sight of myself. Then at 6.03, after a day of sullen silence, the phone rings. I grab it like a drowning man grabs at a twig.

'Hello?'

'Hi, Natalie, it's Sally at reception.'

'Hello, Sally,' I reply, trying not to droop.

'I have a gentleman here to see you.' Her voice drops – 'I guess he's to blame for your *intriguing* appearance today.' And then at her normal pitch, 'Shall I send him up?'

The comments on my lack of lipstick are starting to unnerve me. Maybe I suffer from inverted body dysmorphic disorder and am twice as ugly as I think I am. But lust conquers all and I cry, 'Yes, yes, oh thank you, send him up now!' I feel ashamed of doubting him.

'My pleasure,' says Sally with a giggle. 'He'll be right with you.'

I slam down the phone and start running in different directions – I fumble for my make-up bag but it is wedged at the bottom of my bag by that great big bully of a book, *Stalingrad*, lent to me by Saul (I keep meaning to start it). Finally I wrench out the make-up bag. I am poised to click open my powder case when I hear a gentle knock. I stuff it out of sight and rake my hands through my hair.

'Come in!' I croak.

My caller strides in, clutching a large bouquet of deep red roses, and my heart sinks.

He looks at me and the smile dies on his face.

'What,' says Saul in a voice I've never heard before, 'is that on your chin?'

Chapter 5

It's polite in modern society not to grow a beard. (In the name of equality this applies to women too.) Beards are musty cornflake-ridden things and should only be grown in emergencies. Designer stubble in particular is hazardous and should be banned. If it was, my chin wouldn't look as if it had been attacked by a cheese grater and Saul wouldn't be staring silently ahead and driving his Lotus at a more geriatric pace than usual. I feel menaced. I slide low in my seat and twiddle with my hair. The last ten minutes have not been fun.

'What's *what* on my chin?' I'd whispered, a slow curl of fear unfolding. My hand flew to conceal the offending spot. Except it wasn't a spot. It was a red patch of crusting scab. An injury sustained by fierce and prolonged rubbing against an unshaven jaw. I had stubble trouble. 'There's something I should tell you,' I said in a small voice.

I waited for Saul to smash his fist into the wall like a normal well-adjusted male and scream, 'You bitch! I'll kill him!' But all he said was, 'You forget that I've booked us a table for 7.30 at the Oxo Tower Brasserie. We can discuss it there.'

I opened my mouth then shut it and nodded. He held open the door for me and I cringed as I ducked under his arm. As we reached the car I realised he'd left the roses to die on my desk.

'How was work?' I shrill.

'Good,' replies Saul and starts whistling softly under his breath. I think it's Celine Dion's *My Heart Will Go On.*

I squeeze my hands tight to prevent them shaking. The tension is hideous. I might pop like a balloon and splat his interior in shards of red rubber. Until recently I thought Saul was a pushover, about as scary as a Meg Ryan film. Now, I revise my opinion. He's Dirty Harry with an abacus. I keep glancing at him sideways to check he hasn't morphed.

'Can I turn on the radio?' I bleat.

'I'd rather you didn't,' he says. I quickly withdraw my arm which has already reached out to turn the dial. I realise that if ever I've wanted something, Saul has agreed to it. When he broke a dirty plate and I asked him to wash it before putting it in the bin because I couldn't relax knowing it wasn't clean in there, he scrubbed it with Fairy Liquid and said fondly, 'We're two of a kind!' He also bought me a new plate. He is kind and forgiving. I hope.

We ascend mutely in the silver lift and walk into the bar. It's full of bright polished faces and I wish I was any one of them. I'd be the piano stool if it meant escaping the cool hell of Saul's placidity.

'Would you like a drink?' I mumble to his left nostril.

'A lemonade, thank you,' he replies. He nods towards some empty chairs. 'I'll get the table.'

I watch him stride towards it. He looks thinner in that dark suit. I pay for a vodka and cranberry juice and dream of escaping to a parallel universe.

'There you go,' I croak.

'I'm all ears,' says Saul.

I chew on my hair and tell him. As I speak I realise that Chris isn't going to call and that I've been tricked into risking a perfectly workable relationship. Did I really think that a man who says 'A little less conversation, a little more action please', without weeping in shame at what he's become, will call when he says he will? I hunch in my chair to ease the ache. I *need* you, Chris, I need to touch you, why, why am I never the one, why is it always like this? I remind myself that it serves me right and that Saul is good

40

enough to be getting on with. I brace myself to be shouted at. I dread Saul's rage, but anything is better than this terrifying anticipation. When 7.30 comes, I want to beg the waitress to let us share a table.

The witch seats us in a remote spot. Saul could decapitate me with the bread knife and no one would be the wiser. In fact, he cuts me off mid-confession to order seared tuna and chat with the waiter about whether the French or Californian chardonnay will do it justice. It's a dead fish, I think, and you're about to eat it. Poseidon leaping from the Gents and spearing you through the heart would do it justice. I peer at Saul's unreadable face and wonder if *I* have speared him through the heart. It's his own fault for being so soft. He always rang when he said he would. Where's the sexual tension in that?

But, no sign of spinelessness now. He's aglow with foreboding. I am too bunged up with fear to eat. I light another cigarette.

'Carry on,' says Saul. I kill my cigarette in the ashtray. I feel like a pumpkin farmer earnestly explaining my alien abduction to Dana Scully. At one point Saul touches me lightly on the arm, indicating that I should stop yapping for a moment while he asks the waitress to bring more pepper! I feel cheated. Yes, *I* feel cheated! Why isn't he jealous? Why isn't he turning green and howling at the moon? Am I so throw-away he barely cares if I cheat on him? What would Simon do if Babs cheated on *him*? Murder them both and go to prison, I'll bet – that's how much he loves her!

I study my plate.

'Is there something wrong with your grilled sole?' Saul asks, making me itch to throw it at him.

'No,' I reply, hating the waver in my voice. 'But it has a face and I've just gone vegetarian.' And he *laughs*.

'What?' I whisper.

Saul lays down his knife and fork. 'Natalie,' he says, soothingly, 'it's not a problem.'

'What's not a problem?' I blurt.

Saul's smile hovers between regretful and concerned. 'Well,' he replies, regarding me over an invisible pair of half-moon spectacles, 'it's not as if this relationship was anything serious.'

'What do you mean?' I say faintly.

'I mean,' says Saul, refilling my wine glass with a generous splash, 'that our relationship was always a bit of fun, but the fun has petered out, and our relationship is now patently over.'

The grotesque four-letter word 'over' resonates between my ears like the twang of a monstrous elastic band. Over. How can it be over? How can *Saul* be saying it's over? He adores me! And since when was our relationship 'a bit of fun'? It wasn't fun!

'But, but—' My voice is out of batteries.

'Natalie,' continues Saul in the same cheery tone. 'We both know that things haven't been right for a while. Be honest. You've devoted so much time in the last few months to helping Babs prepare for her wedding that I've hardly seen you. And when I do see you, she's all we talk about. Don't misunderstand me, I'm a big fan of hers, she's a smashing girl. But this neverending chat about her relationship, it's made me realise there's no *us*. However' – a consoling pat on the hand for the loser – 'if you want, I'd be happy to remain friends.' I am so shocked that my eyes itch. He's so indifferent that he's happy to remain friends!

'Chin up,' he murmurs. 'This Chris of yours sounds like a good chap.'

I could burst out crying but I'm dammed if I'm doing it in the Oxo Tower Brasserie. My suddenly ex pours me a tall cool glass of water and suggests that if I'm feeling 'under the weather' perhaps he should call me a taxi. I nod snufflingly, and mutter that I'm going to the Ladies to wash my face. Saul pauses for an appropriate second then adds, 'Now are you going to eat that sole or can I have it?'

*

'Cheer up, love,' says the cabbie. 'It might never 'appen.' I smile my gratitude for this fabulous rare jewel of insight and think, 'It just did.'

I can tell he's dying to talk at me, so I dig out my mobile and ring Tony.

'Speak,' he says imperiously. There is a fuzz of blurry chat and shrill laughter.

'It's Nat,' I holler. 'Saul just dumped me!' I await his condolences.

'What champagne you got, darlin'?' he says.

'What!' I squeak.

'Aw, floozie,' says my brother. 'Bowcock was never going to set the world alight. You'll have forgotten him by tomorrow. You'll be fine. You always are.' I nod gratefully into the phone. 'I wouldn't tell Mum though – she'll be gutted,' adds Tony. 'Keep the change.'

I sigh. 'Thanks,' I say, beeping off.

I flop in my seat, and the cabbie says, 'Hard day? You finished work, av ya? Day over for ya?'

I reply, 'Not quite,' and ask if he wouldn't mind taking me to Holland Park. Then I ring the speaking clock and affect animated chat. When the driver swerves to a sulky halt outside the smart green door, I shove notes at him and leap out. As I press the buzzer it strikes me I haven't even checked if she's in. When she opens the door in an apron I'm so relieved, I burst into the tears I prepared earlier.

'Oh my God,' gasps Babs. 'What happened to your chin? Are you all right?'

'I'm fine but it's all gone wrong!' I wail. 'Chris hasn't rung and I've just been dumped by Saw-haw-haw-haaul!'

I plan to sink weeping into her arms but she pats me briskly and sidesteps my trajectory.

'Sorry for not ringing first,' I sniff, stumbling. 'I was in a state.'

Babs looks at me. 'You're all right,' she says. 'My *hus*band – oh ha ha, I can't get used to saying that – is playing rugby. My brother's here though. Come in. Mind the boxes.' My pleasure at Simon's absence is cancelled out by Andy's presence. I pick my way past the Kilimanjaro of John Lewis merchandise clogging up the hallway and follow Babs into her steel and wood kitchen. Andy sees my mascara-streaked face and leaps from his chair.

'Shall I go in the other room?' he says. I cover my chin with my hand and will Babs to say 'yes' at the instant she says, 'No.'

I ignore Andy and sit down.

'You look like you've just joined the paras,' he says in a remarkably ill-conceived attempt to cheer me up.

'No, she doesn't,' says Babs immediately.

'No, you don't,' agrees Andy, as my smile turns to mush. 'I meant that your um, eye shadow has run. Er, I'll be in the other room, shall I?'

He exits the kitchen at a swift trot. I glare after him. Babs prods lovingly at a slab of raw meat in a pan and says, 'Andy's a bit on edge right now.'

'Really. How strange, after a year's holiday. I didn't think you ate red meat,' I say, unwilling for the conversation to be diverted.

'I do now. Although this is for Si,' explains Babs. 'He'll be back any minute.' I marvel that you can know someone so well – *think* you know someone so well – then be confounded by their choice of partner. They're not who you thought they were after all. You're not half as intimate as you boldly presumed. 'Poor Andy,' she adds. 'He's staying with Mum and Dad. They're driving him up the wall.'

'I thought he owned a flat in town,' I say impatiently.

'He rented it out while he was away,' she replies. 'There's still a few months left on the lease. He's looking for a room to rent short term, but London's so pricey it isn't true,' she adds.

I vaguely sense that Babs wants to communicate more than her words imply. I grope for a secret meaning but retreat empty handed.

'Has he tried Streatham?' I say politely. By the look on

44

her face, I have failed as a special agent. I feel hollow and awkward. *I* am the damsel in distress and I resent Andy trying to steal my conical hat with the floaty bit on top. He has short hair and it doesn't suit him.

'Is he still upset about his fiancée?' I ask dutifully.

'He was a bit more than upset, Nat,' says Babs. 'He and Sasha were together for three years.'

Yes, and my parents were together for sixteen years. Time for – as Matt would say – a two-faced moment. I heap my voice with hammy woe and sigh, 'Poor Andy, it must have been so hard for him.'

Privately, I think it's high time he relinquished his teen queen title. The big ballyhoo about Andy is that he was engaged to a girl who left him for another guy a month before their wedding. While this was certainly a great blow, he received lashings of sympathy and got to keep all the presents. Plus the minute she scarpered, he quit his megabuck job as a broker, leased out his chrome-and-leather-stuffed penthouse in Pimlico, sold his Audi, and went on a twelve-month boohoo sunshine jaunt, working in beach bars, swimming with dolphins, no doubt beading his hair, and *finding himself* – what a martyr! The men I know find themselves by lolling on the sofa and sticking their hands down their trousers.

I can barely believe that the sympathy wagon still trundles on. If he were female, the world would be gleefully sorry for about a week, pompously urge him to get on with his suburban little life the next, all the while covertly fanning rumours that he was a shoddy cook and spent too much time furthering his career. If a woman bales she's a hussy, while a bloke is practically encouraged to leg it. So Andy is treated like a big brave abandoned baby, whereas a jilted woman is tarnished, as if the man's infidelity is her fault, no wonder he—

'So,' says Babs, handing me a cup of bionic tea. 'Saul gave you the big E.'

I'm unsure if her phrasing is compassionate, but decide

not to question it. 'Babs,' I say. 'You wouldn't believe how nasty he was.'

'Would his nastiness have something to do with Chris, by any chance?' she replies.

I grit my teeth. 'Possibly,' I say.

'*Quel surprise*,' says Babs.

I stare at her. I feel like Julius Caesar with a knife in his back. Meanwhile Babs is Brutus, watching me bleed to death with interest.

'Babs,' I squeak. 'I have been binned by *two* men in *one* day!'

I burble out the whole sorry tale (excluding the orgasm bit as I don't wish to detract from my grief).

Babs's mouth shrinks and shrinks until it becomes a chicken's bottom. Then she says, 'Ah Nat, I'm sorry. But face it, Chris was a fantasy. Everyone flirts at weddings. You just took it a bit far. Si says Chris is notorious. When you're driven by ambition or drugs – and Chris is driven by both – you are not *reliable*. You weren't to know. You were tempted – we all get tempted, we wouldn't be human otherwise. But you knew the risk. Bottom line, you cheated on Saul and he found out. What did you expect? I know we've had our laughs about Saul, but he's not an idiot. Think how hurt he must be.' Babs squeezes my arm and adds in a softer tone, 'Come on, Nat. You know I adore you, and I hate to see you upset. But what do you expect me to say?'

I make a face and scan the room for a large purple hat, as she has obviously ordained herself as an archbishop without telling me. Even my mother in collaboration with the Pope wouldn't have the gall to come out with a sermon like that.

I blurt, 'My life's just fallen apart!'

Babs clunks her mug on to the table. 'Your life hasn't "just fallen,"' she says. 'You dropped it.'

I want to speak but the words are gummed to the roof of my mouth. I stare at my bitter tea in its brittle new

Wedgwood Jade thimble-sized cup and wonder how to run away and retain dignity. To my amazement – I assumed she'd carve an A on my forehead and cast me out before I contaminated the marital home – Babs rises, bends, and hugs me. I clutch her. 'Give Saul time, Nat,' she murmurs. 'He might come round.'

I nod and scream inside, 'I don't want him to come round! I want Chris! I don't want you to be married either!' What a brat. I tell myself not to be so silly and selfish. I *am* pleased for her. I'm just gutted for *me*. I smile at Babs and say, 'You're right. Thank you. And by the way, the new kitchen looks great. I – I like the way you've framed your seating plan.'

'Arr! Do you? You sweetheart.' Babs beams, and for a second she's my old Babs again. Next thing I know, she's trapped my shoulder in an iron squeeze, vanished and reappeared in the time it takes me to dab my eyes, and announced, 'Andy'll give you a lift home. You're on his way.'

I don't want to go home and I don't want a lift from Andy. Yet here I am, rattling down Elgin Avenue in a tatty blue Vauxhall Astra, hoping no one sees me, and indulging Andy's schoolgirl take on romance which I'll bet he purloined from an aged copy of Australian *Cosmo*. Here it is in all its glory: 'I reckon you should treat a new bloke like high risk stock – you know, imagine your emotions are your savings. The best strategy is to invest 10 per cent. Invest all your savings instantly and you're stuffed!'

He's been talking nonsense since Babs waved us off. I knew I was in for a long ride when he said, 'So, Natalie. What do you do to relax?'

What a stupid question! 'I go abroad for two weeks every summer,' I replied. (I wanted to add, 'although Simon has recently pinched my hunting partner.')

Cue, a lecture – if you can believe this – about *yoga*. Blimey. Being dumped by his fiancée really has hit him hard. And after nine minutes on the wonder of Sivananda yoga (apparently it's not all about humming with your legs crossed) he suggested I found a relaxation technique – if not yoga, something 'to take you out of yourself'.

I'd barely grappled with this affront when he said, 'I've got this picture in my head of you, Natalie, of when I last saw you. It must have been about four years ago. A load of us went go-karting with Babs, remember? You were insane! You were going to be first round that track at all costs, and I can just *see* you, this blur in a white helmet and green overalls, screaming with laughter as you made the finishing line, and then running away from Babs who was trying to spray you with Diet Coke, you were a fast runner, and now, and now . . . you're a different person. You seem so *muted*.'

So I reminded him that I'd just been involved in a multiple relationship pile-up and he had the gall to come out with the line about 'high risk stock'!

I look at his tanned face side on and marvel at his short memory. So, Saint Andrew, I want to say. You don't remember. Babs's fifteenth birthday party, kissing me numb in your parents' linen cupboard (I've not looked at linen cupboards in the same way since), mumbling a stream of testosterone-fuelled rubbish about me visiting you at college, you'd write, you'd phone, we'd go out, I'd stay over, I was so shy, but God I was gorgeous – I was fifteen, I *believed* you! – and so I waited and dreamed and planned my dress and silence. I couldn't tell Babs and I couldn't tell Tony. Thanks, Andy, you lying git. That snog-and-go reverberated in my head for years.

High risk stock. I reply, 'I think that's so wise.'

Andy looks at me and laughs. 'No you don't,' he says – all green eyes and perfect skin. 'What's wrong Natalie? You've been giving me the evil eye since the wedding.'

Chapter 6

I was such an *easy* child, as my mother never tires of boasting to the dentist, the lady in the bank, Mrs Parekh in the corner shop, the man in the post office, her fellow receptionists at the surgery, and a great many other people who couldn't give a toss. Tony – surprise! – was the difficult one, the baby who screamed so long and loud that my mother would often shut him in the front room and run to the end of the garden to stop herself from hitting him. Naturally we don't talk about that, but I was told it once by an indiscreet relative. I suspect that my mother harks back so persistently because my failure to marry and spawn and shin up the career ladder without chipping my nails makes me less of an easy adult. If she could see me right now she'd be more disappointed than ever. A perfectly good son-in-law has been wasted and instead of hurling myself on a burning pyre, here I am scuttling to the studio to watch Melissandra rehearse with a full-beam smile on my face because the man who displaced my prospective husband, the man who my great friend assured me was more likely to donate his penis to a sausage shop than call me, the man who constitutes a blatant misuse of my horizontal resources, has just called me (better three days late than never) and we are meeting tonight. So there.

Altogether, today is turning out to be an excellent day. The Italian State Tourist Board press office responded to my fax, and while the essence of their response was 'pay for your own bloody jollies' they were kind enough to pass on the number of the L'azienda turistica di Verona. I am researching flight details and hotels and liaising with the *Telegraph* picture desk. Matt is delighted and I am teacher's pet again. His pleasing verdict on the Saul and Chris saga was, 'A person who dislikes animals is one step away from a serial killer.' (Saul was frightened of Paws.) Then he advised me not to call Chris until my scab cleared. But Chris called me and we are meeting at *Poncho* at 10.30. Normally I wouldn't be seen in a body bag at *Poncho* – it makes Taco Bell look like the Met Bar – but I didn't want Chris to think I had nowhere to go on a Friday night. The party is a welcome back party, organised for Andy by his pal Robbie. Andy invited me – a sympathy invite – when I was captive in the Astra. I didn't have the nous to refuse. (I didn't have the nous to refresh his memory either.) I'm going because Babs is going. Presumably Simon will be there too, so at least Chris will know someone. I didn't tell Chris it was karaoke, but I did say that my brother Tony – Vice President of Marketing at Black Moon Records – might turn up, and Chris said it sounded 'boss'.

The only monster blot on the landscape, I think, as I slink into the studio to meet Mel as arranged, is this scab on my face. I feel the urge to hack off my chin with a knife. I wish it was fancy dress, I could go in a yashmak.

I sit on a chair by the pianist, and gaze at the dancers. I want to leap up and shout 'Oh my God, you're so clever!' I will never get over the beauty of classical ballet. I've seen *Swan Lake* – technically known as a 'grind' – fifty times and at the first flutter of a feathered tutu I dissolve. When I first joined the company, I watched class and asked Matt to identify the god in the headscarf. He replied, 'I have a rule: Don't shag the payroll.'

Like I have a choice. Dancers aren't generally keen on civilian bodies. As Julietta reportedly said, 'Once you've driven a Merc you don't want to drive anything else.' I watch Oskar now, fiddling with his headscarf in the mirror. This week, the company is rehearsing for spring.

Mel is sitting on the floor in what looks like a babygro, cutting up plasters and sticking them on her calloused toes. Her feet are ugly. It fascinates me, the graft and mess and tears behind the cool serenity of this purist art. Dancers are the only athletes who can't show the viewers how much it hurts and I'm in awe of their discipline and poise.

Then the Artistic Director swishes in and orders everyone to 'Get your junk off'. The AD is slightly more feared than a vengeful god and the dancers scurry to remove their layers. You can always tell if they're feeling fat by what they wear to class. Some days it's like walking into ski school. The répétiteur – whose job it is to breathe life into a production and betray people to the Artistic Director – is already taking the principal couples through their paces.

Today, the répétiteur has the Herculean task of translating into English the instructions of Anastasia Kossoff – former star of the Kirov – who is 'staging' our presentation of *Romeo and Juliet*. Anastasia is sixty-seven with a body like a wasp, and will never be able to infuse these British pears with even a breath of her genius. The problem is, she literally scares them stiff. Mel scampers into place – 'sorry, sorry!' The AD watches like a bird of prey.

The pianist plays, the dancers dance themselves dizzy, and Anastasia starts shouting: 'It looks like you working! Here' – gracefully executing the step herself – 'is dignity. *Here*' - mimicking the dancers like a stiff wooden puppet – 'is not dignity! Use grace! Not jerky! Urgency! I not see the shape of your arcs! Can we do the *écarte* step again! Control!' – the sweating, panting principals stare dejectedly as she demonstrates – 'Softly, soft . . . come up! Come up! Control yourself! Squeeze, squeeze, now carry yourself! Carry, carry, little *ronde de jambe* – small, huh? On the top of the ground! As this goes forward, this goes out but not too much! Yah! OK lez go, don't drop that! How' – she turns to the répétiteur – 'do you explain this in technique?'

*

51

Forty excruciating minutes later, the class is dismissed. Mel looks crushed, and I ache for her. Ballet is all about correction. And all ballet dancers are perfectionists. It's not what you call a horse and carriage partnership, and it's no mystery that most dancers are a mash of desperate vanity and low self-confidence. As Mel passes the AD, he murmurs, 'Nice try, darling.'

She is wan as we walk to the corner café. I hate to say it, but her dancing today was less than wonderful. She did not – as they say in ballet – 'move big', and she stumbled twice. And although she has the frame of a spring onion, her thighs looked pappy. Suddenly she blurts, 'Oskar is holding me back! He's just not there on the lifts! He's dancing like a plank with rigor mortis!'

I am not about to skewer my baby friendship with a principal dancer by disagreeing. I present a consolation prize. 'Poor you,' I say. 'But guess what' – I cross my fingers – 'I've spoken to the *Sun* and they want to do a feature on you!'

Mel does a bunnyhop of joy. 'When?' she gasps, squeezing a lifetime of hope into one short word.

Even as I smile, my heart flips uneasily. But I ignore it. That's what you get for selling your professional soul to the devil. Anyhow, it's worth it to see the look of gratitude on Mel's face. In her world right now I am Number One. I tell her it will be this Sunday, and it's for their health & beauty section. 'They're going to compare your fitness with a rugby player's. So that should be a laugh, and they'll take gorgeous pictures of you in a tutu, with the hunk, and there'll be a shoot, with a hair stylist and a make-up artist, and the *Sun* has so many readers you'll be even more famous than you already are!'

Mel's toothy grin lights up her face. We sit in the café and she buys a Mars Bar and a Coke.

'This is the first thing I've had to eat in two days,' she announces.

'Oh!' I say. 'How do you feel?'

Mel smiles again. 'High as a kite.'

I think of when our nutritionist told a junior soloist to eat more or reap the whirlwind aged forty. 'Forty!' she scoffed. 'Who cares about forty? I'm not going to live that long!'

I smile tightly and try not to wonder if my *Sun* story is actually a good idea. I *should* have OK'd it with the AD, but I haven't and I know that Matt assumes I have.

'You know,' I say, 'you should eat.'

Mel frowns. 'Natalie, my thighs are enormous. And my legs are short, and I've got no neck – I can't *afford* to eat like a horse!'

I didn't say, 'eat like a horse,' I said 'eat.'

'I want to see bone!' she adds, quoting a late revered choreographer who married four of his ballerinas. (In this industry there's a quick turnover.) I sigh. Mel's insecurity is exhaustive. Last year, one of the GLBallet's guest artists was a twenty-three-year-old Serb – a wonderful lyrical dancer though a tad stocky compared to, say, a bamboo stick. Mel watched her dance Odile in *Swan Lake* in a black tutu and scoffed, 'I bet she thinks black is slimming. You might as well ink in the white bits on a killer whale.' I know that makes her sound mean, but she isn't – just scared. Mel reminds me of a dog that's been ill-treated; everyone is a threat until they prove they can be trusted, and then she becomes sweetly, irrevocably fond.

I see the café owner glance at us, and foolishly, I feel proud to be seen with her. When I was small I confused ballerinas with fairies – beautiful, mystical creatures in pink and white and able to fly – the breathless sum of my little girl dreams. I've never outgrown that awe.

Mel grips my hand. Her mood has bounced from stormy to sunny. As we chat she darts from this to that like a tiny tropical fish, confiding that she is bored with Oskar and wants to have a fling with a 'civilian' (ie, not a dancer), that the new ballet mistress is a total bitch and once made a senior soloist dance with a broom tied to her back so she'd stand up straight, and that – dramatic pause here and hoarse whisper to maximise impact – while Anastasia seemed pleased with Julietta today, yesterday she was overheard saying, 'There's nothing wrong with your dancing, have you tried not eating?'

'Really?' I gasp. Julietta has a Formula One metabolism. Her 'problem' – if you can call winning the body lottery a problem – is keeping her weight *up*. While Mel chainsmokes and chews gum, Julietta carbo-loads and remains sculpted. Matt says she doesn't yak it up either. I can't believe Anastasia would say such a thing.

'Well, that's what *I* heard,' purrs Mel.

Three hours later, snug in a cosy purple room and allergic to silence, I repeat this piece of gossip to a charming stranger at Andy's party. He says he's called Jonti and feigns an interest in ballet. He asks a brisk stream of astute questions, then wanders off. It *was* something I said. I look around, and see Andy talking to a short, muscular guy encased in an FBI jacket. He must be a detective. I swirl my wine and peruse the karaoke brochure. Entertaining though this is (Goldfinger and Footloose are two of my favourite songs, I'm afraid), I wish I hadn't been so prompt. No matter how long I loiter in the street fiddling with my mobile phone, I am always the first to arrive at parties. I think I caught it off Saul.

'Natalie.'

I look up. Andy is waving me over. I can hardly disobey, although I imagine mouthing *Me?* and legging it. He looks all right with a tan but does himself no favours with a shirt apparently made from scraps of curtain.

'What did you say to Jonti to make him disappear like that?'

'I have a knack,' I say.

Andy doesn't get it. He grins, and asks if I want a drink. 'Natalie, meet Robbie.'

FBI man grips my hand and squeezes.

54

'Natalie is a big friend of my sister,' explains Andy, as the blood makes a slow return to my fingers. 'And Robbie is a small friend of mine.'

Robbie rolls his eyes at Andy and says, 'Gimp Boy is jealous of my superior muscle tone.'

Andy snorts. 'Jealous? You've got arms like my nan!'

I try not to smile until Andy walks off to greet some guests.

'So will you be singing for us tonight?' says Robbie.

'I'd love to,' I reply. 'I really would. But I wouldn't be so cruel.'

Robbie laughs. 'We could sing together if you like. My voice is so bad it would divert attention from yours. We could do something easy. Bohemian Rhapsody?'

I laugh. I am a foot taller than Robbie and can see that the crown of his head has one hair per five follicles. But while he is no oil painting – or finger painting even – there's something about him I like.

'What do you reckon?' he says, rummaging in a pocket and producing a small pale green object. 'It's for Andy to put on his dashboard.'

I admire it. Robbie grins. 'You're joking. It's a fluorescent Virgin Mary, it's rank!'

It emerges that Andy and Robbie compete to buy each other disgusting presents. Andy now has four china shepherdesses, a commemorative plate, an alien baby in a jar, and a cut-glass vase adorned with gold leaf. And Robbie is the proud owner of the Windsor Gentleman's watch, a pine woodpecker doorknocker, a fake rabbit head on a plaque, a large green plastic iguana, and a life-size metal Doberman pinscher. I am laughing, when a voice like nails down a blackboard enquires, 'Natalie, who's your friend?'

I hang on grimly to my smile. Frannie at a party. Weedkiller on a lawn. Then I recall that Frannie *half* extended the hand of friendship this week and that I turned her down. I smile properly. 'Frannie! Great to see you! This is Robbie, a small friend of Andy's. Frannie is—'

'A close friend of Andy's sister,' says Frannie. Robbie stretches out a hand. He doesn't know that Frannie sees the handshake as 'a literal male stronghold' and has perfected a squeeze that would crush rocks. I watch, terrified. Someone could get hurt. Then Robbie squawks, 'I surrender!' and Frannie *giggles*.

'Drink, anyone?' I ask, relieved.

'I'll have a pint of bitter, please,' says Frannie.

'White wine and lemonade for me,' grins Robbie. I leave them to it and head for the bar.

'Natalie,' says Andy, blocking my path.

'Andy,' I reply, as politely as I can.

He takes my hand and leads me into the corridor. 'Now,' he murmurs. 'You're not going anywhere until you've told me what's wrong. I haven't seen you for, what, years, and you seem to have developed a grudge against me. What have I done? Is it what I said in the car? Is it to do with Big Tone?' He treats me to a smile which I'm sure works wonders on his mother and secretary but makes me want to smack him.

'No,' I say stiffly. 'Nothing to do with Tony. No.'

'Natalie,' he says in a cooler voice. 'Whatever it is, I can take it.'

I'm not sparing *your* feelings, I shout in my head, I'm sparing my own. My insides churn and I blurt, 'It's nothing, OK? Happy birthday. I mean, welcome back. It's nice to see you again.'

'But no welcome back kiss?' he says cheekily.

'I'd love to only I have a large festering scab on my chin,' I retort. 'I wouldn't want to transfer it.'

'Shame,' sighs Andy. I step daintily over his foot and scurry to the bar.

When I return to my original party position, the first words I hear are, 'The pointe shoe is merely a phallus.' I tense. Ballet is another crime Frannie holds against me.

'I didn't realise,' says Robbie. 'Is that why me mum's so keen?'

I hold my breath. Frannie peals with laughter.

'You're the expert, I'm told, what do you reckon?' says Robbie to me.

I say carefully, 'I see Frannie's point – classical ballet *is* sensuous, but it's sexless too. Upright and prim. The centre of gravity is in the upper chest. Modern dance is more focused on the, er pelvis.'

'Upright!' nods Frannie, '*Exactement*! The female ballet dancer is merely an erect phallus being manipulated by the male for his own pleasure!'

I look about for deliverance and to my relief see that Babs and Simon have arrived. Babs looks luminous, as if she is lit up from the inside. Her curls gleam in the green and blue disco lights. As I wave at her, a waitress digs me in the ribs with a tray of pizza.

I shake my head. Frannie takes a slice and says, 'What is it, Nat – scared your belly button might detach itself from your spine for five minutes?'

I squirm. 'I don't like garlic.' Nor do I wish to greet Chris with breath so potent it could power a jet plane.

'So you're a midwife?' says Robbie politely, to Frannie. 'I admire people what do that job.'

Her face softens. '*Do* you?' she says. 'Well, I appreciate that. It can be so thankless. People scream at you when you're only doing your best – I'm always relieved when the partner faints because then he's out of the way and you can step over him – the trouble is we're constantly short-staffed and what with the heat and the mess and the smell, it's all too easy to lose your sense of amazement but – oh, hello!'

Andy looks through me, and drags Frannie off to join him and Babs in a rendition of *Wives and Lovers*. As this is a song warning women not to let themselves go after marriage, I can only conclude that Frannie has a sense of humour, even if she doesn't waste it on me. To me Frannie is like a thistle, prickly and dour, and has been ever since we vied for Babs's friendship at school. (When I was twelve classrooms were full of double-desks. Those double-desks caused a lot of grief.) To Babs, Frannie is gruff, but loyal. A serious person who you *do* things with, visit exhibitions, attend talks, a friend who is low on frills but stands by you.

Frannie admires Babs for her strength and courage. But Frannie and I are like two magnets repelling each other. We try to get on but I find her brash and intimidating. I am the kind of woman she disapproves of. The day I got my degree results (a Desmond, as we so wittily called a 2.2 back then) I donned black stilettos and a short tight skirt, drank most of a bottle of Warnink's Advocaat, and reeled round the college bars with Kathy, a companion pisshead (she was swigging Lambrusco), snogging whichever men fell into my path. I've since modified my drinking and dress sense but, like most people who know you from your teens, Frannie judges me on my past. Occasionally she'll attempt to educate me – recommending books by Susie Orbach, Erica Jong and 'your kind of feminist, Natalie' Naomi Wolf – and I'll glimpse a flash of her kindness. But generally she regards me as beyond help.

'So how do you know Andy?' I ask Robbie.

'We met at college,' he says grinning. 'I suppose you know him through Babs?' he says.

'Not really,' I say. 'He was a friend of my brother's but they didn't really associate with their sisters. They'd rather have played with nuclear waste. And then, when we were older, he went to university, then he worked in the City, and didn't he work in Aldershot for a bit? Anyway, I haven't really seen him for years. I know he lived with his girlfriend, and then he went travelling, after Sasha, er . . .'

'Left him,' says Robbie. 'Yeah, Sasha, mixed-up kid.'

'Really? I never met her. I know Babs was fond of her. It's funny, isn't it? A person can be part of a family, and then a couple split, and the family never sees that person again.'

Robbie nods. 'I think I saw her the other day,' he says.

'Sasha?'

'I was on me moped,' he replies. 'She was crossing the road. Kensington way.'

'That's near where I work,' I cry. (This is a bad habit of mine – grabbing at things that are blatantly *not* coincidence. It's a sad reflection of my desperate need to bond with the whole world. I'll see a guy on the tube with a black umbrella and want to tap him on the arm and exclaim, 'Incredible! – *I've* got that umbrella!')

'Oh right,' says Robbie. 'So would you've liked to be a ballerina yourself?'

I giggle. 'Do I look like I could be? It was a fantasy, when I was four. They wear such pretty dresses.'

We are laughing about this when I'm tapped on the shoulder by Babs. So, she came over.

'Hello, Nat,' she says. 'Hi, Robbie.' Then, to me, 'I take it all back. Your prince has come. Or should I say, Charlie's turned up.'

I twist round fast enough to crick my neck. Charlie? Chris! A vision in a sheepskin jacket, raggy jeans and Van trainers. He is talking to Simon. I beam at Babs, and speed over.

'Princess!' says Chris, nuzzling his face into my neck. He pulls back. 'What did you do to your chin? You look like you had a fight with a lawnmower.'

'What did *you* do to my chin?' I reply.

Light dawns. 'But it was worth it, eh, gorgeous girl?' he grins. 'At least *you* don't have to look at it.'

I sag. His honesty is commendable but I work with women and I'm not used to it.

'You need a livener,' says Chris, peering at me. He looks aghast at Andy belting out a falsetto version of *Anyone Who Had a Heart*, and adds, 'Let's go. You all right with that? These people haven't got a bone of funk in their bodies.' He steers me out of the door. 'We're going to see a man about a dog.' My heart jigs in triumph. He's going to introduce me to his friends. I translate this to middle class and decide it is on a par with being introduced to his parents. He must like me.

'What's his name?' I say happily.

Chris shoots me a mischievous look. He says, 'Well, his mates call him Chaz.'

Chapter 7

Some people will never be cool, and Puff Daddy and myself are two of them. He overdoes it on the jewellery (bracelets *or* rings, is my mother's rule, and nothing too heavy round the neck) and I have too much respect for authority. I'm the only person Tony knows who calls the police 'the police'. I am the kind of girl who succeeds by sticking to the rules, not breaking them. Others live on the edge but if I tried I'd fall off it. That's why I've never taken drugs. I've always felt that while everyone else got high, I'd get a blood clot. That's why the last twelve hours have been surprising. I've actually done cocaine.

Chris scraped the powder into a neat white line with his Tesco Clubcard and my mouth went numb and it tasted like earwax and I gagged and gagged and gagged and then I felt a great whoosh of blood and I was clutching the sink and my whole being was a massive boom boom, warm pulsating power and I looked in the bathroom mirror and I was deathly white but strong, and I laughed at the black shadows under my eyes because I was bright, bold, beautiful – a girl in a stained-glass window – I was scared of nothing and second to no one and for the first time in my life it was a thrill to be me.

The other surprise is that 'Never speak to strange men' is a good rule, even for twenty-six year olds. Not because my father told me, but because this morning at 8.25 as I slumped on the side of my bed wondering if I could possibly have been run over in the night without noticing, the telephone rang, its peal slicing through my head like cheesewire through Brie.

'Natalie?' said a crisp voice.

'Matt!' I whispered, 'what's wrong?'

He took a breath. 'Get your ass into work,' he said. '*Yesterday*.'

A cold drool of fear slithered down my spine and I croaked, 'Why?'

Silence.

'I've got to go into work early,' I told Chris who'd just stepped from the shower, his hair as slick and shiny as a seal. I tried not to mind that a great gloop of my pink E'Spa hair putty had been scooped from its tub. You're only meant to use a blob, I thought. Men have no idea about denying themselves, they see what they want and take it.

'All right, princess, I'll give you a shout,' replied Chris.

'Oh. OK,' I said, surveying my untidy flat in quiet horror (it is *always* pristine but Chris is a magnet for mess). 'Wh– when you go will you double lock the door with the spare key – it's on the top hook in the kitchen – then post it through the letterbox? I don't feel well,' I added. 'I think my body's gone on strike.' The guilt was engulfing me in sickly green waves, but I didn't want to sound weak.

Chris grinned. 'A night on the charles is gonna do that to you, princess,' he said.

Never again, I'm not cut out for it, I thought as I crawled into the office. I need water. I'm close to collaspe. I mean, collapse. All the moisture has been sucked out of my head. Then I saw Matt's rabid face – and Paws cowering red-eyed under the desk – and terror whitewashed pain.

'Read it,' demanded Matt, shoving today's *Record* at me. I looked at the print and for one wild second prayed he was playing a trick on me. Heading the diary page was a piece about GLBallet's dancing star Julietta, and how she was – 'said a spokeswoman' – 'piling on the pounds'. The phrase I'd parroted to a stranger the night before – 'There's nothing wrong with your dancing, have you tried not eating?' – leapt out at me. Next to the byline *Jonti Hoffman* was a photo of a thinner, younger, better looking man than the one I'd met at Andy's party.

'You're not exactly a sylph yourself,' I muttered.

'I took four calls at home this morning, before eight, shall I list them?' says Matt. I nod. 'The AD, the Director of Public Affairs, Julietta, and a *Guardian* reporter. We are s-o-o-o in the cak! What were you thinking of? This is so unlike you!'

Matt rubs his eyes, and Paws and I stare at the floor. My brain feels so parched and swollen it might burst from my head. I chew my hair. What is wrong with me? I don't make mistakes. Not at work. Never. Matt's always praised me as 'the acceptable face of nitpicking professionalism'. Not recently, though.

'How did you know it was me?' I whisper.

'The source is described as "chewing her hair in agitation". Who else could it be?'

I sink into my chair. The thoughts scramble – Andy is a moron, how dare he invite a tabloid hack to his naff bash and not warn me, and Mel, why did I believe her, and why didn't I keep quiet, why do I always take on the social grunt-work, am I – shudder – a PR to the bone?

'Do the ballet police know it's me?' I ask.

Matt glowers. 'I convinced them it was fabrication. Luckily for you, our President was at Oxford with the paper's Chief Exec.'

This is code for 'grovelling puff piece ahoy'. I smile at the thought of Jonti having to eat his press hat.

'Thanks, Matt,' I say. 'I'll start back-pedalling anyway, if you like.'

'I like,' he replies.

I spend the rest of the morning working like a dog – although the one occupant of the office truly entitled to that name (or maybe I flatter myself) spends a solid four hours sprawled and snoring on the floor. I don't come off the phone until the *Sunday Times* has agreed to a Life in the Day of Julietta Petit, and the *Telegraph* Italy trip – booked for Thursday week – is 95 per cent in the bag.

'I'm going for lunch,' declares Matt, at ten past one. Paws gives me a cold glance that says, Look who's in the doghouse.

I purse my lips and nod sadly. My brain is no longer swollen – in fact it's shrunk to a walnut and is rattling tinnily around my skull and giving me a headache. I feel listless but I can't keep still. I'll go to the gym. I stand up and trip over my sports bag. Usually I run, but today I need a distraction. I'll do a class. I scamper out of the building and across the road to my gym (small, functional, full of gay men, and though Matt 'wouldn't be seen dead in there' I love it because I'm as invisible as a child's wish floating up to heaven).

Fifty minutes of jumping about later I'm hunched on the changing room bench, slick with sweat, rasping for breath, my face mottled white and scarlet. Well, now I know I'd never make it in ballet.

'Do you want some water?' says a voice. It's the kind of dipped-in-cigarettes husky voice that makes me long for laryngitis. I look up to see a curvy woman gazing down at me, frowning and smiling at the same time.

'Please. My legs have stopped working,' I wheeze. She hands me her water bottle and I drain it in two gulps. 'How come you're not sweating?' I whimper, nodding at her mid-riff (I don't have the strength to lift my head any higher).

'I wasn't working as hard as you,' she replies. This is an endearing lie. Why is it that women love to evoke envy but would rather die than admit it? I smile. I've noticed her around the gym. Sure, the men watch her, but she gets a lot of attention from other women. When *that* happens, you know you've arrived.

'I think you're just fitter,' I croak.

She replies, 'If I am I should be. I teach Pilates matwork here. You might know it. It's non-aerobic but tough.'

'Oh,' I gasp. 'I know what Pilates is – I work at GLBallet,

64

a lot of the dancers do it. Julietta Petit – you've probably heard of her – she's always going on about it. I've, I've not tried it myself, although I'm sure it's – er, great. I'm Natalie, by the way.'

'Hi,' she replies. 'Alex. I see you here pretty often.'

I feel grateful for her attention and I want to hang on to her kindness. I say, 'Do you want a coffee? I mean, I owe you a drink.'

She glances at her watch. 'Yeah, ten minutes, why not?' We shower and change – me into a cable-knit navy top and long skirt, her into fresh gym gear – and march next door to the juice bar. I learn that Alex used to be a solicitor, lives in Shepherd's Bush, and is recently divorced.

'But you're only twelve!' I exclaim, before realising this could be construed as impertinent. She booms with laughter at my worried face. She has a rich hearty laugh, like being given a present.

'I'd better go,' she says, wrinkling her nose, 'I have a meeting at 2.30.'

I shuffle to my feet. 'Well, thanks for the water,' I say shyly. 'Maybe see you at next week's class – if I live that long.'

Alex beams, and as she walks away, calls, 'You'll be back before then!'

I smile after her, confused but warmed by the fading sunshine of her presence. There's a glow about her that reminds me of Babs. I'm so childishly pleased to have made a new pal, I forget I'm in disgrace and tell Matt.

'And did you,' he says, 'tell this new best friend that Paws has gained four pounds through his addiction to peanut butter basset biscuits?'

I redden but decide that if he's cracking jokes about my blunder, I'm half forgiven. This, plus the insufferable smugness of having exercised, puts me in such an excellent mood I call Babs.

'Sorry to bother you at the station, only we didn't get a chance to speak last night,' I gabble. 'And I've got so much

65

to tell you. And, of course,' I add quickly in deference to her recent moodswings, 'I want to hear your news. Have you got your wedding video back yet?'

'As it happens, it's at my parents',' she says. 'I'm going to get it tonight. Si's working late, poor love – shall I bring it round?'

'Oh!' I say – I want to be on standby in case Chris calls, but Babs won't stay long, not these two-by-two days – 'Definitely. You get off at six, don't you? Why don't you come straight over?'

'Well, I'll be at mumandad's till about half-seven, I reckon, so I could be at yours fifteen after that. The video's an hour and a half but we don't have to watch all of it.'

'Fine, brilliant, can't wait,' I crow. I put down the phone and make a face. An hour and a half! It's Babs's wedding but in my experience, all wedding videos are alike: endless footage of people milling about or dancing badly and a series of middle-aged men telling plotless tales and bad jokes. Still, the Italians might compensate. And Chris, of course.

I take a taxi home from work – I feel as fragile as scorched paper, like I might crack and crumble at the slightest touch. So I'm not about to trust myself to public transport. I'm pleased, if surprised, to find that Chris has double-locked the door as I asked him to. I look for the key but it isn't on the mat. Then I squint at the afghan rug and breathe deep. He – he – he has *vacuumed!* I sweep into the lounge and run an incredulous finger along the mantel-piece. Not a speck! 'Unbelievable,' I murmur to myself, '*Un*believable.'

I run into the bedroom. Spotless. I shake my head in awe when I see that even the used condom he dropped on the bedroom floor last night has vanished. In my experience, the most devoted men have trouble with the concept of 'tidying', and even when they *do* clear up after themselves, it's with an absent-minded sloppiness that makes you feel that if only you were Robert De Niro or Muhammad Ali,

66

they'd have put some elbow into it. So if this isn't proof of Chris's infatuation, I don't know what is. I skip into the (gleaming) kitchen and see he has left a little note on the table. Funny, his handwriting is exactly the same as that of my . . .

Mother.

'Why does she *do* it?' I moan into my hands, as Babs shakes with silent laughter at the condom tale – she can barely hold her coffee mug she's sniggering so violently.

'Does she know about Saul yet?' she chokes.

I wince. 'No, but that's no consolation. I swear, half the reason she likes Saul is that she can't imagine him doing anything *vulgar* to her little girl.'

Babs bites her lip. 'You shouldn't have given her a key. Then again, your mum is a hard woman to refuse.'

'Tell me about it. I can hardly confiscate it now, can I?'

'Well, it's a scary idea but you could *try*. You could suggest a key amnesty. It's your home.'

'Yes,' I say. 'Bought with money given to me by her and Dad.'

'Na-at! Whose side are you on?! Si says a gift is unconditional. You're a grown-up. Tell her you'd prefer her not to barge into your flat, even if it is to slave after you. That said, rather you than me.'

'Can you imagine? I couldn't! Anyway, it makes her happy. She means well.'

'Aw, I know that,' replies Babs. 'Your mum has a heart of gold. But what she does isn't what you want. Or is it? And can I have milk and sugar?'

'Gosh yes, sorry.' I open the fridge and squeak. 'Alien fridge alert!' Babs jumps up and we stare into the (ex) abyss: apples, pears, mangoes, pineapples, avocados, a mushroom risotto (labelled 'home made button mushroom risotto'), a vat of soup (marked 'home made carrot and coriander soup'), an enormous chicken (covered in foil but labelled 'roasted chicken'), a great bowl of mash (labelled 'home made butter mash'), three packs of fresh sugar snap peas from Marks & Spencer, and a cheesecake the size of a football pitch (no label – because, as my mother is fond of saying, her cheesecake 'speaks for itself').

'It's hard for me to say anything,' I tell Babs after we've established that, right now, my brother will be staring into an identical bulging fridge. 'Would you like some cheesecake?' I add.

'Nah. Tell you what I do fancy,' says Babs. 'Roast chicken. If you're having.'

I make a face.

'What?'

'I've gone off chicken,' I say. 'I don't like the cut of a chicken's jib.'

Babs pouts in mock alarm. 'Nat. If you don't say something, how's she to know what she's doing is wrong? By the way, you've been stirring your coffee for four minutes and you have it neat!'

'Sorry,' I mutter. I wash and dry the teaspoon which gives me time to think.

And what I think is, when you're too young to know better, your parents are flawless, they fight dragons and win. Then you get a little older and notice the cracks. Your heroes are frail. They need protection from the extent of their offspring's depravities because despite their protestations of 'I was young once too!' you know they couldn't hack it. (I'm not referring to myself here, more Tony.)

Maybe a little bit me. How can I tell my mother she's out of a job? It's much easier to need her, to pretend I haven't moved on. I earn a modest £24,000 and yet I live in a sunny flat in luscious leafy Primrose Hill, a spot which – except for the dog poo (rich people own big dogs) – is as darling and desirable as it sounds. It would have been treason to rent a basement in Vauxhall. My mother would have been less mortified if I'd poisoned the Queen. She had the money off Dad, what else would she do with it? And it wasn't as if I was a high earner like Tony.

Her purpose in life was to marry well and provide for her kids who would in turn marry well and provide for their kids who ... It's bad enough that Tony and I broke the cycle. (Sometimes I feel like I've accidentally extinguished the Olympic flame.) I'd feel wicked telling my mother, 'I'd like to earn it myself, I prefer to clean my own flat, and by the way, don't cook for me.' She'd feel hurt and it would make no sense to her. Or to most people. Even when I told Matt, he drawled, 'We should all have such problems.'

I glance at Babs.

'How's she to know what she's doing wrong?' she repeats.

'OK, OK,' I say. 'Let's not talk about it, let's talk about nice things.' I grin winningly.

'No,' says Babs. 'I think we should talk about it actually.' From nowhere, my heart is hammering.

'Guess what – I took coke last night.' It emerges as speech before I've approved it as thought. I giggle as I remember the scene. Chris saying, 'Do you want a line?' and my blushing refusal and his shocked realisation that I was a coke virgin. 'Oh my God,' he'd murmured. 'I feel like a pervert hanging round the school gates!' When he said that, I changed my mind. I mean, the stuff looked like talcum powder. He'd chopped it out on his ironing board, how bad could it be? And the truth was, I felt proud. I was flattered to be asked, 'Do you want a line?' *Me*, ten years behind everyone else, but finally being invited to join the party.

Babs looks angry. I gulp. I can't look at her.

'You know,' says Babs slowly, 'that taking coke, for you, was a very bad idea.' She drums her fingers on the table.

'Wh-why?' I quaver. I feel defensive and decide not to tell Babs about the aftermath. (I'd been on the brink of a heart attack and Chris had said, 'Take some Night Nurse.')

Babs stands up. 'No offence, Nat,' she says sadly. 'But you haven't had the training. You can't even say no to your mother. Do you really think you've got the strength to deal with a class A drug?' She looks at me, picks up her wedding video and walks into the hall. 'Natalie, I'm seriously worried about you,' she says, with the loftiness of a person whose life is all sewn up. 'I so want to talk to you about what's going on with you at the moment. But Nat – and please know I only say this because I value our friendship, not because I'm being sanctimonious – it's hard to be close to you when you're so shut off. You're not honest with me, Nat, and if you're not honest I can't help you. I know you were raised to keep a stiff upper lip, put a brave face on, and all that. But it's done you no favours.' She wrenches her lips into an apologetic smile, then shuts the door behind her so softly it doesn't make a sound.

I stagger backwards into the kitchen like I've been shot in the chest. The first thing I see is the Married One's coffee mug, a smug kiss of red lipstick staining its rim. I smash it on the floor and watch the milky coffee crawl along the tiles. Then coolly, methodically, I pick up the shards, and plop them in the bin. I suck a bloody finger and say dully, 'It's only a graze.'

When the floor is immaculate I press 141 and call Chris. I let it ring forty times, then wait five minutes and call again. I call his mobile, but it is switched off. So I call his home again and again and again, hitting redial with my leaky finger like a broken robot.

On the sixteenth attempt he answers. 'Did you just get in?' I blurt. (Good grief, what if he was in the bath all this time? And why do I only think of these possibilities *after* I've pressed the nuclear button?)

'Just,' he replies.

'Can I come round?' I breathe, sliding to the floor with wobbly relief.

Chris hesitates and says, 'I've got a bit of a mad one.'

And you're speaking to her, dear. I squeeze my hand into a fist and keep my tone breezy. 'I can tag along,' I sing as if I am not standing in a lions' den and his thumb signal, up or down, makes no odds to me.

After what seems like an age, he laughs and says, 'I can't resist you, princess. Yeah, go on then.' I take down his address then smirk into the pale blue silence. Babs is mistaken. I can say no to my mother. I can say no to everyone.

Chapter 8

If you date a man for a year and he doesn't propose, dump him. He's wasting your time. When I was twenty my mother told me this every other day (not realising that the whole point of under-twenty-one dating *is* to waste your time). But now I'm twenty-six and galloping headlong towards forty she is a lot less rash. Which means that when I confess the life-shattering truth about Saul over a Sunday morning coffee at Louis Patisserie in Swiss Cottage, her mouth turns downwards in such a droop of dismay, it prompts the elderly waitress to ask if there is something amiss with her almond croissant.

'So, so who . . .' Even my mother, who has the social delicacy of a dog on heat, cannot bring herself to complete the mystery-condom question. We each crumble our food and die a million deaths in our heads. (Although my food proves hard to crumble – without asking, my mother has ordered me a large yellow sweating Danish pastry, a garish confection that might have appealed to me when I was five and a half years old.)

'So who what?' mumbles Tony, through a mouthful of apple cake. He is wearing Cutler & Gross sunglasses and last night's Duffer of St George shirt and vintage Levis. ('Mad night at the Met,' he explained loudly on arrival, 'with Noel Gallagher' – a boast sadly lost on the patisserie clientele who might have been impressed had Tony's mad night taken place at Blooms with Neil Sedaka.)

'The thing is, Saul and I weren't really suited,' I say apologetically. 'But I am seeing a lovely new man.' (And if

72

my mother chooses to interpret 'new' man as 'does the ironing, attends a men's group, discusses his emotions freely' rather than 'recent' that's fine by me. Unfortunately, it doesn't look as if she's processed the information that far.)

She twitches. 'You don't look after yourself,' she sighs eventually. 'I don't know what to do any more. Look at you! You look a state.' This is an old trick of hers. If she disapproves of something I've said she won't acknowledge I've said it. Instead, she'll pick on me for something unrelated. Then, when the insult has simmered and my self-esteem is zero, she'll pounce on my original statement and tear it to bits. (I believe terrorist organisations deal with their hostages on the same principles.)

Tony lifts his dark glasses. I stare back anxiously, because yesterday Chris told me I dressed like a librarian and hauled me to Urban Outfitters where he encouraged me to choose a yellow T-shirt with a picture of a tiger on it, and a voluminous grey skirt made from tent material.

'*Ye-es*,' says Tony approvingly. 'But she looks a designer state.'

I smile gratefully at my brother. Our Sunday morning patisserie meetings once a month are always a trial, but they are family tradition. Which I suppose is the same thing. But they do allow our mother to check up on us without breaking into our homes.

'So who is he?' she says tightly. Tony whistles and clicks at the waitress for another hot chocolate.

'He's called Chris,' I reply meekly. 'Chris Pomeroy. He was at Babs's wedding.'

'What!' exclaims my mother. 'Not that man named after a poodle?'

I grit my teeth. She'd criticise a rainbow for being bent and although I'm used to it, today it grates. 'He's an old friend of Simon's. He works in the music business,' I add, raising my voice as Tony's attention wanders.

'Yeah?' says Tony. 'Doing what?'

I sip my coffee and say, 'He was on our table, remember?'

Tony shakes his head. 'Doing what?'

I sit on my hands and say, 'It would be nice for you two to meet properly. He, he manages a band. Called, er, Blue V' – on impulse, I castrate them – 'Called Blue Fiend.'

Tony snorts. 'Never heard of them.'

My left hand shoots up to twirl my hair. 'I mentioned you to him the other day,' I say, 'and, and, he was very impressed—'

'This band of his is unsigned, right?'

'Yes, but Tony, I think you'd get on. He's so dedicated, and his band, we were with them last night, they had a gig at The Red Eye—'

'Pay to play?'

'Er, I don't know, but it was really good, Chris said the response was even better than when they played at –'

'So who are they like?'

'Chris says they're a loose genre, sort of New Romantic Rock, the first Romo Metal band, think Iron Maiden meets Spandau Ballet with a dash of Rage Against The Machi . . .'

I tail off as I realise I am not being heard. My mother, who has been sitting in silence, follows Tony's mesmerised gaze to the patisserie door where a tiny Eskimo with dark glossy hair and huge blue eyes is standing in a long puffy black coat, a faint line of anxiety clouding her dolly features.

'Mel!' I cry, leaping to my feet. 'Well done for making it, you're early!'

'You know her?' murmurs Tony.

'She's one of our principal dancers, she's being interviewed and shot by the *Sun* today, and I'm the nipple police, we're due at the gym in, oof, one hour – Mel! The taxi picked you up okay? knew where he was going? I told him precisely where it was, great, sit down, would you like anything? This is my mother, my brother, Tony, this is Melissandra Pritchard, star dancer of the GLBallet.'

Mel shakes hands with my mother and bats her

74

eyelashes at Tony. Should she ever fancy a career change, she could bat for England.

'Delighted,' says my brother sizing up Mel with a reverence he usually reserves for expensive cars. He even takes off his sunglasses.

'Hi,' replies Mel, tilting her head so that her dainty chin all but disappears into the collar of her coat.

Tony spies a whiskery woman hobbling towards a faded gilt chair, leaps up, intercepts the prize and presents it with a flourish to Mel. My mother looks on in silence as I fetch another chair for the woman who has stopped to catch her breath and is leaning hard on her walking stick. 'Sorry,' I say, wincing, 'my brother didn't see you.'

I return to the table in time to hear Tony asking, 'Can you do the splits?'

I glance at Mel who giggles and says, 'Yes!'

Tony – whose knowledge of ballet is nil – purses his lips, impressed.

Mel giggles again and lisps, 'That's the least I can do!'

My brother narrows his eyes and says throatily, 'Sounds to me like you're the cleverest girl in your class.'

Mel shudders in delight and cries, 'Oh, do you think so?'

I look at my mother. Her face is an exquisite clash of pleasure and pain, reminding me of the time Tony explained, aged fourteen, how he was able to afford a stereo with woofers like slabs from Stonehenge. (He'd spent his holidays chasing ambulances, fire engines and police cars with a camera and selling the pictures to our local paper.)

'It must be so wonderful, dear,' says my mother eventually. 'Dancing in a pretty dress in front of all those people, all adoring you.'

Mel gives her a pitying smile. Her gaze keeps flickering towards Tony. 'Oh it is,' she replies. 'It's addictive. Although an audience will go wild at any cheap flashy dancing with an odd spin thrown in. The best thing is when you dance for someone whose opinion matters.'

My mother's smile is 20 watt. 'You're such a delicate slip

of a thing,' she says, 'you're almost translucent. Do you eat?'

If I dared, I'd kick my mother under the table (not just her ankle, I mean I'd kick her right under it – what *does* she think she's doing?). Mel flutters as if this is an almighty compliment and says, 'My body is my tool of work. I have to be light enough to be lifted. I have to be disciplined.'

'I think you look crackin',' exclaims Tony, interrupting my mother who is muttering something about skin and bone.

'I think we'd better go now, Mel,' I say. 'We don't want to be late.'

I kiss my mother and Tony goodbye and – to her surprise and his amusement – Mel does the same, flinging her pipecleaner arms tight around them and singing, 'Lovely to meet you, I hope to see you again, you must come and see me dance!'

My mother dabs her mouth with her napkin and says quietly, 'That's a very kind offer.'

Tony adds, 'You say when, darlin', I'll be there,' and arranges his hand into an imaginary gun shape which he fires at Mel.

'That was a friendly gesture,' I explain as we walk to my car.

Mel beams. 'I know that, I've seen chat show hosts do it on television, I can't believe he's your brother, he's so cute! I wonder what he'd be like to kiss – oh Natalie, I can't believe I just said that! I'm outrageous! What does he do for a job?'

I tell her and her reaction is such that I wonder if I accidentally said he was Chief Exec of the Royal Ballet. 'You *must* bring him to see me dance,' she says in a tone that is an order not a suggestion, 'and we could all go out afterwards.' I look at Mel to see if she's joking. 'Although probably your mummy would get bored,' she adds, checking her reflection in the car mirror.

'Now,' I say as I floor it, 'we're going to the gym first for

76

the stamina tests – the personal trainer will test your resting heart rate, flexibility and all that, compare it to the rugby bloke's, it shouldn't take too long, and the journalist will be watching and taking notes and the snapper – the photographer will take pictures. You remembered your kit, didn't you? Remember I rang twice to remind you? Then we go to the studio, where all you've got to do is put on the gear – I've got a swan tutu, tights and shoes in the boot – and they'll do your make-up and hair. I think it'll be great fun.' I glance at Mel who is nodding vigorously.

I take a deep breath and add casually, 'Now, you can chat to the make-up lady, that's fine, but if she or the journalist asks you any leading questions about food, you just tell them that you eat cereal and fruit for breakfast, a sandwich and a banana for lunch, snacks when you can fit them in, like yoghurt, and fish or pasta or a baked potato and cheese for dinner, chocolate and er, lots of water. The reason you're slim is that you do five or six hours of dance exercise daily and burn up to 600 calories an hour. I don't know if you heard about the *Recorder* diary piece – that was a bit of a boo-boo – but we don't want anything else appearing in the press that suggests the GLB dancers aren't healthy.'

Mel screws up her face and says, 'I couldn't possibly eat all that!'

I say firmly, 'That said, you're representing the company, and the Artistic Director will read it. If he thinks you don't eat, he won't cast you in the big roles, will he?'

Mel considers this and says, 'Yes he will!'

I say sternly, 'Not after the Julietta fiasco, he won't.'

Mel nods meekly. Then she murmurs, 'Poor Julietta, now everyone thinks she's fat!'

'And don't say anything today about Julietta,' I add. 'This story isn't about her, it's about you. This is *your* chance to shine, so we mustn't let her steal the limelight, must we?'

Mel thinks about this and replies, 'No.'

I sigh with relief – Machiavelli was a tactless berk compared to me – and light two cigarettes, one for each of us. Although I'm tempted to smoke them both, at once.

Five torturous hours later I make it home. The interview didn't go too badly. Unless I'm deluding myself. Best not to think about it. I'm sure it will be fine. I rub my eyes and press the Play button on my answer machine in the hope that at least one message will be from Chris. Sadly, all three are from my mother. I feel she should have her own flashing light on my machine so that I'm spared those three seconds of false hope. As her voice fills my hallway, an ugly feeling starts to swell inside me. Why isn't she sitting quietly with a bar of Dairy Milk watching any television drama starring Jane Seymour? I'm sorry if that sounds uncharitable but since the uneasy dinner celebrating Tony's promotion, our carefully neutral relationship has acquired an acidic tinge.

Today, her tone has an edge. The first message is to say that I 'looked peaky' and it was a shame that I had to 'rush off like that' and to call her when I get in. The second is an octave higher and suggests that 'it might be a nice idea' if I arrange for Tony to attend a ballet because he is 'quite smitten' with my friend and to call her when I get in. The third is as high and unsteady as a card tower in a gale, and begins, 'I'm worried about you' and ends 'I don't mind if you don't have time to call me but I'm surprised you can't do this one thing for your brother, you were such a good little girl and now . . .'

And the ugly feeling in my chest grows like an alien child, ripping and clawing to get out. I *am* a good girl. I am so fucking good Mother Teresa could have taken lessons from me. I am so fucking good I didn't have an orgasm until I was twenty-six years old. I am so fucking good that until last Friday the baddest thing I'd had up my nose was a tissue. I am a good girl and while I see that my Nordic-jawed brother is a more beauteous boastworthy proposition than me, he is not the chocolate box perfection my mother thinks he is.

I stand over the wittering machine like a dark shadow and think bad thoughts. That's what good girls do. Nice on the user-friendly outside, nasty to the gristle and bone. When the train grumbles into the station every morning, I could extend a pink pearly polished fingernail and tip that limp celery stick of a man on to the track. When I approach the zebra crossing in my car and a woman hurls a pushchair into my path, what if I pressed my kitten heel to the accelerator? And when I know that my brother is the father of an eleven-year-old girl, the flaxen-haired result of a nine-month fling during his year out in Australia, what if I told my mother – who aches to become a granny – that she can stop mourning my lack of procreation with such operatic grief because she already is?

Chapter 9

I woke this morning and was *aghast* at myself. Yesterday! What a nut. Feel free to disregard everything I said, I must have lost control of my hormones. Now they're in line again, I ring my mother to grovel for making her worry, and she is gracious in victory. Especially when I tell her that Mel is keen on Tony.

'I'll call him the minute I get into work,' I add.

'He's in a meeting,' says his PA, as she invariably does. 'He should be out by eleven.' When he hasn't rung by twelve I call again. As 'it's your sister calling' cuts as much ice as a cardboard ice-cutter, I ask his PA to say, 'It's your sister calling about the ballerina.' Seconds later, Tony's on the line.

'Yo,' he says.

'Hi,' I reply, stiffening as I realise I'm on speaker phone. 'Listen, I'm calling about Mel. Er, can people hear this? She's dancing tonight, Thursday night and Saturday matinée, and I thought it would be great if I invited Chris too and then we could all watch the show together. It's *Coppelia*, a really sweet ballet, you know, peasants dancing round a haycart, and you and Chris could get to know each other and then Mel would come out with us and we could go to see Blue Fiend, they've got a couple of gigs—'

'Floozie,' says Tony. 'I like it but I'm balls to the wall for the next two days, could you put it on a fax?'

'What a splendid idea,' I say, but as I am rarely sarcastic and Tony is immune to it anyway, he booms, 'Cheers easy,' and disconnects me.

*

'Tony can do Thursday,' I tell Chris, when my brother's PA gets back to me on Tuesday afternoon.

'Boss!' says Chris. 'The band are playing at the Monarch.' However he does not say 'Boss!' when I add that prior to watching Blue Fiend at the Monarch we will be watching Mel in *Coppelia*. 'Shit. I might have to leave early to help the band set up, they're on at ten,' he says.

'Oh, sure,' I say, unwilling to admit that it isn't *that* easy for me to secure free tickets nowadays. When I asked Matt for three seats, he said tightly, 'Press, are they?' I think he's anxious about the *Sun* health piece which is out this Friday. ('I'm not doubting you Natalia, but I can't believe the Ballet Police sanctioned it.')

But he relents and so on Thursday at 7.10, Chris strides into the lobby of the Coliseum, and Tony follows ten minutes later. Chris looks different, and I realise with pride that he's actually shaved. Tony – who wins Black Moon Records' Ligger Of The Year Award at their Christmas party *every* year – is hungover in Helmut Lang but dashing even so.

'My two favourites!' I sigh, linking arms with both of them.

'You big wuss,' says Tony, not unkindly. He hands me a fifty to buy the Bollinger, and I hurry back from the bar to apprehend any conflict. It's a relief to hear Tony say, 'So he's authorising these regular petty cash withdrawals, it's going on for months, people trotting in asking for "money for a shirt for a party" and the guy can't figure out why these shirts are always costing sixty quid!'

Chris laughs so hard he turns mauve. 'Reminds me of when I went to, er, Soho House with the guys from Uranus' – I see Tony twitch at mention of a rival label – 'We all chuck our credit cards on the table at the end of the meal, and there's a blue cotton tablecloth, right, and, for a laugh, yeah, I swipe everyone's credit card across it and, I'm telling you, man, every card left a faint white line!'

I look nervously at Tony, but he chortles, and says,

'You're having me on, mate, I heard the same tale from one of *our* lads—'

I glance at Chris and notice a deep red flush creeping up his neck, so I say, 'The show's starting in a minute, maybe we should go and sit down?'

We file into the blue and gold faded grandeur of the auditorium, the polite buzz of chat floating in the air like dandelion spores, the muted dress of the audience punctuated here and there by a child in a tiara and an elegant woman in emeralds and velvet, the rustle of programmes and the bustle of people jumping up to let others squeeze past to their seats. A smart voice courteously requests that all mobile phones be turned off. Tony and Chris look horrified.

The lights dim, a hush descends, and as the orchestra strikes up, Chris whispers, 'So how long does this malarkey go on for?' Five minutes later, Tony declares confusion at the plot. I feel like a nanny juggling delinquent twins.

'It's simple,' I whisper. 'Dr Coppelius is a toymaker, Coppelia is his mechanical doll—'

'Ooh er,' says Tony. 'Sounds a bit suss.'

And when I say to Chris, 'What do you think of Mel pretending to be Coppelia?' he replies, 'No offence – I think her dancing's wooden!'

Both men perk up briefly during the interval. Tony, gasping for caffeine, whistles at the usherette rather than walk two steps to the front row, and Chris chirps, 'How much padding did that gay ballerina have in his pants, it's like he stuck a pillow down there!'

He doesn't leave early to help his band set up, because he falls asleep at the start of Act III and remains unconscious until the curtain.

'I told Mel we'd meet her just inside the stage door,' I say. 'Will the band be okay without you?' I add as I see Chris glance at his watch.

'Oh yeah,' he replies. 'They're pros, they soundchecked earlier, and they know I'm meet— er, I thought we'd take

82

my motor, you know, if Tony wants to have a few jars. How much longer is Mel gonna be?'

'Here she is now,' I say, as the star of the show scampers towards us in tottery pink heels and a silver mini-dress. Tony's eyes bulge.

'Hello, Tony!' she cries. 'Hello, Natalie, oh! and who are you? How was I? I thought I was terrible! But Oskar was more terrible! Did you see him fail on that lift?'

'This is Chris, remember?' I say hastily. 'It's his band we're going to see. And don't be silly, you were great. You were fabulous, and the show was fabulous!'

Chris smiles at Mel – who is sucking up the praise like a whirlwind in a church – and says under his breath, 'It was two and a half hours of rivetless entertainment.'

Mel claps her hands and says, 'Oh goody, did you love it, Tony?'

Tony cries, 'You were stormin', darlin', you were wicked, you were massive!'

'I was . . . *massive?*' repeats Mel in an incredulous tone.

'He means you were wonderful, Mel,' I squeak, before I have a situation on my hands, 'not large in the physical sense.'

'Are we off then?' says Chris.

Five minutes later, we are standing in front of a large battered Volvo, burgundy except for a single panel which is beige. Chris tugs open the back door, winks at me and says in a mockney drawl, 'Laydeez.' I scramble in and Mel follows. 'Should be a great gig tonight,' he declares to Tony, revving up. 'The NME was talking about a feature on the band, and some of the A&R boys said they'd come down—'

'*Some* of the A&R boys?' says Tony. 'They're like a flock of sheep, mate, it's all or nothing with that lot.'

'Yeah, yeah, I know, but between you and me, three majors are interested but I'm playing it cool—'

'This noise is horrid, Chris, it's so loud I can't bear it, it's giving me a migraine, please turn it off!'

As the noise in question is Blue Fiend's demo tape (I've heard it forty times in the last fortnight so I know), I shrink in my seat. Chris pokes his finger at the eject button, as if it were Mel's eye, and it spits out the tape. He stuffs it into his pocket.

'Thank Christ for that,' says Tony. 'Talk about dad rock. Who the fuck were they? Whoever they are they won't sell a fucking unit.'

'Er, no one really, bunch of chancers, what with the buzz around Blue V—, Blue Fiend, word's got round and they want me to manage them. Yeah, right!'

'So,' I say, 'the place will be packed tonight. How exciting!'

'Oh Natalie, that reminds me, all those free tickets you gave me for the concert tonight, I've still got them in my bag, I did ask people but they didn't like the sound of the band, Blue Veined Fiend, it sounds so rude!'

A silence ensues, alleviated only by the piteous sound of the Volvo's engine fighting for breath. Tony bursts into a harsh laugh. 'Mel,' he says. 'I like you a lot. Will you marry me?'

Mel giggles. 'That depends,' she replies, 'on whether you promise to obey.'

Tony turns around and grins at her. 'You bring the whip, I'll bring the handcuffs, darlin',' he says.

Mel squirms in delight. 'That's not what I meant, you naughty boy,' she says. 'Oh Natalie, your brother is outrageous!'

'Here we are,' says Chris suddenly. 'My word, I mean bleedin' hell, will you look at those crowds! The birds – ten deep – *pushing*! Like the last days of Rome! And – snappers!'

There is indeed a scrum of fans and photographers barging and Chris is so shocked he nearly swerves into them. Tony looks at Chris with sudden respect. 'Seems like you've got a bit of an organic buzz going here,' he says casually. Pause. 'Street level, of course.'

Chris – dizzy with visions of Lear Jets and desperate to park the Volvo – burbles, 'I knew it! I knew this'd be the breakthrough gig! They're *it*, man, I'm telling ya – everyone loves 'em – kids into metal, frilly shirt fans, anyone under fifty who doesn't work in a bank, skateboarders, I tell you, they've got a cracking tune for their first single, you'll hear it – once it's out the box it's really gonna go off, and they're visual, goddammit they're pure theatre, I gotta think about the press photos, I'm seeing gritty, grainy, black 'n' white, the boys in front of a derelict building, or maybe grouped in a stairwell looking up, no, I've got it, the guys spaced out in a field, Tarqy, the frontman, close to camera, and a cow, a goat! no a cow, yeah a cow – Jersey! Friesian? Jersey! Friesian's a cliché, in the background, and the vid, I thought, the boys, in the Mexican desert, red Cadillac, MTV'll love it—'

I am speechless with joy on his behalf, which isn't a problem as he doesn't stop talking until the Volvo is parked and we are battling with the peasants outside the Monarch.

Chris pushes through the glut, plops out in front of the doorman and says, 'All right, mate, Chris Pomeroy, the guys' manager, yeah?'

The doorman – a primate in a tux – murmurs, 'Guest list closed.'

Chris cries, 'It can't be, I'm the manager!'

The doorman's right nostril lifts. 'You manage The Manic Street Preachers.' He isn't asking.

Chris's mouth drops like a trapdoor and he stammers, 'The – Muh, Muh – The *Manics?*'

Seven minutes later, after a text message to the right person on Tony's mobile, my brother, Mel, Chris and I access the Monarch, where one of the biggest rock acts on the planet are staging an impromptu set – a secret warm-up gig before their one huge UK arena date tomorrow night – and where Blue Fiend were shunted on ninety minutes early before their core fan base (i.e. their mums) arrived, and ignored by an elite audience until they slunk off twenty minutes later.

Tony instantly spies ten 'good friends' and vanishes into the fug, clutching Mel to him. He's so well-built and she's so bijou, they look like a very glamorous Laurel and Hardy. I sigh. The picosecond Tony discovered that the furore was in honour of the Manics, Chris dropped off his radar like a pebble off a cliff. I hunch my shoulders in a pointless attempt to protect my eardrums and light a cigarette, though the air is so choked with smoke I hardly need to. All my internal organs are rattling to the beat like pans in a drawer and I'm concerned a kidney might come loose.

'You supported the Manics!' I bawl at Chris, who has recovered from the doorman's slight and is delirious.

'I can go to any agent,' he shrieks, 'and tell 'em the boys have supported the Manics!'

Then he catches up with some A&R stragglers in the toilets. He leaves the Gents as wretched as a cat in a bath.

'What?' I screech in a voice as loud as the Big Bang but rendered noiseless by the Manics' sound system. It emerges that the A&Rs only made it in time to hear Blue Fiends' last track. And their collective response to *Flawless Gems and Snarly Beasts* was not ideal. The most constructive comment: 'Bands like that are *so* last century.' The less constructive: 'Bands like that are going nowhere', and the least constructive: 'They look and sound like a warthog farting.'

I try to interpret this verdict positively, and fail.

Chapter 10

My mother rings my mobile the next morning at 7.30, apparently to enquire, 'Juicy bolognaise mint.'

'Pardon?' I say.

'To see how last night went!' she roars.

'Sorry,' I say yawning and blinking myself awake. 'The gig was quite loud. I'm still deaf.'

She advises me to syringe out my ears. 'Where are you, dear? I rang you at home but you didn't answer.'

'I'm – um, staying with Chris.'

There is a delicate silence. 'You haven't heard from Saul then. How did Tony get on with that girl? Funny little thing, she was, it was like shaking hands with thin air.'

'Very well indeed,' I say, grinning. '*Very* well.' I glance at Chris, asleep beside me, and cover the mouthpiece. 'He and Mel seem really taken with each other. Although it was a bit awkward with Chris, his band got depressed and threatened to quit because they didn't go down very well with the A&Rs.'

My mother sniffs. 'Oh well, that lot,' she says dismissively. 'They change their minds from one week to the next. Tell him not to worry. An identical act will get signed and then they'll all come running. What are they? Funk metal? Death? Speed? Thrash?'

'Chris calls them Romo metal,' I say.

'That's a new one on me,' she replies tartly. 'Do they hammer on and pull off?'

'Mum, that's quite a personal question, I mean—'

'Natalie, you are funny! Does their sound feature any Van Halen style guitar solos?'

'Of course, er, no.'

'What amplification do they use?'

'Gosh, I'm not quite su—'

'With metal you've got to use Marshalls, dear, you can't use those old Vox AC30s, they feed back terribly.'

I smile grimly at Lenin, courtesy of an Andy Warhol print on Chris's bedroom wall, and wonder if my mother involves herself too keenly in her son's career. I wouldn't mind but last week she asked me if a pirouette was a puppet.

'How was Weight Watchers?' I ask, to change the subject.

'Fine, thank you dear. I took off my chiffon scarf before I stood on the scales.' She stops, then adds, 'Although I must say, it isn't the same as it was. In the old days if you lost weight they'd ring a bell. They'd say how much you lost and everyone would give you a clap. Things have moved on a bit now. No one rings bells.'

'And – ah – how are you doing?' I enquire carefully.

'Not bad. I lost one and a half pounds last week. But I gained one the week before. One on, and one off. One on, and one off. Tony says it's like listening to the football results.' Her high tinkling laughter sounds false, and when I join her, so does mine.

'Oh well,' I say. 'Easy come, easy go.'

'Easier come.'

'Have you spoken to Tony?'

'Natalie, I couldn't call him at this time of the morning! He'd be fast asleep!' With that, my appetite for chat tails off. I switch off my mobile. Then I lie back, and try to drift into sleep, but Chris's nose whistles as he breathes. It's like sharing a bed with a collie. If he was Saul I'd pinch it quiet but like all bullies I'm a coward. (Chris hates being woken up and will happily string out a revenge sulk for twenty-four hours.)

Stealthily, I sit up. The only available reading matter is a pile of *Kerrang* magazines, a rhyming dictionary, and two books: *Quotations from Chairman Mao Tse Tung* and *How to Write a Hit Song*. I roll on my stomach and catch my reflection in the antique mirror headboard. It is smudged with girls' fingerprints, and my hair is greasy. Great. Maybe a bath will wake me up. I tread over decaying shirts, creep to the bathroom, and softly turn on the art deco bathtaps. I place a sponge under the gushing water to muffle it.

I sink into the cast iron monster, squeeze a dot of Aveda shampoo on my hair (Chris has more beauty products than the Queen of Sheba) and rub it in. Then I rinse off the foam in the tub instead of using the shower head, so as not to wake sir. I don't pull the plug for the same reason. It's only when I am patting myself dry with a towel that I notice. I stiffen and my hand freezes. I stare at the bath in disbelief. There's a sudden tightness in my throat. I stoop until my face is an inch from the soapy water and I can hear the blood rush to my head in panic. What *is* this?

Hundreds of long blonde hairs, floating like bodies, in the water. *My hair.* I stare for a moment longer, but the sight is obscene and I yank out the plug. Then, slowly, I raise my hand and gently pull. Five hairs. I pull again. Seven hairs. Again. Four hairs. Again. Eight hairs. Eight. My heart is bopping along to the Manics and I feel like a woman in a horror film come real. Oh God, if only this was a dream. (Except I know it isn't, because when it *is* a dream, you never think 'oh God, if only this was a dream.') I swirl around to the huge mirror, snap on the showbiz lights, and inspect my scalp. The white skin between the strands, sick milk-white skin . . .

'What are you doing? Have you got nits?' says Chris, a greyish irritable ghost in the doorway.

'I'm going bald – my hair is falling out!'

Chris snorts and says, 'Don't be mad, women don't go bald.'

'But look!' I shriek, pulling at my scalp. Three hairs obligingly come away in my hand.

'Well, of course it'll come out if you *pull* it out,' he says. 'Don't pull it.'

'But look at the bath!' I plead. Chris walks over to the bath as if it's a long way, and says, 'Ur. You're moulting, princess.'

I start to twirl my hair – oh God, maybe that's why – and stop.

'Could be stress,' adds Chris. 'I reckon you're due a sickie.'

A *sickie!* I don't take sickies! I'm Employee of the Month, every month! (Well, if the GLBallet was McDonald's I would be.) I don't do things like that, but then . . . I stare at the bath and think, what do I care? My hair is falling out, Babs says I can't say no, she isn't even speaking to me, I feel lost without her, I'm exhausted from the gig – or rather, from spending till 4 a.m. humouring Chris who was up and down like a yo-yo – and I don't want to go into work. I carefully dry my hair with Chris's huge stainless steel hairdryer – it's powered like a jet engine and transforms me into Bonnie Tyler – and at 8.45 leave a message on Matt's voice mail.

'Matt, I'm really sorry, but I think I'm seriously ill,' I whisper, as Chris listens in, nodding. 'I've got a terrible migraine, it's making me sick, I'm staying at my mother's, she's looking after me.'

Chris makes a 'stop' gesture, and cuts me off. 'Princess. Too much yap, it's a dead giveaway.'

I stare at him, aghast. 'But I said that so he wouldn't ring me at home and get suspicious when I wasn't there,' I squeak.

Chris laughs. 'I take it back then. You're a pro,' he says, ruffling my *Dallas*-meets-*FrightNight* hair. I fight the urge to lurch away from his hand.

'Do you really think it's stress?' I say, touching my hair, almost, softly, then away again, like it's an ice sculpture.

'Yeah, man, it's gotta be,' replies Chris. 'Don't think about it or you'll make it worse.' I smile at him, he looks so thin and boyish in his boxer shorts. I'm desperate to believe him. But I keep seeing those hundreds of hairs gently swirling in the bath, every one a symbol of doom. I mustn't worry. If I worry, it'll come out in tufts and I'll be bald in a month. I need to get away from myself. (Sometimes I see myself as others see me and I don't like it – I feel it's one problem I should never have to deal with.) But I'm stronger than my fears.

I size up Chris and say, 'So, what shall we do today?' I want him to take me to bed and make me feel good again. After he's cleaned his teeth, of course.

The trouble is, he isn't going to feel like it today, not after last night, he was off his head. Today – as I now know – is comedown day, a wretched no-fun snappy day, the burlesque beauty of yesterday faded to grey. *I* didn't have any. I've gone off coke, ever since I sneezed and literally blew a hundred quid in one second. Also, I wanted it, so I knew I couldn't have it. (I've decided I have an addictive personality. I'm not allergic to wheat or peanuts, I need *something* to make me special.) Chris grabs my hand.

'Tell you what,' he says. 'I'll fix us something for the weekend.'

My heart sinks but I decide not to hurt his feelings. And two surprisingly dull hours later, he has today's entertainment wrapped. (As exciting as it is to play wild child with a bad boy while everyone else toils, I am shocked that buying drugs is so *menial*: a long trundly drive to Wimbledon where Chris's white middle-class dealer resides in a neat semi, and a decade of stultifying hairdresser chat before we can make our getaway. Secretly I was hoping for something more sordid.)

'After you,' says Chris, and when I hesitate, he adds, 'Coke is a clean, safe drug!'

I hesitate again. Tony says only gibbons die on drugs but knowing my luck, my inner self is hairy, says 'oo oo oo!' and has knuckles that trail along the ground.

Chris murmurs, 'You're more of a prescription drugs kinda girl, aren't you?'

I'm goaded into doing a line.

'It's very moreish, isn't it?' I giggle, as we fall into bed, young and in love with our new personalities.

Chris is otherwise engaged when his mobile rings. 'Y' ello!' he says gruffly, pinging up and whipping the microphone on his hands-free headset down to his mouth. (His motto is 'Stay Connected.')

'It's for you,' he says accusingly. I widen my eyes, shut my legs, and, sniggling, purr, 'He*llo*?'

'Miller, what the fuck are you playing at?' says a voice. The joy drains away. I gulp and the taste is bitter.

'How, how did you . . .?' I trail off.

'Your mum rang.'

I sniff, and dab my nose on my wrist. (I don't want the coke showing down the phone.) 'Right,' I say. 'But this number. How . . .?'

'In your Rolodex. You're just too efficient for your own good, Natalie,' adds Matt.

'I'm really really sorry,' I whisper. Sniff, dab. And I am. Sorry to be found out. Thank you, *Mother*.

'Did you see the *Sun* today?'

'Not yet,' I mutter. Sniff. Dab.

'Mm, well, I suggest you have a look. Because today, for the amusement of their ten million readers, they ran that little health piece you organised for Mel, complete with the doctor-stroke-nutritionist's expert conclusion that her body fat is extraordinarily low, his reluctance to make an on-the-spot diagnosis, and his diagnosis nonetheless, that such low body fat is symptomatic of patients presenting with FUCKING ANOREXIA NERVOSA!' he bawls in my ear.

Metaphorically, I faint clean away. In reality, I say, 'Ooooooooooh!', which isn't useful to anybody.

'Are you doing coke?' he adds suddenly.

I sniff, dab, guiltily. It's like hiding a parrot under your jumper and it squawking 'Arraaaakk!' and you insisting, 'Actually no, that was *me*.' The excuses jostle in my head

92

then collapse in a heap before my brain has time to convert them into speech. 'Jesus, Natalie,' sighs Matt. 'Don't do it.' His voice is as soft as warm butter and it makes me want to cry. 'You've screwed up.'

I curl my legs and pull the duvet up to my neck. Matt pauses, and when I say nothing, adds, 'God knows. Sometimes I look at Mel and I think, there is a woman writing the longest suicide note in the world. It's one thing *us* knowing, the company knowing about Mel's little problem, the poor kid's had it for years, we've tried to help her but she isn't changing, she likes it, it's her way of trying to be perfect. But in PR terms, the world knowing is bad news. I know she's your new buddy, but this is your job. You could have picked any dancer but her. Most of them are gannets compared to Mel. I'm sorry, Nat. I can't protect you this time. The Ballet Police are rabid, and I have to tell you, it doesn't look good.'

My heart pumps horror. 'W— what do you mean?'

He sighs. 'Nat, you know the situation, they're *searching* for excuses to make redundancies. But look. I don't think they're going to make any decisions immediately, and if the *Telegraph* trip is a success, I'll make sure you get all the credit. I'll do my best for you' – I cross my fingers. If only I had long velvety ears and breath like a drain I might be able to charm him – 'but, Nat,' – he pauses – 'I've got to do what's best for my department too.'

'I know,' I whisper. The fear pounds, yet a small squiggle of hope dances in my chest. As far as I know, I've done an excellent job on the Italy trip. Matt and Julietta are booked to fly to Verona on Wednesday evening, the photographer and make-up artist fly out in the afternoon – the hotel rooms are booked, the shoot has been sanctioned by the authorities and will take place early Thursday morning, giving the *Telegraph* ample time to slap the picture of Julietta poised on Juliet's balcony on its front page for Friday: Valentine's Day, and the opening night of GLBallet's *Romeo and Juliet*.

'—left, now might be the time to take it.'

'Pardon?'

'Nat! Get it together, will you! I said, you've got all your holiday left for this year, and I suggest you take a few days now. Lie low, sort your head out. Yes? I'll expect you back Wednesday lunchtime.' Then he rings off. I stare at the mobile, numb and frozen except for my heart, bop bop bop.

Chris plods back into the bedroom in a stripper's gown. Or boxer's robe, but frankly, it looks like a stripper's gown. 'Can I have my mobile back?' he says. 'You were on it for ages.' He peers at my brimming eyes and adds, 'What's up? You're not going to get emotional on me, are you?'

I grit my teeth. Emotional on *him*? Last night this man was C 3PO in a flap! Then I say, 'Don't worry, I don't do emotional. But aren't you going to ask me what that was about?'

'No, but I'm sure you'll tell me anyway.'

I keep the tale short, in accord with his attention span. Chris wipes a hand down his face as if erasing it and says, 'He's exaggerating. He's pissed off because you took a sickie.' Then, 'You've killed the mood, doll. The mood's dead, you killed it.'

I don't have the will to argue so I say I'm sorry and his mood softens, and he offers to call me a cab. (He also, rather sweetly, tells me that it's my *duty* to take sickies, that ideally I should be taking ten a year, since if we all did our bit, it would make it that much easier for everyone else.) I'm neither consoled nor convinced. An hour on – after boring the cabbie to death with my woes – I fall into my flat. I don't know if it's me or the coke but I feel dead inside. I hover over the phone and glare at it, like a vampire tempted to order a garlic pizza. What am I scared of? I grab the receiver and speed dial.

'Hey!' says Babs happily, forgetting we've argued. 'I was mowing the lawn.'

'Sorry,' I reply (sorry is my auto-response these days). I picture Babs cutting a square of grass the size of a table mat while her neighbours look on appalled, wondering why she can't hire a garden design consultant like everyone else. I'm about to start bleating about work when she adds, 'I was going to call you. You've got a fan.'

'Really!' I squeal, vanity crushing my more urgent problems under its elephantine foot. 'Who?'

'Robbie!' she cries. 'He's mad about you, and he's such a lovely bloke. He—'

'He's balding,' I say – somewhat hypocritically, as I am too. 'Anyway, I'm seeing Chris.'

'Him,' says Babs, dragging this small, modest word through an ugly swill of meaning. 'He ignored the dress code and he never bought us a wedding present. Si only invited him to make up the numbers.'

'You mustn't take it personally, Babs,' I say, straining to be nice. 'The thing about Chris is . . . Chris, er, doesn't believe in wedding presents. He's not very big on tokens.'

Babs reacts like a religious bigot judging an atheist's taste in furniture. And amid the huffing, I gather that 'token' wasn't a wise choice of word.

I realise, with a jolt, that I'm not going to tell her about work – I no longer feel her understanding is guaranteed. I want to deprive her of *my* intimacy. And to think our relationship used to be so *easy*. I feel awkward around her, like an alien impersonating a human being. To calm her down, I say, 'You are right, though. Robbie is a lovely guy.' To my relief – I suppose – Babs replies, 'Look, give him a bell, go for a drink, it doesn't have to mean anything.'

I note that while coupled female friends are constantly, kindly eager to pair up their unattached peers, their generosity rarely extends to seeking out taller, sexier men than their own. That said, I called to make peace, and offended instead. I silently take down Robbie's number, and promise to ring him.

Chapter 11

What gets me is that the world is full of chancers who gamble and win, whereas *I*, who have adhered primly to the rulebook since the day I was born, come unstuck the second I shut it. What will I do now? For the last sixteen years, Babs has got me through it, whatever *it* was. When Dad left, even though I was fine, Babs shared double-desks with me for the entire school year (Frannie tried to stir up trouble between her parents to no avail). I never had to *edit* myself with Babs. She gave me confidence. Now she's been taken away, I'm falling apart.

I'm not falling apart, I'm fine. And to prove how fine I am, I'll go to the gym. Or I could go for a swim. I haven't swum for ages, and I love swimming. There's an Olympic-sized pool near Hendon, and when I lived at home I'd swim a hundred lengths every Sunday, then go home and fall asleep. I have good stamina. You knew it would be the gym, I think, as I walk in to the cramped reception area. Even though it meant going back into town. I can't resist the running machine. Babs will jog along the hard shoulder to avoid the running machine – it gives her the sense of 'going nowhere fast'. I like it.

'Not *again*,' says a husky voice.

I press the red 'STOP' button, and turn around to see a goddess in black and white lycra.

'Alex, hello!' It's all I can do to stop myself hugging her. I adore friendly people – you know, the sort who raise a hand when you stop to let them cross the zebra crossing, who catch your eye and smile when a religious zealot starts preaching on a train, who say, 'You dropped a fiver, love,' when you drop it – the sort who spread a little casual happiness because while they know that universal hostility is understandable, it isn't necessary. There aren't enough of them.

'You're a permanent fixture on that machine,' she says. 'I think that getting you into the Pilates studio will have to be my new mission.'

'Oh! Thank you. I'm flattered.' Over my dead body. Non-aerobic. Zzzz! No way is she *ever* going to get me into the Pilates studio, what a shocking waste of precious endorphin time!

Four minutes later I'm lying on a blue mat, getting acquainted with my corset muscles. I'm not sure I like it. There's very little in the way of sweat, and the class is full of fat old ladies, one of whom farts like a trombone while reaching for her toes. I just about bite through my lip to keep from laughing. The exercises should be easy but aren't. Even an order as simple as 'sit on your sitting bone, with a straight back and your legs stretched out in front of you – taller! Straighter! Engage the stomach and back muscles!' proves an excruciating form of torture. Stretching is agony and a bore, and I can only deduce that I've been sensible to avoid it. Another manoeuvre requires you to sit on the floor with your fingertips on your bent knees – 'don't let your toes touch the floor!' – to scoop in your stomach and roll on to your back in a ball shape, *then* to haul yourself up into a sitting position using your 'transversus abdominis' which, I guess, is a posh term for stomach muscles. I manage it, by cheating.

Alex shakes her head and grins. 'You're using your legs to gain momentum, Natalie. Forget your legs. Imagine you have no legs!'

I hate not being the perfect pupil immediately. And there's a tedious emphasis on 'correct' breathing. My feeling is, I've breathed my way all my life and not suffocated. That's got to be good enough, surely? At one point

97

I realise I feel dangerously calm – which leads me to believe I'm not working hard enough. So I introduce a little pace to a lower back exercise and Alex tells me to take it easy! (Her exact words, 'You don't have to kill yourself – Pilates exercises don't *look* strenuous but they are – they're deep and strong, so a little goes a long way.') I don't believe her but when the class ends I find I'm exhausted. It must be boredom.

'It was great,' I tell Alex afterwards. 'I loved it!'

'That's a relief – after I committed the cardinal sin of dragging you off the StairMaster. I'm really pleased. Listen' – she checks her watch – 'are you free for a quick coffee?'

I watch Alex drink a hot chocolate and eat a caramel and raisin flapjack. She grins at me and says, 'My New Year's resolution was to incorporate chocolate into every meal. How about you?'

'Oh gosh. I had millions! To do more exercise, eat less rubbish, drink more water, spend less money, be more tidy – um, I'm sure there were loads more but I've forgotten them. I think I wrote them down somewhere.'

Alex smiles. 'My sister Louise is like you, Natalie. She was going to give up crisps, wheat, drinking, smoking, and exercise four times a week. She rang me on the fourth of January to say she'd broken all five resolutions in one day. To be honest with you, Natalie, I was surprised she'd held out that long.'

I giggle, although privately I suspect that Louise and I couldn't be more different. I say, 'It's all about self-control, I suppose.' Instead of adding her opinion, Alex waits for me to continue. Suddenly, I feel bashful. 'I did like Pilates,' I blurt. 'I'm just annoyed that I couldn't do that roly-poly thing right.'

Alex bursts out laughing, and squeezes my arm. 'Natalie. Don't be so hard on yourself! You did brilliantly. It was your first class for goodness' sake. And there's no real right way of doing Pilates – it's all about what's best for *your* body. That's why I like it so much – it's customised. I hope you come again. I think I might make you! A few more classes and you'll be an addict.'

Not likely, I think, as I stuff my dry and unsullied gym kit into the washing machine at home. Although Alex herself is a sweetheart. I feel as if I've known her a lot longer than I have. *She*'d have sympathised if I'd told her about being laid off. Oh hell. I'd forgotten about that. I flop at the kitchen table and pass the time by pulling at my hair and watching it fall. At ten past five, the phone rings.

'Dear, how *are* you I called you at work this morning and Matthew was under the mistaken impression you were ill and were staying with me well I was so concerned I rang you back instantly but your mobile was off and I've been going out of my mind all day, what are you doing tonight?' Without waiting for a reply, my mother adds, 'I'll make you dinner, why don't you come round at six thirty if you're not at work?'

After seeing Alex, I *was* feeling relatively balanced. Not any more. On the way to Hendon I drive through a shaft of sunlight and jump because I think I've been snapped by a speed camera.

'Get it together, Natalie,' I growl. I force myself to sing along to the Pet Shop Boys and tell myself that my redundancy is a threat, not a certainty. But when I share this thought with my mother she disagrees.

'Oh Natalie!' she cries, dabbing at the corners of her eyes with her knuckles and staring at me as if the 'Hungry And Homeless' sign is already visible. 'Whatever will you do now? You'll be unemployable!' With these cheering words, she deposits a sailboat-sized plate of liver and onions and mash on my side of the table. On her side, she deposits a glass of white wine, a small bag of salted peanuts, and a low-fat chocolate mousse. (This is patently *not* a dinner recommended by Weight Watchers, but my mother is an expert on points and mistakenly believes she can cheat the system.) I inhale through my mouth to avoid smelling the liver. Tony is the one who likes liver, remember? I shout inside my head. As for me, the idea of eating a chicken's *liver* – anyone's liver, in fact, I'm not fussy – makes me want to puke.

'Mum,' I say, soothingly (although I want to scream: I'm the one who needs soothing here!), 'I haven't been kicked out yet. It could be all OK.'

She bites her lip, as if she cannot understand what she has done to deserve such a stupid daughter. Then she blurts, 'It could be, but it never is!'

'It might be,' I say in a low voice, because I barely trust myself to speak.

My mother throws down her napkin. 'I knew Chris Poodle was a rotten influence,' she exclaims. 'But it's too late – Saul won't have you back now! I wouldn't mind, but you don't even give the nice ones a chance!'

I think of Saul. I want to screech, His boobs are bigger than *mine!* And he's got a tongue like an anteater!

When I don't reply, my mother jerks out of her poor-me pose and stares accusingly. 'I don't understand, Natalie,' she says. 'You haven't even explained what it is you did. It must have been terrible for Matthew to do this!'

I'm unsure if she means that my crime must have been severe, or if she is commiserating with Matt over the agonies he suffered in shopping me to the Ballet Police. I scrunch up my napkin until it is invisible to the human eye. And I say dully, 'I made a few silly mistakes.'

'What mistakes?' she shrills. 'They must have been extremely silly for this to happen!'

I tell my mother about Mel and the *Sun* piece.

She gasps, 'Not *Tony's* Mel?'

'Yes,' I hiss through my teeth. '*Tony's* Mel.'

Sheila Miller picks up her napkin and throws it down, again, *on* to her chocolate mousse – a sign of how upset she is as she considers it shocking manners not to clear your plate and has been known to reproach offenders with the words, 'Didn't your mother teach you anything?!'

100

When she replies, her voice is hushed (the Cancer Voice, I call it). 'Oh Natalie, how could you? How thoughtless, how exceedingly thoughtless. I can't believe you could be so thoughtless. So embarrassing for Mel! And for—'

As my mother says the word 'Tony' for, at a conservative estimate, the billionth time in six minutes, I feel a sharp tear rip across my chest, as surely as if a part of me has broken. Before I know what I've done, the liver and onions and mash are sliding down the magnolia wall and I am screaming so loudly that the neighbours won't have to bother to fetch a glass.

'Why is it always, always about Tony? I'm sick of it! Tony this! Tony that! He's so bloody wonderful and I'm such an abject failure' – it annoys me that even when I lose my temper I use words like 'abject' – 'Well, I tell you what – he's not so wonderful, mother, why don't you get your precious Tony to tell you about his secret bloody daughter he's kept a bloody secret for eleven bloody years, get him to tell you about that, oh I love it, so bloody perfect he picks the perfect bloody woman, doesn't he, a sorted sweet-natured girl, in frigging Australia, could she be any more convenient, sends him a picture once a year, doesn't harass him for money oh no, he gets to bury his mistakes, live his perfect fucking hedonistic life, drive the car, so successful, so bloody—'

'Natalie,' interrupts my mother in a low voice. At the sound of it my mouth snaps shut like a pair of castanets, reality hits with the force of a speeding juggernaut, and I stare at her in terror. My mother is a big barrel of a woman but at this moment she looks tiny in a giant world – a little chump, sitting in front of a mess of mash and onions slithering down the magnolia wall. 'Hand on my heart,' she continues in the same expressionless tone, 'I have never been ashamed of you in my entire life. But today, right now, I'm sorry to say that I am.'

101

Chapter 12

It's like complaining of a stomach ache and being diagnosed with a baby alien. You might sense a twinge but you have no understanding of the rampant ugliness inside you. I don't hear myself until I stop talking, and then I can't believe such filth came out of my mouth. I feel invaded and half expect a green claw to burst from my belly button. Who *put* it there? She can't believe it either. We remain frozen, staring warily at each other like two cats gauging whether to leap into a fight. (If we had tails, they'd be swishing.) I don't dare move, until my mother drops her gaze to the tablecloth and says numbly, 'I probably need to clear up.'

I turn and run.

What have I done? What *have* I done? It's her fault, though. I hate liver. I sit in traffic and the driver behind me hoots because the lights are green and I didn't accelerate from 0 to 60 on amber. I give him the finger then worry that he'll leap from his Nissan Micra and attack me with a crowbar. Mind you, he'd be doing me a favour – Tony probably wouldn't shout so loud if I was in intensive care. I feel like I've swallowed a volcano. I fumble with the door, lean over, and retch on to the road. I'm sweaty and shaking. Which would I prefer: serious head injuries or my brother's rage? Brain damage, of course – there's no contest.

The phone shrieks as I walk into my flat and I want to rip it out of the wall. Right now I could *do* with an alien – he could make himself useful and zap me into space. It occurs to me that if I was Paws, I wouldn't have to deal with any of this. My existence would be an endless picnic of farts, naps, and being fussed over. Dreaming about life as a basset hound – Gucci accessories and being wrenched from your family at six weeks – I lift the receiver to my ear like a gun.

'Princess,' says Chris.

I just about weep with relief and croak, 'Hi.'

He sniffs. Then, in staccato bursts, he says, 'You and me. Sunday. Three thirty. My gaff. Be there.'

It's like talking to an AK47 which, in my present condition, is a pleasure. I want to tell him what I've done but I can't. He's not interested. (My dilemma: I'm attracted to Chris because he's wild, yet I want him to care about the bumfluff of my life. And these twin desires come from my *brain?*) It's nothing to Chris that my mother is ashamed of me. My mother is ashamed of me. Oh God. Sometimes you suspect it, but to actually *know* . . . The ugly feeling is back, heavy in my gut. It's her fault. I drift into the bedroom and lie stiffly on my bed until the phone rings again. It's like waiting for a train when you're late for work but tied to the track.

'Hello?' I falter.

'You stupid little girl,' says my brother – mild words but his tone is scathing – 'I can't believe you did that.' His voice starts off quiet and grows louder and louder. I cringe, as he yodels on. His complaint – which if I exclude the swearing is brief – is that I have complicated things. It's true. Tony's life is as straightforward as a Topsy & Tim book. I've turned it into *War and Peace*.

Because this was never about morality (I know I said I was square but, please, I'm not Ann Widdecombe). I've never thought it an outrage that Tony has a daughter from a passing affair, because the woman he had the affair with was so happy to have the baby (indeed, Tony running back to Blighty was probably a bonus for her). On the irresponsibility scale he's a Two, compared with some.

Frannie has seen one guy impregnate – or rather seen the results of one guy impregnating- *five* different women in one year. My brother's fatherhood is not a scandalous secret, despite what the neighbours in Hendon will say.

It *is*, though, a situation he has preferred to ignore, because family involvement is vastly inconvenient. One reason my brother is so successful is that he has a borderline schizophrenic talent for dividing his life into separate compartments. Things get in the way otherwise.

'Tony, I'm so, so sorry,' I whisper.

'Do you fuckin' know what this means?' he yells in my ear.

I nod. While Tony seems to indulge our mother's obsession with his every move – not that tough as he enjoys talking about himself – he's only ever let her skim the surface. While dispensing informatory snacks at a generous rate (Mum, don't tell anyone, but So-and-so refused to land at Luton airport because Luton isn't very rock 'n' roll . . . Mum, you shoulda seen it, this unsigned band hired a topless double decker, did it up like a set, played outside Black Moon till they got moved on by a traffic warden), Tony keeps the gourmet facts back. He's in marketing. As if he's honestly going to say what he thinks. My mother scrapes at the hard shell of his private life like a mole digging at granite.

'This,' he shrieks, 'is the tip of a great big fat granny iceberg invading all our lives!' He never spoke a truer word. I nod dumbly at the phone. The granny iceberg is now adrift and its hulking destructive might is floating this way, crushing all resistance in its path. Tony didn't *want* any of this. Since our father eloped to LA, Tony has been his own man. He plays the dutiful attentive son and brother, yet he keeps his distance. *He's* never asked me if I want a line. Despite the chat, Tony keeps to himself. That's how he operates. I only know about Kelly and Tara because he rambled out the tale one Christmas when he was as mashed as the parsnip purée.

Secretly, I'd love to meet them. I've always been fascinated by Tony's secret family. First, I thought a secret family was glamorous (you grow up in Hendon, you get your kicks where you can), and second, I think we'd get on. Kelly is an artist, and she sounds great – sensible, but fun – and Tara sounds like a nut. In annual letter number five, Kelly wrote that when Tara grew up she wanted to be 'a Hoover'. Tony told me this while in a cocaine haze, and sniggered, 'Just like her dad.'

He showed me a photo, and I thought, how can he *not* want to see this little mouse, with brown skin, white blonde hair, and bright blue eyes, her father's eyes? My niece. I think of Tara and I know that until Tony surrenders every last detail of the pair of them – including their preferred breakfast cereal and Kelly's mother's maiden name – our mother will be at him like a Fury fighting over handbags at the Harrods sale. And that's just the beginning. My brother's time is up and it is my fault.

'She'll have 'em over here, living in Hendon!' he bawls. 'My bloody *soul* will be public property!' While this is blatant artistic licence for Tony who – as far as I am aware – doesn't possess a soul, I know what he means.

'Are you sure?' I quaver. 'I mean, swapping Bondi beach for – for Brent Cross and Blockbuster Video, they might not—'

Tony screeches, 'Mum's on her way here! I'm going to New York tomorrow morning! This is going to be endless! It is going to be no end of hassle! It'll be like fuckin *EastEnders*!'

This, I fear, is not an exaggeration. I try very hard not to cry, and succeed.

'I tell you one thing,' he growls. 'That berk you hang around with, his shite band, they are *so* over! Bands come and go, and his are *gone!* Tell him this from me, darlin – you can't polish a turd!' He slams down the phone so hard my eardrum nearly ruptures. I pull at my hair – three hairs, I think without feeling. I want to call my mother and make

105

it better, but I can't. She's on her way to Tony, anyhow, the scourge of other road-users, driving her blue Metro at the pace of a wheelbarrow, bolt upright, nose an inch from the windscreen, both hands gripping the wheel at ten to two. She'll have done her make-up before leaving the house. No one puts on lipstick like my mother does. She applies it once, blots it with a tissue, and applies it again. Then she sticks a finger in her mouth and pulls it out smartly with a pop. 'Otherwise you get red on your teeth, dear, and that's vulgar,' she explained once. I think of her long-suffering powdery face, lined with years of worry and watching *Murder She Wrote*, and I feel ashamed. It isn't her fault. None of it. The ugly feeling shrivels, and a custardy dollop of guilt settles in its place. She has always meant well, yet I wanted to hurt her. I did, but I hurt myself more. In a bolt of lunacy, I believed I could prise Tony off his pedestal. Like some priggish Victorian, repelling her with dastardly tales of illegitimacy and shame! Instead, I've fuelled her Oedipal obsession. And shown myself to be small-minded and pea-brained to boot. I'm the forgotten godmother trying to scupper Sleeping Beauty's marriage prospects. My mum is ashamed of me.

But the guilt can't wash away the injustice of it all. I admit I brought it upon myself, but I can't help thinking, I'm in disgrace, why is Tony untarnishable? I'm not the one who, when River Phoenix died, sent an email to half of London which read 'Fucking lightweight'. I'm not the one who escaped jail because a sniffer dog checking a large black Beamer at Reading Festival got confused by a bag of cheese buns on the back seat. I'm not the one who discarded a pregnant woman like a bag of old cabbage because she was 'inconvenient'. And yet my mother is ashamed of *me*.

I wait in for her to call. At eleven, I ring her. I ring again at midnight. No answer. I realise that she is screening her calls. The idea is absurd. My mother worships the phone. Its shrill ring means that someone – even a pervert conducting a lingerie survey – needs her. I call her on

Saturday morning at 7.30 a.m. No answer. I bite my lip. There are three levels of rage: screaming rage, spitting rage, and silent rage. Silent rage is an advanced method of psychological torture. I know Tony gave her the KGB Training Manual for her birthday. I didn't think she'd *read* it.

I call Tony on his mobile. No answer. I even call Mel, no answer. I feel as if I've been punched in the stomach fifty times. I suck it in. It aches. I press it. Ouch! It must be psychosomatic. Wow, I'm impressed! That's serious. But I suppose losing your job and becoming an outcast *is* serious. Possibly for the same reason, my legs have seized up. I can barely hobble. I ignore the pain, and I spend the weekend pounding the treadmill like a hamster. I run until my kneecaps grate. It takes my mind off things. On Sunday morning I see Alex – she bounds through the gym as I sweat on the StairMaster. She clutches her head and makes an I Can't Believe It's Not Pilates face, but doesn't come over. I'm glad. I'm so awkward in my skin I feel like a robot masquerading as me. I can't fit a normal expression on my face, and small talk is a hazard – I'm terrified I'll short circuit and say something odd.

On Sunday afternoon I drive over to Chris, who reveals that he has an appointment with an A&R manager at Black Moon tomorrow at 10 a.m. and would I like to bunk work and come along. He won't say how he got it, but I suspect it involved lying.

'That's brilliant, Chris,' I say.

He grins, 'Yeah, I'm made up, me.' I try to smile but it won't happen. 'What?'

'I – I'm a little surprised, that's all,' I sigh.

He takes huge offence so, as I lack the strength to improvise, I tell him the truth: I've accidentally alienated Tony, who has sworn vengeance with, alas, express reference to Blue Fiend (I have the sense to leave out his comment about polishing). Chris stares at me, as if I've just shouted, 'Michael Bolton is the best solo artist in the world!'

'Don't worry,' I stammer. 'I'm sure Tony didn't mean it. He doesn't hold grudges.'

Chris looks frantic, and blurts that during the ballet, my brother said that the A&R manager at Black Moon was 'not your typical A&R', and Chris decided Tony was suggesting he make an appointment. That, and the magic words, 'We supported the Manics', secured Chris a meeting. Now what? What if they get talking in the lift and Tony slags the band?

'Look,' I say, trying to stay calm. 'Tony is in New York, he'll probably be there for a few days, so you're all right. And I don't think any Black Moon boys were at the gig, so it'll be fine.'

Chris scowls. 'No thanks to you.'

And while I think, *Au contraire, all thanks to me*, I keep this to myself, and agree to meet him in reception at Black Moon at 9.45 a.m. tomorrow. I'm shunned by my family and barred from work – what else am I going to do?

'Princess,' says Chris, who is perched stiffly on the silver Philippe Starck chaise longue trying to look relaxed. He is wearing a burgundy leather jacket, a Che Guevara shirt, and dark blue jeans.

'Hi,' I say, nodding at the pretty receptionists and trying not to stare at their phenomenal bosoms. 'I'm with him.'

We spend the next thirty-five minutes staring at framed covers of *Dazed and Confused*, and flicking through this week's NME, until a pale etiolated creature with slicked back hair and a metal spike through his ear appears, and croaks, 'Ben Buckroyd.'

He holds a hand out to Chris, and his eyes flicker over me. We are halfway up the oak stairs when Chris says, 'Er, Ben – no offence mate, but – er, I thought my er, meeting was with a geezer called Jon.'

Ben rakes a hand through his hair. 'Jon's tied up,' he rasps. Chris glances at me. Ben leads us into his office with a flourish. It smells like a stale ashtray and is the size of a broom cupboard, which means that Ben is a talent scout – the lowest of the low, with as much sway as a tree in a box.

Ben plops himself behind a small cluttered desk, gestures for us to be seated in two orange plastic chairs, then swings up his legs and sticks his feet in our faces. There is gum stuck to the soles of his Nikes. My foot kicks against something, which turns out to be a box of demo tapes. I look around and count eleven boxes crammed with cassettes and CDs.

'So you know Tony Miller?' says Ben. 'Shaggin his sister, are ya?' Chris pales and he smiles weakly at me. Ben looks at me too, a small pellet of understanding fires in his brain, he coughs, and says hurriedly, 'Let's hear it.'

Chris hands Ben the CD, he sticks it in a monster stereo, and presses Play. We are aurally mugged by the Blue Fiend classic *Lend Me Your Ears*. Chris dances in his seat (I'm reminded of *Rain Man*). While it would show solidarity to jerk my chin back and forth, I don't want to look as stupid as I feel. I know the first few seconds of the track are important, so I scrutinise Ben's face. Chris is staring at him like a rabbit at an oncoming car. Ben inspects his fingernails. Then he reaches out – time seems to ease into slow motion – and flicks to the next track. Chris looks stricken but bravely taps his foot to *Bitch out of Hell*.

'Sounds a bit ropey,' growls Ben. 'Where did you record it?'

Chris knows the question is a courtesy, and mumbles his answer. I sit there, mute and useless. I feel as small and silly as a wool jumper in a boil wash. Ben zaps through four tracks. He progresses from 'I'm not getting it', to 'Yer singer sounds like a drain.'

I hunch miserably, and gaze at the many photographs on the wall of minor pop acts and Ben, larging it. Finally Ben snaps off the sound. He rocks back on his chair, rests his hands behind his head and husks, 'Most people buy three albums a year – Celine Dion, Simply Red, and Travis. Which shows dodgy judgement. Even so, they ain't gonna buy this!'

Chris locates his voice box. 'If you met the guys you—'

'Sorry, mate. Between you and me, we don't have an active signing policy at the moment. I'm A&Ring two important bands, they're in the studio.' Ben removes his feet from the desk as a goodbye gesture.

'Thank you for your time,' I say as we kowtow out of his cupboard.

'All fuckin' four seconds of it!' spits Chris as he stomps into the street. 'I'm going home! Black Moon Records are crap!' Stomp stomp. Another burst – 'The rude bastard! He wouldn't know talent if it shagged him up the arse!' On which delectable thought, we part company.

I walk towards Camden tube, and try to feel Chris's pain. It's like trying to feel Saddam Hussein's pain. The – admittedly eighties, but – inescapable thought: *You were in there as a dolly bird!* thunders around my blonde head and I don't like it. My heart bops with the realisation. I don't like it! I am . . . I test the daring thought on the tip of my brain . . . *dis*pleased with Chris. I feel foolish. I had no business in that broom cupboard, Blue Fiend are nothing to do with me, I was dragged along as an ornament.

'Well, he's got poor taste in china,' I growl as I turn the key in the lock.

Once inside, I glance longingly at the phone but there are no messages. My mother hasn't talked to me for two and a half days. In appeasement terms, I am the Neville Chamberlain of the family. But this situation is unprecedented. I don't know what to do. I chew my lip (I've moved on from chewing my hair – those days are gone, baby) and suddenly, I do. I check a number on my notepad, dial it, and cross my fingers. Five minutes later, I leave a message on my mother's answer machine.

'Mum, it's me,' I say, trying to sound meek. 'I am very, very sorry for what I did. I feel ashamed, I really do. I wondered if you – I know it's not a great thing for, for a parent – I know it's not like when you came to see me star as a sheep in my infant school Nativity play, but maybe you could come with me on Wednesday morning to the, er, Jobcentre.' I have no intention of seeking employment from the Jobcentre, but know that my mother will appreciate the gesture. 'Not that I *am* going to be made redundant, but as a precaution. Also, I thought about what you said, about not giving the nice men a chance. And so I've just arranged to meet with a nice friend of Babs's brother. He's called Robbie. I'm seeing him tomorrow night.'

I expect this call to elicit a rapid response, and it does. I am standing in the bathroom baring my gums – to check if my teeth *are* lemon yellow or if it's the light – when the phone rings. My mother stonily informs me she's pleased about Robbie. Oh, and she won't be able to escort me to the Jobcentre. But my father will.

Chapter 13

'He's flying in tomorrow afternoon,' she says in a defensive *what have I done?* voice. She knows very well what she's done.

'He's staying at the St Martin's Lane Hotel.'

He would be.

'He's coming over for a number of reasons.'

I don't believe this.

'I thought you'd be pleased.'

My mind is goulash.

When my father wrenches himself from the unyielding embrace of surgically-curvy Kimberli Ann and his palm-balmy home in hot super-blue Malibu to visit his plump suburban *pre*-midlife family in drizzling England, you know it's serious. I dread to think what my mother said to him. I'm surprised she dialled the number. She speaks to him about once a year, and even then it's a short call. Possibly she derived pleasure from informing him that he was a grandfather, and that Kimberli Ann was – I imagine my mother failing to keep the glee from her voice – a step-grandmother. Quite a shock for a twenty-five-year old, I imagine.

I speak to him about once a month. I like my father. He is so affably unashamedly true to three decades of repressed teenage fantasies that it's hard not to like him. He's so touchingly content living his safe rich American Dream which – in its sunny sanitary form – has infinite advantages over the British Nightmare (two dentally-

112

challenged kids, a dumpy wife, a nondescript semi in a nondescript street, a Renault Megane). And the one time I met Kimberli Ann I had to conclude that – apart from her curious habit of punching you painfully hard on the arm every time you said something funny – she was a reasonable human being.

But my father is making this guilt trip alone. Kimberli Ann hates to be parted from Tweety, her bichon-frise, and furthermore, fears flying in case her implants explode (Kimberli's, not Tweety's, although if surgical enhancement for fluffy white dogs did exist, make no mistake, Tweety would be enhanced). Also, my father is reluctant to *graphically* remind Kimberli Ann of his first life – and meeting my mother would be as good as planting a large billboard in front of the Fairbush Gynecology Clinic inscribed with the taunt: DR VINCENT 'VINNY' MILLER IS PAST IT.

'When is he – er – expecting to see me?'

'He flies in at 4.30 p.m. and he and I have a great deal to discuss. As I'm sure you can imagine, in light of recent developments,' she adds stiffly. 'I said he wouldn't be able to see you until Wednesday, but you could go to his hotel for breakfast.'

'Right. Um. Did he, did he – what did he say when you told him?'

As I don't specify quite *what* she might have told him, I don't know which of this week's family kerfuffles her answer refers to which, to be honest, is how I prefer it.

'He said,' says my mother, her voice taut, 'it could be dealt with.'

I wake the next morning with an urgent but blurred thought niggling for attention. I blank and wait for the niggle to loom into focus. Mum. Kid. Dad. Here. Oh. No. I roll over and inspect my pillow for hair. Seven. The start of a long day. Still, I don't have to go into work. *Me*, a lifetime swot. With my job on the line. My stomach flops like a badly cooked pancake. I wonder what Matt will tell our assistant Belinda. She's back from Crete today, no doubt the colour of a radish. (She has auburn hair and pale skin and the word 'melanoma' means nothing to her – except, maybe, a fruit. Last year she went to Ios and got so burnt she puffed up like a Cheesy Wotsit and had to be carted off the plane in a wheelchair.) I'm very uncomfortable, having nothing to do. I need to be achieving. Maybe I should buy shoes? High heels would placate my mother ('Flat shoes give you thick ankles!'). Babs would be pleased too: she says I don't know how to treat myself. (She especially says this when her overdraft is the size of a house and all she has to show for it is a bile-green velvet blouse or fake zebra-skin stole, bought in under ten minutes in a non-refundable Dickins & Jones sale.) And I'm seeing Robbie tonight. Even though it is *not* a date, Babs would be peeved if I didn't make a token retail nod towards the occasion. I pull on two jumpers – the heating is turned to nuclear and I'm still freezing – and consider going shopping.

I should call Chris and tell him about Robbie. Tell him what? We'll be sharing a table. I'll be dressed. It's not disloyal to laugh at another man's jokes. I'm not attracted to Robbie. Am I an emotional cheat? If I meet him knowing that *he*'s attracted to me, am I guilty by association? I think of how I justified seeing Chris when I was going out with Saul. That was different. I was bad, I was punished. I made a fool of Saul a long time before Chris and I got horizontal. My intentions towards Robbie are platonic. I call Chris and tell him anyway.

'Fancies you, does he?' is his first question.

'Oh no!'

'Why else would he want to meet for a drink?'

'Because of my biting wit and charismatic personality,' I reply, deflated.

There is an impertinent pause. 'I'm meeting an agent tonight at Soho House,' he says casually. 'I was going to

114

ask you along. I reckon we're on for a wild one – booze, chat, bit of hokey-cokey!'

I pride myself on getting along with difficult people. But I'm still recovering from the revelation that as I own a fully functioning vagina, my biting wit and charismatic personality are superfluous. I also note that, despite the potent presence of a token vagina to lure his judgement astray, Ben still concluded that Blue Veined Fiend were rubbish.

I find myself saying primly, 'Is there no other way of communicating in the music business than by snorting coke together?'

Chris laughs. 'No,' he replies, 'there isn't, princess. It's the mobile phone of the industry.'

'You were right,' I tell him. 'I *am* a prescription drugs kinda girl.'

'Whatever,' he replies.

Chris puts down the phone and suddenly, sadly, I feel like I've lost everything.

I go to the gym, check the class schedule, and run my anxieties into the ground. Then – drugged on adrenalin and safe in the knowledge that the Pilates class ends in three minutes – I peek round the studio door and wave at Alex.

'Don't lie to me, girl, you timed that!' she says, as I help her roll up the mats.

I can't stop the grin. 'Guilty as charged.'

'How are you doing? I didn't come over on Sunday because I didn't want to harass you. Did you feel any effects from Friday's class?'

'Oh no, not at—' A possible cause of the crippling 'psychosomatic' stomach ache that plagued me all weekend suddenly dawns. 'Er, maybe a twinge here and there.'

Alex guffaws. 'You are *such* a liar, Natalie. I can see it in your face. Saturday morning, you were in agony. Admit it!'

'There's no need to be smug, Alex!' I reply. I grin like a moron all the way home.

A chirpy message from Robbie awaits me. He assumes we're still meeting at Ruby In The Dust in Camden at seven. There is also a series of friendly squawks from Belinda, asking me to ring when I get in. Matt can't have said anything. Nervously, I dial her number.

'Belinda? It's Natalie. How was Crete?'

'All right, Natalie. Ah, gorgeous, drank me weight in vodka an all me freckles have joined up!'

I smile. 'It sounds brilliant. What's up?'

'Oh, yeah' – a note of uncertainty creeps into her voice – 'Matt says you're workin from home today so it'll probably be easier if I make the last minute checks on the Venice—'

'Verona.'

'The Verona trip. I'm lookin at your paperwork, looks fine to me, but Matt's sayin it's gotta be micro-managed cos Italian bureaucracy stinks so I'm givin it the once over. Is there anythin I should be lookin out for?'

I tell Belinda she might want to confirm with the hotel again, and check that everyone received their tickets and flight details.

'I'm on it,' she trills. 'See you tomorrow then,' and rings off.

I don't go shopping.

I call Babs.

'I didn't wake you up, did I?'

Babs yawns. 'I was napping. I'm on at six. We had a bit of a night last night.'

'Really?' I say in surprise. As far as I can tell, fire fighting mostly entails attending alarms that go off for no reason, putting out fires in skips, and rescuing twits stuck in lifts. Burning buildings are as rare as four-leaved clovers. The most dramatic element of the job is the battle to secure a women's toilet that doesn't double as the cleaner's storage room, and finding trousers that fit. Until Babs kicked up a fuss she was expected to make do with the regulation *male* uniform when, as she told the Union, 'There's nothing uniform about the human race.'

'What happened?' I ask.

'Three shouts,' *call outs*, I translate in my head, 'and a mickey' – a false alarm. 'And then at eight in the morning, we're in the watch room, and this woman, well oiled, fake tan, spray-on skirt, stilettos, the lot, keeps staggering to and fro past the station flashing her tits at the lads and bawling "I want to slide down your pole!" It's daylight! She's got her bloke with her! He was so embarrassed. The lads were loving it, and then I tell her to clear off and she screams, "Oh shut up, you're just jealous because you look like a man!" I mean, Jesus! After four years the lads finally lay off – and the women keep going!'

'Babs,' I say solemnly, 'you know what some women are like. They can't stand another woman doing well – unless she's been hit with the ugly stick, then it's okay. You have Pre-Raphaelite curls and a fine bosom. You do *not* look like a man.'

'Huh,' says Babs.

'Guess what.'

'Tell me.'

I tell her *some* of my news. About Robbie: she's thrilled – slightly *too* thrilled for my liking. About my granny revelations (Babs knows about Tony's kid – I tell her everything).

Babs says quietly, 'Why did you do this, Nat? My God.'

I hesitate. I don't like being judged and I'm constantly grateful that most friends judge you behind your back. But Babs has a stunning amount of faith in her own opinions and an equally stunning habit of voicing them to your face. She says what she thinks without check. I marvel at her. To me, society is a minefield and if you don't keep to the designated path, several acres of manure blow up in your face. I shuffle slowly with bound feet while Babs strides along like a general, yanking the pin out of etiquette, hurling verbal grenades at the least provocation, all the while remaining invincible. I trail after her, picking up the pieces.

'It just came out,' I whimper.

'But *how?*' demands Babs. She sounds like a five-year-old on hearing the dubious news that babies emerge from navels. I decide she isn't capable of dealing with the truth so I skip, or rather long jump, the part about my teetering career and tell her that my mother and I had a row about Tony. I cringe, anticipating a reproach but to my surprise, Babs sounds pleased.

'You've had an *argument!*' she cries. 'Well done! You're telling her how it is, you're communicating! Finally! It's *so* what your family needs!'

I'm confused. As consequences have shown, this is the *last* thing my family needs. Nor do I see how hurling mash at the wall is communicating, and Babs doesn't seem to understand how much I hate and fear upsetting my mother. There is nothing worse except, maybe, this. I feel torn apart from my ex-best-friend and it's like trying to scream in a dream and realising you are voiceless. The energy seeps from me like sweat so I explain my father's arrival in as few words as possible. Babs can tell that I'm shutting her out and the spark in her voice fades.

'Well, I'm sure it's for the best,' she says, reading curtly from autocue. 'I hope you have a pleasant evening with Robbie.'

'Pleasant' is a middle-aged word and yet one more sign that our beautiful relationship is flagging. But despite my worries, pleasant is what my evening with Robbie turns out to be. When I walk into the restaurant, he is lounging in a squashy sofa at a low table, studying the menu. He is wearing a tight*ish* white T-shirt – which shows remarkable belief in the British weather system, considering it's February. He turns the page and his triceps shift like steel sausages beneath his skin. I've never been a fan of brawn and I want to turn and run. I march up to him.

'You look like you're waiting to be shot,' he remarks.

'Funny – right now that would be preferable,' I say. I play this back. 'Not because I'm meeting you. I – er, I've got a difficult day tomorrow.'

Robbie wants to know why, but as my big mouth has already got me into enough trouble (that cabbie's probably told everyone), I don't tell him. Instead, I ask him about *him*. A safe subject with most men. 'You obviously work out a lot,' I begin. 'Do you train in a leather belt?' (I fear when Paxman retires, Newsnight won't be calling.)

Robbie is considerate enough to keep his answer short. No, he doesn't wear a belt, and yes, he works out three times a week. 'It used to be more,' he adds. 'Three hours every day and five on Sundays.'

'But, what, how did you do your work?' I say, intrigued.

'I could, still can, pick my own hours,' he explains. 'I'm freelance. A web designer.'

I *nearly* say, 'Like a spider!' Then I think *Would Jeremy say that*? and nod politely instead. I murmur, 'You make me feel lazy.'

'I was overdoing it,' says Robbie. He stretches his mouth to one side in a grimace.

'What?' I ask.

Robbie shakes his head. 'I was just remembering what I was like. At one point I was taking nineteen diet supplements. I was obsessed. I used to drink this liquidised tuna mix every day. I'd liquidise two tins of tuna and half a pint of orange juice and drink it while I was at the gym. My breath smelt like a minke whale's.'

'I'm sure it wasn't that bad,' I say, wondering why he didn't just take a toothbrush in a little pouch. There's nothing worse than running on the spot next to a man panting sulphur. You can't move treadmill in case you hurt his feelings. So you're forced to jog along with a blocked nose, horribly conscious of being *breathed* on.

'It was,' grins Robbie. 'I wasn't seeing mates and I was turning down work so I could go to the gym. Mental.'

'But,' I say, 'you must have felt fit.'

Robbie shrugs. 'I was ill most of the time. I kept getting flu, I'd knackered meself out, but I couldn't stop. If I wasn't working out, I'd feel itchy.'

'Itchy?' I squeak, trying to keep my voice on a level. Nosiness is similar to seduction. You have to ape indifference or the victim will back off. I adopt a glazed expression.

'Yeah,' says Robbie. 'Like me body was shrinking. In the end I saw me GP, and he said I had to calm down or I'd do meself a mischief. Took a while, though. It was like coming off smack!'

'Oh!' I gasp, shedding my sheep's clothing and turning predatory. 'Why do you think you were like that? I mean, why were you so – so compelled?'

Robbie turns coy (what did I tell you?) but eventually mumbles that at school he was bullied for being short.

'Napoleon complex,' he adds, with a little shrug.

'I see,' I say, not understanding.

'Being short,' explains Robbie. 'For men, being short is a curse. I did everything. I wore cowboy boots. Swore a lot. It was a Ferrari, or biceps, and Nat West wouldn't give me the loan.'

'Bastards,' I say.

Robbie grins. 'So biceps it was. I grew biceps like watermelons. I looked even shorter. Shorter and wider.'

I blush inwardly. 'You're not – er, short,' I lie.

'Five foot three,' he smiles. '*And* receding.'

I was being polite. He's not colluding. Eventually, I say, 'It's only unattractive if you fight it.'

'What?' replies Robbie. 'Being short?'

I giggle. 'Receding hair,' I squeak. 'You've got to cut your losses. Shave it all off. Then it looks like you don't care.'

'Even if you're crying inside,' says Robbie deadpan, smoothing his sparse hair. His sparse hair. Oh good grief. I've called him ugly to his face. I struggle to make amends.

'Unless you're a woman,' I blurt. 'Then you've got to hang on to your hair at all costs. Your head hair, that is.' The words ooze and gel and I feel like a puppy stumbling over Sticklebricks. 'Unless you want to be an outcast, you've got to be bald all over except for your head.' Robbie's monobrow gathers in a faint crease. 'I know how you feel – about the balding bit,' I say. (Yet another gem to add to my bulging file, *Infallible Seduction Lines*.)

Happily I don't want to seduce Robbie, and so we embark on a long and informative chat about anti-balding weapons and wiles. We talk about hair stimulants and scalp surgery and vitamin B and vaccinations and antibiotics and slaphead genes and wigs and hereditary alopecia and flushing the system with six glasses of water a day and iron in the blood and the Pill and androgen sensitivity and deep breathing and zinc and blackcurrants and thyroid dysfunction and high temperatures—

'High temperatures?' I say, alerted to a hitherto unknown hazard.

'Oh yes,' says Robbie, grimacing. 'A high temperature can thin hair – I read it in *Sunday* magazine. So the last time I got flu after killing meself in the gym, I sat for ninety minutes in a cold bath. Nearly got pneumonia!'

'And' – I finish the sentence with him – 'serious illness can cause hair loss!'

We laugh together and I wonder if now would be a good time to slide the conversation round to Andy. Because it strikes me that he and Robbie are such good friends that if Robbie fancies me they must have discussed it. I'm keen to know if Andy *sanctioned* this drink. According to Babs, Andy is useless at hiding his feelings. And I've been thinking about his request for a welcome back kiss at the karaoke party. I know it was only a joke, a bad taste joke, but it makes me wonder. That's all.

121

Chapter 14

I have never told a man 'No.' Don't hold your breath, I still haven't. But when Robbie sweeps me home on his Vespa and insists on seeing me to my doorstep, expectation hangs heavy in the air, and I feel obliged to speak. I bleat that I had a nice time but if it's okay with him I'm very tired so I won't invite him up although I do like him and everything but I'm going out with Chris and – Robbie holds up his leather-gloved hands in mock surrender.

'Wo wo wo!' he says. 'Natalie. I'm not asking you for anything. Chill.' Then he grins and zooms off like a wasp into the cold night. I gaze after him, red-faced. I think, most people want *something*.

My father wants me to meet him at 8 a.m. 'My dear, how *are* you?' he drawls on my machine. 'Your mother's knickers are in a twist.'

I play back the tape and even though I know his concern is genuine, it sounds contrived. He doesn't sound like any father or gynaecologist I've ever met. To be fair, he has an excellent reputation as a gynae, albeit a terrible one as a father (in Hendon, at least). *I* think he did his best. Only he was hopeless at fatherhood, in the way that some people are hopeless at maths. He did the weekly shop once, returning triumphant from Waitrose with bacon, custard, and a Cornflakes packet the size of a horsebox.

'No one in this house eats *any* of these things,' said my mother wearily.

'They don't?' replied Dad, surprised. 'Not even for breakfast?'

Mum visibly drooped. 'Frosties,' she sighed. 'We eat Frosties for breakfast, Vince. Even you.'

Dad scratched his head and grinned his dozy boyish grin which, a long time ago, might have charmed her. 'Ah well,' he said. 'Never mind.'

That was the problem. He never minded, she did. If he drilled a hole in the wall she minded that he never got around to buying a Rawlplug. When he left, the house looked like it was made of Emmental (until two years ago, when Babs came round with her triple-decker tool kit and plugged, plastered, and put up shelves, pictures, light fittings).

I arrive at Dad's hotel on the dot of eight. I haven't been sleeping well and, while I resent being bad at a basic biological function, it's easy to be on time when you've been ceiling-watching since 6 a.m. My father, though, is an expert sleeper and marches into the cool white lobby a good twenty minutes after the sleek receptionist alerts him to my presence. My innards flip as I wonder if he might be cross, but Dad is so good at being unbothered I can't imagine it. He is the western capitalist epitome of Zen now that he owns what he wants in life. A shrug-offable relative in Sydney won't trouble him so long as she stays remote and doesn't demand money.

'Good gracious!' he cries, raising his hands in mock-shock and beseeching the attention of an invisible crowd. 'I say, will you look at her!'

I glance around before realising he means me. Although the lobby is deserted I shrink inside my coat. My father spoke like a normal person until he moved to LA, whereupon he acquired an accent that hovers somewhere between Stephen Fry and Dick Van Dyke. While I have overcome my shame at his Hollywood English, his greeting baffles me. The words are joyous but the tone is appalled. No doubt I have committed the cardinal Californian sin and put on weight. Compared to Kimberli Ann, I am Augustus Gloop.

'You look . . . young,' I say, hugging him. Dad is dressed in what I believe Americans term 'leesher wear' and appears to be sponsored by Ralph Lauren. For a man who once bought jeans from Pepe in a bid to seem funky, his style is remarkably coherent. The tan deck shoes, the fresh pink shirt, the cream trousers – he might have stepped from the fashion pages of *Which Yacht?* magazine. His hair is very black and crisp, his face is the shade of a goatskin bag my mother once had, and his skin is suspiciously taut.

We sit in the restaurant on stiff chairs and his first words are, 'My dear girl, you can always sue.'

I am about to ask why I'd want to sue Kelly and Tara when I realise that Dad is referring to my employers.

'Oh!' I exclaim, and then, 'I don't know, but I – thankfully it's nowhere near that stage yet, it's not definite, and – er, to be honest I have made a few mistakes recently. If they do decide to shelve me, I don't suppose I can blame them.'

I stir my espresso to free up the carcinogens, and fight the urge to light a cigarette. My father ruffles my hair.

'Nonsense, poppet,' he cries, 'I won't have it! My girl is but an angel!'

I smile indulgently at this paternal blip, poke some toast around my plate, and give Dad an explanation-lite of why my job is on the brink.

'I'm here for you, my dear,' he declares.

'Thanks, Dad,' I croak. 'But it's fine, I'm in control.' Though it's impossible to faze him, I am equally creative when relating why I let the grandchild out of the bag. There's no point in revealing what a wicked girl I am to my doting dad when I know that my mother will have snipped the shocking tale from an X certificate to a U. She would never let her ex-husband know that mother-daughter relations are less than perfect.

'Poppet,' says Dad, sipping at his freshly squeezed orange juice. 'I'll be frank – this news about the girl, it's quite a curveball. Yet your mother assures me the woman has never demanded money.'

I tense at the implied slight on Kelly but understand that the comment reveals more about my father than it does about her. I also note that Dad has begun to process his new status, in theory at least.

'Will you – will you try and speak to Tony?'

He shrugs. 'My son has made it known he wants nothing to do with me,' he says briskly. 'What can I do?'

I search his smooth brown face for signs of disappointment but they are expertly hidden. 'I'm sure he'll come round,' I say, as I've been saying every month for the last fourteen years.

'No doubt he will,' agrees my father, as usual. His shoulders stiffen, just a little, and he exclaims, 'Tony gave your mother a collection of photographs. Nice looking girl.'

'Yes,' I murmur, delighted. 'Yes, they both seem ... lovely.'

My father claps his hands suddenly in dismissal, and booms, 'Your mother is dreadfully worried about you, poppet, and I must admit, so am I. Tell me, dear, are you taking sufficient care of your health? How is your diet? Is there any way in which I could be of use to you?'

I dip my head, grateful yet mortified. I must be more of a porker than I thought. I feel dizzy. Possibly because we're leaping from one subject to another like a pair of frogs. 'I'm fine, Dad, really I am,' I say.

'If you feel unable to confide in me,' he replies gravely, 'I know that Kimberli Ann would be overjoyed to discuss any issues you have. Our personal trainer-stroke-nutritionist-stroke-herbalist is a delightful chap, and if you have any queries, Kimberli Ann would be happy to pass them on.'

'Dad,' I say, wishing Babs were here to witness the moment my own father accused me of being a lardarse. 'It's a kind offer, thank you and – er, thank Kimberli Ann. But, um, I've just seen the time, and I think we'd better get going to the Jobcentre. I think otherwise we might have to queue.'

'My dear,' replies my father. 'I am not here to help you choose between a paper round or junk mail distribution. My concern is what is *wrong* with you. I find it hard to believe that anyone would dismiss a young lady with your qualifications. You were an 'A' grade student; you excelled at school from the age of four! You might have slipped up at university, but we all have our off-days. And you established a superb reputation in PR within a year of joining the profession. The industry magazine referred to you and your subordinates as 'the crack publicity team!' This ballet company head-hunted you, for heaven's sake! This talk of redundancy is absurd! Absurd, I say! Unless the cause is of a personal nature. Which I suspect it is. And I'd like us to talk about it.'

I mentally remove myself from the St Martin's hotel. I feel that Dad has embraced the American way of Talking About It sixteen years too late.

'It doesn't matter,' I mutter. I feel like a witness to a stranger's fate. Dad stares at me, eyes wide. I'm wondering if this is surprise or surgery when he cries, 'Natalie, wake *up!* What in God's name are you trying to achieve?'

I stare back. I believe that parents only have the right to yell at their children if they've done their time. As Dad only did half of his before escaping to Malibu, I feel he is morally required to address me at normal pitch.

I say, 'I'm sure it'll be fine.'

He shakes his head. His hair remains impassive and I wonder if I will go bald before he does. I know I should appreciate my father galloping to my rescue like an orange knight, but I don't. I blame my mother. She magnifies the severity of any given situation, to the power of ten. I dread to think what she said to lure him to London. I sigh. I am tired of being bothered and wish to sink into a green smoke of nothingness, the Wicked Witch of West Kensington. All I want is for Babs to be my best friend and Chris to be kind and Tony to be not cross and Andy to be contrite and things to be how they were. I want to rewind the years.

126

I won't care about work. I can't care about work. I don't care about work.

'I don't care about work,' I whisper, testing the thought on my tongue tip like mustard.

'Beg pardon?' says my father. He shifts in his chair and I can tell he's given up on me. Eventually he murmurs, 'If your job does go belly-up, which looks likely, I can twist a few arms.'

I think, I don't want to be such a dead weight that Dad has to twist people's arms to make them employ me – particularly as he's not enough of an international mogul to ensure there's no comeback – but I smile and say, 'Thank you.'

'Poppet,' says my father. 'I mean it. I didn't quite comprehend how serious matters were. I don't mind telling you, I feel most uneasy.' I smile again, seeing past his brown face and stiff hair, to a safe dark world of not very much. He sighs, looks at his Patek Philippe watch and then at me. 'I wish you'd spoken up. I'm flying home in – what? – five hours from now, but if I'd known the severity of the situation, I would have most certainly stayed longer. I could always ask my secretary to postpone my flight if—'

That's all I need. 'It's really not necessary, Dad,' I say. 'But thank you. Look you'd better go, you don't want to miss your plane.'

My father pinches my cheek. 'Now,' he intones, 'if that redundancy does materialise and you want me to get my attorney on to it, I will – that fellow can detect a case for litigation at twelve thousand miles, although I doubt even he – well, no matter. I'd like you to give me a tinkle tomorrow, and I shall be speaking to Kimberli Ann about the matter we discussed earlier. I trust you'll update your mother. I assume she will be in touch about the girl, anyhow.' He hesitates, then adds, almost shyly, 'If you see Tony, be sure to send him my warmest regards.' Concern comes easy when you live half a planet away from the problem. I hug my father goodbye, then take the tube to the GLBallet. It's not yet lunchtime and I can't face Matt. Or rather, I can't face his reluctance to face *me*. Who can I face? Mel. I haven't seen her since the Manics. I don't dare ring Tony, but Mel will have seen him. She'll know if I remain banished from court. I jog to her dressing room. There is a full dress rehearsal for this evening's press showing of *Romeo and Juliet*. On a normal day, I'd be at my desk, fielding urgent enquiries from the second cousin of the assistant sub at *Budgerigars Today* (can he have tickets for tonight?).

Then again, so what? I'm at that stage of drowning where the water is soothing you to death. I knock.

'Yeth!' cries a voice. I peer round the door. 'Oh hello,' says Mel. Her greeting is less fizzy than usual. She is sitting on the floor, a small wraithlike figure, naked except for knickers, and I can see fine downy hair covering her tiny body like a shroud. She is horribly thin – all sinew and skeleton – and for no reason, I'm irritated. I want to snap, *You look revolting!* But I don't.

'How are you?' I say shortly.

'Fine, thanks,' she replies, tossing her hair. 'Can you pass me the sticky tape?' I pass the surgical tape to her outstretched hand and watch. She has peeled a pile of flat round cotton wool pads into halves and pressed them over the top of each foot – from the ankle to an inch above the toes. The first time I saw this ritual I thought she was doing it to protect her feet.

She'd burst out laughing. 'I don't have a good instep,' she'd explained. 'My feet are straight, there's no arch. They don't make the correct shape when I'm *en pointe*, so the ballet mistress said, "Let's try padding". The Artistic Director loved it so much, I'm not allowed to be without it. It exaggerates the curve of the foot, it's much prettier. Lots of people do it.' She'd dabbed brown foundation over the mounds of cotton wool, then stuck the false curves to her skin with surgical tape. She does this now, then rises like a small ghost, pit-pats to the mirror, and lifts her left leg high

128

until her body clock reads 'ten to six'. Satisfied that her DIY arches are perfect, she pulls on her tights and retrieves her shoes from the top of the radiator.

'Show us yer arches then,' I tease when the pink satin ribbons are tied. She lifts herself on to pointe with a grin. 'Oh my, you are *so* glamorous!' I squeal, and she giggles.

'I will ring Tony,' she says abruptly. 'But I haven't sent him a Valentine's card. I'm too stressed, I'm working so hard, not like some dancers I could mention, swanning off to Verona!'

I've forgotten about the Verona trip, and I've forgotten that in two days it's February the 14th. Or rather, I've buried the fact in concrete. Matt and Julietta must be flying to Italy this afternoon. But my ears are twanging for other reasons.

'Have you – er, not rung Tony then?' I say, trying to sound casual.

'I think he's a sweet boy,' she huffs. 'I *am* fond of him, but being a dancer is like being a nun!'

Further enquiries reveal that Tony has rung Mel an unprecedented four times since Friday and she has yet to get back to him. And while Tony's former flames – most of whom found themselves burnt out after twenty-four hours – might call this justice, I feel a twitch of sympathy for my brother. Four calls in five days. That's about *my* lot for the year.

I run back to the office where, to my relief, Belinda tells me that Matt is in meetings until he and Julietta leave for the airport at five. I float through the rest of the day, untouchable. I see off the chancers clamouring for press tickets ('fax me a copy of the *Builders Weekly*'s dance page and I'll see what I can do'), I tell my mother what she wants to hear ('That rave about his metallic gold Merc convertible did seem forced, you can tell he misses Hendon'). I don't brood about Chris ('I won't brood about Chris, I won't brood about Chris, I won't etc.'), and I don't ring my brother (though I realise with a selfish rush of hope that if Mel is being coy, Tony might need *me* to divert the path of true love to his door).

At 6 p.m. I switch off my mobile and leave for the Coliseum. Belinda natters and chatters – as Matt says, she's a lovely girl if only she'd pause for breath occasionally – but I don't hear her. I am watertight, airtight, as cold and impenetrable as a spaceship, my hatches whirring down against alien invasion, lights red, alarms wailing, wah, wah, wah. Belinda and I stand in the foyer handing out tickets and programmes to the press like bread to a gaggle of geese. I fawn, flirt, and foist drink on the hacks in the interval, then I take the tube home and fall like a brick into bed. I remain stiffly awake until four, then sleepwalk to work the next day. My bottom has barely brushed the seat of my chair when the phone rings.

Six minutes later, I am leaning blearily against the wall of a toilet cubicle wondering how I managed to book Matt and Julietta on to a plane that *arrived* in Verona at 20.25 rather than – as I'd stated in a neatly printed itinerary – *left* Gatwick at 20.25 and thinking how unlucky it was that the next plane to Verona didn't depart until eight this morning and that Matt had to book himself and a distinctly underwhelmed Julietta into a flea-bitten Travelodge while their soft Verona hotel beds lay frivolously bare.

It was also unlucky that Matt had to pay a surcharge to switch flights and spend forty minutes soothing the irate photographer (who'd wanted to shoot Julietta reaching from her balcony bathed in the golden kiss of the early morning light, but would now have to settle for the less affectionate bog standard lunchtime light).

It was even more unlucky that, despite the dozen faxes I'd sent, the Italian authorities dramatically claimed to know 'niente' about a British newspaper photographer taking pictures, and only gave their surly permission when Matt summoned his dormant theatrical resources and declared sorrowfully, 'How am I going to break it to the Italian Ambassador, whose idea this was?'

And not unlucky but inevitable for the idiot whose brain blips led to this great bobble chain of blunders, that her continued employment is now an impossibility. And I don't doubt that talking about myself in the third person is a symptom of my decay. I mean, I'm clearing my desk, today. I'm free to watch *Wheel of Fortune* for the rest of my working life.

Chapter 15

Matt has told Personnel that I'm not to be escorted from the building. I'm to leave in my own time. I don't cry. Why should I? I glance at Belinda, reading the *Daily Express* and attacking her mid-morning lunch, and wonder what to say. Belinda is so gloriously immune to the emotional temperature of the workplace, I'd swear she was inoculated against office politics along with measles and rubella. I'm about to make my announcement, when Chris calls, touchingly cool. I still don't cry.

'Did you see that Robbie bloke, then?' he asks gruffly.

'We met for a quick drink,' I say, amazed that I'm up to normal conversation. 'He's just a friend.'

Chris growls, 'That's what they all say, until they stick a hand up your skirt.' Depending on whether this fantasy forecast is envy or ego, I should be either fuming or flattered. I can't decide, so I whisper the news of my redundancy. I'm superfluous. I'm the green bit at the top of the carrot. So what. I light a cigarette as a token of my disregard for the rules. Emphysema and unemployment, a cheese and tomato lifestyle.

'I wanted to tell you,' I hiss, expelling the smoke through my nose like a teenage dragon, 'but I didn't think we were talking.'

Chris is quiet. Then he says, 'Sorry. I should've rung earlier. I've let you down again, haven't I? I'm such a git.' An admission touching in its frankness but I feel obliged to protest.

'Not really,' I say.

'No, I have.'

'You haven't.'

'I am a git, though,' he insists. 'I've let you down.'

A polite squabble later I realise he is determined to be a git, so I concede the point. I replace the receiver, and see Belinda gawking at me. 'You! Avin a fag! In the office! Woss goin on?'

I hesitate. Belinda's lunch smells vile. That's one thing I won't miss. Belinda eats like a fat person – full cream milk, peanut butter, chocolate bars, crisps, potato waffles, roast dinners, fruit tarts, cheesecake – yet remains offensively thin. She's been spat at in Top Shop's changing rooms. 'It's me genes,' she explained once to Mel, who went through a phase of sitting with her at lunch to pinch chips off her plate while ostentatiously doodling over a wilting salad. (The phase ended when Belinda went off chips and on to macaroni cheese. Mel asked brightly, every day for a week, 'Aren't you having chipth today?')

I stare at the floor and say abruptly, 'I've been let go.'

There is no response from Belinda except a strangulated gargle. I glance up to see her face is brick red and her mouth wide open, with a steaming lump of baked potato falling out of it. 'Hoh hoh hoh!' she puffs, fanning wildly.

'Hot?' I enquire, unnecessarily.

Belinda nods dumbly, tears in her eyes. I fetch her a glass of water and she signals her gratitude.

'I'm leaving today. Now. So, um, it's been fun working with you. Maybe see you around.'

Belinda stares. '*Now?* So what you plannin on doing?'

'I'm not quite sure.'

Belinda digs at her chilli con carne, and says, 'You should sign on.'

I stifle a splutter – it's always heartwarming to discover your colleagues have faith in you – and murmur, 'That would really make my mother happy.'

'Yeah, but you gotta eat,' says Belinda, who is proving to be persistent, a talent she makes sparing use of in her work life.

133

'Dole or starvation,' I say dreamily. 'I don't know which she'd prefer.'

I arrange all my belongings neatly in a cardboard box, and Belinda helps me to the front door. We pass the wardrobe mistress, who stares. Belinda glares and snaps, 'What *you* lookin at?'

'Thanks, Bel,' I say.

She winks. 'You take care, Nat. You can do better than this place, anyway. Be in touch, yeah? We'll ave a drink sometime.'

I hug her, and stagger to the gym with my cardboard box. The receptionist kindly guards it while I train. I think less about losing my job than the fact that Chris rang. I didn't think I'd hear from him again and was preparing for martyrdom. But this zigzag uncertainty is cool. Chris and I are toying with each other, and that is fine by me. I am his well-connected bit of posh. And he is an escape from the Alcatraz of my good girl's life. He represents everything my mother hates. He is the wild wicked opposite of Saul, of marriage, of a respectable responsible show-offable husband with smart hair and sleek suits and a solid job in the City. And I know Babs dislikes him and I'm glad. Chris would rather hang himself than settle down. His hedonism taunts her. It nips at the matronly heels of I-do.

I pull on my trainers and think that once, this would have upset me. What! This man doesn't love me for the wonderfulness of *me*, he doesn't love me enough to spend his drug money on a glaring diamond ring that I can twiddle and flash at the rest of the world – look, everyone, three thousand sparkly pounds of how much he loves me! – he doesn't appreciate the very special human being that I am, he doesn't want to snap me up like a priceless piece of Elvis memorabilia, I'm just another bit of Spice Girl tat, boo hoo what's wrong with me that he doesn't want to keep me for ever, how dare he! (Not that I'd want to marry *him*, he's feckless and unreliable.)

No, none of that. I feel detached. I'm out of love with

him. Quite able to live with the ego-crunching knowledge that this arrangement is one huge use. In fact, it pleases me. Chris is irresistible because he doesn't care. I despised Saul's neediness. It made a bully of me. He had to reject me to prove himself a man. As for Babs, I pity her. I think she's weak. Sure, the day job is heroic. But out of hours she is dependent on Simon and his double cuffs. I am self-sufficient. *I* am a modern woman. Frannie would be proud.

Simon and Frannie, my main competitors.

I punish the treadmill, smirking at the recollection of the first time Frannie met Simon. She took one look at his affluent cornfed smugness, decided he hadn't suffered enough and was that particular breed of shallow blinkered male who needed dragging back to vicious reality. Hence her detailed and vivid reply to his token enquiry, 'What do you do?'

'Of course, Simon, the worst thing about an episiotomy is, the scissors are always blunt. You give them a local anaesthetic, jam the needle deep into the flesh, then you cut at the height of contraction – they're in so much pain, aside from hearing a scrunching noise, they don't feel it as such. It's like cutting bacon rind, Simon. It's quite thick. It's best to make a decent incision, but that depends on how sharp the scissors are, it can take a few chews. The last thing you want is it tearing, because if it leads to a third degree tear, that involves the rectum . . .'

I feast on the image of Simon's tall slender figure falling gracefully to the floor, his bottle of designer beer trailing a farewell arc of droplets in the air. (She tried the same tactic on Tony once but it backfired when he interrupted the saga with, 'Birds! No pain threshold! I've had shits that'd make you faint!'). I am wincing at the memory of Frannie turning a ripe purple, when a figure appears in front of me, taut brown midriff, belly button like a gasp. I jerk myself back to the present.

'You run like you're being chased,' says Alex.

Much as I resent slowing my pace – my joints set like

135

cement – it is patently rude to keep going. So I stop. 'Well, you caught me,' I reply, smiling.

She rewards me with an easy laugh. Even though her amusement is always so willing, I feel a tweak of pleasure at having prompted it. Babs is the same; she makes you glow, unlike Chris or Tony who make you slave for their approval like a pair of Pharaohs. I once asked my brother why he never smiled on meeting people, and he said, 'They've done nothing to please me yet.' How different to his sister, so full of puppydog smiles, I can't give them away.

'So what's new?'

'A lot actually. I – ah, I've just been let go.' I grin stupidly (as well I might – talking about myself like a badger released back into the wild by the RSPCA).

Alex clamps a hand to her mouth. She says, through long pink nails, 'You mean, your job?'

I nod. 'I was told today. I had to clear my desk,' I blurt. I know such intimate disclosure smashes the gym-chat blandometer but I can't stop myself. I feel that telling one or two people a secret is like a vaccine – it's harmless and prevents me falling ill with the strain of keeping scandalous information to myself.

'You're joking!' says Alex. 'What did you do? If you don't mind my asking,' she adds quickly. I tell her, *ish*. She replies, 'How do you feel? *Are* you okay?'

I give myself a mental once-over and find my state of mind unbruised. 'I'm fine,' I say, to her disbelieving face. 'Really.'

Alex shakes her head. 'I don't want to speak out of turn,' she says, 'but you don't look like you're fine. You look like you could do with a break.' My smile is brittle enough for Alex to add, 'I did speak out of turn. I'm sorry.'

I take a cab home, playing over the exchange with Alex in my head, worrying that I didn't reassure her heartily enough. She is the kind of woman I gravitate towards. Balls of steel, as Tony would say – his ultimate accolade to a chick. Alex reminds me of Babs, hard shell, soft centre. Caring but not – unlike some women I could mention – a sacrificial lamb, woollishly bleating after everyone else's welfare in the pathetic hope that just one person will turn around and exclaim, 'But who's looking after *you*?'

I scowl. Babs hasn't rung to see how it went with Robbie, or my father. I need to see her, I need to talk to her properly. No one else will do. There is no compensation for the loss of a best friend.

I get home, and call Tony.

'He's in a meeting,' says his PA.

I ring my mother and tell her I'm unemployed.

'Oh, my God! What are you going to do now?' she asks, her voice wobbling.

What am I going to do now? What am I going to do now? What *will* I do? What can I do? My mother's shrill panic drills through my skull. I have fought off the truth but now it swarms all over me like an army of ticks, wriggling and burrowing into my flesh, attacking me, picking and pricking at me, worming under my skin until I am caught in the vicious grip of reality, barely able to snatch a breath. I sit with a thump on the hallway floor, gasping, grasping at the pale blue walls which tilt and shift alarmingly. I've lost control, I thought I had it but it's gone, and in its place is anarchy, I'm consumed by it, eaten up with fear, oh Babs oh help me please I need you.

Babs just about bursts through the door, her forehead a comical map of anxiety. 'Natalie, you scared me, are you okay? Oh, look at you!'

She grasps me in a soft warm hug and I float away in a far-off dream, snug as a wish inside a fortune cookie. I shut my eyes and the room bobs up and down. She rubs my back and I lean limply towards her with dangling hands, resisting then sinking into the comfort of her strong arms. I am sunk, literally, cannot go lower, I feel so wretched and that screechy strangulated shudder, like water being sucked down a drain, wrings out my ears, until I realise the noise is me.

Babs lifts me to the sofa, and gently strokes the hair from my face. Then she disappears and reappears with a Caffeine Queen mug of water and a length of kitchen roll as long as an electoral list. 'There you go,' she whispers, crouching at my feet.

'I'm not crying that much,' I snivel, using several acres of roll and crying some more. I gaze into her dark eyes and see the kindness there, and the tears fall hot and fast. If only she was cruel I could have kept them in.

'Natalie,' says Babs, taking my hand in hers as if her touch will make the words less wrenching. 'We need to talk.' I nod slowly, and the room ripples. 'Hang on, let me open a window,' she adds, loosening her red scarf. 'It's stifling.'

She flings a window wide, then heavily plops down next to me on the pale suede sofa (which makes a surprised '*pouf!*') and says, 'Nat, this has been coming on for a while, and I think you know that.' I stare at my feet in their sensible shoes, not daring to speak. Babs pauses for a second, then adds, 'Nat, I'll say what I think. I don't think you're crying because you've lost your job. I don't think you're crying because of the Tony thing. And' – her voice thickens – 'I don't even think it's because you feel I've abandoned you.'

Babs stops talking and I flinch. Ugh, how does she do it? *I* am a fawning fan of the Emperor's New Clothes ('*Love* the jacket, Your Excellency! Armani? Christian Lacroix?'). Babs speaks the unspeakable! I gaze unseeingly at the hardwood floor.

'Nat,' murmurs Babs. 'These – these crises are consequential, they're not the seed of your problem, they're the fruit of it. Your Mum didn't drag your Dad back from LA so he could wail about your redundancy. *She* can do that! The job's not it. Yes, it's serious, losing your job is serious, but you are not your job. Your parents know that. Your job is not who you are. And that's what she, they are worried about. They're worried about *you*. Losing your job is not your problem, it's just a by-product of your problem.'

Babs glances at me. I tense my jaw and look blank. (What can I say, it's easier when you're blonde.)

'Nat,' she says, 'I know you don't want to hear this. I know your mum has tried to talk to you . . . and your dad. I know it's been hard for you, me wrecking the status quo, but I can't apologise, I won't, I can't be responsible for how you feel about that, Natalie . . .' Babs hesitates while I make a strangled squeak, but when nothing more lucid emerges, resumes:

'I know you're trying to say something, to everyone, with how you look – who isn't? – but sometimes Nat, almost always, it's better to come out and say it, even if it's going to hurt people, and I know that whatever you want to say to us, to me, to everyone, I know that what you've got to say has got to be pretty lethal, because keeping it inside is killing you.'

Babs is holding my hand as tight as a farmer choking a chicken. She blinks, angrily, to blot the tears. Slowly, she gets to her feet. 'Come with me,' she says, and leads me, a Pied Piper leading a rat, to my cool white bathroom. She positions me in front of the mirror and says, 'Take off your jumper.' I stare at her beseechingly, but she repeats, 'Take it off.'

I am trembling, all over, and my legs are paper.

'Go on, Natalie,' says Babs, her voice so firm that I obey. In the same dominatrix tone, she orders off my skirt, and my tights, and my long sleeved T-shirt, until I'm standing in front of my best friend in my underwear.

'Christ, Nat,' says Babs. Her bravado is gone, the words wobble. We peer into the grimy mirror – a small oasis of dirt in my immaculate desert bathroom – as if it has all the answers, as if we might step through the glass, like Alice, to another life. Well, I do.

139

'There's a saying,' declares Babs, her chin at a tilt. 'I think Mrs Simpson said it – "You can never be too rich, or too thin." Well, on my pitiful salary, I agree with the rich bit. But as for the rest, woman, will you look at yourself? You've practically dissolved.' She hesitates, as if to ensure my full attention. Then she says, 'You can be too thin, Nat.'

Chapter 16

Thin is what works for me. Thin is the only thing that works for me. And I'm *not*. I wish I was. I peer at the filthy mirror and a great swollen balloon of a fat girl stares fatly back.

'I'm not thin,' I tell Babs.

Babs looks at me as if I've just confessed to a passionate affair with Frannie. 'No, Nat,' she agrees in a voice slick with sarcasm, 'you're not thin.'

I glance at her suspiciously.

'You're skeletal. It pains me to look at you. Your hip bones. Your collarbone. Your ribs. They jut so sharply through your skin I'm scared they're going to pierce it. I'm serious, Natalie. You need to eat.'

I don't *need* to do anything. 'I do eat,' I say.

'What do you eat?'

'I eat masses. I – I have coffee and crispbread with a bit of butter for breakfast, and an apple and nuts and raisins for lunch, and salad and cottage cheese and vegetables for dinner, and probably more only I can't remember. I eat a lot. I feel full.'

I feel bloated, huge, disgusting, ugly, a monstrous lumbering sow of a woman, a greedy revolting red-faced creature, and with every bite I feel myself swelling, I'm punished for breaking the first commandment, don't eat more than a small bird because it's unladylike and you'll get fat and no one will like you, but it's too late, I can feel the flat sharpness of my cheekbones sinking, swamped under spongy bulges of flesh, my thighs spreading like warm lard and sticking together, so it's much safer not to eat.

'Let me tell you what *I* eat in a day,' says Babs, perching on the side of my bath. 'For breakfast, I have a big bowl of Shreddies, and two slices of buttered bread – I like the butter so thick it makes teethmarks – tea, and orange juice. For lunch, I might have pizza or a chicken sandwich or a jacket potato with cheese and beans, and a packet of crisps. I'll probably have snacks, maybe chocolate, or a banana, and for dinner I'll have spaghetti bolognese, and salad, or fish, chips, and vegetables, or beef stew and dumplings, or roast chicken, or a curry, and afterwards I'll have dessert, maybe apple crumble, or chocolate cake and custard, or fruit salad and ice cream, and a glass of wine.'

I shudder. That is an *obscene* amount of food. What a pig.

'That's normal, Nat,' says Babs. 'I get hungry otherwise. And I like eating.' She glances at me, and something seems to jolt. When she speaks, her voice is honeyed with lust. 'That gorgeous sensation,' she purrs, 'that delicious moment when you snap a creamy chunk of milk chocolate out of its shiny silver wrapping, and it melts over your tongue, that soft glut of sweetness – why deny yourself that casual pleasure, Nat? And spaghetti! Spaghetti with bolognese sauce so rich and thick it glitters – the joy of slurping it, sucking it up from the plate in a long splatty squiddle, the juiciness, the chewy satisfaction, my teeth ache just to think of it! And buttered toast! The oozy oily crunchiness of buttered toast, that taste is sublime, it's a basic human right!'

I feel like a pervert panting on the end of a telephone sex line. Babs sees my popping eyes and returns to earth. 'Calories are just *energy*. I need that amount of food to be healthy, to do my job,' she adds, the evangelical ring less resonant. 'If you don't obsess about what you eat, you end up eating pretty much what you need. I eat a decent amount because my job is so physical. I burn most of it off.

I'm telling you, one doughnut, two doughnuts, won't make you fat. To get properly fat you've really got to put the work in, Nat! We're talking dawn to dusk noshing – a strict regime! We're talking twelve doughnuts daily, on top of normal meals. Look' – she flicks her red scarf over her shoulder and lifts up her sweatshirt – 'Am I grotesque?' She tips like a pink teapot and her torso concertinas into rolls. 'N-no,' I stammer, goggling.

'Nat,' says Babs quietly. 'I'm five foot eight and I weigh eleven stone. I am *average*.' She says 'average' like it's a good thing to be. 'Go on,' orders Babs. 'I can tell you want to disagree. I can always tell. You get that politely wretched look, like you're meeting the Queen and there's a frog on your tongue.'

I wrestle with my thoughts, but they are too fierce, too fiery to crush. 'I don't want to be average,' I snarl. 'I can't think of anything worse. I – I hate average. Who wants to be *mediocre*? It would be the worst. Who in the world is sad enough to be satisfied with that?' I whisper so that Babs doesn't detect the hissing venom, but I follow her gaze to my lap and see that my hands are shaking violently, as if I've used them to kill someone.

Babs wills me to look at her. 'But Natalie,' she says. '*You* are not what you weigh. Your body is just the – the container. What makes you special, *not* average, is what's inside. Your wit, your intelligence, your charisma, your quirks, your stupidity even. You were never average, Nat. You were – you *are* – my best friend. You didn't need to starve yourself to prove that you weren't average. Look at you, you're a wisp, a pale ghost of a girl. I have to hand it to you – you don't look normal. But are you happy? I don't think so. If it's happiness you're after, you won't find it because you're thin.'

'You won't find it if you're fat either,' I tell her, bluntly. 'And anyway, I don't feel thin.'

'Anorexics don't feel thin!' she shrieks. 'Everyone knows that! The way you're going, you'll never be thin enough.

It's never enough, it won't be enough until, one morning you'll wake up and you'll be dead!'

I'd question her logic, but I'm reeling from this reckless slap of a word she's thrown at me.

'I'm not,' I gulp, 'anorexic.'

Babs glares at me. 'You might not be Ally McBeal yet but you're on your way. You are *shrunken*. Even your head is thin! Your skull looks too big for you. Frankly, I'm not surprised you've lost your job. I'll be honest – no one is. You're just not *there* any more. It's like talking to a zombie. You're barely present physically, and mentally, you're absent. You hardly go out, and the last time you came to dinner, you mashed your potato pie around your plate like a four-year-old—'

'I don't eat pastry,' I say.

'Nat, that's an excuse. It's like saying you don't like the cut of a chicken's jib.'

'I feel fat,' I hiss.

'But that's your answer to everything!' she cries. 'Nat, I'm asking you because I want to know. Don't you – don't you ever get *hungry*?'

I'm not sure if I know any more.

'I want a body with sharp edges,' I say, after a while, because she won't let me wriggle out of an answer. 'Sometimes I am hungry. I'm always hungry. But when I don't eat I feel good. Pure. I feel empty and it's wonderful. I feel so powerful. Like I could fly.'

Babs shakes her head, and her vanilla crunch hair frames her anxious face like a dark halo. 'Nat,' she murmurs. 'You're not a saint, you're a human being. You're not meant to be pure, or perfect. I wish, I *so* wish, that just once you could leave the fucking washing up. Stay calm if someone rucks up the carpet. The minute anyone steps out of the toilet you're in there hurling gallons of bleach down it. And if they get off the sofa – you're there, straightening cushions. You don't allow yourself to have fun! No casual sex—'

'I'm having sex with Chris.'

'That's *coke* sex! Coke, the drug of low self-esteem! That's cheating! God knows where *he* fits in, but that's not Natalie Miller shagging – it's the drug!'

I want to scream at Babs that I've gone off coke anyway, it makes me paranoid that I've got a snotty nose, and that I know she resents Chris because he isn't Saul, safe, boring Saul, as dull as a woman can get without tying the knot and having a lobotomy. I'm getting my ear chewed off for Not Having Fun, yet Chris Poodle – bacchanalian Chris who spits in the eye of marriage – is dashed aside as a bad influence! What does she want from me?

'Losing control doesn't count if it's drug-induced, Nat,' scolds Babs, who it appears could teach the Dalai Lama a thing or two about the meaning of life. '*That* sort of losing control is just an escape. I want you to relax, be comfortable with who you are, and that means facing yourself, *accepting* yourself. There's no joy, no triumph in being an iron woman. If I'm honest, I'm glad you've lost your job. Because that job of yours, I don't think it helped.

'I know you love ballet, but being around that sort of discipline, that superhuman willpower, is not healthy for someone like you. You can't compete with a bunch of elite athletes. I know it's an art form, and it's awesome, breathtaking, but it's also about perfection, it's narcissistic, anal, it's all about physicality, looking in the mirror all day long, and that's the last thing you need. You need to be in a freer environment where you can eat a few biscuits, gain a few pounds and it won't be a massive guilt vortex that sucks up your existence.'

I wish she'd go. She doesn't understand.

'Babs,' I mutter. 'It's okay for you. You're okay. But me, I'll be uglier, I'm ugly, I feel ugly—'

'You're not ugly, Nat!' shouts Babs, so loud and shrill I nearly topple into the bath. 'You're lovely, you are, my God – Andy and Robbie think you're gorgeous, the pair of them drive me mad! But *you've* got to believe it, believe you're gorgeous, but not just to look at, as a person. That's what matters. Beauty is surface, it means so little, it's transient. Looks are nothing. It's what's inside that counts, and you have that.'

I'm surprised that a large godly finger doesn't poke through the bathroom window and strike her down where she sits. Looks are nothing! Then explain Estée Lauder and her zillion-dollar cosmetics dynasty, my bronzed born-again father and his trainer-stroke-nutritionist-stroke-herbalist, every celebrity back in shape three days after giving birth, my diet addict mother discarded for a younger model, all our cosmetically perfect film stars – we force them to be what they are, and what they are is our punishment – Kimberli Ann and her inflatable breasts, a million airbrushed cover girls, pint-sized Robbie and his exercise addiction, the students who after fifteen years of dedication and desire and maniacal toil are rejected from the GLBallet because while their talent is unquestionable their bodies are the wrong shape for classical ballet. Oh no. Looks are nothing.

I splutter, 'How can you *say* that? How can you pretend that looks don't matter?'

Babs says, 'I'm not pretending they don't matter. I'm saying that looks matter less than you think they do. Yes, if you want to be a supermodel, looks matter. If you don't, they're less important. If you want to attract the sort of man who sneers when you eat cake and tolerates your opinions, then yes, you'll need to be ravishing. If you want to make insecure women hate you, then yes, be born beautiful. But the kind of people you want to be around won't judge you on your looks for longer than five minutes. And I swear it, Nat, you wouldn't want them to.' She pauses. 'But this isn't really about looks, is it, Nat? This isn't about looking ugly. It's about *feeling* ugly. Is that what you feel?'

She speaks so softly I could fall asleep on the sweet fairy whisper of her breath.

I reply stiffly, 'I feel nothing but ugly through and through.'

'Oh Nat,' says Babs sadly. 'You break my heart. How can you feel that? What else do you feel?'

The agony of this interrogation is turning my spine to chalk (this may also be linked to perching on the side of the bath for an hour). 'I feel . . . nothing,' I say. 'I feel . . . not nice.'

Babs holds up a hand. 'Nat,' she murmurs. 'Let me remind you of something. Not so long ago, you and I were walking to the station. I can't remember why. Anyway, we're walking along and you shout, "wait!" And you crouch down and I see this hideous fluorescent green caterpillar on the pavement. It's the biggest bloody creepy-crawly I've ever seen, I wouldn't even dare stamp on it. And I watch you *pick up* this creature . . .'

'Oh yeah,' I say. 'He was really cute, he was a bright green pudgy thing, he was stranded—'

'And I watch you flap around looking for the right *leaf* to place this thing on, and eventually you find one, and the caterpillar won't stick, and I hear you say – hear you, with my own ears, say – "Come on, darling, you've got work to do, you've got to become a butterfly!"' Babs pauses. 'Now *that*,' she adds softly, 'is a person with a beautiful soul.'

Everything blurs. After a long time I whisper, 'It doesn't feel like that. I don't know why. But it doesn't.'

Babs flops her head in her hands. I glance at her luscious hair, rich with dancing curls, playful twirls, chocolate ripples, vanilla streaks. 'You're a liar,' she states. 'A liar, and you don't even know it. I don't think you *want* to accept what you feel.' She stops for a second, then blurts, 'You're so stubborn. I think when I got married, you were angry, but you were angry way before that. My engagement might have been the trigger, Nat, but that was just an excuse. If kids don't feel valued by their parents for themselves, they grow up looking for other ways to be valued. And Nat, when your dad pissed off you suffered the emotional equivalent of being dropped on your head. But you won't admit it.

'You just replay the scenario with every man you've met since – good men some of them, but you push them and push them until they leave you. You don't feel valued but you're blaming all the wrong people. Yet you won't admit you feel angry. You're as thin as tissue paper, but all you allow yourself to feel is "fat". It's a codeword for something else.'

I'm trapped in a cod psychology class with no doors. 'Fat is *fat*, Barbara. There is nothing in the western world – apart from paedophiles and murderers – quite so reviled as a fat woman. Except a fat woman talking with her mouth full. Fat is poor, Babs. Fat is stupid, greedy, indulgent, and disgusting.'

'I don't think fat is any of those things,' she replies coolly. 'That's just your warped perception. I know lots of big women who are smart, powerful, ha—'

'If you say "Dawn French" I'm going to scream.'

'Natalie,' snaps Babs. 'I'm not talking about celebrities, I'm talking about women I *know*. But when you say "fat", Natalie, *you* don't mean women who are clinically obese. You mean women who weigh over nine stone. That's 90 per cent of the female population. Has it occurred to you that what you think is "fat" is normal?'

'People feel sorry for you if you're fat, it's seen as failure.'

Babs replies primly, 'So being Miss Skeleton Head shows your success and sophistication, does it?'

'Pretty much,' I snap. 'Pretty, being the operative word.'

A nasty thought occurs to me. Babs nabs it. 'Oh Christ,' she says. 'You think I'm jealous. Natalie. Please. I care about you. I want you to be well. And I know that thin doesn't work. The one time I went on a diet, years ago, the Cabbage Soup Diet – I smelt like a bog and farted like one. And I looked a right state! Like a thawing snowman, my top half melted away. I had a chest as flat as Holland. It took me a while, but I realised, I like my body how it is. It works for me. I use it. I enjoy it. I want to smell a rose, run up a hill, pat a dog, watch a sunset, make love to Si – it sounds naff, but my body lets me do those things. It's perfect for what I need it to be. What does your body do for you, Nat? You treat it like a prison.'

I shake my head. As far as I can see, I'm in the dock for not clearing my plate and we're looking at a life sentence. All this fuss. 'I was *not* angry when you got married,' I squeak. 'I was pleased for you. I'm sorry,' I add silkily, 'if it came across that way.'

Babs grits her teeth. 'Nat,' she says. 'You play this game, this polite, meek, pardon-me-for-speaking game. But there's a lot about you that isn't meek. There's a lot about you that's powerful. You're a wolf disguised as a lamb. And sometimes I feel that you're taunting us with it.'

'Who's *us?*' I say coldly, displeased at the wolf analogy.

'Me. Your mother. Your dad. Even Tony, if he ever bloody opened his eyes to notice.'

How she has the nerve. 'Please don't talk about Tony like that,' I say. I dig my nails into my skin until the pain is gaspingly sharp. 'This is nothing to do with you or my family. You and they are fine. I am quite aware that you have less time for me now you're with Simon. Admittedly, my mother is hard work, but she is kind and caring and I love her. And I love my dad and I adore Tony. He might not be touchy-feely, but so what?'

'They are fine, *you* are not fine. Starving yourself is not a good way of communicating that you're sad and angry, Nat. You've got a voice. Use it.'

I need to shut her up fast. 'Babs,' I say. 'Don't worry about me. I'm just a vain foolish silly little girl who wants to look like a supermodel.'

Chapter 17

No one likes to have their charity thrown back in their face. They've gone to the great trouble of stuffing their stained old fashion mistakes into a plastic rubbish bag so that those less fortunate can shuffle about Kosovo in *Frankie Says Relax* T-shirts, striped A-line skirts and purple snoods, so to have their generosity rejected hurts. Babs jumps up and I watch her, heart hammering.

'Fine,' she says, her tone so chilly it would have a polar bear reaching for his puffa jacket. 'If that's how you want it.'

She marches into the hall with long haughty strides, me scampering after her like a puppy. She reaches for the latch and adds crisply, 'I tried.'

Then she yanks open the front door, and slams it roughly behind her. Which would be all very soap opera, were it not that her red scarf catches in the door and, judging from the surprised yelp, hauls her back by the neck as she tries to flounce off. I listen to Babs struggling with the scarf for about thirty seconds, and consider waiting for the rude shrill of the doorbell and the bitterly spat 'thanks' – no compensation for the shrivelling of dignity that follows making a sod-you exit then being forced to crawl back again.

I open the door. Me in my pants, her scowling in fury, we stare at each other for a fragile moment and burst out laughing. We shriek and howl so much I have to squeeze my legs together and do a Mick Jagger walk to prevent an unseemly accident.

'Stop it!' I gasp. 'Stop it or I'll' - *squirm, wriggle, Jumping Jack Flash* - 'Oh, it's okay, it's gone back up!'

Babs teeters on the edge of hysteria, and blurts, 'Bloody bastard scarf!'

I grin, shy suddenly, as our laughter drains to a trickle. 'Don't go,' I mumble. 'Stay for a bit, and we'll, we'll' – I squeeze out the words – 'talk about things.'

Babs smiles at me, a luscious full-cream crinkly-eyed smile.

'On one condition.'

'What?' I say.

'That you get dressed. You'll catch your death of cold,' she adds, aping my mother.

I realise that my teeth are chattering and my hands are blue and I'm in my pants. 'OK,' I say, 'but let me make you a cup of t—'

'*I'll* do it,' says Babs. 'I know where the kettle is, be off with you.'

I grin, and trundle towards my bedroom. I don't want to wear the clothes I was in when Babs outed me. Oh God. I feel like a heavyweight boxer with a closet interest in needlepoint. Am I even a little of what she says I am? She thinks I'm angry with her for getting married. How selfish am I? I see myself as she must see me, a fat, selfish, red-faced girl, stamping her unfeasibly large foot at the world. Ought I to have spent more on her wedding present?

If this is the truth, it makes me feel small. At least something does. But I can't stand to have Babs think badly of me.

I rummage through my wardrobe, and snatch the soft clingy pink top that Matt chose to hasten my first step to infidelity. I pull it on and it hangs off me, like a sheet off a scarecrow. More or less since Babs got engaged, I have avoided squaring up to the wardrobe mirror. Now, I force myself to meet my own eyes. My hair is tufty – my *head* hair, my armpits are bald, thank you – where I've back-combed it, to make it seem thicker, and my complexion is

151

the shade of natural yoghurt. Hello, Edward Scissorhands. I stare as if seeing myself for the first time. I am ugly. And knowing that Babs is right, that I didn't want Simon to take her away from me, makes me feel uglier. But she did abandon me. We were a unit. We were two peas in a pod, until Simon, a great big flashy stringbean, swaggered greenly on to the scene and stole her from me.

At this point I thank heaven that some thoughts are private. Did I think Babs should have refused all romantic proposals because they'd inconvenience *me*? I'm a monster! I'm one of those lunatics you read about in the tabloid supplements. I ought to be ashamed of myself (I would add, 'and go to bed without any supper' – if it wasn't unnecessary). I *am* ashamed of myself. Ashamed of myself in many ways. Ashamed of growing up in Hendon. Ashamed of not getting top grades at university. Ashamed of having size seven feet. But this is a new blend of shame to add to my list. I fiddle with the zip of a pair of navy trousers and blush. Did I expect Babs to put her love life on hold until I sorted mine out? Have I blamed Babs?

On the other hand, it is not her place to criticise my family. What am I? Sad? Dislocated. As for anger, I don't know what that is. But, if I reach into my soul and wiggle my hand about, slime clings to it. I am full of white hot ugliness. I am not what little girls are made of. I'm slugs and snails. Even puppy dog tails are too cute a composite for my brand of nastiness. I prod my stomach, hard. This inner rot is surely more than confetti-envy. But *what*? I'll make it up to Babs. I'll do something to prove that I still deserve her friendship. And I know what it is I'll do. It would be sixty per cent kind, thirty per cent selfish, and ten per cent curiosity. I'll suggest it to her.

Then again, have I been that dreadful? A little cool, a little ungracious. But Babs has to remember that she's the winner, I am the loser. She's the bride, I'm the one left behind. She brushed me off like a crumb from the top table, and I find the best way to cope with rejection is to jump in there first. I smooth down what remains of my hair, and decide that I will demote Babs in the friendship league. She drops to second division. She is ousted as Best Friend, and the position remains vacant until further notice. Inwardly I'm getting even, but outwardly I'm humble. And while this might not adhere to religious notions of contrition, it's a start. Repentance is an acquired taste, like dieting. What concessions will I—

'Are you okay in there, Nat?' booms a voice outside the door.

I jump. 'Yeah, yeah, I'm fine, hang on, I'll be with you in one sec.' I pull on the brown snakeskin boots Matt made me buy – they're high enough to make even my feet look small, but the payoff is backache the next day. I can't help feeling sorry for myself. With me, there's always a price. Babs's favourite shoes would induce vertigo in mountaineers, yet she never suffers. I'm sure I'm the odd one out. Example: I'm always seeing other women in pretty coats – red mohair, or brown suede with a sheepskin ruff – and I think, where do they find coats like that? The only coats I ever see in shops are coarse and navy and look like they've been issued by the council. And coats aren't it. I've always been unlucky. I was the only child in my school denied the once-in-a-lifetime experience of unwrapping a KitKat that was solid chocolate (not that I care now of course). Wait a minute, I'm supposed to be repenting. I take a deep breath and burst into the hallway, tingling with good intentions. Babs hands me a cup of coffee.

'Black, no sugar,' she says.

I feel a throb of gratitude. I hate black coffee. It's so bitter it's like biting into an apple pip. Babs knows I prefer it white but won't drink it that way because milk is fattening and if I add so much as a splash of it, the remaining buttons on my slinky pink top will pop off me as I morph into the Incredible Hulk, and that when I next lumber through Primrose Hill, the entire size eight community will run away screaming.

'Actually,' I say quickly, 'I'll have it white.' The coffee cup wobbles in Babs's hand. 'Just a splash. I'll do it.'

Babs bears the coffee cup back to the kitchen like a knight bearing an infidel's head back to the king. I don't have to drink it. Forty-nine calories per hundred millilitres of semi-skimmed, nearly six times that in a pint. I can always do a double run tomorrow. Or after she's gone.

'You've got a frog in your mouth!' shouts Babs, as I dribble milk into the mug. I glance up, guiltily. I know she's using our private shorthand (meaning 'spit it out') to make me feel better. 'Nat,' she adds softly. 'It's very brave of you to do this.'

I feel ridiculous. 'Yes,' I say. 'Five-year-olds are fighting cancer, but it is very brave of me to add a drop of milk to my coffee.'

Babs pouts. 'Feel the pain, Nat,' she declares in a bogus Californian accent to disguise the mortifying fact that she's in earnest. 'It's relative, but it still hurts.'

I smile, remembering a phase Tony went through, of cracking down on people who used silly voices to say things they were embarrassed about ('Are you leaving work early or is Peter Rabbit leaving work early?'). Babs tilts her head, to beckon me into the lounge. I feel a flutter of fear as I trot in behind her. I want to please her, to avert a telling-off.

'Babs,' I say. 'How's Andy?'

If Babs is surprised, she doesn't show it. 'He's okay. He's fine.'

'Has he –' I resolve to ask the question tactfully but, as ever, my tact receptacles tangle with my tactless receptacles. '– found anywhere to live yet or is he still living with your parents?'

'He's still looking,' replies Babs. 'I've said he could stay with me but the truth is, I don't think Si's that keen. Newly-weds and all that,' she adds, her voice laced with sarcasm.

I exclaim, 'Oh that's brilliant! I mean, it's perfect

because, well, I've got a spare room. If he likes he can come and live here for a bit!'

I hope the edge isn't taken off my charitable gesture by the glaring fact that, as of today, I do actually *need* a lodger if my home isn't to be repossessed in the near future. Maybe Babs won't twig.

'Oh!' she says, medium to joyous. 'What made you change your mind? Oh sorry, yes of course, money.'

'No!' I bleat, 'It's not that! I mean, yes I do need the money now, more than I did, but honestly, it's not that. It's just that . . . Well.' I stop. That you're prepared to eat humble pie isn't enough for some people. They want to feed it to you.

'Iknowivebeenabitsulkyrecentlyandifeelbadaboutitandi knowandyslookingforaplacetoliveandyouthoughthecould livehereandiignoredthehintandiwanttomakeituptoyou.'

'Run that by me again,' says Babs, crossing her long legs.

Did I say feed it to you? I meant, forcefeed it to you with a shovel.

'I know,' I sigh, reluctantly granting each word its full complement of syllables and consonants, 'that I've been a bit sulky recently, and I feel bad about it. I really do. And I know Andy's had trouble finding a short term let that's under a million pounds a month, and I've been – er, thoughtless in not asking if he'd like to live here. So I wanted to make it up to you.'

I don't mention that since the Karaoke party encounter, my interest in her brother has been growing. (I never did have the nerve to mention him to Robbie.) I wouldn't mind observing Andy at slightly closer range. For purely scientific reasons.

Babs clunks her mug down on my glass-topped coffee table and I try not to shout, 'Careful!'

'That's so nice of you, Nat,' she cries. 'So bloody nice. I'll ask him tonight, shall I?'

'Yeah,' I say, pink with pleasure and praying he's less of an almighty slob than his sister.

Babs keeps grinning at me until I don't know where to look. Then she twists her Ayers Rock of a ruby ring (she wanted understated but Si wanted overstated) and blurts, 'And I'm sorry if I haven't been that friendly towards Chris. I know you like him, it's just that I – I suppose I felt sorry for Saul, and Chris is so – he strikes me as so phoney, but Si says he used to be different, but as long as you like him and he's good to you, that's what matters.'

I can tell we're heading for a girly backtracking contest ('Oh no, *you're* wonderful, *I* am useless, why ever did I give the impression that I thought *you* were useless when you're so *wonderful* etc.') and decide not to fight it.

'Thanks,' I say. I defeat the urge to give her a verbal rap on the knuckles.

'Frog!' yells Babs.

I clap a hand over my mouth. 'It's awful that you can tell,' I gasp. 'It's like you've got a built in lie detector.'

'Out with it,' orders Babs.

'Well, okay,' I say, gripping my mug. I feel hot and cold at the same time. 'All I was going to say was' – I try not to insult her – 'you keep going on about me lightening up and yet, when I ditch Saul for Chris, you have a go at me and try to matchmake me with Robbie!' I cringe. The glass vase of tact lies shattered in a million pieces. Again. 'I mean –' I start.

'No,' exclaims Babs, 'that's good, that's good, you must *say.*' She elongates 'say' into a great stretchy sausage of a word. 'You're right,' she adds, frowning. 'You're right. Shit, I was out of order with Robbie. I'm sorry. I just want to see you with a nice guy. I suppose, what I mean is, there's losing control in a reasonable way, and then there's losing it in a destructive way. And I think that Chris is the destructive way. With him, it's about reaching oblivion.'

'So what you're saying, is that I must lose control in a controlled way?'

'Yes!' says Babs. Then she snorts, 'Oh, piss off! Though,' she adds, 'that *is* more or less it. I'll be honest, I don't know

156

much about eating disorders' – she mumbles this as if tasting the awkwardness on her tongue – 'but I can see how hard it is for you to – to let yourself eat a proper amount. And I do know that it's more than just wanting to be thin, this feeling ugly business and all, but Nat, would you try and manage a little more food, get a tiny bit more energy, just for me?' She has the wheedling tone of a mother bribing her five-year-old daughter with sweets. Or rather, she has the wheedling tone of *my* mother bribing her five-year-old daughter with sweets. I want to please her. I don't want to disappoint her.

But I don't want to be fat.

'Nat,' says Babs, shuffling in her seat. 'I've been doing my homework. And, this is just a gobbet of information that I'm going to toss into the air. And the gobbet is, it takes 3,500 extra calories more than normal for a person to put on a pound. That's twenty Mars Bars! A squiddly little pound! There's fourteen of them in a stone!'

'Actually,' I reply, 'that's not even twelve Mars Bars. But,' – I smile to let her know I appreciate it – 'thank you for the tip.'

To the casual observer, I am sitting on the sofa, arms and legs neatly crossed, but in my head I am trapped in a plush private all-you-can-eat hell, screaming, 'Get me out of here!' I want to snatch back my offer to Andy. Sod the intrigue, I don't want him here, prying, spying for Babs. Three thousand five hundred calories? Is that all?

I glance at her safe, solid frame perched on my sofa, so full of hearty honest concern, and wish away the irritation which creeps across my face like a crab. I force the mug to my lips as if it's brimful of arsenic, and take a minute sip. I swallow, and my mouth feels tacky, the milkiness clings like napalm. I swallow again, but it's still there, coating my insides in a white smelly film. *Milk*. It's revolting.

'Are you okay?' asks Babs.

I shake my head.

'Nat,' she says gently. 'You are not going to swell into a

sumo wrestler. But eating more *will* stop your hair from falling out. You need to support your body. Work with it, and – er, keep your hair on.'

Babs grips the sofa to stop herself giggling. (She often laughs at inappropriate moments and had to walk out of her grandmother's funeral so as not to offend the priest.) So I don't take it personally. Apart from anything else, I *want* to keep my hair on. How can I succeed in the world without it? Fat and hairy, or thin and bald? The choice is not encouraging. I feel like a spinster being tried for sorcery. If I float I'm burned at the stake as a witch, if I drown I'm just a middle-aged woman who never married – oops, sorry, our mistake.

I fantasise about washing my hair and not shedding like a cat.

'I've got to get it together,' I say, more to myself than Babs.

She nods, slowly, and reaches out, slowly. I feel like a mental patient who might lash out with a fork. 'It's okay, Babs. I will try to eat more, and to be well. I absolutely will.'

'Nat!' cries Babs, beaming. 'That is fan-bloody-tastic!'

She smashes her coffee cup down on my glass table again and crushes me in a hug. I try – think, a raisin in a nutcracker – to return it. As my arms are pinioned to my sides I feebly pat the side of her hip, the furthest I can reach. And my chin is being tickled to death by that sadist of a red scarf. It's hardly comfortable, and yet, out of nowhere, I feel more peaceful than I have in a while. But the wonder is that when I promised Babs I'd try to eat more, I think I meant it.

A truth. You don't get many of those to a pound.

Chapter 18

A good intention is a wonderful thing. It allows you to bask in the warm anticipatory glow of your own merit without shifting off the sofa. It's the Joining a Gym = Exercise factor. So when Babs leaves I am floating on a blissful pink cloud of resolutions.

I'll find the perfect new job, I'll be the perfect daughter (second helpings – just say yes), the perfect sister, the perfect girlfriend, the perfect *ex*-girlfriend (it's about time I apologised to Saul), the perfect friend, the perfect landlady (no rebuking lodgers for rucking up the carpet or leaving teabags in the sink). I'll eat just enough to stop moulting, I'll be what everyone wants and I'll be happy.

First on the grovel list is my mother. I dial with the fervour of a convert. 'Upper Ground Surgery,' declares a bored voice. 'Hello?'

'Mum, it's me,' I say. 'I just wanted to tell you not to worry, because everything's going to be okay. Andy's going to be my lodger – the brother of the bride! – so that will help pay the mortgage, and I'm going to start looking for a new job straight away. I'm not – not quite sure what – what I want to do, what I could do, but at least now you don't have to worry so much.'

'That's wonderful, but you will charge Andy the going rate, won't you, dear?' replies my mother anxiously. 'I know he's a friend of sorts, but now you've lost your job you need the money. I don't know what people charge for a double room in an upmarket area of London these days. Fifty pounds a month? Sixty?'

159

'Something like that,' I say, refusing to sag. 'It's nice, though, isn't it? It's one problem solved, isn't it?'

'Sixty pounds! I suppose it's one less thing to worry about. It's good to have a man in the house, it makes burglars think twice. A man or a peke – the smaller they are, the bigger the racket. As for a new job, you've hit the nail on the head, Natalie. What *can* you do? That's my biggest worry.'

My biggest worry is whether the polar ice cap will melt and drown the whole world, but I suppose the possibility of me spending the rest of my days watching *Wheel of Fortune* and calling it 'educational', is an equally legitimate concern.

'I thought I might –'

'There's nothing here, so I spoke to my colleague, Susan, and as luck would have it her husband Martin owns a dry cleaning firm, you know Martin, big jolly man, known locally as something of a raconteur, he's looking for a junior to help out behind the till. It might not sound much but it's a fairly responsible position, and there are prospects of promotion. They're based in Borehamwood, so it wouldn't be too far to travel, and you could start next week. I know it's not ideal, dear, but beggars can't be choosers, and you might enjoy it.'

I am speechless. I feel as mortified as a cat in a floppy red bow. I envisage a life of scrabbling amid other people's dirty linen. A *Groundhog Day* existence of smiling patiently and pinging a button and declaiming, 'That will be twenty four pounds and fifty pence please!' A deadly job in the suburb of Boringwood under the gimlet-eyed supervision of Susan's husband Martin the raconteur (an old fart who bores people professionally), who would joyfully detail my every move to his snoopy wife (who wears a green sun-visor all day, every day, because she thinks it makes her look like a professional golfer), who would dutifully pass the informational baton to my mother. Cheaper than government surveillance, but every bit as effective.

160

'Mum,' I bleat. 'It's nice of you but ...' I tail off, paralysed by a flashback of the last time I set foot in a dry cleaner's. A thin-lipped woman nudged me and sniffed, 'See that crimson velour trouser suit hanging there? That belongs to my sister-in-law. She comes in here every week. Mind you, she can afford it.' Much as I want to be perfect for my mother, I'm not saintly enough to sacrifice myself to Martin Pipkin's Eeesy-Kleen empire. How to break it to her?

'Mum,' I chirrup, inspired. 'It's a brilliant idea except for one thing.'

'Wh-at?' she says, her voice cracking with hurt.

'*Till* girl at the Borehamwood branch of Eeesy-Kleen! I'd be a laughing stock for every eligible man this side of Reykjavik! No self-respecting professional snob would dream of dating me ever again.' (Not that the legal, financial and medical fraternities have been wildly fantasising over me in my current state of employment. And not that I'm bothered.)

There is a terrifying pause.

'I see what you mean,' she says finally. 'I'll call Tony. Maybe he'll find you something.'

Not if I call him first. I speed-dial the number and wonder what I can offer him. Tony is like a B-grade celebrity in that you can't bother him on a whim, he'll want to know what's in it for him and how much you're paying. I don't have any supermarkets for him to open (though I might have access to a dry cleaner's if I play my cards wrong) but I do, for the moment, have access to Mel. Anyway, he's shunned me for a week so he should have worked off his fury by now. Tony shouts, threatens, intimidates, then – as you crawl bloodily to a corner to lick your fatal wounds – finds it in his heart to forgive you.

'Could you tell him,' I beg his PA, 'that it's a matter of life and death?'

'Excite me,' says Tony. He yawns, for effect.

'Well,' I say, relieved to be granted the royal pardon

(implicit in not having my head bitten off). 'The good news is, Mel likes you but she – er, also likes a challenge, so if I were you I wouldn't do anything – ah, demonstrative for Valentine's Day—'

'What, so she'll turn down a weekend in Paris?'

'Er . . .' I am briefly stunned by this as the most my brother has ever given a woman for Valentine's Day is the boot. 'Ah, what I meant was, if I were you I wouldn't do anything demonstrative for Valentine's Day except take her to Paris for the weekend.'

'Thought so.'

'And the bad news,' I shrill, before he cuts me off, 'is that I've lost my job and Mum wants me to start work as a till girl for a dry cleaner's in Borehamwood.' I regale him with a pruned version of the messy tale (time is money). Tony whistles.

'Floozie,' he murmurs. 'A question. We're throwing mash at Mother, we're gobbing off about classified information isn't our business, we're getting fired by the tutu factory, and we're hanging with managers of dodgy bands. We're the faint breeze that grows into a hurricane. Are we, by any chance, losing it?'

I allow my gut retort time to dissolve. 'As far as I know,' I reply eventually, 'I'm sane.'

'Christ,' he exclaims.

'What?' I ask.

'In *Catch-22* terms,' he says gravely, 'that means you're a psycho.'

My brother is speaking to me, I tell myself, as I look up the number of the Fairbush Gynecology Clinic. Even if what he says isn't that complimentary. Still, my resolve is weakened – I feel as if a large rat has chomped through it and all that remains is a thread – and I dial the number slowly.

'Fairbush Gynecology Clinic!' tweets a receptionist who has obviously worked on her motivation and given her all to this precious line. 'How may I direct your call?' (Clear

162

diction, gentle yet searing emphasis on the 'direct', the 'call' fading to a Monroe-esque coo, well-paced, unobtrusive breathing technique, altogether very convincing.)

'Oh, hello. May I speak to Dr Vincent Miller? It's his daughter.'

'One moment, please, I'll put you through to his assistant.'

I go through the rigmarole again, but Dr Miller is with a client.

'Could I possibly leave a short message?'

'Sure,' says his assistant sourly, obliterating – again – the myth that Americans are polite. I can't understand it. I am always obsequious to foreigners – I'm a lone ambassador, I'm representing my nation!

'If you could say—'

'Hold it! . . . OK, go ahead.'

'If you could just say' – I grit my teeth – 'that Kimberli Ann is welcome to call me any time to discuss the issues.'

'Pardon me?'

'The *issues!*' I boom. 'Now you say *bless you!*'

'Pardon me?'

'Never mind,' I mumble, wondering why I continue to humiliate myself by turning out jokes a Christmas cracker would be ashamed of. 'Thank you so much, bye.'

I have no intention of paying the slightest heed to any New Age nonsense that Kimberli Ann cares to garble, but the gesture is all and my father will be delighted. I slump in my chair and decide that blissful pink cloud or no blissful pink cloud, good intentions are an ordeal and I don't have the strength – mental or physical – to call Saul. I picture his cheery face. I miss him, a little. He's a gentleman. A gentleman that *comfort eats* – his phrase! – like a middle-aged housewife. No. I don't miss him at all. I ring Chris instead.

'Is there, um, any chance you're free tonight?'

'I might be,' he replies. 'Why? Slaphead blown you out?'

I titter wearily. 'You know Robbie's just a friend. Not

even a friend! An acquaintance. Anyway, I thought, seeing as it's Valentine's Eve, I could cook you dinner.'

'Dinner?' says Chris.

I know he isn't a great foodie – he's skin and bone and I rarely see him eat – but he sounds positively *insulted*.

'Er, yes,' I say, hoping I haven't unwittingly said something terrible in rhyming slang.

'Valentine's *Eve*?' he says, his tone confirming the worst.

'It was a joke,' I gabble, realising too late that I have committed a heinous sin – I have dared suggest that tomorrow, February 14th, is a special occasion. I have wielded the axe of fake romance over his innocent head and our defenceless relationship, I've put G-force pressure on him to translate his feelings into garish bouquets and slushy cards and soppy gifts, I'm forcing him into an (expensive) public display of how much he rates me – a display which can and will be measured against other displays, that will be judged and criticised by colleagues and friends, that will make him resent me, despise me, and dump me the following day.

'What I meant was,' I add in a rush, 'it's Valentine's Day tomorrow so don't bother doing anything.' I just about manage not to choke on the words.

'If you insist,' drawls Chris. 'I'll be round at eight.'

'Yes,' I mutter. 'Great.'

Blast.

I am charging around Tesco like a bull with a drawing pin in its butt, when my mobile rings.

'Hello?' I say, screeching to a halt by the endless rows of cream, double cream, single cream, extra thick single cream, clotted cream, whipping cream, soured cream . . .

'Natalie!' cries a voice, distinct from the majority in being friendly not furious.

'Yes?' I say, warily.

'It's Andy. Babs told me! So I'm forgiven for whatever it was I did? Ah, Natalie, you star! One more week at my

164

parents' and I'd have turned into a bloke who wears a patterned sweater stained with egg and stalks the hair-dressers off *Coronation Street*.'

'You'd have racked up a fortune in train fares,' I suggest. 'You'd have spent your whole life rushing from London to Manchester.'

'You saved me,' he replies. 'But I tell you – it was close! So – ah, when do you want me?'

I'll say one thing about Barbara's family. They're not backward in coming forward. If *I* had been offered a room by me, *I'd* ask if I was sure it was still okay – as a courtesy if nothing else. To blithely assume that people mean what they say! It's like swearing undying friendship with the couple you meet in the Algarve, enduring the necessary charade of exchanging addresses, promising to visit them in Huddersfield, and then, a month later when your tan has faded and you've forgotten they existed, receiving an insolent and over-familiar call from two strangers, inviting themselves to stay at your home for the weekend!

'Sunday?'

'Good for me,' replies Andy. 'Any particular time?'

'Oh, gosh, I don't know – er, you say.'

'Three?'

'Yes, that sounds fine.'

'Great. And you can tell me what I'm paying and run through the house rules – no five in a bed orgies, class A drugs only, curfew eight-thirty?'

'Curfew, eight *fifteen*,' I say sternly. 'And strictly no more than four in a bed.'

When I blip off, I'm smiling.

Chris is not smiling. I have spent the last three hours preparing an elaborate meal: guacamole with paprika-toasted potato skins (from Nigella Lawson's *How To Eat*), cod wrapped in ham, with sage and onion lentils (Nigella again – the woman's a genius), and seven-minute steamed chocolate pudding (ditto, if it ain't broke don't fix it), the fresh coriander and lime infusing my kitchen with a glorious burst of sharp-scented sunniness, the hot crispiness of the potato jackets, so crackly and satisfying, the thick creamy green avocado pulp, the cool slippery white fish, the sweet pearly pinkness of the ham, the shiny brown lentils, such pretty colours, a delicious piece of modern art, the overpowering smell of the warm rich oozy chocolate clinging to my senses like a vampire to a neck. I have chopped and scooped and mashed and peeled and stoned and pulped and sliced and baked and watched Chris juicily devour every bite. I'm not that hungry so I just sip a little white wine.

But Chris is not smiling because as he scratches the last scrape of brown gluey pudding from its smooth china bowl, I tell him that Andy is moving in on Sunday. The timing isn't wonderful but, after my discussion with Babs, I feel a little braver. Also, I now know I'm getting nothing for Valentine's Day, and if I'm going down, I might as well go all the way. (This opinion, I confess, is borrowed from Tony, who once sparked a debate at Black Moon Records on the topic, Which Serial Killer? Head of A&R said he'd like to be murdered in a relatively quick and painless fashion, preferably injected with morphine by a mad doctor. My brother was keen to be gorily dispatched by a more flamboyant psychopath: 'I want to be clogging up drains, I want double page investigations in Sunday newspapers . . .' It wasn't a tasteful discussion, but the gist was, if you're going, go out with a bang.)

'Who the bleedinell is Andy?' says Chris.

'He's Babs's brother. It's purely a business decision,' I bleat, quaking inwardly. 'He's only staying for a couple of months. Until *his* lodgers move out,' I add. 'He's got a flat in Pimlico. He's all right, just a bit dull. Thing is, I need the money, and I – I owed Babs a favour.'

'Right,' says Chris tonelessly. He shoves away his bowl, and sparks up a cigarette. He doesn't offer me the packet so, fumblingly, I light one of my own.

'So what's this geezer do?'

'I'm not sure. He used to be in finance.'

Chris snorts. His subtext is easily legible as 'capitalist pig'.

'You, we, we went to his birthday party at that Mexican place, the karaoke, remember?'

Chris expels a disdainful jet of smoke.

I tap my ash into my silver Heals ashtray and consider reneging on my offer to Andy. I don't want to upset Chris, but nor do I want to offend Babs. I am about to apologise for my thoughtlessness, when Chris rises from his chair and declares, 'Gotta go.'

'You're *going?*'

'Your point?' he says, in a tone that would wither a forest.

'No, no,' I stammer. 'Nothing.'

'Know this, princess,' he snaps, on his way out. 'I won't be messed with. *Capisce?*'

No one has ever said 'capisce' to me before, and in a silly middle-class way I feel quite glamorous. Which isn't to say that I don't sit at the table and mope at my clunky tactlessness and wasted cooking and pointless effort and the certain gloom of a barren Valentine's Day and my inability to do anything right and my knack of upsetting people and being shouted at and walked out on. But when, at ten past midnight, I stop grizzling, it occurs to me that this is the first time a non-geek has ever accused me of 'messing' with him. And, soggy as I am, I can't help taking a little pride in that.

Chapter 19

I set my alarm early for Valentine's Day, but when it starts shrieking at seven I'm already awake. I couldn't sleep after Kimberli Ann called, at 1.10 a.m., to discuss my issues.

Kimberli Ann is actually intelligent, but she is interested only in herself and how the world relates to her, and that makes her stupid. She imagines she has empathy but can only see things *her* way. She won't help you because she cares about you, but because she wants to spread the word of Kimberli Ann (she certainly converted my father). She will get what she wants eventually – a film deal – because that's all she cares about. She isn't brilliant but she's good enough.

Anyhow, I lay in bed, limp and puffy eyed, and we had an interesting chat. Though, I suspect, not quite the chat my father had envisaged. Kimberli Ann was blown away to hear about my weight loss, but from what 'Vinny' *(gik!)* said, my situation was 'sub-clinical', more a 'lifestyle disorder', like, I was this tall and so many pounds, so in point of fact I was a 'cheeseball anorexic', I wasn't thin enough to be rushed to hospital and force-fed a calorific dinner by experts.

Right? Er, right. So if I wanted to shape up, Kimberli Ann had the skinny on how. I shouldn't fast. That's way unhealthy, she informed me. The body loves to store fat when it's fasting. It's like you're stranded on a desert island so, like, your metabolism slows and you gain fat. Had I heard of fat-blockers? Like, they block the absorption of dietary fat. Pop one of these babies and I could eat candy, cookies, I could sin all day. OK, I might need the bathroom without warning, I might experience gas with discharge, oily spotting, fatty stools with an orange uh coloration, and an inability to control my bowels but hell, I sure wouldn't have to control my sugar budget!

Having relieved herself of this wisdom (and heaven knows what else), she tells me to get a good night's sleep, as lack of sleep is considered to be a factor in the current obesity epidemic in the United States.

I *think* this is a joke, but the eerie possibility that it might be true keeps me bolt awake till morning. Despite feeling like molten lead has been poured in my ear during the night, when the alarm shrills, I'm pleased to get up. I conclude it's good to have options – isn't that what democracy is all about – but that fat-blockers are for people devoid of willpower. I have enough challenges, I don't wish to welcome orange pooh to the fray.

Besides. Today I keep my promise to Babs. I will eat enough to keep my hair on. Hence the alarm call. I faff around getting dressed, delaying the point at which I have to sit down at the table. I set out my plate, my Caffeine Queen mug, and remove a slice of bread from the freezer.

'Even one piece of toast is better than crispbread,' Babs said yesterday. 'Crispbread is bulked-up air, there's nothing to it.'

Funnily enough, this didn't put me off it. But 'wholegrain bread is busting with hair vitamins', encouraged me to make the leap. A scrape of butter. A scrape of Marmite. I eat as slowly as a snail with its jaw wired, but I eat.

My heart bops all the while and I feel my stomach recoil at the assault. Chew. Chew. Chew. Chew. Swallow. The toast sticks drily in my throat, and scratches on the way down. I sip water but the pain remains. My weak useless hair. Other women lose weight and *their* hair doesn't fall out. Typical. I even fail at dieting. My eyes start to prickle and I feel heavy, like a sodden washcloth. I stare into the mud of my thick black coffee. The cheat's laxative. I drink it, and a wispy blonde hair falls on to the table's white surface. I've got nowhere to go today, why did I even get up? Suddenly I am pulling yanking tearing at my hair, panting, vicious, ouch, impotence.

I unclench my fists and inspect them, listlessly. Eleven hairs. Oh genius, Natalie. The kitchen scissors are in the drawer, why not hack off the rest? I speed to the bathroom mirror to inspect the damage, carefully lifting and parting sections of my hair, like a chimpanzee hunting for nits. I blur my vision to avoid sight of my blotchy face so, not surprisingly, I don't spot any bald patches.

'You gibbon,' I tell myself. Then I step on the scales. Exactly the same. I try not to smile, but the satisfaction ripples through me. I smooth my jumper, splash my burning cheeks with cool water, destroy all evidence of my bizarre autotussle – I must have looked like a woman with a bee in her ear – and walk to the newsagent. Before the postman can disappoint me.

Hair, hair, glorious hair, I think, squeezing my knuckles. I am still breathing hard, like a claustrophobic pot-holer. At least I don't have to suffer the tube – all those other women, bouncing glossy shampoo ads the lot of them, all grinning like death masks in smug expectation of the fat bouquets that await them at the office. (Rigorously trained men *always* send their bouquets to the office, there's no point otherwise.) I need to speak to Babs, I need to be reassured. She'll be home from her shift at 9.30-ish.

The toast sits inside me like a lump of metal. I feel dragged forward by it, my belly – ugh, vile *swelly* word – has become a bowling ball. To accommodate its bulk I need to walk with a stoop.

I buy the *Telegraph* - Julietta smiles mournfully from the front page – and a new pen. I wander aimlessly up and down Primrose Hill High Street for an hour, trying to enjoy the freedom of fecklessness, then slouch home again. That heartless postman hasn't delivered my post. I'm wondering whether to call the sorting office, when my phone rings.

170

'Natalie? Frannie.'

I jump and hold the phone like a rotting banana, between a finger and thumb, a safe distance from my ear.

'Frannie,' I croak. 'Happy Valentine's Day! How are things? How did you know—'

'They said you no longer worked at the GLBallet. I presume you left of your own accord?'

'Of course!'

'I'm stunned. I didn't think you had it in you.'

I am tempted to bang my head against the wall in case I'm dreaming. Back-handed, yes, barbed, undoubtedly, but was that . . . a *compliment*?

'So, Natalie. What are you wearing for Babs and Si's dinner party tomorrow?'

What? That burst of humanity was brief. First, what I wear has as much relevance to Frannie as it does to an Albanian refugee. Second, Frannie regards appearance queries as demeaning to both parties (in the same way that she objects to women who claim a dependency on chocolate: 'Men like it as much and eat more of it than women, they just don't make such a big deal of it!'). And third, Frannie would join the *Baywatch* fan club before asking my advice on, say, any subject in the universe.

Babs and Simon are having a party and I am not invited! The thoughts stampede. Did Frannie ask who else was coming? Or did Babs tell Frannie to keep it secret? Did Babs forget to ask me? Did Simon ask her not to? Was it because Babs objects to Chris? And why am I left out when I bit the frigging bullet and asked her big smug brother to stay in my flat? Is *he* invited? Did I offend her yesterday? How can I answer Frannie's question without conceding match point?

'I'm – I'm busy tomorrow night, unfortunately, so I won't be going,' I mumble.

'Oh! Weren't you invited then?'

I grit my teeth. Frannie's sort are incredible: if you have a weakness, they'll hunt it down and tweak it.

171

'Natalie,' she adds. 'You do *know* why you weren't invited?'

'N-n-no.'

'Because you wouldn't eat anything.'

My lips gum together in shock. Babs . . . Babs wouldn't tell Frannie about yesterday . . . would she?

'I . . . I don't know what you mean.'

'Yes, you do,' cries Frannie. 'You know full well!'

I can't stop myself. 'Wh – what did Babs tell you?' I stammer.

'That's not for me to say,' replies Frannie. '*Thags nok for me to say*'. I want to rip her self-righteous head off. Hers and Barbara's. The traitor.

'I am fine,' I say in a small voice. 'I do eat.'

'Well, if you do, the news hasn't reached your hips. If you ask me, it's high time you pulled yourself together. It's criminal, behaving like that when people in Africa and parts of Manchester are starving!'

'I –'

'You know the other reason you weren't invited?'

'No.'

'Your resentment of Simon is palpable and embarrassing. The trouble with you is, someone always has to be Number One. You've got to learn, Natalie, not everyone is a threat to your position. You've also got to learn that sulking is for children.'

The receiver wobbles in my hand. I'd like to snap back with such verbal wit and ferocity that Frannie would be tongue-tied and mortified until her dying day. Sadly, my creative mind is a desert, its heat-parched earth cracking with creeping desperate weeds and the odd shiny beetle. In other words, the old witch puts the phone down on me before I've thought of anything.

Chapter 20

'The vagina,' said my father once, 'is like an old sock. The heel goes and you darn it, but that doesn't stop something going wrong with the toe. The vagina can be defective in many different areas. You repair one thing, something else develops.'

I feel the same way about friendship. Babs and I struggle to mend our differences, and then she thrusts a secret dinner party into the equation, ripping a large hole in it. I feel the urge to get out of the flat again. Anyhow, I need to buy a book on downsizing. I march along the road, and fantasise about dropping in on the night in question – 'Hello Babs, I was just passing, thought I'd say hello, oh! Fee fi fo fum, I see you've got company, I'll go then, shall I, no, no, don't worry about me, I've got a nice lumpy bowl of gruel, some delicious tap water, and the dog to talk to' – I'll hire Paws, OK? – 'I'll be fine . . .'

That would be acceptable, wouldn't it? It's only sulking if you don't talk! Oh God, I've been branded a sulker! And everyone knows I resent Simon. But then Frannie is hardly impartial. Reassuring me that no one is a threat to my position, when she's diligently threatened my position for the last sixteen years! As for complaining about someone always having to be Number One with me – I don't deny it! Someone *does* have to be Number One, and I want it to be me! What's the point in being second best? That's failure.

Hang on, I've just lost my job. *That's* failure. I browse along the bookshelves, and pounce on *Downshifting – the*

Guide to Happier, Simpler Living. Probably the first copy ever sold around here. I reject *Easy Ways To Make Money* as I don't wish to look too desperate in front of the sales staff, who are worryingly friendly. I waste £25 on house-porn, *100 Luxury Interiors*, to put them off the scent. It might impress Andy – he's my lodger, as from tomorrow! This cheers me enough to admit that I do *half* understand why I'm not first on Babs's dinner party guest-list. I haven't exactly welcomed Simon to my bosom (it hardly seems appropriate). And the last time they invited me round, didn't I sit there toying with my food like a petulant child?

This puts me in a mood again. I can't get away from the feeling that everyone is trying to make me fat. I do my best to deflect it – I'm always urging other people to eat. Once I fed Paws a whole pack of chocolate digestives, purely for the pleasure of abstaining while another creature put on weight (although he was subsequently sick in the GLBallet lift). My other gripe is that Chris hasn't rung. February 14th and not a sausage! Not that I *want* a sausage – it's hardly a romantic gift – but he might have sent a card. But perhaps this is his way of showing he likes me? If only I was better at deciphering the code.

I unlock the front door, plod into the kitchen and stare. There, on the white table, stunning the room's quiet colour scheme, is a small terracotta pot of passionate purple blooms. I unpick the envelope stapled to the cellophane and open it. A trip to Paris? The message reads, 'Dear, at least give the Pipkins a call! I've put some food in your fridge for the weekend – shop bought, forgive me, it's been crazy at the surgery this week – you'll have to tell me what Andy likes! I'm at bridge tonight, but I'll call you tomorrow. Mum.'

I slump, and – it would be childish not to – tenderly water the flowers. Then I about-turn and yank open the fridge. The squash of produce makes me giddy. Tuna and sweetcorn, salmon and cream cheese in dinky pots, smoked salmon, crab pate, sushi – good lord, the sea must be an empty tank! – pasta filled with asparagus, spaghetti, four cheese pasta, ricotta and spinach pasta, cheese and sun-dried tomato pasta – wheat allergy, anyone? – a pineapple, two mangos, green pesto, red pesto, fresh tomato sauce, cottage cheese, mushrooms, onions, minced beef, pepperoni pizza, and four squat cans of M&S lager – oh my goodness, Man Food!

I shut the door and back away. Normally at this point, I take a large rubbish bag from the second left hand drawer and methodically throw every morsel into the bin. I want to scrub the fridge clean, I itch to get the food out of the flat, away from me. I can't see it but its malign presence infests me like the smell of a decaying corpse. I squeeze my hands into fists, digging my nails hard into my palms until the pain relocates. *I'll* get out of the flat. For the third time this morning. I walk to the video shop, puff puff puff, choose three films suitable for today's theme, and walk home again.

Now I have a plan.

I imprison all the food in the freezer except for the fruit, the spaghetti, and the fresh tomato sauce, which I place in an orderly line on the side. Then I vacuum Andy's room with the Dyson, boil some water in my Porsche kettle for a peppermint tea, sit on my Heals suede sofa, put *The Nutcracker Suite* on my Nakamichi Soundspace 8 stereo, light an Aveda scented candle, and read *Downshifting – The Guide To Happier, Simpler Living*. It's very informative. I *could* save money on salon facials by staying at home and rubbing my face vigorously with a warm flannel. As for approaching the council to register my interest in an allotment – Primrose Hill is a big park: they could easily afford to cordon off a small plot.

I jot down the address of Original Organics Ltd, in case things get really desperate and I need to buy a wormery. Then I stick the first part of my Valentine's entertainment in the video. *Full Metal Jacket*. I take a half-hour break for dinner – a half bowl of spaghetti cooked with no oil, with a tablespoon of fresh tomato sauce on the side to add in. I slice the pasta into a neat criss-cross of cubes, and slowly, grimly force it down. Four hundred calories, approx. Another hundred for the mango. The numbers reassure me, but the process bores me. I don't like eating. It's so dull. Nothing even *tastes*. It's a chore. I want to do a Joan Collins – divide the food on the plate in two and leave half – but each concession to abstinence sees a hair loosening its grip on my scalp. Babs had better be grateful.

I squeeze down the last slither of spaghetti – hoping each strand makes its way directly to a head follicle – and wash the bowl and saucepan until they shine. Then I spend the dying hours of the day watching *Thin Red Line* and the full extended director's cut of *Das Boot*.

I wake up purged by gunfire and go straight to the gym. London is subdued at eight on a Saturday and I pelt along the roads feeling superior to its slothful population. I bounce in to the gym, beeline for the running machine, and soon the bliss of emotional stasis descends. Thump thump. Will Alex be here? Thump thump. Are there Pilates classes at the weekend? Thump thump. It would be nice to see her again. Thump thump. But you don't know her that well. Thump. Inappropriate desire to access other people's lives. Thump. Not receiving you, over.

I shower at home – in communal changing rooms women gawk at me and I feel like Gretel being sized up for the pot. And I've stopped taking baths because I hate the sight of all that floating hair. I'd heave myself out of the water and strands would coat me like a web, their sly insect tickle telling the repellent truth. In the shower, they fall, are washed away and I wallow in ignorance. I pump the dregs of conditioner from its bottle and console myself that if Chris and I are over, at least I'll save on grooming products. I leave my hair to dry naturally – I don't want my remaining locks burned off by the hairdryer. My elaborate precautions let me believe that hardly a hair has been lost.

I've run long enough to eat breakfast. Brown toast. Marmite. Coffee. The same as yesterday. My new regime and I won't deviate. I don't like surprises. As I work on the toast I add and subtract – calories gained, calories spent, eating it on, running it off – the sabotage is involuntary. I should gain weight but as Liz Hurley once said, if I was as fat as Marilyn Monroe I'd kill myself. What do people do, who don't think of food? Their lives must be gaping holes, chasms of nothingness punctuated by random meals. What would I think about, if I didn't think of food? I'd think the unthinkable. So food is what I think of. I gnaw the toast and do my sums.

I leave a square, I need to. I pick a crumb off the floor and catch myself. If Chris saw me doing that! I throw the crumb back on the floor and put my plate and cup in the sink and think of Babs. Just once, leave the fucking washing up! Well, I will. I'll leave it until tomorrow. Or until this evening (no need to go mad). I feel this break-through gives me a valid reason to ring Babs. Anyway, I was thinking of asking her to come round while Andy moves in. I can't help it if she feels guilty at my hospitality in the face of her non-hospitality, can I?

'Party on,' murmurs Babs, when I tell her about the washing up, making me feel foolish.

'Would you and Simon like to come round for tea tomorrow, while Andy moves in? Simon's invited too, obviously,' I add, so my generosity is not misunderstood.

'What a nice idea,' she replies. 'I'll see if he's free.' There is no trace of surprise, or guilt in her voice. In fact, she sounds sunny, playful, carefree. Probably she's just had sex. I want to ask, 'So what are you up to tonight?' but I'm too much of a coward. Instead I say gruffly, 'I've been trying to eat more, like you said.'

'Have you? I'm pleased.'

I wait for more praise but there is none. I can't believe it. It's like the love of your life announcing himself as a one-night stand the following morning. But what about our

177

deep and meaningful talk? Me baring my soul and my underwear? All that and now this! No reassurance, no well done? I need *feedback* (my sort of nourishment). It's enough to drive me to my mother. I am cooking up a suitably cool retort, when Babs chirrups, 'All right then, Nat, have a nice evening, we'll see you tomorrow,' and rings off. I stare at the receiver and consider being more spontaneous.

Sunday afternoon, the pinnacle of a bland weekend. I am bleaching the toilet bowl for the third time when the doorbell rings. Ten to three. Andy. He's early, which is better than late. I fret when people are late. I bare my teeth in the mirror, rip off my apron, hang it on its hook, and pull open the front door.

'Wotcha,' says Chris. He leans against the doorframe, all harsh cheekbones and sharp edges. Dark eyes, red lips, sent from hell.

Oh, go away, is what I should say but my common sense short circuits. I might as well press 'defrost' and crawl into the microwave. He has the same effect on me.

'I bought you something,' he mumbles, handing me a white plastic bag. 'I was busy Friday.'

A present. He bought me a present! The greatest gift of all! I open the bag. A CD. 'The Offspring,' I say. 'Wow,' I simper, not daring to admit I've never heard of them. 'Thank you.'

Chris smiles. 'They're Yanks. They're great. Blue Fiend are very, er, inspired by them.' He trips into the lounge. I watch him approach my CD player in his complicated trainers and loose jeans. Why do I find it endearing that the man has no arse?

'You know,' I say, nervously, 'my lodger is moving in, in one minute.'

I brace myself for fuss but Chris nods and says, 'Yeah, I know, princess, you said.' He grins. I grin back, but even as I do so, I feel like a tourist smiling at a timeshare salesman. Just me is not enough. What does he *want?*

'So, what have you been up to?' I say.

Chris grins again. I've never seen him smile this much. Unless a scowl is imminent, his image will soon be toast. 'This and that,' he replies, lifting my hair and licking my neck.

'Euw!' I say, breathing in the smoky scent of him, and trying not to wilt. Suddenly he hoists me over his spindly shoulder and hauls me, gasping and flapping like a fish on a line, into my bedroom. 'Chris,' I bleat. 'We can't, Babs and Andy'll be here in a sec—'

He answers me with a kiss. I watch his pale slender hands travel over my grey top, under it, tracing cold patterns on my colder skin. I lie there passive. He kisses me again, his eyes wide, pupils huge and needy. And I give in. It's not so much the physical release, which feels like a dream, lifting me out of myself. I love it but I distrust it. What I crave is to be desired. It empowers me (if only for ten minutes). As for desiring, the doing is fun, the feeling alarms me. When Andy rings the door, I'm in the throes of living dangerously.

Chris lights a cigarette, and watches me, amused, as I leap from the bed and dress in a blur. I restrain my hair in a pert ponytail, pat my face to eradicate all X-rated traces, and wipe the sin off my lips.

'How do I look?' I ask.

'Post-coital,' he replies smugly.

The doorbell shrills again. 'I'm coming!' I shout.

'Again?' drawls Chris.

I beam, rush to the bathroom, squirt a blob of toothpaste into my mouth, and bound to the door. My new lodger is standing there in jeans and a T-shirt clutching a bag of wires.

'Hi!' I cry, blushing to the hilt. 'Sorry, I was tidying up.'

Andy smiles the curt smile of someone who dislikes to be kept waiting.

'Not for me, I hope,' he says.

'Only partly,' I reply, and his smile gains warmth.

Andy glances beyond me and I turn, as Chris pads towards us, barefoot and tousle-haired. I sigh inwardly. He might as well bowl up naked with the words 'Just Been Shagging' scrawled on his forehead. 'Um, Chris is here, you've met, haven't you?' I bleat.

Chris nods tersely, sucks on his cigarette, and extends an unfriendly hand.

'All right,' says Andy, and I sense the unspoken words *You wanker* fogging the air. I am reminded of two tomcats fluffing up their tails, so it's a relief to spy Babs bounding up the stairs, two at a time.

'Scandal!' she cries. 'We're polluting Primrose Hill with cheap motors – it's like Deals on Wheels out there!'

'Babs!' I exclaim. 'And oh, Simon. Hi, come in. Chris, look Simon's here!'

Chris unbristles and Andy's hard expression softens.

'How nice,' I croak thankfully (I was waiting for the pair of them to down trousers and compare penis size). 'Andy – shall I show you your room and you can, um, put that bag of wires down?'

Babs looks at her brother and laughs. 'You had a bag of wires, didn't you, Si?' she teases.

Simon – the dictionary definition of colonial chic in a thin linen shirt and cotton trousers (or, for short, the dick) – offers me his cheek to be kissed, and says, 'All men over twelve have a bag of wires, Bee, it's a rite of passage.'

Andy says, 'I've got two bags, what does that say about me?'

Simon laughs a deep baritone laugh probably copied from his father and says, 'I dread to think.'

Pompous twit. I glance nervously at Andy and, before I know I've said it, I blurt, 'You've got superior equipment?'

The joke escapes with a suggestive shimmy and for a second I don't breathe, as if a lack of oxygen will grab it back, and everyone looks at me and laughs. Everyone, except Simon and Chris. I smile at Andy. Even though I

180

want to, it's surprisingly hard to resent him in the flesh. Part of me wanted to taunt him, parade my relationship with Chris to punish him for his so easily forgotten teenage crime. When he made that joke about the kiss, I felt the power balance shift – ever so slightly, but the nastiest part of me wanted to make the most of it. Yet, now he's here, clutching his bags of wires, I feel the venom start to melt. Laughter transforms his face. I want to watch him, but Chris is acting the Ice Queen so I don't dare.

'So, Natalie, are you going to show me to my quarters?' Andy asks in a teasing voice – put on, I suspect, purely to irritate Chris. I think we can safely conclude it's hate at first sight. And what, I am dying to ask Babs, is up with her brother and Simon? I thought they were pals and yet here they are practically at each others' throats.

'Oh sure,' I say, wondering if I've introduced the match and petrol to the paper factory.

'I'll do the tea, shall I?' suggests Babs.

Simon grunts, plods into the lounge, and flops on my suede sofa. I'd object, only his white linen and beige cotton complement my colour scheme. Chris, nose in the air and clashing, follows him.

Weary, I force a smile at Andy, and say, 'The guided tour.'

He trots down the hall behind me, his heavy boots clunking on my painted floorboards, and says, 'Your flat is like a show flat! Are you renting?'

My proud grin disintegrates and I splutter, 'No!'

Andy sees his mistake and adds, 'After months of shagpile and chintz, this is awesome. It's so, sort of, seventies minimalist I'm tempted to leave that second bag of wires in the boot. I feel like clutter already. Christ knows how you put up with Babs – no joke, the woman's a fire hazard!'

This is a nice try, so I grant him a smile and he smiles back. He has orderly teeth, a wide jaw, slanted green eyes. His nose is straight except for a slight bump in the middle, and his hair is dark blond. I stare at his affable open face and think, bag of wires or not, you'll always look like you've just trekked round India on a trust fund. 'Do I have lipstick on my teeth?' enquires Andy.

'Oh! No. No, I, er, was just thinking how you and Babs look nothing like each other.'

Andy raises an eyebrow. 'True.'

'Your room,' I cry.

'A glitterball! Very Austin Powers.'

I smile. 'You can thank your sister,' I say.

'It's great. It's going to be great. What a cool room. I like big windows.' He lollops to the window and flings it wide. 'We must celebrate!' he shouts. 'Dinner in Primrose Hill! KFC! My treat!'

He's joking, of course, not to mention that I wouldn't set foot in a fast food joint for fear of absorbing rogue oil particles through osmosis – but Chris sounds a swagger away from hurling Andy through the bay window.

'Sorry, mate,' he growls from the door – in a tone that suggests he isn't sorry at all. 'That's my bird you're coming on to and tonight she's got a date with *me*.'

Andy and I swing round. It's all gone a bit Ilford, as Tony would say, and for a childish second I hope the two of them will start fighting over me, like mongrels scrapping over a chop. My heart hops and I yearn for a lace handkerchief to flutter over my lightly glowing brow. So what if Chris is goaded to affection only in the face of imaginary competition? It's the affection wot counts. He's taking me on a *date*. I doubt he's ever said the word before.

I am so caught up in the impossible romance of the moment that I deflate like a cold soufflé when Andy snaps, 'I'm sure Natalie can speak for herself. And why not do another line, Chris? You're not paranoid enough, I think you need it.'

Talk about bludgeoning the mood stone dead with a claw hammer. I mean, where are the violins and sunsets in that?

182

Chapter 21

When my father first arrived in LA he stayed at the Beverley Wilshire, and one day decided to walk three minutes down the road to get some teabags. A Shogun drove past, and the driver leant out and bawled, 'Hey buddy! Why don't you fuck off and buy a car!' My father pretended not to hear. The truth is, my parents are not big on confrontation. My mother's finest moment was saying to a woman in the supermarket, 'Can't you control your child?' The woman replied, 'No,' and my mother scurried off. I have cowards' genes, and it takes me seconds to realise I don't want Chris and Andy fighting over me.

'Chris,' I simper, dreading his anger, 'it's fine, it was a joke.' I smile in horror at Andy – stupid stupid boy! – and ask, 'Do you need help getting the rest of your stuff out of the car?'

Andy shakes his head. 'I'll manage.'

His petulant air, plus a tuft of hair that sticks up on his head, renders him six years old for a second. I don't know what's wrong with him. I've reluctantly dismissed the idea that he suddenly adores me and that he *did* want a welcome back kiss at his party. I've watched him closely since he arrived and he doesn't look at me in the right way. (I am expert at covertly watching men covertly watch me.) He doesn't flirt. There's no dragging out of eye contact. He's treating me like a pal. So it can't be that he's jealous of Chris, it must be something else. Could it be that, in scientific tests, Chris was found to be a wanker?

'Is Andy, er, okay?' I whisper to Babs, ten minutes later,

183

as I arrange a pack of boudoir biscuits on a plate. 'He doesn't seem to like Chris that much.'

I hold back from saying what I want to say, which is: You'd think he'd be chilled after poncing round India for a year but I've never seen anyone so rude in my life!

Babs makes a face and boots the kitchen door shut. 'Ooh,' she squeals, 'sponge fingers!' She swipes one, decimates it with a crunch, and says, 'He, well, actually – it's because of Robbie. I wouldn't have said, Nat, but Robbie is *mega* keen on you, and you gave him the brush-off. Rob is Andy's best mate, and Andy sees Chris as being in the way.'

My expression says what I don't: that's all very touching and *Stand By Me* but what business is it of his? What is he, a pimp?

Babs's face displays a portion of the guilt I'd like to have seen earlier. 'I didn't help,' she mutters.

'Pardon?' I say.

'Last night,' she sighs, 'we had people round and Andy was there, and what with him moving in here today, the subject of Chris came up, how he's changed since Si first knew him, for the worse, frankly, and I'm afraid I said' – here her tone becomes defiant – 'that I thought, as far as you were concerned, he was bad news. It's only because I worry about you, Nat,' she adds fiercely. Her voice cracks and 'Nat' comes out as two syllables.

My heart melts so hot and fast I expect it to ooze viscous red through my navel. I whisper, 'No, no, it's fine, I understand.'

Babs pauses. 'I know he's good in the sack,' she says at last. I quail – *how* does she know? It's nothing to do with her! Who the hell has she been talking to? What shameless gossip with no respect for anyone's bedroom business spilled the beans? Actually, I think it was me. 'I know he reached the parts no other man – or you, for that matter – could reach, ' she continues. I cross my eyes in alarm and slide low in my seat. 'And that's great,' she declares, oblivious. 'I'll grant him that. Well done, Chris. But he was the stabilisers. Now you can ride the bike on your own – wham bam, thanks, Pomeroy, you've served your purpose!'

Babs finally notices that I'm mortified. She flicks a curl out of her face, cracks another boudoir biscuit in half and says, 'I'm sorry about Andy. Look, this is strictly confidential but – there's a bit of tension between him and Si right now. God knows why, Si won't admit to it and I don't want to get involved. That might be part of it. Chris being a mate of Si's. But please don't say anything,' she adds quickly.

'Oh! no, of course I won't,' I cry, hugging this nugget of privileged information to my chest. I surprise myself by snatching and wolfing a boudoir biscuit. It dissolves in my mouth like fairy dust and turns my speech sticky. I'll burn off every last calorie tomorrow in the gym. I brush the crumbs off my lips with the urgency of Lady Macbeth scrubbing the blood from her hands, and say to Babs, 'Shall we go into the other room?'

The next thirty minutes are a challenge as the conversation doesn't flow so much as stagnate. A few choice samples:

Chris: 'Pass me the Jane.'
Andy: 'The what?'
Chris: 'The Jane Asher.'
Andy: 'Sorry?'
Chris: 'The flippin ashtray!'
Andy: 'Oh right, you should have said.'

Me: 'Would anyone like some boudoir biscuits?'
Chris: 'Boudoir biscuits! They're not boudoir biscuits, man, they're sponge fingers!'
Babs: 'Everyone *I* know calls them boudoir biscuits.'
Andy: 'So which part of Manchester are you from, Chris?'

Chris: 'You what?'

Simon: 'Chris isn't from Manchester! What a hilarious notion! Last I heard, Chris was a Hertfordshire lad, isn't that right, Chris?'

Chris: 'I spend a lot of time in Manchester.'

Simon: 'Still making waves at the Hull Adelphi?'

Chris: 'There's a big buzz around Blue Fiend, man.'

Andy: 'A big buzz? As in, flies around –'

Chris: 'Piers Allen. Of Piers Artistes. One of the biggest agencies in the biz. Sent him the demo, and he called yesterday, hot for it. We're meeting tonight.'

Simon: 'What, on a Sunday night?'

Chris: 'At a gig. You've been a suit way too long, man.'

Me: 'But, but I thought we had a date?'

Chris: 'We do, princess. You're invited. You'll love it.'

Babs: 'Ooh. Lucky you, Nat. You'll have to wear your prettiest frock.'

I wear what I'm wearing – a grey top, long navy skirt, and navy boots. Chris suggests that I change into something a little more 'street', and I say, 'Like what, a wheelie bin?'

He looks at me in surprise – because when am I ever terse? But eating that sponge finger has made me irritable. I feel loathsome. Uncomfortable. The shame of wanting it. I blank these thoughts and kiss Babs goodbye. I nudge the air in the region of Simon's cheek, blocking my nose against the waft of his Chanel *Homme Allure* aftershave.

'See you later,' I say to Andy from a cool distance, as we leave for the gig.

I'm quiet in the Volvo, and amused to find Chris attempting to *jolly* me.

'How's our Tony?' he asks.

'*Our* Tony?' I say, thinking *Have him, he's all yours.* 'He's fine, thanks. Why?'

'Why not?' jollies Chris. (Jollity doesn't suit him. I feel uneasy.)

I try to make an effort. 'So, good news about Piers Allen. It'll be great for Blue Fiend' – I am tactful enough to ignore the fact that Chris, despite initially shunning my advice to drop the 'Veined', seems to have done so – 'to have an agent. Especially one like him.'

'Yeah. Your . . . Tony, he a mate of Piers at all?' Chris strains so hard to sound casual he nearly gives himself a hernia.

Now I understand. He's petrified that Tony will rubbish him to Piers before the deal is done. Chris wants to keep me on his side as he thinks I have power over Tony. He thinks Tony would never diss his sister's boyfriend. I almost laugh. How little Chris knows about my brother. If anything, it would encourage him! From nowhere, I feel the urge to annoy Chris.

I itch to ask if this sudden interest from Piers (the kind of shark that makes Jaws look like a small goldfish) is to do with a band-wagon. There's a law in the music business that states you are nothing until an act three million times more gifted than you get successful and then – because you too happen to be, say, Welsh – the A&Rs start courting you (if it worked once, they'll work it again, they'll build the Taj Mahal with egg cartons!), and before you can say Britpop, you the impressionist and your crime of an album – call it *Art Forgery* – are big on the back of someone else's talent.

'Do you think it's anything to do with *Acitate* going to number one on Thursday?' I murmur. 'And Dodge Kitty being signed by Uranus?'

Chris reacts like I've poked him in the eye with a drumstick. 'No! What! What the fuck do you mean by that?' he gasps.

'I mean,' I say, as an unseen presence takes the words right out of my mouth, 'that they're both from Doncaster, they have the same groggy haircuts, the same *King of the Hill* dress sense, their sound is being described as Trashrock and, by remarkable coincidence, Blue Fiend fulfil all the same criteria, except the last, and that can be worked on. They're practically a tribute band.'

Chris turns a mortuary shade of pale. I sit on my hands, and hope he doesn't hit me. Without warning, he swerves the poor beleaguered Volvo into the kerb. The blood boils in my veins. It's like there's rocket fuel in there. I said what I thought to Chris. I said it, because I thought we had a date. And because if I knew I was tonight's eye candy I don't think I could stand it.

Now I know that's a bit rich, coming from me. Me, who craves perfection, shrinking from my walk-on part as object of desire! Do I want to be beautiful but not treated as beautiful? And is that because people treat beautiful as stupid? Maybe it's because I want to have it all: the looks, the brains, the status, the respect. In that case, I should drink Coca-Cola and upgrade car. Chris (who should also upgrade car) crunches the handbrake like a breaking neck, and it occurs to me that this is no time for a Christmas wish list. I hunch my shoulders. I should have kept my mouth shut.

'Natalie.'

'Yes?' I squeak, twitching at the sound of my name. What happened to princess?

'You don't have to come along tonight if it's not your scene. Why don't I drop you in a cab?'

I glance at Chris and see that he wants to drop me in a cab very much indeed.

'Good luck with Piers,' I manage, fumbling with the door handle.

'Thanks,' he replies. He looks me in the eye and says it like he's actually heard me.

I creep home and catch Andy standing in the kitchen with a new iron in one hand and an instruction booklet in the other. '"*Getting To Know Your Iron*",' he murmurs as I peer round the door. 'Fuck orrrrff!'

'You didn't have to buy one, you could have used mine,' I say shyly.

Andy smiles. 'Now you tell me,' he replies. 'I hate spending cash on frivolities like irons. Why are you back? What happened to the guy from Piss Artists?'

'*Piers* Artistes!' I squeak. A rogue giggle escapes but at the same time I feel anxious. He's like a nanny!

'We decided that it might be better if Chris spoke to him in private,' I say primly. Andy opens his mouth to reply but the doorbell interrupts him.

I frown. 'I wonder who that is, I'm not expecting anyone.'

'I am,' grins Andy, speeding past me. I watch with concealed disapproval. Please, make yourself at home!

He opens the door and the high voice of a young teenage male squeaks, 'All right, mate. Fourteen fifty, yeah. Ta, mate!'

Ten seconds later Andy marches into the kitchen wielding two large pizza boxes. The sweet greasy smell of cardboard and burnt cheese is like an assault. 'Ground beef,' he announces, 'and Vegetariana, which is really salad on toast. You'll help me out, won't you?'

'I, no, oh, I don't –' I begin, my hands fluttering in panic, the smile dead on my face.

Andy doesn't reply but he opens the top box. I don't want to look but it's compulsive viewing, like a car crash.

'I'll get you a plate, shall I?' I croak.

'Where are they? You sit, I'll get them,' he says. I gesture wordlessly to the cupboard. Andy pulls out two large dinner plates.

'I, I can't, I don't eat off those,' I bleat. 'I use a smaller plate.'

'Oh, okay.' Andy bends and retrieves a side plate and I think, I didn't say yes, but I fetch him a knife, and he cuts into the thick dough and it yields and oozes like a lover, and I watch.

'Which would you prefer, beef pizza, salad pizza or both?' he demands, knife poised.

'Salad,' I hear myself say. 'One slice is enough.'

I wait for the cry of, One slice! Is that all? You can't just have one slice! One slice isn't enough! Have more, look have five slices, and there's more in the box, one slice etc etc . . .

But Andy slides one slice on to my small plate without comment. No escape now.

I sink, defeated, into my seat, like it's an electric chair. The slice of vegetarian pizza lies before me, a fat poison slab, its warm hot scent clogging my nostrils and sticking to my clothes, the tang of green peppers sharp and distinct against the dense oily reek of the cheese. I don't eat cheese. Cheese is fat with a bit of protein thrown in for effect.

I don't want to touch it with my hands, taint myself, but I can't use cutlery, I'd look like my father trying to 'get down with the kids'. So I pick it up with prissy fingertips – I've never eaten food this heavy! – and take a small bite. And another. Bigger this time. And another. And another, and another.

'Buon appetito!' says Andy with his mouth full.

Chapter 22

The thing I admire about Babs is, she always finds an excuse to do exactly what she wants to do. The purchase – against her parents' advice – of an unwieldy cappuccino machine which took four hours to dribble out a small weak coffee and seven hours to clean, was justified with, 'One day that'll be a valuable antique.' The ill-fated staking of a week's wages on lottery tickets was waved away with, 'If I hadn't I'd still be torturing myself wondering if I would have been a millionaire by now.' And the eating of an airport-size Toblerone between lunch and tea was dismissed with, 'I obviously needed the energy.'

I follow her impressive example and try to legitimise the pizza:

- It's not what you eat, it's how much. (No, don't like that one.)
- No food is intrinsically bad. (Unless it's cooked by a kitchen terrorist who isn't paid enough to wash his hands between the toilet and the chopping board.)
- One enormous honking pig of a meal can't make you fat.
- Andy ate more than me.

After lengthy consideration of these thoughts and skipping breakfast, I feel better. I walk to the newsagent to avoid seeing Andy before he leaves for work, or whatever it is he does, and buy myself *Vogue*. According to the *Guardian Against Fun*, it's the only women's magazine that doesn't descend to the level of its readers. Also, one of its writers has had a boob job, and I'm keen to see if she can match Babs in defensive flannelling. There is a lot about symbols of womanhood and failing the pencil test but the words that stick with me are, 'It took me a while to accept that nobody could ever describe me as "skinny" now; to live with the fact that I'm not an eight any more, I'm a ten . . .'

The jumbo challenge of living as a size ten occupies my mind and won't budge. To what advanced level of Zen must a woman clamber to 'accept' that nobody could ever describe her as skinny? How *can* you accept it? My parents dying – yeah, okay, that has to happen. But ballooning to a size ten! How can you 'accept' a tragedy that could have been avoided? I am tense and preoccupied as I walk back from the newsagent, rueing the day that meals were invented, fretting over how to atone for the pizza, aware of the globs of dough oozing through my gut, settling stodgily on my hips, and feeling green and bitter to the core, a walking gooseberry of ill-will towards those women who can self-whittle without side effect.

I walk in the front door, trip over a large brown sausage lying in the hall, and scream. Paws slowly raises his head and looks at me with sad red eyes. Eh? Matt!

'Where's your Daddy then?' I say, hoping to ingratiate myself and avoid being bitten.

Paws yawns and says, 'Behind you, dear,' and I squeak and whirl around to see Matt hanging off the kitchen door frame, trying not to smile. 'A *very* fanciable blond let me in – it's okay, he's gone out. I presumed he was Chris which didn't go down at all well. I forget how fast you operate, Natalia, I can't keep up with you. I brought you your cheque,' he adds.

I blush, run and hug him, in that order. 'The cheek of you! That's Andy, my new lodger. What cheque?'

'Your redundancy cheque, sweetheart. Three months' salary and not a penny more.'

'Oh my gosh! I didn't even think!'

'Why am I not surprised?'

'You're very clever indeed?'

'I must be.'

We grin at each other. 'I can't believe you,' I say. 'I've caused you all this trouble, I've messed up again and again, I've done the opposite of my job, made the whole of our department look gormless, and yet you come round – hang on, aren't you supposed to be at work?'

'I took the day off. I wanted to make sure you weren't suffering an existential crisis. The first Monday of being between jobs can be a bit of a downer.'

'Oh *Matt*. On your day off! You're a guardian angel!'

'I prefer fairy godmother.'

'I'm so sorry, Matt,' I say. 'And I know I've said it before. This time I mean it. I owe you big. I should have been sacked.'

Matt waves away my thanks. 'I'll be calling in the favour when you're rich and famous, I promise. In the meantime, I'll write you a reference. Have you organised yourself any work?' He nods at the copy of *Vogue*. 'Or are you settling down to a life of idleness?'

'Er. No, and no. I thought I should get myself into a 9 a.m. routine of going to the newsagent. I'm lost without a routine.'

'Bless. Well, I've got some bits for you.' He digs an envelope out of his rucksack. 'If you could get these blurbs into shape in the next few days. And as soon as Stephen's back at work – in a couple of weeks, please God – I'm sure he'll have something for you.'

'Thank you *so* much! He's going back to work so soon? That's great! He's got a good recovery rate. Is he still in the wheelchair?'

'No. Although if it were his choice, he'd have sat in that hideous chair flicking through glossy magazines till he dropped dead, the big queen. The physio had to practically tip him out of it.'

I bite my lip. I'm not sure if you're allowed to laugh at

these things. I say instead, 'Hang on – I've got a present for Stephen.' I run into the lounge, snatch up *100 Luxury Interiors* and hand it to Matt.

'Oh dear,' he sighs. 'This will only encourage him.'

I beam.

Matt says, 'Darling, Belly and I want to take you out – any excuse for a piss-up, obviously – so we'll have to arrange something.'

'Definitely! But I – I will be seeing you anyway, won't I? As a, er, friend?'

'Paws and I intend to dog you all our lives,' says Matt gravely.

I hug him again. 'Matt, I will make it up to you, I will. I know it's too late for you, for the department, I mean, but I kind of know what's been, well, wrong with me, and I'm working to make it better. So I won't embarrass you, if you do give me a reference.'

Matt flaps his hands, as if batting a fly, and says, 'Oh stop.' He pauses. 'What *has* been wrong with you?'

I feel awkward. I respect this man. I want him to respect me. I don't wish to be classed in the same bracket as Mel. She's up to her neck in it. I'm just paddling. So after hesitation, I say, 'Women's problems.'

'I won't pry,' says Matt, regretfully.

I work on Matt's press releases for the rest of the day, and I'm grateful for every minute. I am disturbed from labour three times. Once by Chris, who calls to report that Piers Allen is meeting the band tonight so, 'Yeah, man, it's looking cool.'

He doesn't ask when we are next seeing each other, and it occurs to me that he has a pathological aversion to making plans. It also occurs to me that I have a pathological aversion to *not* making plans.

My second caller of the day is Mel. I hear her lisp and presume her ears are on the waggle for intrigue. But she actually sounds upset. 'Natalie, I am *distraught!* What will

194

I do without you? You're the best PR in the world!'

What! After I outed her as an anorexic and prompted the company to pay for her to see a nutritionist? I'd presumed that was why she was offish when I popped in on her dressing room last week.

'Really? You don't mind about the, er, *Sun* piece and the, um, nutritionist?'

'Natalie, you made me famous! Who cares what that silly doctor says? And as for the food woman, I don't have to listen to her! If they want to weigh me, I just drink a ton of water! But how are you, you poor thing, how are you feeling? It must be awful, losing your job. Is it?' she adds, hopefully.

'It's quite awful,' I say, unwilling to disappoint her. 'But I've got some work.'

'Oh goody,' she replies, unconvincingly. 'Guess what – though – I saw Tony at the weekend, and he's such a sweetie [*thweetie*] and I haven't seen you properly for ages, and I thought it would be so nice if you and me and Tony all went out together and had a nice chat, and I'm not dancing tomorrow night so then would be perfect, we could do something fun like go and feed the ducks in Hyde Park!'

I check my wasteland of a diary, then, for lack of anything more interesting to do, agree.

I'm touched at her concern, and warmed by Matt's generosity. The only spoilsport kicking over my sandcastle is Babs. You would have *thought* she would call to see how it was going with Andy. She hasn't, and I can't help feeling used. She fussed and cooed until I bought the dress. Now the sale's gone through the smile's wiped and she's back to filing her nails. I'm stewing over this, when the phone rings.

'Hello?' I say, hoping.

'Natalie?'

'Yes.'

'It's Andy.'

Three minutes later I click off and scowl inwardly. All

the men I know and love – Tony, Dad, Chris even – have no emotional attachment to food. That is how I like it. They eat what's there. They don't own recipe books, preferring tomes where the name of every character is preceded by rank. They have no interest in menus, are more concerned in appearing at the right restaurants. So why is Andy such a *girl*? He's rung from work like a new wife, asking me to join him and a friend for 'supper' in my own home! He's not been here twenty-four hours and already he's hosting dinners! I can't be rude so I'm forced to attend. I feel like a *foie gras* goose. My mother couldn't have planned it better. I go for a pre-emptive run around the park. I return to chaos.

'You look cross,' says Andy, waving a wooden spoon in the air. 'Are you annoyed about the kitchen?'

I survey the bombsite. 'No,' I lie, deftly stepping aside to avoid a splat of gloop off the spoon. It's all very well taking in lodgers to pay the mortgage, but the downside is, they think they're entitled to *live* with you.

'You are,' replies Andy, wiping his hand on his jeans. 'I'll clear up. But don't worry. I'm not a full-time wok-wielding maniac. This is a one-off, to say thanks for having me. Robbie's also going to stop by – not that I'm slaving over a hot stove for that little sod. You don't mind, do you?' he adds, as my eyes flicker.

'Of course not,' I croak, wondering if it can get any worse. Will my mother jump from a cake then make me eat it? 'What are you making?' I ask, to disguise my ill grace.

Andy whirls the spoon again. Splat, splat. 'I forgot to ask if you were vegetarian, so I thought I'd make tomato bread soup. It's a bit of a bastard, because you have to de-pip and peel the tomatoes, but it's gorgeous. And there's something irresistible about primary-coloured food. Do you want a drink?'

Why be a hero? 'Yes,' I say. 'OK, whoa! thanks. Great. Well, I'll just go and, um, have a shower.' I plod down the hall, carrying my wine glass and feeling suburban. I half expect him to shout after me, 'Eee, I looked up from *Kilroy* before and that hussy next door was hanging out her washing in a slip!'

The first thing I notice on entering the bathroom is that Andy has placed his shampoo, razor and shaving cream on Babs's old shelf. And Clinique moisturiser, bless. I keep *my* box of tricks in the bathroom cabinet as I feel the more beauty products you have on display, the less excuse you have to be ugly. The first thing I notice on leaving the bathroom is that Robbie has arrived. This is because I tiptoe out in a towel and run smack-bang into him. For the second time today, I scream.

'My darleenk, eet's been too long!' he cries, arms flung wide. I repeat the scream, and rush into my bedroom.

'Pervert!' I shout, slamming the door. I hear him laugh, and I laugh too. I'd forgotten how much I like Robbie. He gets better looking as you get to know him. And he's not a sulker. Although, maybe he just wasn't 'mega keen' on me. I think it'll be okay tonight.

I dawdle over what to wear and twenty minutes later emerge transformed, in an orange wool jumper, black trousers, brown boots (I know I should wear brown trousers to match the boots but there's something about the concept of brown trousers I can't get along with), and meticulous make-up. I'm not like some women, such diehard professionals that their smooth foundation and flawless lipstick are not so much applied as created. But nor am I a total disgrace. I sidle into the kitchen like a crab.

'You look nice,' says Robbie, coughing. Andy, fussing over the saucepan, doesn't comment.

'Do you need any help?' I say.

'No, it's all done,' he sings. 'Although you could put some plates on the table. Actually, no, why don't you sit down. Rob!' he adds. 'Pull your finger out, you lazy git, get out the bowls and spoons and grate the parmesan.'

'Yes, all right, Jamie,' replies Robbie, pretending to bustle. He rolls his eyes at me and mouths, 'Twat.'

'I heard that,' says Andy, without turning his head. I sip my wine to stifle a giggle. 'Okaaaay! Here it is.'

He dollops a steaming red glob into my bowl, and rips up a leaf of basil, which he places prettily on top. He starts to do the same for Robbie, who pipes up, 'I can rip me own basil, ta very much.'

'Then rip it,' says Andy, affecting huffiness. 'See if I care!'

'It smells fantastic,' I say, scarcely believing my own ears. Tomato, bread, basil, these are ingredients I can deal with. I breathe in the rich scent and my stomach rumbles. A bold statement, for me. God, I – I – I actually want to eat this. My fingers creep towards my spoon, and I catch Andy frowning at me.

'We will, of course, say grace,' he says sternly. My spoon clatters on the table and I blush as red as the soup. 'I jest,' he adds.

'I jest can't help being a pillock?' suggests Robbie.

'At least you can admit it,' replies Andy smoothly. 'Isn't that the first step?'

I want to laugh, but am speechless at this *spell* of a recipe. My tastebuds are dancing the tango on my tongue. No. My brain clogs with the terrible implications. What am I doing? This isn't what I trained for! I have a talent for deprivation, that's what I'm good at. And here I am, lured into a greed trap. My stomach stops rumbling and boils with resentment. How dare he barge into my home and force himself and his pan upon me?

'Leave me alone!' splutters Robbie.

'What?' I say, keeping the edge out of my voice with effort.

'I *did* wash my hands,' cries Robbie. 'Natalie! Tell him to leave off!'

'What?' I ask Andy.

'Well, Robbie's a good lad,' says Andy, leaning on both elbows like a small boy. 'But he's forever—'

'And! Do me a favour!' squeals Robbie.

'No, carry on, I want to hear, what?' I exclaim.

'He's forever fiddling with himself, to make sure it's still there!' Andy grins and stuffs a glob of tomato bread soup in his mouth.

'I'm only doing what the doctors advise!' shouts Robbie. 'Anyway, you're no great model of hygiene. What about you at college? Your room! Did you tell Natalie about the pint glasses of—'

'Robbie!' bawls Andy. 'That was twelve years ago, I was sodding eighteen, the toilet was down the hall!'

'Mm-mm,' I say, fighting a swell of laughter. 'I'm so enjoying this meal.'

'Yeah, pack it in, Rob,' growls Andy. 'You're putting Natalie off her food. Let's be *ad*-ult. It was a lie,' he whispers to me. 'Anyway *he* used to pee in the sink. Middle class pretensions.' And in a louder voice, 'I see the Dow Jones is up sixteen points . . .'

Happily, the Dow Jones is accorded short shrift and we move swiftly on to juicier topics. Such as, Andy's glittering new career. (He has managed to wangle himself a weekly financial column on an internet magazine site – 'I think they need someone to predict when they'll go bust'. And he's doing freelance work for the City desk – 'and it is *one* desk' – of a London freesheet. And he's earning a thirtieth of what he earned on the stock market. But he doesn't care – as a broker it was 'work work work with no life at the end of the tunnel'.)

He also wants to know if Robbie and I saw the picture in today's paper of the richest person in the world. (A software businessman worth $50 billion. Apart from a fancy beard and good teeth, you'd never tell just by looking at him. You'd think he'd be wearing a tiara.) And Natalie, what about the way Chris smiles? Yesterday! He kept doing a funny thing with his lip. I say I think it's meant to be a rueful smile. Like Billy Baldwin. Andy's sorry but it really wound him up.

I confess that I've been reading the *Daily Express* sports pages to impress Chris with my fake expertise on football. Andy and Robbie are appalled. Stop immediately! Does he read the *Daily Express* beauty pages to impress you with his fake expertise on lipstick? You sexist baboon, Rob, Natalie might be a rugby nut for all you know. Um, it's okay, I'm not.

Talking of unreasonable behaviour, what about the time Rob dated a woman who forbade him to drink water after 9 p.m. because she hated being woken in the night by his trips to the toilet. Hang on a sec, Andrew, didn't Sasha used to make you walk her chihuahua? It was a Yorkshire terrier, I'll have you know. Had a terrible habit of eating other dogs' pooh. Name of Miffy. Miffy, I love that name! And when Rob bought his Vespa and Andy dared him to ask the big hairy bloke in the bike shop if he had 'an extra-large purple helmet?' And what are you up to now you've left the ballet company? (Freelance dance PR, although the work doesn't exactly thrill me. What would you like to do? *Like* to do? I never thought. I, I should think, shouldn't I?) And then, finally, casually, so it comes across as a great big joke, does Andy remember his sister's fifteenth birthday and kissing me in the linen cupboard a dozen years ago?

The momentum falters slightly, and Andy looks horrified.

'Christ, we did, didn't we?' he blurts. 'You were this adorable fifteen-year-old and I was a big greasy lout slobbering all over you! I made the mistake of telling Tony that I thought you were a babe. He beat me to a pulp.'

'No!' I gasp.

Andy grins ruefully. 'I was a wimp, I admit it. I spent far too much time listening to Morrissey. I didn't dare go near you after that. I snuck off to college, tail between my legs, if you know what I mean. Not that you weren't better off without me. Bloody hell, I'd totally forgotten. You've got a good memory.'

There is a brief uncomfortable silence. Then, 'Urgh you

filthy perv, preying on innocent fifteen-year-olds!' cries Robbie, monobrow stern. 'Natalie, what a creep, he's disgusting!'

I stare at Andy, struggle to keep a straight face, and the remainder of that cherished venom dissolves. We talk and talk, laugh and laugh and my shoulders lose their stiffness and I glance down at my plate and it's empty.

I honestly think for a second that I'm seeing things. But no, there it is, scraped clean. An alien heaviness in my stomach confirms the truth. I was aware of eating. I allowed myself. I made myself. For Babs. It reminded me of being spoon-fed when I was little. 'And a spoon for Mummy. *Good* girl! And a spoon for Daddy. *Well* done! And a spoon for Tony. *Goo*- Tony, don't be silly, of course your sister can have a spoon for you. What? It's your spoon? OKokayokay! No tantrums! All right, all right. Please darling, get up off the floor now, there's a good boy [*sigh*]. And a spoon for Teddy . . .'

What's the big deal? After all, I skipped lunch. I went for a run. I watched my dinner diminish, I measured the remaining quantity with every scoop. But to actually *finish*. Clear my plate like a pleb. What next – *snacks*? Natalie, did Andy tell you about the time he went about saying 'Get the photo?' because he'd read it in *The Man with the Golden Gun* and fancied himself as Scaramanga? (Christ, Rob, you're allowed to be a dickhead when you're nineteen years old. I'm talking about last week, pal . . .) I cover my mouth to stifle a giggle fit, and try to forget my immaculate plate.

When I answer the phone I'm still laughing.

'What's so funny?' says Babs.

'Oh *hi!*' I squeal. 'Your brother! Your brother's funny. Him and Robbie. They're like a pair of bickering old women! I, I think it's going to be nice, him living here.'

I expect Babs to be pleased. Particularly as I am tactful enough to blur the subtext: I thought Andy was a grumpy New Age twit, smug on cod philosophy filched from other

201

backpackers and *Wisdom of the Dalai Lama, Abridged,* but after an evening in his company I've almost revised my opinion.

But all she says is, 'Yeah, well. I thought you'd get on. What with your matching mood swings.'

'Oh,' I say. What I ought to say, what I should say, what an assertive woman would say to such a snide little dig, is, 'And what do you mean by that?' But all I say is 'Oh.'

I think Babs realises she's out of line because she adds hastily, 'Ah, don't mind me, Nat. I don't know what's wrong with me today. No, it's great, Andy living with you. I think it will be nice, you'll get on great. The only thing is, he's still pining for Sasha, so all I'm saying is, watch out.'

Chapter 23

Watch out. I don't say it out loud, but I say it at least twenty times in my head that night and the following day. What do you mean by that? I excuse myself and go to the bathroom and brush my teeth and floss and gargle until all taste and trace of tomato bread soup is eliminated. What do you mean by that? I tear off my orange jumper and black trousers, dirty with the scent of greed, and scrub until my skin tingles. I bow to the modern equivalent of a Roman emperor and step on the scales. (The same. I live!) I huddle in bed and try to sleep. What do you mean by that?

I know precisely what she means by that. Don't go getting any funny ideas about my brother. The cheek of her. Demoted, but still reckons she's the General. Sorry, Babs, you're a foot soldier now. When you stopped phoning five times daily, you lost your right to give orders. I wouldn't mind but you've already broken rank once. Get this: you're my ex. When people are intimate, they can say exactly what they think of each other, no matter how sadistic. It's one of the perks of a close relationship. But when they split, it's back to being civil. So. I can do whatever, whenever, and my mistakes are none of her business. Well, some of them, anyway.

I wonder what it *would* be like to kiss Andy.

Mel has suggested I meet her in the GLBallet reception at 6 p.m., which isn't ideal, although it does mean I can hand-deliver Matt's press releases.

'Going-home time!' she tinkles. 'How are you coping? You don't look too downbeat! How was your Valentine's Day? Mine was such fun! I got heaps of flowers from fans, but look what Tony gave me – I am so, so lucky!' Mel digs in her purse, flaps a first-class Eurostar ticket at me, and does a perfect pirouette of joy. Her blue eyes shine bright in her pale face. 'We're going to stay in an amazing hotel – it's called Hotel Costes – it's on the rue St-Honoré, and loads of celebrities go there! And his PA checked with the Ballet Schedule so I don't miss a single show, isn't he sweet? Oh Natalie, your brother is so clever, shall we go for a coffee and talk about Paris? I said to Tony we'll meet at his place at seven, it's too dark to go to the park. Oh please say yes!'

Two excitable minutes later, Mel and I are sitting in the shabby corner café on poky metal chairs. Mel asks if I've ordered carrot cake with my peppermint tea.

'No,' I say, still raw from the gluttony of last night. I glance at Mel's hopeful face, and a twist of spite escapes me. 'Are *you* having carrot cake?'

'No,' says Mel quickly, her entire body a spasm of panic. 'I've had lunch. I'm stuffed.'

This goads me. Why should *I* be forced to eat because my stupid hair starts shedding? 'Are you sure, Mel? You should eat. I don't mean to be rude but you're, you're looking a bit, a bit' – I search for a non-derisive term – 'scraggy.'

A frightening expression settles on her face. Nervously, I wait for her to speak. When her rosebud lips part I flinch.

'I love boys who make romantic gestures!' she cries, as if I'd said nothing at all. I sag with relief as she rattles on about Tony and Paris.

That's one mistake I won't make again. I light a cigarette with shaking hands. What a fool! Mel doesn't want to be rescued. She yatters on and I watch but don't hear a word. No, I will *not* be having carrot cake with my tea. I sit there stiff and sour, warming my ever-frozen hands on the teacup, until Mel says, 'Natalie, are you okay? You look all funny.'

I say brightly, 'No, yes, I'm fine.'

'You can tell me, I won't tell anyone!'

While not convinced, I am beyond caring. Anyhow, my fast fading friendship with Babs has no bearing on Mel. She probably *won't* tell anyone. I regurgitate the tale, with express reference to the various dinner party affronts. I avoid reference to my, hm, issue. It's like trying to dodge raindrops.

'I don't get it!' squeaks Mel. 'Why is she being so mean?'

I sigh. What is the point unless I relate the whole story, fresh, plump and unfilleted? And if so, how do I broach the taboo? I am not a taboo-broacher. I pride myself on my ability to tiptoe around the elephant in the living room, the hippo in the lounge, and the anorexic in the coffee shop. It's safer that way. Wild animals and obsessional women are unpredictable and – as I know after a single prod – best not tackled by amateurs.

'Well,' I begin, focusing on a chocolate-brown crumb on the table. 'We had a row. Babs sort of accused me of, of – er, not eating.'

I fully-flesh the story, without looking Mel in the eye once. I've taken a paintbrush to the elephant, and daubed him red from trunk to tail.

I stutter to a halt. Mel hisses, 'Tony says that your friend Babs is a big beefy girl, so it's obvious she's jealous of you! You're naturally thin, Natalie, you're very feminine – Babs must be as jealous as hell!' I nod vigorously, yes, yes, this is what I want to hear, sod eating more, I am *right*. If a little grossed out at the word 'feminine'. But. I don't feel right. As Mel rants on, I notice the grey tinge to her teeth, and the dreadful pink rawness of her knobbly knuckles which, though tiny, seem giant and bulbous compared to her twiggy fingers. Her hair is dry and lustreless. And I realise that no one in their right mind would be jealous of either of us.

205

I'm relieved when it's time to go to Tony's.

The cab draws up in front of my brother's crumbly white stucco-fronted penthouse (or, for laypersons, 'top flat') in Ladbroke Grove. Mel rings the buzzer, and we plod up the Prussian blue carpeted stairs, her tracing a finger along the dark red flock wallpaper. Faded grandeur is the charitable way to describe the hallway. Grubby and threadbare would be meaner, but more accurate. Today, its fustiness is overpowered by the smell of fried meat. 'Poo-ee!' cries Mel, waving a porcelain hand in front of her button nose. She raps hard on the white door and, after a fashionable sixty-second delay, Tony yanks it open.

'Hey, sugar pop,' he murmurs to Mel, who tilts her cheek to receive a kiss. I stand patiently behind her in the cold dim hall – my best smile primed to burst into bloom – until my brother deigns to greet me.

'Hi, Tony,' I say hopefully, as our eyes meet.

'Hi.' The word drops from his lips stillborn. He turns back to Mel and I follow him inside, my heart a pebble of impending doom.

Mel settles in Tony's white leather sofa between two blue Elvis-print cushions. She lies on her back, her head hanging off the seat, her legs gracefully propped against the back of the sofa and up the blood red wall. As Tony doesn't question this bat-like arrangement, I assume he knows she's 'draining' – the revolting ballet term for getting rid of the lactic acid that stiffens your muscles after exercise.

'My back hurts,' she says suddenly.

'Poor Ikkle Lambkin,' cries Tony. 'Does Ikkle Lambkin want a rub?'

Mel smiles from her upside-down position. 'No fank yoo, Big Daddy Bear! Iss too sore. It feel wery hot.'

'Does Ikkle Lambkin want Big Daddy Bear to get her some ice?'

At this point, I would dash from the room to vomit, but aural trauma pins me to the spot.

206

'Oh *no!*' cries Mel, in her normal voice. 'I'd better drain, otherwise I'll get all puffy and stiff and probably injured. And then they won't let me dance, and I'll feel like an elephant and I'll miss loads of performances and then when I start dancing again I'll feel all fat and tired and it'll be like I'm moving in slow motion.'

'Christ,' says Tony.

'But will you light the candles?' lisps Mel. 'It's so pretty when you do that!'

My brother crosses his ebony wood stained floor in three strides, and skims his lighter across the row of black candles that line the mantelpiece. I sigh, and plop into a black furry beanbag (pardon me, a £1,500 Black Mongolian sheepskin beanbag). A shortlived squeeze once told Tony his flat was a cross between 'a tart's boudoir and a gothic dungeon'. He was thrilled. I think it bought her an extra day.

'Can we have a joint?' asks Mel, lighting a Camel.

I quake at her audacity but Tony purrs, 'Coming right up.' He gets to work with a Rizla, smiling at her and scowling at me in one look. I sit stiff and miserable and bum-level with the floor, spinning my fag packet over and over between two fingers, like a rectangular wheel, flick, flick, flick.

'Will you stop messing with that friggin' fag packet!' growls Tony.

'Sorry,' I mutter, dropping it.

'Is there champagne?' squeaks Mel, who appears to have acclimatised to Tony's louche lifestyle in record time.

'Sure, sweetheart,' smiles Tony – back to Dr Jekyll. 'There's a bottle in the fridge. Want me to get it for you?'

'Oh no, its okay,' says Mel, on her gnarled feet in one fluid move. 'I'll get it.'

I feel a lurch of terror as Mel exits the room, as silently as a cat. Alone with the killer who knows I suspect him!

'Did I tell you, Piers Allen is interested in Blue Fiend?' I gabble, to save myself. Tony smirks. 'Have you – have you talked to Piers?' I ask, confused.

'Mm,' says Tony. 'I have. And you're right. Piers is very interested in Blue Fiend.' He cackles, a short venomous burst. Very Captain Hook.

'Wh – what?' I stammer. 'What's the joke?'

'You'll have to wait for the punchline,' says Tony sharply, pinching a great tampon of a spliff into shape.

Mel pads back into the room, holding a bottle and three old-fashioned champagne bowls. 'I'm back!' she cries. 'I hope you talked about me!'

Tony takes the champagne bottle, prises it open with a loud pop (Mel acts the part and squeals) and pours the frothing liquid into the bowls. 'Sweetheart,' he murmurs to Mel, 'why don't you go into the bedroom? I went shopping today. There's a little surprise for you on the bed.'

Mel gasps. 'Is it a present? For me!'

'Might be,' says Tony gruffly. 'Neglected childhood,' he tuts as she speeds out of the lounge. 'Criminal. Needs lots of attention to make up for it.'

He brushes a hand across his eyes. I nod slowly, wondering at this spectacular display of fluffiness from the man who, by reputation, makes Clint Eastwood look like a big girl's blouse. And that obscene babytalk. In front of me! If I didn't know better, why, I'd think he was in *love*! Mel as a sister-in-law. I take a medicinal gulp of champagne and choke.

'I'm not happy with you,' says Tony, watching me clutch my throat, turn purple, and wheeze for air. He inhales deeply on the spliff, and doesn't pass it to me.

'Wh – what have I done now?'

'Did you think it would just go away?' he says, his blue eyes as cold and dark as the North Sea.

'What go away?'

'When did you last speak to Mum?' he asks.

'I, I, I speak to her every day, er, this morning. She phoned to see how Andy was settling in.'

'She wants to write to Tara.'

Of course she does.

'She wants to fucking go and visit them.'

She wants to turn *The Simpsons* into *The Brady Bunch*.

'You are in serious shit with me, Natalie, I do not need this hassle. I like my life and I do not want it complicated. *You* have complicated it. Do you get what I'm saying?' My brother is hunched and breathing smoke through his nostrils and looks poised to spring at me like a gargoyle come to life. I am praying that the spliff will reach his brain in the next millisecond and paint the situation Disney when he suddenly roars, 'SAY SOMETHING!' and I jump clean off the Mongolian beanbag.

What *can* I say, Tony? Your drugs are inferior. I did a bad thing. On my list of regrets it's right up there with:

* confidently introducing a friend of Saul's to Babs by the wrong name

* resisting for a year then submitting to the stifling hype and wasting a hundred and fifty quid on a big hairy pashmina, *just* as they were outed as scarves and kicked out of fashion

* greeting Kimberli Ann and my dad and his bright black hair at Los Angeles airport with the words, 'Dad! What have you done to your hair?' and – when he croaked, 'Ah! I accidently spilt something on it' – whimpering the feeble addition, 'Because it looks terrific!'

But as my life's errors churn around my head, I realise that if I had the chance to yell 'Surprise! Secret grandchild!' at my mother again, I would. I am not sorry. I regret annoying Tony. Rather, I regret making Tony annoyed with me. And I feel guilty for hurting my mother. But she deserved to know. It was short-term pain for long-term gain. And she *will* gain. I'll bet that large pointless pink scarf at the back of my cupboard that Kelly and Tara will welcome her to the underground branch of the family without so much as a 'Where were you?'

209

I know though, that I didn't do it for my mother. I blabbed for *me* reasons. And how can I say that to my brother? Tony, who has always come first. Tony, who never struggled to be golden because he just *was*. Whereas me, I'm silver girl. I was born second and that's where I've stayed. Mediocre, nothing special, average, ah well you did your best. I couldn't even come last and fail in style. That fleeting mash and liver madness wasn't madness at all. I wanted to knock the king off his throne and scramble up there myself.

But how can I say that? I look at my furious brother and all I can think is, when I was eleven I made scones with lard in home economics and brought them home for tea. Mum took one bite, made a face, and spat my love into the sink. But doubtless if they were your scones Tony, she'd have eaten the lot.

'I'm sorry,' I whisper, 'I've got no excuse. I'm an idiot.'

I claw my way out of the beanbag just as Mel charges into the room waving a flimsy pink cardigan and gossamer vest in one hand and a mass of deep pink tissue paper in the other and squealing, 'Oh, dese are so beautiful, Big Daddy Bear, oh dey fit Lambkin perfectly, oh Big Daddy Bear, he iss so kind, Lambkin love dem, she will be so pretty, she iss going to wear dem to Paris!'

I smile queasily and say to my brother, 'I'm sorry. I'll go home now.'

There are several sorts of crying. One is the loud wailing snotty see-what-you-did-to-me disciplinary sort – i.e. performed in front of the guilty boyfriend who reaps the snivelling whirlwind of his cruelty and neglect and is traumatised into solicitude for ever.

Another is the quiet headachy screwy-faced self-satisfaction sort: a luxury, strictly speaking, forced out even though your tear ducts are parched, because you believe you deserve a blub and are determined to feel sorry for yourself.

And the third is the mournful mopey weeping Madonna sort (the Virgin Mary, just so we're clear): shedding innocent tears of woe against a harsh world – NB it helps to have lank hair for this one – that roll sorrowfully down your face and plop unchecked (your disposition is too mild for tissues) on to your wimple.

The only disadvantage of number three – my boohoo of choice – is that it is uglifying. It makes my eyelids and, oddly, my nose and mouth, deepen in colour and swell and puff until I look like Verucca Salt on becoming a blueberry. Naturally Andy walks in at the final monstrous moment of metamorphosis.

'Shit!' he yelps. 'Are you okay?'

'Oh gosh, yeah,' I sniff, hurriedly smearing the grot off my face with my sleeve. 'I'm fine.'

He regards me suspiciously. 'Are you sure?' he says.

I assess him from behind my hand and a decade of *reasonably* well-founded prejudice shrivels. Since yesterday this man is confounding his rude and stroppy reputation with charm. And – as I always take nice people for granted but gratefully fawn upon nasty ones who slip out of character for five minutes – I find this quite beguiling. And he *was* apologetic about the kiss in the cupboard. 'Are you sure you're okay?' he repeats.

My lower lip trembles. 'Yes!' I manage, in a hysterical warble.

'No, you're not,' says Andy.

I surrender to his impressive observational powers. My shoulders start shaking and the tears gush through my hands. 'Toe-oh-ny! Is an-noyed with me!' The injustice of my dignity being smashed to even tinier pieces because this wail accidentally rhymes makes me sob louder.

'Tony?' says Andy stepping closer. 'But he's annoyed with everyone. He's been annoyed with me for the last ten years! Don't listen to him. It's just his way of reminding you he's important.'

'B . . . b . . . b . . .' I embark on the ambitious word 'but'.

It proves too challenging. I shut my eyes tightly to block the tears, and a warm hand strokes my hair. My *hair. Andy's* hand! I'm not sure whether to open my eyes or keep them shut. If I open them I'm sure I'll do something inappropriate like stick out my tongue and shout 'Gerroff!' So I keep them shut. To my surprise, my blood starts from its usual sluggish meander and begins to speed round my system. I don't move as Andy tightens his arms around me and *kisses* the top of my head. Please let there not be a bald patch.

I am shocked out of my crying fit. I stand still, and he pats my back and says, 'So what was he annoyed with you about?'

'Oh. I said something I shouldn't.'

My face is flat against his chest so when I open my mouth to speak I nearly champ down on a nipple. Andy loosens his grip and rubs my arms briskly, as if to warm me, and says teasingly, 'I can't imagine that.'

I want to smile but feel reluctant to look him in the eye because mine are so red he might mistake me for a bloodhound. Oh God, he hasn't let go. We're on the line. Anything could happen. My skin feels raw and hot where he's touched it and I stare down at his smooth brown forearms and want to lick them. My insides ooze like melting chocolate. And what about Chris, you great trollop? snaps my conscience. Have you no self-control?

Have I no . . .? Have *I* no . . .? Bar querying the Pope's Catholicism, I doubt I could have asked a more insulting or superfluous question. I pull violently away from Andy at the precise moment he lets go of me, totter three steps backwards, flail like a cartoon chicken walking off a cliff, shout, 'Woo o oh!' and land with a thump on the floor.

'Oh! let me—'

'No, really, I—'

'Sorry, but I thought you—'

'No, it's my fault, I—'

We blunder on as Wooster and Jeeves until our mutual

humiliation wears thin and Andy regains enough composure to announce he's 'late for a drink with a friend in the pub'. I accept the lie gratefully and wave him off. Then I lean against the door, shudder with embarrassment and outlaw all thoughts about kissing Andy.

Chapter 24

Which doesn't preclude thoughts about Andy kissing *me*.
Did he want to? Was he planning to? Did I imagine it? Am
I presuming? Did he think better of it? Is that why he let
go? Why didn't he want to? What's wrong with me?
Should I act disdainful when I next see him? Or airily
indifferent? What would make me more desirable? Would
it help if I bought one of those brown and white Himalayan
pompom shawls?

I stamp around the flat wanting to talk to someone. The
obvious person isn't going to want to talk to me. Not about
this. Not when she told me to 'watch it', only twenty-four
hours ago. But she can't have it all her own way. She got
the handsome man, the puffball dress, the white and
turquoise honeymoon, the gravy bowl in Wedgwood Jade,
the garden flat with window boxes, the fitted kitchen with
halogen lights, the John Lewis clubcard, everything so neat
and perfect, all our Barbie Doll dreams fulfilled. She has so
much, she can't begrudge me a little nothing with her
brother. Because nothing happened. I only want to *talk*.

I debate whether to call her for two full minutes before
picking up the phone. It rings five times then clicks on to
answer machine. A cool male voice drawls, *'Hello there,
you've reached the home of Simon and Barbara Freedland'*
– good Lord, I think, forgive the tribute phrase but that is
so last century! – *'We are out or busy but please leave a
message and we'll return your call as soon as we can.'*

Pardon me, but what a prat, is the message I'd like to
leave. And if you ever have a girl, Babs, be prepared to call

her 'Simona.' Or Simone, even. But I restrain myself and say, 'Hi Babs, it's Na—'

There is a short clatter and a muffled voice husks, 'Nat?'

'Hiya!' I squeal. 'Oh my gosh, I'm dying to speak to you!'

'What about,' says Babs. It is barely a question, which riles me.

'Don't be cross,' I say, 'because nothing happened, but I sort of had an accidental close encounter with Andy.'

'Oh, for God's sake,' snaps Babs.

Suddenly I feel like a cat upon spying an upstart kitten at its food bowl. 'Sorry,' I squeak, the hairs on my neck bristling and my voice four octaves higher than shrill. 'But why exactly is that such a problem for you?'

I realise what I've said, cross my eyes, and stick my left fist in my mouth as far as it will go. I never but *never* invite confrontation (the mash incident was a first), I just don't. So what the hell am I doing? I cringe and wait for verbal extermination. I take my fist out of my mouth and add quickly, 'Nothing happened.'

There is no sound from the earpiece.

'Babs?' I say fearfully. Maybe she's fainted. 'Babs?' I gulp. 'Babs, are you okay? I promise you, it was a big nothing, I was upset and he rubbed my back, just a friendly thing, only me being silly, reading things into it, I—'

'Nat,' whispers Babs. 'You're all right. It's not, it's not . . .' she tails off and I hear a hiccup. Not a happy sound.

'Babs,' I say, alarmed. 'Do you want me to come round?'

'Yes,' she replies. 'Come now.'

'Brownie's honour, I'll never so much as look at the guy again, Amen,' I bleat to the pale blue walls, as I grab my coat.

I am one step from the door when the phone rings. Good grief, what now?

'Hello?'

'Princess.'

'Hi!' My enthusiasm is in direct proportion to my guilt.

'We gotta talk.'

'What's wrong?' I say, glancing at the clock. Nine-thirty. Of course. Today's favour. I think, don't push it, I've already done you one favour this evening.

Chris is silent. I'm thinking, Hurry up! when he speaks again. 'Something's up with Piers. Something serious, man.'

'What do you mean?' I say.

'He's not returning my calls.'

A bell tinkles faintly, daintily at the back of my head. Something Tony said about waiting for a punchline. 'Well, maybe he's away.'

'Nah. He's around.'

'Well, maybe he's busy and, I mean, taking on a new band is a big commitment, maybe he—'

'The band aren't returning my calls.'

'What?!'

'Look, princess, I need you to speak to Tony for me, get him to take my call, he knows this geezer, right, knows how he operates, I gotta speak to him, it's serious man, there's some heavy shit going down and I don't know what.'

I take a deep breath. Problems. One, Tony is in no mood to be doing me favours. Two, three and four, I am not a man, I'm in a rush, and did anyone ever tell Chris about the word 'please'?

'Chris,' I sigh. 'I want to help you, but can it wait for – for a day?'

'No,' says Chris and slams the phone down.

'Moron,' I murmur as I crawl through London at the pace of a hedgehog with a limp. 'Sort out your own problems.' I light a cigarette and wish I could afford my own helicopter.

'God knows what's wrong with Babs,' I say aloud, stopping at lights that stay red for as long as sunburn. 'Good enough to be her friend, not good enough to flirt with her brother. Can't even believe I'm thinking about it. You hated him, remember? Posture like an old tulip. Sullen on the phone. Forever locked in his room listening to REM. Only emerging from the stupor once, to snog you then vanish, leaving you mortified for the next eleven years. Though who'd have thought he'd have such beautiful forearms?' – here I employ my best Tammy Wynette impression – 'A *mayyyn's* forearms!'

Instinct makes me turn to my right, and I see the male driver in the adjacent Saab look quickly away.

'Everyone talks to themselves in the car!' I say, chastened.

But I say it in my head so as not to alarm any other road users. I finally reach Holland Park, scamper up the path and ring the doorbell. 'Helloo!' I coo, bending and peering through the letterbox. The door opens. 'Eeek, you scared m— gosh, Babs, what's the matter?'

Babs looks ill. She is dressed in a shapeless *I Killed Kenny* T-shirt and baggy grey tracksuit trousers – like a Kosovan, in fact – and is clutching a mug of tea as if it were a lifebuoy. There's no sign of tears but her face looks drawn, older, and she has dark weary smudges under her brown eyes. Her rippling hair has been scraped back into a severe ponytail. She *really* doesn't want me to tangle with Andy.

'Listen. I swear it won't happen again, I—'

'Christ, Natalie,' snaps Babs, jerking her hands wide and sloshing tea on to the tiles. 'Not everything revolves around you! This has nothing to do with Andy, it's about Si!'

'*Simon?*' I repeat inanely, staring at her.

For a second Babs's features pinch as if she's considering sarcasm – 'Yes, Simon, my husband, remember?' – but then she nods limply and exhales, 'Mm.'

I lunge and catch the mug as it drops from her grasp. 'Babs?' She says nothing but her pain is as tangible as a scream in the night. 'I'm so sorry, what, what is it?'

Babs shakes her head, her jaw rigid with the effort of

holding back. I have never seen her this way, and the horror roars through me like a chill wind, gusting away the meaner emotions that have lurked inside for so long. I feel ashamed of my sour lack of generosity. 'Please tell me what it is,' I whisper. 'I'd do anything to help.'

Maybe she senses the genuine feeling, buried for so long under polite artifice, because she smiles, a pale fleeting ghost of a smile, and nods me towards the kitchen.

'Can I make you another tea?' I say, as she sinks into a steel chair. Babs is a hefty woman but the way her long limbs fold into themselves reminds me of a spider curling up to die. She shakes her head and waves towards the shiny new married-person's kettle, which I assume means: But help yourself.

I sit opposite her and wait, buzzing with dread. Please don't let it be too bad, for her sake. And mine. I don't think I'm up to dealing with that level of guilt. She presses a hand to her temple and squeezes. Then she spits, 'Everyone says, "Oh how's married life treating you? how's married life treating you?" it's all they fucking say and I'm going, "Fine, fine, great thanks," because I'm a *newly-wed* and I'm supposed to be screwing five times a night seven nights a week – that's what they want to hear, that's what I'm meant to say, when the truth is, it's treating me like shit, "It's shit, thanks," and I don't know what to do, and oh God, I can't speak to him, he's not listening to me and oh Christ, I'm. . . I'm so *desperate*.'

'But Babs, poor darling, why?' I splutter. Apart from sounding like the bespectacled librarian stooge in a bad 1950s film, I can barely crank out the words. My friend sits there, cracking her knuckles, crunch, crunch, and I grab her hands and hold them tight in mine.

'He . . . he . . . I don't know. It's lots of things.'

She pulls away, and crosses her arms. Then she laughs, a hard bitter laugh, and says, 'Natalie, if you're ever on honeymoon and your new husband watches *Seven Samurai* on video two nights running, take it from me, it's a bad sign.'

'Wh – what's *Seven Samurai*?' I whisper fearfully. I suspect from her tone that it isn't a jaunty Japanese version of *Seven Brides for Seven Brothers*.

'It's a three-hour black and white film about bandits in sixteenth-century Japan,' she replies. 'And then he watched *Shogun*. That's nine and a half hours. Of pretty much the same.'

I am stunned to silence. Bandits? On honeymoon?

'I wouldn't have minded if *I'd* gotten to see his samurai sword more than twice in two weeks!' Her attempt at a laugh is more of a sob. She adds suddenly, 'It's so fucking unfair. The guys at his work –' I'm still absorbing the outrage of the honeymoon bandits but I nod to show I'm keeping up. 'Bastards. You know, not one of his colleagues said congratulations. It was all stuff like, "Another one bites the dust." And – can you believe someone said this – "You're making the biggest mistake of your life!" This fucker's never even *met* me and he said that to Si! And when they found out I was a fire fighter – well, that was the beginning of the fucking end, wasn't it? "You're getting hitched to a lezzer, mate" – and that was the *best* of it. Didn't stop them coming to the wedding and getting wasted on his parents' money though, did it? And I'm thinking, nah, Simon loves me, he can take it, he's not going to listen to a bunch of prats, but then, I was speaking to Annelise, you know, the other woman at the station, and she only goes out with other fire fighters, and we were talking about that and she said she wouldn't get involved with men outside the service because "Who's going to be the hero in the relationship?" and, and I can't stop thinking about what she said. I thought, it won't be like that with Si, he'll be different, and I thought he was – he *was* – different, he admired what I did, he was proud, I mean, Christ, he earns twenty times what I do, he's still the bleeding *breadwinner*, you know, he still gets to beat his chest and bring home the woolly mammoth, I'm not altogether robbing him of his masculinity by not being a, a, a *nursery school teacher* but you know it seems I am, because he's angry with me, he's hostile and it's been going on for weeks, and I hardly see him, he's always working late or leaving early and out with the lads and coming home pissed and it's like everything I do is a personal insult to him, he's so distant and cold, and what if he's having an affair, I'm scared he'll do it just to teach me a lesson for, I don't know what, agreeing to marry him, not knowing my place, making him look a wuss in front of his mates, making him, God forbid, different from them because they all live in fleapits and don't do a weekly shop, it's like they resent him for joining the enemy camp and he's taking it out on *me*, and maybe he *is* cheating on me, can you believe it, two months in and I'm already checking his bloody pockets! Oh Christ, Nat, I'm so bloody miserable, I'm sorry to land this on you but I don't know what to do, what *can* I do?'

At which point she looks at me with big sad eyes, as if I have the power to magic away three decades of hardcore bloke-training and make it all nice again.

Chapter 25

We were thirteen and Babs and I were eating tea in her kitchen. White bread dripping with chocolate spread, the dark syrupy sort you can't get any more. It must have been the weekend because her father was sitting with us. Anyway, Babs's mother was reading a book on the sofa (my mother wouldn't dream of having 'lounge furniture' in the kitchen) and she *farted*. Our horror knew no bounds. Farting in front of your husband! The ultimate no-no! Didn't she know men went off you if you did that? *My* mother would rather combust than parp in front of my father. Imagine our surprise when my dad left and Mr Edwards stayed.

When I say goodbye to Babs at half past one (no sign of Simon) I am in shock. You think you know and you don't. I've done three hours of counselling and, in the same timescale, months of purgatory. I realise I want her to be happy, and I'd do anything to repair her marriage. I know she'd do the same for me. I've told Babs that the first year is the hardest (according to the *Mirror*) and that honeymoons are a nightmare and should be banned, as they can never live up to your expectations. I've told her that Simon adores her, but signing on the dotted line has given him the jitters. I've advised her not to fart freely, to be on the safe side.

I've not told her that one in three marriages fail (the *Guardian Against Fun*.) And I've struggled with pertinent advice for Simon. You have to be careful when criticising a friend's partner because the second they kiss and make up, *you* are the baddie who slagged off the love of her life.

I am snug in bed before I even think of Andy. Babs doesn't want him to know. ('He's useless at hiding his emotions, Nat, he'd go and punch Si's lights out which I don't think, at this point, would be helpful.') She won't confide in her parents either ('They gave me twelve grand to help with our new flat, how can I do it to them?'). I feel useless. I am the Liz Taylor of marriage guidance, my grasp of man management extends to hiding the remote control. Who could I ask for help? Tony, Mel, Chris, a trinity of clowns. But there is someone else. Could I?

Frannie?

Admittedly, if I had to name the person most likely to become an Angel of Mercy, it wouldn't be her. I've always felt she was destined for a less saintly career. Let's compare. Jeffrey Dahmer, for instance, was a cute baby. Blond, dimpled, the whole works. Nice parents, too. When Frannie was born, she looked like Christopher Walken. Her mother has the get up and go of a matzo ball, and her father once advised her that attending college was pointless as 'You'll only come out and start having babies.' Talk about a training camp for psychosis!

That said, she has been trying (*very* trying). In her own, profoundly irritating way, she wants to help. Despite receiving no encouragement, she persists in her attempts to better me. Frannie has a good heart, even though I suspect part of it is cooked through. And she worships Babs. I have no doubt that if she knew of Simon's behaviour, she'd bite off his balls. Which is why I have no intention of telling her about Simon. None. I'm going to pretend *my* relationship is in trouble, and ask her to advise *me*. She'd love that. The chance to patronise and educate will be irresistible. For once I will put Babs before my own selfish considerations. I am a genius.

The next day, I do a forty-minute run at the gym to psych myself up, return home and page Frannie.

No sign of Andy. When the phone rings, I fall on it.

'Hello?'

'Chris.'

'*Chris!* Oh hi, hi, um, how is everything, look I haven't had a chance to speak to Tony yet but I—'

'I spoke to Piers.'

'Oh that's great! So I don't have to—'

'He's nicked the band.'

'Pardon?'

'He wants to be their agent, and he wants one of the guys on the management side of his company to manage them. I didn't fucking know there *was* a management side to his company.' Chris's voice lifts to a whine.

'Oh no!' I gasp. 'That's outrageous, what – what happened?'

'Last week, yeah, he wants to know all this shit, what's the story, how committed are they, have they got more than one song, what the buzz is, what do they look like, and I answer all his shite questions, yeah, and he acts really keen, hears the demo, drops round the studio, and, yeah, he's gonna take them on and then – nothing, man! I call him ten times. Nothing. And then the boys go quiet on me, and today, Piers gets on the blower, says, "I'm sorry, but it's not working out with the band. Blue Fiend have decided they want a different manager and we've agreed to give it a shot." Not working out? First I've fucking heard of it!'

'Oh Chris, you poor th—'

'And! And the fucker goes, "But if you've got anything else you want me to hear, bring it in!" Not a sniff of guilt, it was like, "'scuse me mate but can you lift your arm so I can twist the knife better?" Jesus, man! And then, two seconds later, Tarqy's on the line, the fucking Judas! After all I've done for him! He'd still be an alarms and installations engineer if it weren't for me! Going on about how I was managing them all wrong! Says, "Piers has put an end to the toilet tour because it takes all the glamour and quality out of our act." I mean, when I got the Fiends a gig at the Berwick-on-Tweed university bar, Tarqy was delirious, man!'

'Oh Chris,' I sigh. 'You poor th—'

'It's like, it's like, what is this, ma—'

As Chris launches into a whinge as long as Route 66, there is a beep-beep on the line. I *know* it's Frannie.

'Chris, I'm sorry to interrupt. Look, I've got to be quick, it's dreadful about Piers, what a total git, but what – what can I do? I, I don't think Tony can help you with this.'

'You gotta call him, princess, he can recommend a brief, or maybe have a word with Piers. I—'

'I can't ask him to do that,' I blurt, jiggling both legs.

'Ah come on, man, I'm not asking much. I—'

It's the 'man' that does it. 'I can't,' I say coldly. And, imperious in a blaze of courage, I press line two.

'Really really sorry to keep you waiting,' I bleat.

'I should hope so,' says Frannie. 'What is it?'

It takes a short explanation – during which I swallow enough humble pie to double my weight – to reel her in. Frannie's shift ends at 10.15 tonight. We can meet near the hospital, in Lambeth, or somewhere along her route home. A bar near Bank tube, where she changes for Bethnal Green, would be acceptable. I'm too uncool to know anywhere in Lambeth or Bethnal Green, so I say, 'That sounds great, Frannie. I know, why don't we meet at the Pitcher & Piano in Cornhill? It's bang in the City, just round the corner from Bank tube.'

There is a cough, as if Frannie is choking on my bad taste. 'Natalie,' she sighs. 'You're so petit bourgeois. I've never been to the Pitcher & Marrow. But I suppose it will be an education. And as for your problem with Chris, I'm sorry to hear it, but it doesn't surprise me. Don't you see that by wilfully resisting an appearance of physical maturity, you pander to the male vested interest in promoting and overvaluing thinness? You help Chris to repress you! It's far easier to subjugate a woman who looks fragile and pre-pubescent like yourself, rather than a hardy

Amazon like Barbara, or a voluptuous earth mother, like *my*self' – that's certainly one way of describing seventeen stone, I think. Has Frannie ever thought of PR? – 'Of course he'll treat you like a toy if you don't have the courage to challenge and confront his primal fears by presenting a mature, powerful image of womanhood. By starving yourself to a husk and never speaking up for yourself, you encourage his persecutory conviction that the powerful woman emasculates. Do you understand, Natalie? You, the compliant child, are permitting his fantasies of potency and authority – thanks to you, these fantasies become *factasies*. If you don't pudge up, of course he'll shag around! By remaining size eight you allow his physical and mental superiority – you are a non-person! Now do me a favour and think about that. I'll see you in the Pitcher & Marrow, ten-forty. Au revoir!'

Two seconds into Frannie's monologue, I realise that ideas devised at 2 a.m. are rarely as brilliant as they appear at their time of conception. But it's too late. The phone lies dead in my hand and I've roped in the biggest meanest troll outside of *The Three Billy Goats Gruff* to help solve Babs's marriage problems. Repressed indeed! And I *am* eating more. (I discovered last week that lack of protein can make your hair fall out. What next? Lack of yellow in your wallpaper? Lack of good TV programmes on a Tuesday at 4 a.m.?)

But I don't dare ring Frannie back, so I spend the rest of the day in a state of creeping dread. At 9.30 p.m., I can bear it no longer and leave the flat. Incidentally and not that I care, *where* is Andy? Out with a girl? I drag my feet to Chalk Farm tube. At least I can count on London Transport to delay me. Every journey takes an hour in this city – there's always a station closed because an escalator is broken or it's the ticket master's birthday. I dream of moving to Bangladesh for a taste of efficiency. The District & Circle Line speeds me to Bank in seven minutes flat.

I emerge from the wrong exit on purpose and pigeon-toe

225

along Threadneedle Street, thinking, it's so grey and smart, oh yeah, doesn't Simon work round here?

I'm so blonde. Of course Simon works round here! How else would I know about a git-magnet like the Pitcher & Piano? In peacetime, Babs forced me along for the rat's birthday drinks! 'It's like his second office,' she'd said fondly.

As I (unfondly) reminisce, a timid thought presents itself. What if he's there? I bet he is. Would I confront him? Yes. Compliant child, my arse! Although there's no need for language, as my mother would say . . . I sweep towards the Pitcher & Piano like a vengeful god, pausing only to apply lipstick.

My legs are jelly as I join the braying fray, as a thousand well-paid eyes sweep over me, assessing and dismissing in one disdainful move. I drop my gaze, knowing that I look cheap (as in the lower tax bracket). I feel like the oik at the ball. There's no point trying to buy a drink as bar staff ignore me in roughly the same way that polite company ignore a dog's erection. What am I doing here? My idea was mad. I can't go through with it. I wrench my mobile from my bag, page Frannie with the instruction: 'Sorry to mess you around but it's OK now.' Right. To the loo, then home, no harm done.

I start slinking through the yattering crowds – ' 'scuse me, 'scuse me' – gently touching my palms to the walls of grey tailored backs to stop them from crushing me like a grape in a winepress, ducking under trays of sloshing pints – 'sorry, sorry' – although it's *their* fault.

'Natalie,' barks a crisp voice only slightly soggy at the edges. 'Woulden have thought this was your kind of hangout, won't you come and say hello?' I spin round as Simon claps a heavy hand on my shoulder and twiddles me towards him. 'Hello, hello,' I stutter, hearing my voice, weak and squeaky, and thinking, *Now* what? I note his slack features and unfocused eyes and attempt a frosty smile.

'Come and meet the gang,' he slurs, his hand slipping

downwards. 'Gentlemen,' he booms – a loud huddle of posh suits part and stare – 'May I introdush you to a fren of mine?'

'Fren'?! Since when are we *frens*? It took him four months to remember my name! I am propelled forward, a reluctant object of curiosity like Tank Girl at an Action Man convention, and various stubbled faces nod and grin and look me up and down. I'd be floored by the alcohol fumes, except that Simon hasn't removed his hand from my back – I think he's forgotten he left it there. I bleat a greeting but fail to perform further.

He drawls, 'We should get you a bevvy, mm, what'll you have? I suggest a pink drink for a lady, a vodka & cranberry or a kir royale?'

The assembled chimps seem to think this is funny, so I invoke the spirit of Frannie and say, 'That sounds pretty but what I'd really like is a pint of Carlsberg Elephant.' (All I know is, I once saw a tramp drink it.) Simon's cronies bend over laughing, spraying each other's expensive ties in lager. 'Where's Babs?' I ask tightly, turning away. 'Will she be joining us?'

Simon – his hand may actually be welded to my back – steers me to the bar and within seconds summons a pink drink from the air.

'My wife,' he titters. 'Maaaaai waayyyyf is out saving lives, she's a lifesaver doncha know.' He rolls his eyes in sarcastic wonder. His hair is a little askew. Simon is as sozzled as a worm in tequila. Go on, tell him. My heart bops in anticipation. I turn around and block his path to the rest of the pack. He smiles and teeters.

I swallow my fear and stare down at his black Chelsea boots. Then I look up and say sternly, if unnecessarily, 'You are drunk.'

Simon's grin spreads slowly across his face like treacle and he says, 'Natalie – you don't mind if I call you Natalie, do you?'

What else was he planning to call me? John Thomas? I

light a cigarette and don't offer him one. 'You *do* call me Natalie,' I remind him curtly.

'I do call you Nadalie! Nadalie, thish is a lovely surprise seeing you here, did I tell you that? Thish is my stomping ground, did I tell you, I woulden expect to see you round here, the girlies round here are all seccies and ball-breakers!' Simon chugs a half-pint of lager down his elegant throat.

'Simon,' I say.

'Whassat?' says Simon.

'Don't you think you should get home to Babs?'

'No!' he blurts, and staggers backwards, giggling.

'Careful!' I gasp, as he slips and treads heavily on the heel of a man with shoulders and neck like a bull. 'Sorry,' I cry. 'Please, Simon,' I shout over the hubbub. 'What about Babs, it's so unfair, you don't want to make her unhappy, she adores you and I know you're mad about her, I know—'

Simon slaps his hand on my shoulder and leans on it – it takes all my strength not to buckle – and bends until his lips tickle my ear. I assume he wants to confess his regret but instead he murmurs, 'Nadalie you don't mind if I call you Nadalie Nadalie did anyone ever tell you you've got sush a pretty mouth only you don't use it mush I could tell you what to do with a mouth like that you're very quiet but I like that, you know what they say about the quiet ones don't you?' I lurch away with such force I headbutt his nose. 'Shit,' he splutters, cupping his hand over his face as the red dribbles through his fingers. 'Shit.'

I stare at him, the ugliness inside spits and boils, and I babble, 'You, you, I'm *not* sorry, Simon, you're disgusting, I'm not sorry, you don't say things like that, you're drunk, you're drunk okay, but—'

Simon drops his empty pint glass on the floor and everyone turns as it smashes, and he uncups his hand and violently yanks my head towards him and presses his mouth to mine, hard, crushing, mashing my lips and

228

clinking my teeth and I flail and push and struggle and snort blood and grip his arm to try and get him off me but it's only when I lift my boot and scrape it hard down his shin and stab it into his foot that he lets go and stares at me in bleary shock and pain and I want to fling my pink drink in his stupid face and over his sunshine yellow silk tie and pale blue shirt and dark blue suit but what would that say to Babs, so I place the sticky half-spilt kir royale on the bar with trembling fingers, wipe the blood and spit off my mouth with the back of my hand, and say, 'Be a man, Simon, and get home to your wife.'

I walk calmly out of the Pitcher & Piano into the dark night and then I start running, shuddering and retching, like a trainee vampire after its first bite.

Chapter 26

According to the Chinese calendar, I was born in the year of the Rooster. I suppose I got off lightly (Belinda was born in the year of the Dog and I think Tony is a Rat) but I've never *liked* being a Rooster. I wanted to be a Tiger, of course (I think the only other options are a Goat, Monkey, Horse or Snake – apparently the Chinese aren't bothered about giving their children complexes). But having resented the Chinese calendar all these years for labelling me, I'm now forced to accept that it was close to spot on. I was born in the Year of the Headless Chicken.

'You all right there, love?' says the taxi driver, glancing in his mirror. 'Boyfriend trouble, is it?'

I rub my mouth and croak, 'No, yes, I'm fine, thank you,' but when I pay the fare he watches my hands shake.

'You wanna watch yourself, love,' he rasps, leaning an elbow out of his window as I hurry up the path. 'Can't be too careful.'

Tell me about it. I jam the key in the lock, fall inside, and stagger to the bathroom. I see myself and shudder. Dried blood round my mouth, I look like a bad-mannered cannibal, and my hair is wild and my eyes, bright in a mad frazzled way, and my face is long and gaunt, is this what I want, ugh, I want to strip off my clothes and scour my skin raw but I can't bear to see myself, this hollow self, because Babs is right, I'm not fat, I am *not* fat, I can see it now, but I feel it, what I am is not good, oh God what have I done, I wash the dirt off my face and clean my teeth and spit spit

spit into the sink and I'm trembling so hard I can't get a grip on anything.

I place the towel back on the rail and it slithers to the floor. I snatch it up and fling it at the rail, whipping it, you bastard towel! whap whap! then hold my breath in case I've woken Andy. *What* would I say if he saw me like this? — 'I had steak for dinner and got carried away'?

I smooth my hair, straighten my shirt, glide to the kitchen and softly lock the door. I want to sleep for a thousand years but I don't think I could ever sleep again. I know what I'm about to do, and the thrill shivers through me like an ill wind. I open the larder door, step on a chair, and lift down a large tin box from the top shelf. I place it silently on the table.

Open sesame.

The contents of the box shine like paste jewels under the bright ceiling lights.

'You'd feel a lot better if you ate something,' I drone, imitating my mother. ('You'd feel a lot better if you ate something,' is what she'd say if I'd been slashed in the stomach with a carving knife: it's her answer to everything. She once watched a recording of Johnny Rotten singing *Anarchy in the UK* and remarked to Tony, 'He'd feel a lot better if he ate something.')

I stare into the box and my insides writhe. I reach out, my pulse is speeding, the urge overtakes me, I'm possessed, I can't stop myself, I'm suffocating in lust.

And then I'm snatching, tearing, a wild animal, ripping at the wrappers with my teeth, the purple, gold, red, silver, bronze, all and everything, the loud wanton colours of desire, cramming, stuffing, jamming, oh it's all gone wrong, this thick gluey lush glut of sweetness it's molten heaven it tastes like a dream more more I'm hungry hungry I'm so fucking hungry rapacious I can't stop it any longer, that emptiness inside like a yawning monster, grumbling, loud and absolute, I'm feeding, filling the badness, soothing it, pressing it back down, making it go away and oh oh yes it feels so good like ice on a wound, until the noise inside is silenced and I am sated.

For about one piddling minute. And then it hammers at my chest again. I stare at the obscene wreckage of sweet wrappers littering my pristine white table and all I can think is, what have I done? I've had a fit. I've had a Roseanne Barr episode in my sleep. More pressingly, my stomach is swollen to the size and weight of a ripe watermelon and there's a good chance I'll split. I glance at my lap and it's sprinkled in brown and white – chocolate and coconut crumbs. When I brush them away they smear, disgusting brown smears like shit on my trousers. They never show that on the Bounty ads – flabby arms and the brown trouser effect. I feel a great welling force, the urge to scratch the skin off my bones. Oh God. The tears ooze and I scrunch up the evidence and bury it in the bin, all the while wailing inside, this isn't paradise, it's hell, and could it be any worse?

I sit at the kitchen table, buzzing. I feel the whole of me vibrating with self-revulsion, although sharing the blame is the accumulated caffeine from a Mars Bar, a milk chocolate Bounty bar, a Milky Way, a Snickers, a mint Aero, a Fruit & Nut Dairy Milk, a box of Maltesers, a packet of Minstrels, and a tube of Smarties. Not that smart at all. I sit and stare at the wall, the words 'ohgodohgod' run through my head over and over again like an endless daisy chain and when I look up at the clock it's 2.17 a.m. I want to go for a run, run it all off, I don't want to go to bed, but considering I don't want to exist either, going to bed is a small surrender. I unlock the door, tiptoe to the bathroom, clean my teeth until my spit isn't brown, and pad into my bedroom. Then I scream.

Andy is in my bed!

The unutterable pervert!

I stare disbelieving at the hump in the duvet and – when it doesn't leap up in horror and shame – scream again. (As you might have observed, I'm good at screaming. It comes from having a nervous disposition.)

232

'Natalie?' calls a bleary voice from down the hall. 'That you? You okay?'

Then who the—? I pick up a candlestick in one hand, then yank back the duvet with the other. *Chris* is in my bed!

I rush to the door. 'Fine, thanks,' I bleat into the dark.

I gape at Chris. What the hell is he doing here? I was rude to him earlier. I'm sweet as custard and he's grumpy for weeks and the minute I'm rude, he can't get enough of me. Or can't get enough *out* of me. Well, not only has the worm turned, it's done a triple back flip. One word from him about Tony and he is history. I mean it. I'm whacked up on sugar and not to be messed with. I poke him in the side with the candlestick. He doesn't wake up. Drunk. I place the candlestick back on the bedside cabinet and marvel. Once I would have been flattered that some loser of a man had chosen to slink home to my bed after overdoing it on the Jack n' Cokes. (Aw! He's all helpless and he's come to *me!* Aaar! He's been sick all over my bedclothes! Cute!) Now I just don't have the patience.

I paddle through my bottom drawer, dig out the biggest plainest scariest Victorian schoolmarm of a nightie I can find – high neck, ruffles, bows, beige, the lot – and put it on. Then I lie there feeling like a sea lion in drag until I fall asleep.

I wake up queasy. After a few squeaks and grinds, my brain crunches into gear and I remember why. And I'm horrified and repulsed all over again. I blame the Edwards family. Babs and Andy pressing me to eat, eat, eat, and so I eat a little more, but it's all or nothing with me, a little will never be enough, and so the pressure builds like steam inside a pan of boiling water with the lid jammed shut. And then, whoooooff! How could I? I controlled it for so long, I had it all under control, until she and her brother interfered. Christ, I feel sick. I blink at my alarm clock and flinch. Arrgh! A box of chocolates! Sitting there! *Roses.* For a second I think it's God playing a joke. Then I realise.

Chris. He might as well have bought me a pig costume and an apple to stuff in my mouth.

'Bloody Nora! What the fuck's that you're wearing?'

I close my eyes then open them. Chris is giving me the sort of look that *Daily Mail* readers reserve for beggars on trains. 'You look like Norman's mother out of *Psycho*,' he splutters.

'It's Duffer of St George,' I lie.

'Oh, right, cool,' he says, reassessing. 'Nice one.'

I scowl. 'How did you happen to be in my bed?'

Chris seems startled. 'I er, I, I've no idea. Oh yeah, I do. I was up Camden way, trying to sort out a – and uh, it got late, and well, you're just up the road. That prick let me in. I don't like him, princess, I don't like him being here.'

My mouth clanks open. 'Chris,' I shrill, 'He's here because I need the cash – I lost my job, remember?' Chris shrugs. 'I don't like him being here,' he repeats sulkily. He swivels out of bed and rubs his eyes. 'And yesterday, you were well out of line. I hope you're cool today though because we gotta talk. Here, look, happy late Valentine's Day' – he waves to the old lady chocolates – 'Right, I'm going to shower, then we'll talk. You'll talk Tony round, princess, you're good like that. Look, man' – pause – 'You're *my* woman, yeah. You and me, babe. I don't want Andy around. He gets in the way.'

Having delivered this imperious address (although I was half expecting him to add, 'We got plans to make, we got things to buy, we don't waste our time on some creepy guy'), he plods off to my bathroom. I stare after him and the queasiness shifts to my throat. I yank off the fright-nightdress and pull on my baggy comfort clothes. All my life I have been dictated to. Told who I am, what to be. And I'm fed up. I am not taking orders from some nit who, as we speak, is dolloping great squirly worms of my priceless Aveda creme conditioner on to his ungrateful freeloading head.

I make my bed, lie on it, and await his return.

234

Fifteen leisurely minutes later Chris pads in, drilling a corner of my fluffy white towel into his earhole.

'That new conditioner you've got stinks!' is his greeting.

'What new conditioner?' I say, sitting up.

'That white stuff, in the shower. I had it on my hair for ages and it stank.'

'*White* stu—?' I start, then stop. 'Chris,' I say boldly, 'I've had a think, as you said—'

'Good girl.'

'Well,' I smile. 'That's the problem. I'm *not* a good girl.'

'What are you talking about?' says Chris in the voice of a persecuted saint.

I clear my throat. 'Well,' I declare. 'I like Andy being here. And I'm not your woman. So.'

Chris, who is towelling his hair dry, stops mid-rub. 'What?' he snaps. 'What are you going on about?'

'I am saying,' I trill, 'that the Big Use is over. Finished. We are done. Yesterday's fish and chip paper. I am not your PA and I will not be speaking to my brother to sort out your business problems, not now, not ever. So you can get out of my flat now, and I don't ever want to see you again.' A 'please' nearly pops out but as it lingers on the tip of my tongue I replace it with – '*Capisci?*' (because, unlike Chris, I didn't learn my Italian from *Goodfellas*).

After much spluttering and 'But what about the band?' and 'you evil little cow' and 'can't I just use the hairdryer?' Chris leaves the building.

I wave him off for ever, whimpering with relief. Sayonara, baby! The power of speech! While these may well be the biggest bravest words I've ever spoken, I am well aware that bravery and stupidity are very closely linked. In this instance, my bravery was fuelled by fear, by the fervent desire for Chris to be far away from me and any candlesticks when he rakes his hand through his dark shiny locks and discovers that the tube of 'white stuff' in my shower was not a new stinky hair conditioner but the finest and most effective hair removal cream that £5.99 can buy.

235

That's the trouble with men. Too damn cocky to read the label.

I lean against the door and breathe in the silence. He's gone, and I ditched him.

'Mornin',' says Andy, bouncing out of his room in a horrible tartan dressing gown and old man's slippers and spoiling the moment.

'Did I hear' – he draws a baroque squiggle in the air – '*drama?*'

'I've just dumped Chris.'

'Good move,' drawls Andy, clapping his hands. 'What a loser.' And then, 'Hope you don't mind that I let him in last night. He said you'd arranged it and I was too knackered to defend the castle.'

'Oh, that doesn't matter,' I say. 'Um, but I think he's going to be very upset.'

'Too right he will be,' exclaims Andy, rubbing at his stubble. 'You were too good for him. You were the, the Breitling Emergency to his fake Rolex.'

Assuming this is a compliment – although I'm not so sure I like to be referred to as an emergency – I grimace. 'Thank you,' I say. 'But actually I didn't mean that.'

I explain about the hair removal cream. We laugh so hard and honkingly that I forget it's supposed to be awkward between us. Andy disappears into the shower, and I decide to write off yesterday's chaos and start again. The wisdom of this resolution is proven when my phone shrills at 9.31 a.m.

'Hello?'

'Simon?'

'No, this is Natalie,' I say, thinking, do I really sound like a man?

'No, *this* is Simon.'

'Oh!' I cry.

'Natalie, I wanted to apologise for last night. I'm dreadfully sorry. I was out of order. This whole marriage

236

malarkey has been – ah – what you might call a shock to the system, and I've not dealt with it as well as I might, but I, I'm not really an AP' – I search my file labelled "poshspeak" and it presents me with "AP = Awful Person" – 'I'm getting it together, no more outrageous scenes like last night, I assure you. Babs is a top girl, I behaved like a prat. So, so this is strictly *entre nous*? I can trust you not to say anything?'

What is he, mad?

'Simon,' I croak. 'Cross my heart hope to die, there's no way I'm going to tell Babs's – *what a pillock she married*, I add in my head. 'You, you do mean what you say, though, don't you?'

'Absolutely,' he says curtly, and puts the phone down. I grasp my peppermint tea in unsteady hands and thank God for deliverance. That's that then, and we all live happily ever after. But I thank the Bully in the Sky too soon because a minute later the phone trills again. This time it's Frannie.

'I saw you,' she says, 'kissing Simon.'

Chapter 27

It's like letting a car out in front of you. There's no obligation, it's your right of way, but you're feeling holy, you want the world to live in harmony, so you selflessly wave them into the traffic. And what do you get for your trouble? Trouble. Without exception, you have let a lunatic into your path who dawdles along at 15 m.p.h., braking erratically for invisible obstructions, rolling reluctantly towards the green lights as if they're booby-trapped, making a mad break for it just as they turn red, leaving you, the benefactor, stranded and late for your urgent appointment, and possibly incurring a £3 fine at the video shop.

Except this is a million times worse. I stare wordlessly at the phone and feel frantic. No, Frannie, you don't understand – it was meant to be a *good thing!*

'No, look—' I croak, recognising my impotence.

'I *saw* you,' repeats Frannie. 'And you know what? I thought you were better than that. But I was wrong, Natalie. You're that self-obsessed I wouldn't imagine you even comprehend the depravity of what you've done.'

'But I didn—' I start.

'Please! don't! make! it! worse! by! defending! yourself!' spits Frannie. 'There *is* no excuse!'

I feel a chill flutter of fear at who I'm dealing with. Anything you say will be taken down as evidence and used against you at a later date. I do as I'm told and shut up. She then takes my silence as an admission of guilt. 'You,' she adds, 'are the most narcissistic creature I have ever encountered, but not for one minute did I think that even you would—'

'No I'm *not*!' I cry – this is one slur too many – 'I hate the way I look!'

'Crap!' shouts Frannie. 'Your whole existence is about the way you look! You take the womanly masquerade to the limit! You define yourself through men! You live only as an object of the male gaze! Your self-esteem is fed solely on the penis! You're so damn ravenous for reassurance you'll even seek it via the phallus of your good friend's husband!'

Frannie, I can't help thinking even at this pivotal moment, is obsessed with penises. I say, 'But Simon w—'

'I am beside myself about Simon!' yells Frannie, 'I am appalled about Simon!' – at last, something we agree on – 'It makes me *sick*, and I wish it didn't, but it goes to show, you could put a goat in a blond wig and men would ask it to dance, how dare he betray Babs like that, how dare he? As for you! You have to prove to yourself that every man fancies you! Robbie and now Simon! My God, I dread to think what you've been up to with him, but I am *so* going to put an end to it, the second my shift is done I'm going straight round to Holland Park, and let me tell you, it will give me great – I mean, *no* – pleasure to impart the vile truth to Barbara, none at all!'

I buckle under this barrage of insults, but manage to salvage a grain of common sense. I blurt six strategic syllables – which I pray reach Frannie's ears before being shot down – 'Don't tell her, for *her* sake!'

'Your sake, more like!' Frannie puts the phone down with a click.

I cover my face with both hands.

Horrible. The thought of Babs *thinking* that I would do that to her. I imagine that surreal nightmarish sense of betrayal, creeping up on her. I picture her bewildered face, the disbelief and the hurt, and a great lumpen pain swells

239

inside me. I want to rush round to the fire station and gush out the truth. But then the truth is as distasteful as the misconception. And I am to blame. I rushed in, a fool, a silly naive fool. Did I really think I was doing Babs a favour? I wanted to be peacemaker because I needed a role in Babs's marriage. I had to stake my claim on their lives. In some way, Frannie was right.

My mother rings three times, no doubt to badger me about Eeesy-Kleen. I let the answerphone deal with her. I sit at my desk, which is in fact my mother's old dressing table, in the corner of the kitchen, but I can't do any work (this is aside from the fact that I *have* no work). I lean on my elbows and stare at the wall. I'm a coward. I can't face a fight. I think of Babs and feel a dragging ache. I try to white it out, but it won't go, it clings. At 1 p.m., I surrender. I snatch my bag and go to the gym. I need to get on the running machine and run. I change into my kit in a blur, arrive breathless at the row of treadmills and – they're *occupied*. I glance at my nearest rival. Stringy leg muscles, lean torso, set jaw, long distance look in his eye. He looks close to death, and I hate him. As Tony says, line a group of marathon runners and a bunch of smack addicts against a wall, and who could tell the difference. This junkie's body language reads, Do Not Disturb.

I assess his neighbour. Glutinous legs, a protruding belly, and the tiniest shiniest shorts you ever saw. A houseplant that's outgrown its pot. At every thunderous step, his body shakes and the sweat flies off him. I can smell his breath from here; sweetly rotten, like compost. He keeps eyeing marathon man and increasing his speed, so I deduce that, even if it kills him, he's going nowhere fast. Get *off*, I want to scream, I'm piling on the pounds just standing here!

'Give up,' murmurs a husky voice to my left. 'I would.'

'Alex!' The sight of her soothes my irritation like a soft breeze. 'How are you?'

Alex grins. 'I'm good. It looks like you're free to attend my class, Natalie!'

I laugh. I am suspicious of any form of exertion that threatens to mess with your head, and my brief acquaintance with Pilates has done nothing to disabuse me of my prejudice. Also, it crippled me for three days.

'I'd like to but I, I need to sweat,' I say. 'There's this big black scribble in my head, I feel like a Jackson Pollock. I need to run it out.'

Alex presses her lips in disapproval. 'Sounds like Pilates is exactly what you need. Go on, it'll be good for you. It's like sex. It's usually a lot better the second time.'

The words, 'It'll be good for you' imply a deeply unpleasant sensory experience. I envision my mother standing over me wielding broccoli.

'Go on,' purrs Alex. 'It is hard work, you won't be slacking. You're working deeper muscles. I know you felt the effects last time.' I hesitate. 'One class,' she wheedles. 'It's like a mental massage. It'll help clear your head. But not in that mindless run-run-whack-it-out-of-you way.'

I sag. I am comfortable with my neuroses and wish to hang on to them. It's why I've never tried yoga. I have no intention of letting my guard down. Pilates, yoga, judo, I don't trust them. I don't want well-honed fanatics poking about my mind, disturbing whatever lurks beneath the murk, changing the way I think. I like my exercise pure, straight up, unemotive, no additives.

Mental massage! It sounds like a cult. But then.

Some of the gunk in my head *needs* clearing. Much as I hate being urged to do things (it's the 'It's a lovely day, you should be outside' syndrome), I admit that, mentally, I need tuning. My brain feels like a congested plughole. My whole existence is about the way I look, apparently. Frannie was close. But Babs knows me better. She said something a few weeks ago, which loiters, however hard I try to shake it off. It's not so much about how you look, she said, it's the feeling inside. That feeling inside, a bored goblin hunched and malevolent, urging me on to further destruction. And, oh my, have I been destructive.

'OK,' I say to Alex. 'I'll give it another go. But then Pilates and I part ways.'

'How did you find it?' says Alex afterwards, as I roll up my mat.

I nod dumbly. 'Painful,' I manage, 'and the breathing is still a problem. But better. Definitely better.'

'How much better?' she laughs.

'I feel like kneaded dough,' I whisper.

'That's what I like to hear,' she says. 'Will we be seeing you at the next class?'

'Oh, yes.'

I drive home, wanting to skip. Pilates was as exasperating as before. My transversus muscle wouldn't behave itself, I couldn't maintain a 'neutral pelvis', and I kept going into an anterior tilt (i.e. sticking my bum out.) But, I feel warm in a way I haven't felt. I sit at the wheel and try to connect with the earth's gravitational force. But I'm floating. Back in that studio I felt . . . capable. Not like in a step class where twenty-nine other women skip through ten thousand knee-twisting moves and I feel like a carthorse. I didn't have to conform to Pilates. Pilates conformed to *me*. It was much the same as last time, all very understated: no sudden lunges, no messing about with huge elastic bands, small focused movements, a lot of torso work, endless punitive stretching. The difference is, this time it felt *right*. It was meditative, without being spooky. And Alex is an excellent teacher. She reminded me of a cat licking kittens into shape (only the fish breath was absent). I feel calm and ruffled at the same time.

This unexpected high grants me ten minutes' grace, then I'm back to agonising about Babs. I pray that Frannie's sense has overcome her rage and righteousness but I fear it hasn't. Then again, Babs hasn't rung my mobile screaming, so I can only hope. I try and block the creeping thoughts of betrayal. I *have* betrayed Babs. Not in the way Frannie thinks, but I have. As an antidote to my soiled conscience, I spool back the Pilates experience and luxuriate in the memory. I'd like to tell Alex that I'm hooked, but I don't want to sound silly.

To be honest, I feel foolish. I've always believed that you need other people to make you feel special. I never considered that you could make yourself feel special (and I don't mean that in a Babs 'I lost my virginity to myself' sort of way). No matter how conceited you are, unless you're Tony, you can't feel special in a vacuum. You need back-up. But then, I suppose you can't feel special if you *are* a vacuum. And often, I am. I feel like a fake, staging a sunny show for friends and family. As if no one really knows the dark, empty me. Yet, that class I did today, it made me feel different. Not *special* or anything Hollywood, but solid, as if I could be something. I felt a ripple of calm, inside. That class might have injected warmth into the emptiness. And *I* made it happen.

I park my car, bursting with Disney thoughts. I'll call Dad, and Kimberli Ann, tell them of my progress. I am eating more, even if my main motive is to stave off baldness. I resent every bite, I feel like I've sold my soul for nice hair, but I am eating more. And Mum. I haven't even spoken to her about getting in touch with Tara and Kelly. I should visit Hendon, show off my new portly figure. Although, I don't know if I'm stable enough to stand her offensively obvious glee at my two pound weight gain. I can't bear how other women are pleased when you gain weight. Even with my mother, it's hard to know what's concern for my health and what's competition. My mother's satisfaction at seeing me eat while she abstains makes me want to slap her. That's *my* trick, making other people eat. Oh, Natalie, stop it. Maybe I'll take up her offer of nepotism and do a few days at Eeesy-Kleen.

I am a step from the front door when I realise that Andy

might be home. A dilemma: if I'm trying to feel good about myself in ways that are not to do with lipstick, is it cheating to check my nose for bogies? I decide no. I reason that you could spend a fantastic evening holding court to a swathe of friends, secure in the knowledge that your heart and soul are second to none, then waltz home, glance in the mirror, realise that your nostrils are gummed green, and be forced to reappraise your night. You now realise that as you regaled the crowd with fabulous anecdotes like 'Guys, did you know Isaac Newton invented the catflap?' your audience was, in fact, preoccupied: 'What a loser, she has a snotty nose!'

I whip out my vanity mirror. Perhaps Andy isn't like me, but I bet he is. I look for other people's imperfections. It makes me feel better about myself. It's an instant kick. Yes, I could learn to appreciate their good points but the truth is, I don't *want* to hang around on the off-chance that one day I'll gain the wisdom to see into their hearts. What, and discover they're better than me? I do what everyone else does – give them a quick once-over then judge them on their choice of jumper. That said, I must be softening a little. Robbie, for instance. And Andy. That dressing gown was a sartorial atrocity, and as for the slippers . . . But none of it made me like him any less. Usually I pounce – any excuse to despise someone before they despise me. But Andy doesn't seem to operate like most people. He's like his sister in that respect. What you see is what you get.

I push open the door, and there he is standing in the hall, with the phone in his hand. Faded jeans, black T-shirt, and the foulest expression I have ever seen. If he was ever chased by a herd of yaks in Tibet, I'll bet that look saw them off. If what I see is what I'm about to get, I'll be needing a mortuary technician with flair. It's all I can do to remember I'm house-trained.

Andy clacks the receiver into its cradle and the rage in his eyes is like a gun aimed at my head. When he speaks I am so frantic to hear, my ears scramble the sound and his voice seems to lag and warp, like a cassette unravelling in the machine. But I understand the words, seconds later:

'That was Frannie.'

Chapter 28

For our first 'anniversary' I bought Saul an axe. And before you condemn me, he was delighted. He'd recently bought his garden flat in West Hampstead and was full of the joys of hacking defenceless shrubs to death. I opened *my* presents and my suspicions were confirmed – he didn't understand me. He'd given me a large pointless stuffed toy dog, a blue and gold arts and crafts mantelpiece clock, and a Tweetie Pie mug. I didn't mind though, it made me feel safe. In my experience, the minute a man understands you, he leaves you. But Andy doesn't understand me at all, and it looks like I've lost him anyway.

'Wh – what did she say?' I croak, when my tongue unglues itself from the roof of my mouth. I am tall, but he looms taller, as menacing as a shadow in an alleyway. I glance past him to my bedroom and consider making a run for it. Andy doesn't answer.

'You know what she said,' he replies eventually.

I read the expression in his eyes and wish I was either blind or illiterate. 'But Andy,' I splutter, 'it wasn't what it looked like.'

I'm aware that the delicate situation isn't helped by the fact that if ever I'm suspected of guilt, I look guilty. I panic, and instantly look like a guilty person trying to look innocent.

Andy laughs horribly. 'Ah come on, Natalie,' he says in mock disappointment. 'That's a bit weak. Can't you do better than that?'

I bite my lip to keep control, and wish I was a better

actress. 'Andy, I would never do that to Babs,' I plead. 'I swear, I wouldn't.'

'Really,' says Andy, folding his arms – which I believe is body language for 'I don't like you any more.' (*Derog.* 'You filthy liar') – 'Frannie saw you with your tongue down his throat.'

'Yes, but—'

'Yes *BUT*?' exclaims Andy in a voice so loud I jump and drop my gym bag on my foot. 'Where does "but" come into it? Jaaysus! She said you had a problem with her getting married, but—'

'Babs told you that?' I interrupt in a very small voice.

Andy looks briefly discombobulated (a silly word which I'm probably only using to make him sound less scary and to make myself less scared). He quickly recovers and snaps, 'We're not talking about Babs, we're talking about *you*, her supposed great mate! I don't believe this! I don't know what's worse, you betraying your best friend or that, that *peacock* cheating on my sister. I knew there was something going on with him. I – God, what have you done to Babs?'

I feel so small and wretched I can't even appreciate his brilliant description of Simon as a 'pea cock'. He glares at me. 'Do you realise what you've done to her? It's treason. How's she going to feel? Do you know what it's like to be cheated on by someone you love? It's like you're filled with broken glass. What is she going to do? You've put her in the worst dilemma you can put anyone in.'

Anger has drained the colour from his skin. I can hardly look at him. I am gobsmacked – literally, I feel numb, as if I've been punched in the mouth. There are simply no words in my head. I want to explain but sheer disbelief at the mess I've pulled everyone into crushes the breath from my lungs. Andy shakes his head.

'Don't you have *anything* to say?' he enquires in a tone which hovers somewhere between bemused and disgusted. 'Because I want to know what you have to say! I want to know how this came about, I want to know how it started,

247

I want to know every breath, every word, I want the whole story, dissected, I want to know how you go about ruining someone's life.'

I can't imagine Tony sticking up for me like this if he'd caught Babs with Saul.

'Yes,' I burst out finally. 'I do have something to say. If you'd give me the chance to speak!'

Andy's mouth thins until it is a line. He nods, once, tersely.

I can't catch my breath and the words burst out in snatches.

'I would not – go *near* Simon – I – she told me he was – upsetting her – staying out late – not happy – she didn't think he was cheating – but – she thought he might – soon – I wanted to help – I promise – I felt bad for – resenting her – I thought she was so lucky – wrong – I wanted to make it up to her – tell Simon off – stupid idea – he was so drunk – he was out of control – and then he started saying these ridiculous things, *not* out of lust, it wasn't a lust thing, it was aggressive, and then the kiss Frannie saw, he just launched at me, but it wasn't lust, it was just vicious, because when he said that stuff I hit him on the nose with my head.'

'With your head,' repeats Andy. This prompts mass panic in my facial muscles.

'Yeah,' I mutter, twitching. I pray it looks like an ingrained nervous tic, a hangover from some distant childhood trauma, rather than a newly acquired symbol of guilt.

'But when did she tell you this? And what – you're saying there's no affair? *No* affair? I don't know if I believe you, Natalie. But why, but then' – he frowns – 'I don't understand, if there was nothing going on, why did you wade in there? What's wrong with speaking to him on the phone? Did Babs *ask* you to go over there?'

'No,' I say, feeling worse than ever. 'No.'

'But don't you see? Barging off to meet him to have a go,

248

you knew what state he was in. Don't you see how . . . how inappropriate that is? Why put yourself in that position, it's like you were—'

'Asking for it?' I say, the boiling ugliness inside exploding into rage, *rage*, RAGE. A blast of heat tears through me, shredding me red and raw and scorched with the force of it. So this is what it is to feel fury, I think as I hear myself roar, the words smooth and fluid.

'I wanted to make things right and he assaulted me and you imply that I wanted it to happen! That's a revolting accusation and if you don't believe me, ask Simon!'

Andy takes a step towards me and hisses, close to my face. 'If you need to think it wasn't your fault then think it! And don't you worry, I will ask Simon, because he and I have *a lot* to talk about! But I tell you this: you made a big error of judgement and Babs is the one who's paying for it.'

He stops hissing, and adds quietly, 'You say you wanted to make it right, but I think that deep down you wanted something else, and whatever your excuse, you've got to live with that. I'm out of this flat, as of now. I'll collect my stuff at the weekend.'

I lean against the wall as he wrenches open the door and storms out.

I did, I plead in my head, I did want to make it right. Didn't I? My skull feels like eggshell. What meanly green part of me enjoyed the drama of Barbara's misfortune? Two per cent? But don't we all want that, in the tiniest part of ourselves? We want our friends to do well, but not so wonderfully well that they spotlight our failings. We're delighted for them to succeed in their special interests, but not those general areas where we're striving alongside, struggling in vain.

But does that mean that I'm so lacking, my latent desire is to see her marriage fail? I don't want *that*! Or is it that I want her to know what it is to suffer? I don't know any more. But if it is then I deserve everything I've got. I walk into the kitchen, drag the chair over to the larder, and remove the tin box from the top shelf. Then mechanically, joylessly, I sate my newborn anger with 4,563 calories' worth of chocolate. Beat that, Bridget Jones. The guilt engulfs me like a dense fog. I'm punished but not purged.

Chapter 29

In times of conflict – according to an eminent expert – men retreat into a 'cave' where they remain, solitary and brooding, for hours at a time, ignoring their poor partner's increasingly bewildered and desperate pleas to emerge and explain, only shuffling sheepishly into the light when they have at long last processed and discharged their dark inner struggle. I've come to the conclusion that 'cave' is a euphemism for 'toilet'.

Anyway, I think they must be on to something, because after my monster munch I feel a curiously masculine need to lock myself in the bathroom for ninety minutes. I sit rigid on the floor – flanked by those dual masters of tyranny, the mirror and the scales – hugging my knees, hoping for salvation, but not expecting it. Maybe if I jumped out of the window, Babs would realise how sorry I am. I fondly imagine this scenario for a lingering moment then grudgingly admit to myself that suicide – unlike flowers and chocolates – is not a way of saying you're sorry. It's a way of making everyone else sorry. Oh. That's not very nice. But, that means I must be *angry*.

I'm so surprised at this, I bob up into a defensive crouch and nearly bang my head on the underside of the basin. Anger? I don't do anger. I'm not an angry person. I am self-contained. I rarely answer back. It's not how I was brought up. Why, I only shouted at a man for the first time this week and there were mitigating circumstances – I had to get Chris off my property before his hair fell out. Is that the behaviour of someone who's angry?

251

I'm not like Frannie – Frannie is angry. She lives in a constant state of anger. Whereas most people need to drive a car to reach that level of aggression, Frannie attains it unassisted. She's like a man who punches you for looking at him in the wrong way.

Once, she invited Babs to a football match in Southampton, and they were travelling back to London on the train, 'lairy and pissed' according to Babs, when a middle-aged man leant across the aisle and asked politely if they'd mind keeping the noise down. The word 'sorry' was halfway out of Babs's mouth when Frannie screamed – *screamed* - 'You wouldn't say that if we were men, and you wouldn't say that if we were with men, you sexist prick! Fuck off and die!' She didn't stop screaming abuse, despite Babs imploring, 'Easy, Fran, take it easy!', until another passenger called the (male) guard, upon which Frannie turned fey and fluttery, cranking out a credible impression of a helpless little girl pig – and I choose my words advisedly – being set upon by the Big Bad Wolf.

Now *that* is angry.

And I'm not like that! I'm well-mannered. I'm controlled. I'm in control. Or at least, I was until my life started to unravel like a cheap jumper. Look at me! Troughing chocolate like a . . . a – my mother. I curl my lip. She has no dignity where chocolate is concerned. She can't resist it. She's a junkie. I remember when Babs's parents invited us for supper, weeks after Dad left. My mother ostentatiously refused dessert, then cut nineteen 'tiny slivers' off the chocolate cake like a bad carpenter shaving wood off a door, until a 'tiny sliver' of cake remained. She then exclaimed to Mrs Edwards – who'd eaten one modest slice with her espresso, *finito* – 'Jackie! You're so lucky with your figure!'

I can't understand how this happened. I lean against the bath and backtrack through my decline. Feeding frenzy – after months of strictly monitoring my intake – prompted by it all going wrong with Simon, then Chris, then Andy.

Oh dear, is it all about men with me? It can't be. No. It isn't. The Simon fiasco was a mere footnote to my friendship with Babs. Which faltered a while back. Around the time Babs met Simon and I went on a diet. Did I feel angry then? I don't recall feeling anything. Stunned, perhaps. Wretched in the presence of a couple so smoochily, blatantly, shamelessly in love. When I was with *Saul*. A decent guy, yes, but not the sensitive brute I imagined for myself. Then I met Chris – the relationship equivalent of piercing my tongue – and threw away my job.

What a mess. Yet as far as I can see, it all comes back to Babs. What do I feel for her? Admiration. Respect. Love. I adore Babs. Except, it's hard to love someone quite so heartily when their taut shiny life reflects the bumps and scratches in your own. But then, that's your problem, not theirs. I've been taking my problem out on Babs. I've been sullen with her. How embarrassing. I've acted as if she was in emotional debt to me for being happier than *I* was. Like she owed me a love life. Well, thanks to my excruciating behaviour, now I owe her. She thought I was angry. She said it, when she had a go at me for losing weight. I must be angry, then.

My head shrinks into my neck like a turtle retreating into its shell. Anger is one of the worst ways of losing control. It's primitive. Anger is such an unbecoming emotion. It makes you ugly. It turns ears red and tips of noses white, it flares nostrils so the hairs show, it squeezes sweat from skin – water and urea – an all-over wee. Sometimes when you're angry, you spit without realising. Unlike, say, when you're afraid: your eyes widen prettily and your chest heaves, tricking onlookers into thinking your bust is bigger and more bouncy than it actually is. Or when you feel joy, which might bless you with dimples and a glowing complexion.

I shudder. I mean, this is like Liberace being told he's a repressed breeder. I feel a peculiar urge to visit my mother. She's great when you're miserable. She won't stand for it.

She says, 'Nonsense, dear!' and harasses you into jollity, even if you're in a subdued mood because *she* put you there. She'd never scold you directly, but get too exuberant and the aura of reproach was like an ice cube down your back. You'd be crushed. Instantly, she'd burst into life, bolstering, cajoling, nursing you into a good humour again.

That's what I need. I heave myself off the floor, and plod to the phone. 'Mum?'

'Hello, dear! I've been trying to call you all day! I was frantic! Are you okay? What's wrong?'

'No, no, nothing, sorry, I'm fine thanks, how are you?'

'I'm all of a flutter, since you ask! When did we last speak? I know you've been busy, dear, I didn't want to disturb you, I don't like to interfere, make a nuisance of myself, you know that, but I've got so much news, so much has happened, I'm all in a spin!'

Could it be that Waitrose have rearranged their poultry shelves?

'Mum,' I sigh. 'Please don't say that, you know you're not a nuisance. You sound differ— you sound great. You'll have to tell me all about it. I was going to say, can I come over?'

'Now? Of course, my pleasure! Silly girl, you don't need to ask! Have you eaten?'

'Oh, er, I—'

'I've got some bits and pieces in the fridge, I'll put them out, and you can take what you want. I've got a lovely bit of lemon sole, fresh from the fishmonger, it's never quite the same from the supermarket, I could poach it for you if you like, why don't I do that?'

I take a deep breath and put her off poaching the fish as diplomatically as I can, then say goodbye and feel terrible. She sounds so horribly honoured to hear from me, as if I'm the lady of the manor deigning to call the servant at home. I fluff my hair about my face and put on my bulkiest cable-knit to stave off the 'you look so thin' onslaught. Maybe I should stick a pillow up my jumper? Even though I feel enormous. The two pounds I've gained aren't me, I feel like a kangaroo carrying a marmoset in its pouch. I drive to Hendon fast, and park in front of the feathery fan of pampas grass that my mother is so proud of (bizarrely, she believes it lends the front garden 'an Egyptian quality').

My mother opens the door before I ring it – doesn't she ever remove that apron? – and enfolds me in a light hug (neck and upper chest touching, bosoms and lower bodies demurely apart). She releases me after two seconds then as I rear back, exerts a sudden slight pressure on my back, which I take to mean 'stay right where you are'. I freeze, as her hands squeeze my shoulders and upper arms – pinchily proprietorial – and she lets me go. I smile, uncertain. Do I meet requirements?

'I'm sorry I haven't rung in the last few days,' I say, to fill the quiet. 'I kept meaning to. So, so what's the big news?'

'Come into the kitchen,' replies my mother, beaming, suddenly. 'Are you sure you won't have something to eat? Just a nibble?'

'What I'd really love is a cup of peppermint tea,' I say brightly, watching her hopes rise and fall.

My mother switches on the kettle, bustles over to the side, places the biscuit tin on the table, and draws up a chair. All the while she smiles and hums. ('*Sweet Home Alabama*', Lynyrd Skynyrd). I am agog. Her favoured style is 'downtrodden', but today she is positively jaunty. I wonder if she's OD'd on the Diet Coke. Or trounced the opposition at Weight Watchers. She clasps her hands and grimaces at her lap, and I realise with dismay that there are tears in her eyes. Will she take offence if I ask her what's wrong? I am steeling myself to make a possible blunder when my mother declares in a tremulous voice, 'Today I spoke to my granddaughter.'

'Tara?' I gasp.

'Yes! Why, are there any others I should know about?'

quips my mother. As she tends to treat jokes with the suspicion that most people reserve for slavering dogs, this verbal frivolity suggests the extent of her delight.

'Oh Mum!' I whisper. 'What happened, what did she say?'

My mother turns away in a quick, practised move and sniffs. Then in a matter-of-fact tone, she declares, 'Your brother showed me all the letters and cards he's received over the years. And the pictures. He keeps them in his kitchen drawer. The number was there – to ring – but I decided it would be more prudent to write. It doesn't take long for a letter to reach Australia these days. Kelly rang me this morning – at 7 a.m.! – five in the evening, her time, she would have received my letter that morning. I knew who it was. We . . . we spoke for seventeen minutes. She's an artist. She has her own little gallery. A soft-spoken young lady, knows her own mind – you can tell, and then she put Tara on, she has the same – it took my breath away – exactly the same *energy* that Tony has, had at her age, a very friendly exuberant little girl, very direct, terribly grown up. She likes body surfing and computer games, she told me. And she recently finished with her boyfriend. At the age of eleven!'

I stare eagerly at my mother, and nod for her to continue. She smiles.

'And then what?' I say.

My mother looks thoughtful, as if searching for something. 'Tara wanted me to email her a photograph of myself,' she replies. 'But I wouldn't know how. I said I'd have to have one done, and then I'd have to post it.'

'I could help you with that if you like. What else did she say?'

'She wanted to know if it was raining here. And if she should call me "Grandma". She calls her maternal grand-mother "Elizabeth". Imagine that!' My mother's voice has dropped to a husk. If I didn't know her like I do, I'd shout: But what was it *like*, to speak to your granddaughter for the first time, how did it feel to hear her voice, to be addressed, for the first time in your life, as Grandma? What else did you talk about? You must be ecstatic, angry, delirious, mournful, joyful – a tutti-frutti of emotions!

But because she's my mother and I'm me, I don't ask. All I say is, 'Will you – will you – would you be seeing Tara and Kelly at some point?'

My mother clears her throat and declares, 'Australia is quite a long way away, and the flights are fairly dear.'

The use of 'quite' and 'fairly' tells me that she has been investigating the price and time of air travel from London to Sydney since roughly 7.25 this morning, and so has had a good fourteen hours to minimise the cost and distance in her head. For one silly second, I want to throw myself on the floor and blub.

I am brought to my senses by my mother saying briskly, 'I'm not used to all this palaver, I feel quite worn out. And you look terrible, as usual. You must eat more, Natalie, you're looking ill.' This is a clear sign that the dangerously emotive subject of newfound grandchildren is now closed, at least for today.

'It's been a difficult week, Mum,' I say. 'But I have been eating more. I've been' – I try not to wince as I parrot a favourite expression back to her – 'trying to feed myself up.'

My mother sighs in blatant disbelief. 'Martin was disappointed not to hear from you,' she murmurs. 'I know Eeesy-Kleen wasn't ideal but I was only trying to help. I don't suppose you've thought any more about what you're going to do?'

I am considering how to answer this question and not precipitate a silence, when the phone rings. My mother, whose relationship with the phone is one more commonly encountered in sixteen-year-old girls, races to it. 'Hello?' she says breathlessly, then 'Jackie! *Pronto!* How lovely to hear from you! I know, you've been at the deli all day, don't worry, I understand, yes, oh yes, that would be lovely, I'd love to pop in tomorrow, what time? Five-thirty, fine. How are you, how's Robert? And the children? Mind you, I hardly need to ask, I've got Natalie standing right here, she can update me on both of them!'

Mrs Edwards has a deep, sonorous voice, and while my mother presses the receiver tight to her ear, Jackie's every word is clearly audible. She asks how I am. I feel myself blush.

My mother clicks to her default setting of wringy-handed mode. 'Not too good,' she declares sorrowfully, her eyes running over me yet avoiding mine. 'Still painfully thin, but what can you do, she won't listen to me, I've tried everything' – hang on, I think, I've gained two whole wobbling pounds of flesh here, talk about ungrateful – 'And what's more, the ballet company gave her the elbow. It's all so upsetting. Jobs are so hard to come by these days. I found a position for her in my friend's dry cleaner but no, no she wouldn't hear of it. I realise it was hardly ideal but surely it's better than *nothing*? Oh Jackie, do you think Natalie will get another job? You know I do worry.'

Purely so as not to run out the door, I employ my Pilates breathing technique (same as normal breathing except each breath lasts five times as long, thus after you've slowly expelled one lungful of carbon dioxide, the possibility of suffocation is so grippingly imminent you swiftly forget all secondary concerns). I take a deep desperate gasping gulp of air and nearly miss Jackie's reply. Happily, her words are emphatic enough to penetrate the wind-suck.

'Of course Natalie will get a job!' she booms. 'She will get a wonderful job, she is such a clever girl! Sheila, it is crazy to worry, you must have faith in her! Ah! *Uno momento*, Barbara is here, she wants to have a word.'

My mother's face falls and reluctantly she passes me her precious phone. I stare at it, in terror. 'Take it,' exclaims my mother, waving the receiver like a rattle. 'It won't bite you!'

Chapter 30

Guilt is a punishment aperitif. A sort of miserable-to-be-going-on-with, until the full-blown three-course punishment is served. It makes you rue the day before the day even arrives.

When my mother hands me the phone, I know the game is up. My legs go floppy and I have to sit down (thank heaven for my mother's hallway pride and joy – a gaudily upholstered Louis XIV chair from John Lewis). If only I was . . . that china basket full of china posies over there, if only I *enjoyed* confrontation: some people relish it – to me, that's like enjoying your own execution. Or sitting through an evening of experimental dance.

'B – Babs?' I stammer, as the nausea laps at my throat.

'Natalie,' says Babs. At her stony tone my entire digestive tract spasms in fear. It's like an anaconda squeezing a goat to death in there.

'Yes?' I croak.

I hear Babs take a deep breath. Then she says, 'I'm very angry with you.'

My stomach heaves and I drop the phone and speed to the toilet – 'We don't say "loo" in this house!' – and gag and gag until there is nothing left to eject.

'Natalie! Are you okay?' shouts my mother, rapping gently on the door.

'Fine,' I gurgle.

'Babs says to phone her when you're feeling better,' bawls my mother. 'Would you like me to call Dr Eastgate?'

'No thanks,' I squeak, wondering if 'when you're feeling

better' is code for *'when you've atoned for your crime'*.

I stagger out of the toilet three minutes later, trembling. Andy must have stropped straight round and told her. My mother feels my forehead and tuts. 'You're all clammy. You must be sickening for something. I *knew* you weren't well. I think you should go straight to bed. Why don't you sleep here? Your bed's made, and I don't feel comfortable with you driving home in this state.'

Normally, the thought of sleeping in my old bedroom would not appeal. My mother hasn't redecorated and it remains cloyingly pink and frilly: the lacy eiderdown, the neat row of bears and Barbies, the doll's house, the tea set, the play cooker, the Sleeping Beauty nightlight, the Enid Blytons – a spooky shrine to Natalie Miller aged seven, as if I'd died in a car crash.

Even spookier, all evidence of my teenage self has been silently removed – the Duran Duran posters, gone, replaced by a Holly Hobbie height chart, my modest collection of nail varnish, vanished, replaced by a clutch of pottery animals, the sort you once got free with petrol. She must have ransacked the attic one wet weekend after watching *Changing Rooms* – her mission, to return my childhood possessions to their original home. Tony's bedroom received the same treatment (blue decor, toy trains, Lego, Scalextric, plastic guns, cowboy hat, water pistols, etc – all intact.) As Babs would say: Ker-eepy!

And Babs is the reason that I am delighted to accept my mother's kind invitation. If I go home Babs might bash the door down – it's her *job* - except she won't have to because her brother has a key. I shudder. For a capitalist turned hippy turned loud emotional incontinent, Andy is a force to be reckoned with. Or, in my case, to be avoided.

'If you need something to wear, your Snow White nightdress is under the pillow,' trills my mother as I climb the stairs. Then, quietly to herself, 'And it'll still fit, more's the pity.' And louder, to me, 'Shall I bring up a mug of Horlicks?'

'Yes, okay,' I say, planning to tip it down the sink.

I switch on the pink lightbulb, which transforms the room into either a fairy grotto or a cheap brothel. I slowly undress, wash my face, and crawl into my ludicrously soft bed and close my eyes. It's strange to be in a single bed again, I feel like I'm lying in a luxury open coffin. I decide not to add to the illusion by putting on the Snow White nightie.

As it happens, I develop a violent migraine and stay in bed till Friday. The day that Matt assigned for my farewell drink. He suggested we meet outside the Coliseum at 4 p.m. and that I 'keep the rest of the afternoon free in case it turns nasty.' This is not a problem as, currently, all my afternoons are free for the rest of my life. I ring him to check it's still OK with *him*. 'Front of house, at four, unless you're standing me up,' he says. I smile for the first time in days.

I should also ring Babs. I know I should, but I physically cannot. It's like that moment with a home sugaring kit, where your bikini line is smothered in sticky gunk, the cotton strip is smoothed over it, there's no way out, you're braced to rip a forest of hardcore hair out of its roots and and and – your arm refuses to budge. Of course it does! It knows that to obey the mad brain order: 'jerk sharply backwards' will cause intense eye-watering pain. It's deserted the obviously defective mother ship to exercise independent sense.

So I don't ring. To ring Babs would be suicide! Fight or flight? What rubbish, there's no option! I'm surprised I wasn't born with wings. Babs has always told me off for being self-destructive, and my decision is a glowing example of how far I've progressed. Or so I tell myself. In fact, I am a porridge of angst. I think, call her, go on, call her, and my heart shrivels and I don't. I can't bear to face up to what she thinks of me. Maybe I'll write a letter.

Matt takes one look at me and pronounces me the image

of heroin chic. I'm pleased, until he adds, 'Put some weight on, girl.' I scowl and tell him I've had a bug. Then I bend to pat Paws, and feel a potato-like object – my brain perhaps – roll ominously towards the front of my cranium. I hurriedly stand straight again. 'Are, er, Belinda and Mel not coming?'

'Don't be daft,' says Matt. 'They've got some things to sort out. They'll join us in the pub in a few minutes.' I nod, and try not to wonder at the irony of being booted out then having my ignoble departure joyously toasted. But as we troop down the road to the Chandos, the ridiculous nature of the situation booms louder and louder in my head until I'm mute with humiliation and unable to think of a word, let alone say it. (Not strictly true – I could ask, 'So, has Paws had any ear infections lately?' but even I have some pride.)

'What's the problem?' demands Matt.

I give him a look. 'Which one?'

He grins, as I hand him a Budvar. 'I knew it had to be more than a bug. Tell Auntie Matt all about it. By the way, Stephen loved the book. He sends a big kiss.'

'I send it back, if you know what I mean.'

We slide into a booth, and I pick a problem. Not the Babs one, it's too private, too raw. Tony? What the hell. I tell him about Tony. His eyes pop, and every so often he squawks, 'Blimey!' I don't want to burden him with the full weight of my woes, so I also tell him about the Ikkle Lambkin/ Big Daddy Bear exchange. He nearly ruptures laughing. 'She's an exhibitionist,' he gasps, 'but that's obscene!' Then he adds, 'As for your brother, someone wants to be a dad more than they let on.'

'They do?'

'Natalia, what else do you think all that googly woogly stuff is about?'

'I thought it was about trying to repulse by-standers.'

'Darling. A basic psychology lesson. There are all sorts of roles one fulfils in a relationship, and being a parent to

262

your lover is one of them.' I try not to look stupid. 'Partly,' Matt continues, 'because one's biological parents tend to botch the job, so we search for a partner who can fix their mistakes. It's a secondary concern, obviously, as our primary quest is for a partner who isn't a founder member of the kennel club. Paws, you didn't hear that. You ever met Mel's parents, Nat?'

I shake my head.

'Her mother is Bronwen West. Now *she* was an exceptional dancer. Mel can put on a show but, well, there's no comparison. Or rather, unfortunately, there is. As for Mr Pritchard – not what you call a hands-on dad. Threw a lot of money at her, got her into ballet school, presumed his job done.'

'I didn't know any of this. Poor Mel.'

'Not at all,' declares Freud, draining his Budvar. 'Clara has found her Drosselmeyer, and Tony likes being a daddy more than he thinks he does.'

I jump, guiltily, as a figure in a fifties screen siren coat smacks a hand on the table and crows, 'It's all sorted!'

'Belly!' says Matt.

Belinda smiles, and I thank *God* my name isn't Belinda, the trauma of 'Belly' would have me hospitalised by now. She slides into the booth and in the name of decency (although it's a bit late now) Matt and I abandon our dissection of Mel and Tony's relationship.

'I've missed you, Bel,' I say. 'Shielding me from friends and family. I don't suppose anyone's rung for me? Anyone who doesn't know I've, er, left?'

Belinda looks heavenward, in a parody of deep thought. 'Ooh, no, not as I recall.'

'If there *were* any messages, might you' – I say the words, knowing their futility – 'have written them down?'

Belinda grins. 'Yeah right!' Matt arches an eyebrow and she deletes the grin. 'I would of, if there were any,' she says. 'But I aven't, so there couldn't of been.'

Silence falls as we ponder this, until Mel bursts in –

263

freezing briefly at the door so that everyone can admire –
walks over, an elegant duck, and starts talking. Last night
– saw the Kirov – *Swan Lake* – and oh! – feels like a buffalo
– all so tiny, so slender, no muscle bulking, the girls – steel
wires ('thteel wireth'), so strong, so well-rehearsed –
GLBallet – never given time to rehearse – and the *corps*! –
like watching a ballet through a kaleidoscope – the lines,
immaculate – not a toe out of place, not a wobble –
apparently drilled, poked with sticks, from the age of seven
– the elegance – drummed in – the GLBallet, dumplings,
amateurs – this pain in her back – murderous, and
GLBallet – doing *Swan Lake* in July – the nerve to follow
the Kirov! – costume – a white all in one – horrifying, you
look ten times fatter – ridiculous that the GLB doesn't have
a full-time Pilates coach – needs to trim her thighs – so
selfish, Julietta – a private coach—

'I know a Pilates teacher!' I cry, thrilled to be of use. 'She
teaches at my gym.'

'Doeth she teach privately? I can't train with ordinary
people. But I need to de-bulk and Pilates is the best way.'

'Is it? I mean, you don't sweat that much.'

'Natalie. It streamlines, it elongates the muscles! That's
why dancers do Pilates!'

'I thought it was to help them recover from injury,' I say
humbly, using my Pilates breathing technique to take an
efficient drag of nicotine. I'm pleased. I shouldn't say it. But
it's like discovering that smoking is good for you.

'You two do not need debulking,' growls Matt. 'You're
as bulky as a pair of pipecleaners. You make old Belly here
look like a prize heifer, no offence, Belly.'

Belinda – henceforth known as Miss Rhino-Hide –
cackles.

'Belly,' coos Mel. 'What's the time? I've got to warm up
for, you know.'

Belinda glances at her watch. 'Five thirty. I'll come with
ya.' They kiss me goodbye, and leave.

Matt says, 'I'd better get back too.' He pauses. 'You

wouldn't do me a huge favour and look after Paws for ten minutes? I've got some running around to do.' I hesitate. 'Rehearsal's over by now,' he adds. 'The place'll be empty.'

'Of course,' I reply. 'No problem.' We trot back to the Coliseum. When I become aware that we are clicking along the road in foolish unison, I give in and bleat, 'So, has Paws had any ear infections lately?' (I'm rewarded with the gratifying answer, 'Yes, two.')

I sit in row E of the deserted auditorium, and Paws – blithely unaware of our dual illegality – falls asleep. The stage is bare, and the blue material on the seat in front of me is worn through. The place is so much smaller empty. But I can't suppress a shiver of excitement. It's a house of dreams. I look at the ceiling. Beige and blue. A bit like my colour scheme at—

The stage lights shine, and the silence is broken by a pianist striking up a suite from *The Nutcracker*. I recognise it as the build-up to the Sugar Plum Fairy's solo. I gulp, and shrink in my seat. The last thing I want is to come face to face with Julietta. Matt promised me rehearsals were over. I stare, torn between enchantment and dismay, as a porcelain figure glides to centre stage in full luscious costume: a deep fuchsia tutu, its stiff frilly layers paling to the lightest pink, white tights, pink satin pointe shoes, and a starry tiara. I sit bolt upright. Mel! It's *Mel*. She looks straight at me, stretches out an arm, smiles, and curtseys.

The gesture is universal. *This is for you.* Confused, I glance at the pianist. Belinda! I didn't even know she could *play* the piano! I can't help it. The tears spill. This music is a kiss of life to the soul. And Mel is magical. For once, she escapes detachment and loses herself to the passion. She glides, weightless, joyful, she seems to hang in the air, her every move as smooth as syrup. I can practically feel the heat off her. I start, as a male dancer in a turquoise headscarf bounds on to stage – for a millisecond I think *Oskar?* Matt!

Matt as the Nutcracker Prince, squeezed into a crimson

velvet and gold brocade jacket, and wearing – judging from his turnip-like crotch bulge – approximately five jockstraps under his tights. His haughty expression as he flings himself about like an ungainly mountain goat is the *spit* of Oskar – whose exquisite talent is a squeak less breath-taking than his superiority complex. Mel's sweet saintly smile, as he hauls her into the air like a sack of celery, doesn't falter. I laugh so hard that Paws wakes up with a jerk.

'That' I say afterwards, hugging them all, 'is without doubt the nicest thing that anyone has done for me, ever, in my entire life.'

Belinda blushes beet, and even Matt looks bashful. Mel cries, 'We wanted to give you a special treat, and it was *my* idea – I thought of it!'

'It was a brilliant idea, Mel,' I say. 'And you're a stunning, stunning dancer. And Bel's piano-playing is amazing! As for you,' I add, turning to the Nutcracker Prince, 'is there no beginning to your talent?'

Matt cuffs me round the head. 'Cheeky cow. Now, go on – disappear, before I start getting emotional. It's Friday night in an hour. I'm sure you have a host of wild parties to attend.'

They wave me off at the stage door. I skip to the tube. Wild parties indeed. I am not a party animal. What *is* a party animal anyway? Paws in a bandanna? I sit on the train, grinning – despite being pinned between a huge American woman and a man whose legs are sprawled so wide they're practically 180 degrees. That's an impressive turn out, and I want to ask if he's a professional dancer. Actually, I want to say, 'Shut your legs, you're on public transport, not relaxing at home on your sofa, and you're squashing me to death!'

Tony – an arch sprawler – believes that if you want a space in this world you must fight for it. That said, he dislikes women sprawling on the tube, as it makes them look 'like slappers'. He once made the mistake (on purpose) of recounting this prejudice to Frannie, who replied – to his grinning face – that it was 'Yet more depressing evidence of a primitive and unhewn mind.' What was it she said about dieting? Something about sanctioning my own repression. But right now I don't feel repressed. I think of this afternoon's performance and, in the soppiest, silliest, girliest, frilliest way, I feel good. I widen my legs an inch.

My mood only dips when I reach home. My flat is dark and silent. I don't shout 'Anyone there?' like shortlived people do in horror films. I knock on Andy's door and slowly, warily, boot it open, as if a bat might fly out. The room is bare, except for the glitterball. No bats either. I shut the door again. I plod into the bathroom. The spare shelf is empty. I inhale deeply. A faint lemony scent of aftershave lingers. I march to the window and heave it open. The cold air gusts in, blowing every last trace of Clinique Chemistry from the premises. 'That's right, piss off,' I say. I sweep into the hall, and when the phone rings, I pick it up without thought, like a mother would a crying baby.

'Hello?' I say, thinking, *damn*.

'Nat?'

Noooooooooooooooooo! 'Yes,' I say sadly.

'It's Babs, you dipstick! I can't believe you didn't call me back! I'm *so* angry with you!'

Chapter 31

Once, I sent Babs to the video shop to rent a 'chick flick' and she returned with *Joan of Arc*. 'It's got history, it's got period costumes, it's got a bird in it!' she cried, when she saw my disappointment. 'What more do you want?'

'It's about FIGHTING!' I bawled. I'd assumed my meaning was obvious to her. I suppose I always do. She knows me so well, it's a surprise when she *doesn't* read my mind. Especially when my thoughts are as guilty as they are now. I am about to cry: We weren't really kissing – Simon was drunk! when Babs adds, 'You're so secretive, why didn't you tell me you were looking for work?'

My jaw drops. The mindwarp is similar to hearing a cat growl. Finally, I stammer, 'What do you mean?'

'I mean,' cries Babs, 'that I'm at my parents' and I hear my mum yapping to Sheila about you having to go and work in a dry cleaner's and not wanting to, when I thought it was all sorted, that you were all set up to be a freelance PR. You're very naughty! When we had that talk about – you know – marriage the other night, you didn't say a word about it.'

I swallow. Think, Natalie, think. He can't have told her. Frannie can't have told her. This is my chance. I open my mouth and the words that emerge are, 'Well, the night we had that talk about, about marriage, was the night we, er, talked about marriage. I didn't think it was right to be bringing up the subject of um, dry cleaners.'

Babs laughs. 'So you're not continuing with PR?'

'Half,' I say. 'I'll be writing a few press releases, that's all

– it doesn't really amount to being a PR. But I don't mind. I've gone off it.'

'So what *are* you going to do?'

'I don't know. I hadn't thought.'

'I knew it!' cries Babs. 'Frozen with indecision! So I thought of something you might like to do, for now, which wouldn't pay that much but would be more of a party than steaming shirts all day. Guess.'

'No idea,' I bleat. I wipe the liquid guilt off my forehead and wonder what the hell has happened to make her so chirpy. I thought she was on the brink of divorce?

'You could – and this is just a suggestion, yeah? – work at the deli!'

'Your *parents*' deli?' I squeak. I'd have been less surprised if she'd suggested I join the Fire Brigade.

'No,' says Babs, 'Sainsbury's deli.'

I can't reply. Me, in a deli? That's like asking a chicken to guard a fox! Good grief, it would be horrible! I'd be surrounded by food ten hours a day! And I can no longer trust myself to resist! I've lapsed! My will has wilted! I'm off the wagon! And I'd be working for Babs's parents! They'd be urging me to eat constantly! I'd be a chick in the nest having worms poked down its throat! I might as well pack my bags and go straight to the clinic.

I say, 'What a kind idea.'

Babs beams down the phone, I can hear it in her voice. 'You really helped the other night. Sounding off to you was like therapy, I feel I've sorted my head out. I think Si felt something was up. I think he sensed I'd called time. I didn't even have to say anything. Get this – the last few days he's got home on time, he bought me flowers, he *cooked* for me – he's more cordon bleugh than cordon bleu but who cares – and he sat down on the bed this morning and said he was sorry he'd gone awol but it was pressure at work and he knows he's taken it out on me and he's deeply sorry, he wants to do right by me. And – guess what – he's taking me to Prague for the weekend! *Prague!* Tonight! For the weekend! We're off to the airport in ten minutes!' Here her voice dips to a whisper: 'Si's packing in the bedroom! I don't actually believe him – about the pressure at work bit – but I, I feel optimistic. Like there's a proper chance that we could work things out. Weird, isn't it, that a relationship can become work?'

'In my experience,' I croak, 'it's work from the minute he spies you across the room and you sit up straight and hold your stomach in.'

Babs giggles and says, 'No that's just you, sweetheart. So what do you think?'

'I think it – mm, bodes well,' I say slowly, thinking, gosh, maybe I *did* (in the least desirable, most ham-fisted way possible) help her marriage.

'We still need to talk about the Captain Caveman problem,' she adds. 'But all in good time, as Dad says. God, I hate it when I find myself quoting my parents. Anyway, look, if you're interested in helping out at the deli, the offer's open, maybe call my mum over the weekend, you know what my parents are like – laid back isn't the word – you could start next week if you want. But, no pressure, it's just that you helped me out. I wanted to do the same for you. Anyway, look, I gotta go, we'll speak, Nat. Ba!'

'Ba,' I say, to thin air.

I walk unsteadily into the kitchen. 'Failed again,' I announce to the kettle.

The trouble with me is, I am not a good *explainer*. I'm so busy thinking 'Don't say X' that I say it. So I suffer in silence because if I spoke up I'd suffer more. And so would Babs. I've just started to sweep the kitchen floor – I feel better when the flat's in order – and the doorbell rings. Like all good city girls, my Pavlovian reflex applies only to the phone. I distrust anyone who has the nerve to show up in person. I squint through the fisheye and jump backwards. What's *he* doing here? Am I to be frogmarched to his sister and forced to confess? I make a rude face, briefly, to relieve tension, then paste on a smile and open the door.

'I forgot my iron,' declares Andy in a false bright voice, addressing the door frame. 'I didn't think you'd be home yet. I was going to get it and go. I also forgot to leave the keys.'

Stiffly, I hold open the door and, stiffly, he walks in. Clinique Chemistry, crumpled T-shirt, crumpled jeans. He did forget his iron. I can tell he wants to speak and I don't want to hear it. So I blather, 'I haven't spoken to Babs yet, she actually just rang, I would have told her but she didn't give me a chance. They're off to Prague.' I want to add: Please don't look at me like that.

Andy shoves his hands into his pockets. He looks as happy as an ant in a wasps' nest. Then he says, 'I feel like a wally, now I've spoken to Simon. I—'

'You spoke to Simon?' I cry, pleased that I am not alone in blurting out squirmworthy words at fretful moments. *Wally?* – hello, Mr 1984!

'Yeah.' Andy removes his hands from his pockets and fiddles with a loose thread on his jeans. 'What a tosser. I wanted to deck him.' My eyebrows nearly shoot off my head. 'I didn't though,' he adds. 'You know Babs. If she thinks he deserves a smack, she'll deliver it herself.'

'Babs knows? But just now, she, she acted like—'

'No no no, Christ, I haven't told Babs! *Simon's* going to tell her.'

'When?' I resist the urge to scream: Aaaaaaaaaaaaaah!

Andy sticks out his lower lip. 'He said he'd tell her as soon as he got the chance. So tonight, I reckon, or over the weekend.'

He says every word like he doesn't want to part with it. He has no idea of what constitutes the *meat* of a story. I feel like an inept zoo keeper trying to make a chimp share a banana. I curl my fists to stop myself from shaking him. 'And is he – will he' – I light a cigarette and drag deeply – 'do you know what he's planning to tell her about *me?*'

Andy replies, 'He's going to tell Babs that he leapt on a

271

woman when he was drunk. He thinks it'd be better that way. I suppose it makes sense. Simon reckons that who he kissed is irrelevant.'

Men. I love it. 'Irrelevant'!

'If' – Andy nods at me and makes an abortive attempt at a smile – '*you* want to tell Babs the rest, it's your choice. Simon admits it was his fault. He said what happened – it sounded disgusting. He was disgusted with himself. And not just about the despicable way he's treated Babs. You could have had him up for assault! He knows that.' Andy looks me in the eye for the first time. 'I really feel bad about shouting at you, Natalie. I'm sorry. The way Frannie told it – it was a different story. I, well, it's obvious, I didn't forget the iron.'

I heave a huge, Pilates-enabled sigh of relief, and say graciously, 'Not that obvious. Don't worry about it. But, do you think he – Simon – means it? Babs is going to be so, so hurt. It's going to be torture for her.'

Andy sighs. 'I don't know. He told me he was committed. He said he was just scared of marriage. He's going to be honest and hope she'll let him start again. What can I say? He's a scumbag, but I can't get involved, more than I already have. *I* can't make him behave, though I'd like to. It's humiliating enough for her as it is. They've got to sort it out between them. They're adults.'

'Mm,' I say. 'You're right.'

There is a long silence, during which I think to myself: You've done enough meddling to put Scooby Doo to shame, you're lucky to have escaped intact. Now leave them to it.

I smile awkwardly at Andy, testing the idea that he's no longer angry with me. I feel I should say something, but Andy speaks first. 'Oh yeah. The other day. When I was packing my things. This woman called round. Henrietta.'

I frown. 'I don't know anyone called Henrietta. What did she look like?'

272

Andy grins – a proper eyes-involved grin. '*Vey* smart,' he says, in a clipped Home Counties tone. 'Very jolly hockey sticks. Had a laugh like a seal. Sensible skirt, Barbour, pink jumper, and a brooch.'

'A brooch!' I boom in disbelief. 'How old was this woman?'

Andy wrinkles his nose. 'I don't know – mid-thirties?'

'Mid-thirties? She sounds more like late fifties. She doesn't sound like anyone I know. Not even a friend of my mother. Did she ask for me by name?'

Andy seems to be holding back a laugh. 'No, actually, no,' he says. 'But she did know you.'

'How?'

'You know her brother.'

'Really?'

'Apparently,' continues Andy, 'he's not very good at ringing home. "Mummy and Daddy get terribly concerned. And what with Daddy's blood pressure it can all turn rather frightful. *Fraightful*." This was one of two addresses she had for him, she was in London for a craft fair, thought she'd surprise him.'

'Craft fair? And I know her *brother*? Are you sure she didn't want the downstairs flat?'

'Nah,' says Andy, who patently finds my confusion hilarious. 'Definitely this one.'

'OK,' I say, knowing I'm being set up. 'So this brother I'm supposed to know so well. What's his name?'

Andy starts giggling. He giggles so hard it takes him a good minute to spit the words out. 'His name,' he sniggers, struggling for breath, 'is Chris.'

'Chris?' I start to laugh myself. 'Chris – Blue Veined Chris!?'

'Happily, I've no idea, but – yes!'

'But,' I choke, 'but – but – Chris is . . .'

'Chris is "me old man worked down the mine, me mam's a dinner lady, I'm a Manc, me, I'm workin' class, do yeh want a sausage for yeh tea!"' booms Andy. 'Or, to call him by his true and delightful given name' – Andy does a little chat show tap dance as if to herald the entrance of a bright new star – 'Crrrrispian!'

Chapter 32

We laugh, self-consciously at first, then louder; it's infectious, like chickenpox. We laugh until we're laughing so hard I feel it would be a pity to stop. Also, I don't want to be the party pooper. I keep thinking of the high-ranking official at a Nazi rally who after a twenty-minute standing ovation for Hitler decided his palms were sore, enough was enough, and sat down. I'm not suggesting that if I cease cackling Andy will have me shot, but I don't want to offend him.

Just as I'm starting to fret, Andy comes to my rescue: he shakes his head and grabs a chair, his laughter subsiding to a snigger, then a smirk. I breathe a secret sigh of relief, and join him at the table. 'Do you want a drink?' I say politely. 'Or do you have to go?'

Andy hesitates. 'Well, if you've got a minute, I'll have a tea.'

'Minute?' I blurt, without thinking. 'I've got the whole night! I mean,' I correct hastily, 'I'm not in a rush.'

To clear up every last morsel of misunderstanding, I gabble, 'I met up with some friends from work today, I didn't know how long we'd be out, so I didn't plan anything. In the end, I got home before sex. Six! I mean, six. So when I say I've got the whole, er, night, that's what I meant.'

Shut up, says a sensible voice inside my head. I obey. I rush to the sink and fill up the kettle. Jesus Christ! Andy says nothing. As he lacks the social decorum to usher the conversation forward, I voice the first thought that wanders brainward, namely, 'It's funny how you and Babs are so *British* in your eating habits, despite your mum. Babs is hooked on tea as well, and you, ordering takeaway pizza that time, it's a – it's like mooning in the face of your roots!'

I turn round, to see Andy smiling at me. *'Bella!'* he cries in a cod-Italian accent. 'What is it-a you want-eh? My mamma, she grow up in Italia, she taste da pizza at Pizza Hut, she say, "Oh my goodness! No please!" but-a me and my sister, we live in-a Stanmore for all of our lives! We like-a da PG Tips, we like-a da Eeenglish breakfast, we don wanna be call "Spaghetti" by da children in school-eh!' Reverting to his normal voice, he says, 'Italians drink tea too, Nat. If you haven't planned to do anything tonight, does that mean you're free?'

My hand jerks and a splash of boiling water spills on to the floor. 'Oops. Yes, I am. Are, er, you?' I brace myself for the biting retort, 'No, Sad Girl, like most functioning young hipsters on a Friday night, I'm glamorously engaged, I was merely Polyfilla-ing an awkward silence.'

'My evening is a void. What would you like to do? We could get something to eat' – Andy seems to recollect himself – 'or not. We could go to the cinema, although that would be a waste, sitting in silence watching a big TV, or – I know, we could go to the Tate Modern – it's been open for years and I still haven't been and the longer I leave it, the more I feel ashamed. Like I'm less of a complete human being. Tea helps, though,' he adds, taking a sip.

'The Tate Modern!' I exclaim, 'I'd love to go there. But where is it? Isn't it on a patch of wasteland?'

'Yeah,' says Andy. 'South London.'

Two hours later, I'm culturally enriched in that I now know to avoid modern art when stepping out with a guy I find attractive but haven't yet kissed, as stumbling across videos of naked men dancing to unheard music merely

276

highlights the issue. When we retreat to the café, believe it or not, I'm glad.

I take a brazen bite of my dark chocolate tart. (Andy kept repeating, 'I'm going to have something but you don't have to,' until I felt obliged to prove my normality. Sort of like allowing Kurt Russell to test my blood for alien content in *The Thing*.) Then I sip my peppermint tea, warming my hands on the mug and – now that I'm no longer the scarlet woman who tore his family apart – tell Andy about the offer of deli work vs. the offer of dry cleaning work. Deli work is the lesser of the two evils (in that it's marginally more acceptable to the outside world) and so I'm psyching myself up to accept.

'It is, believe it or not, a laugh,' he says. 'It's like a paper round, we've all done it. It's such a friendly place. You just have to be able to put up with Mum bitching and moaning about British food and British eating habits and complaining that all the English customers demand the same sandwich day in day out, never trying something new, and always wanting to cram in fifty different fillings – salami and pastrami and cheese . . . In Italy, you stick to *one* so you can taste the flavour. It drives her mad, and she goes on and on about it.'

'Oh,' I say, smiling. 'I wouldn't mind, I've had worse than that.'

Andy takes a gulp of beer. 'So have you got anything else lined up or are you going to take it easy for a bit? You mentioned the PR work, but you said you were sick of it.'

I smile, surprised. Most of the men I know are identical in their ability to delete great chunks of information twenty seconds after you've slashed open your psyche like a pomegranate to share it with them. *My* brain clings to trivia like a bogey to a finger. Nine years ago, my first 'love' – incidentally, a bold and mocking parody of that word – mentioned the name of the guy who helped out on his parents' farm. Nine years later, the ghostly identity of 'Bunny Grimshaw', a man I've never met, never want to, and never will, continues to hop about my consciousness, occupying valuable disk space. *Why?*

'Well remembered,' I say, stunned by the realisation that I *am* sick of PR, and lighting a cigarette to help myself think. 'I'm doing it for the paltry cash, but it's not my life's dream.'

'So what is?' asks Andy, leaning forward.

I pause. The quickest way to kill a fantasy is to make it real. Oh, what the hell.

'There is,' I say, 'one thing that, well, interests me. But, it'll sound ridiculous, I'd have to train, and it would probably cost a fortune, and even then I might not be good at it, I might not get a job and my mum would be devastated.'

'Well,' says Andy. 'That's the positive side. What about the negative?'

I laugh. 'I'm just being realistic.'

Andy shakes his head. 'You haven't even told me what it *is* yet.'

I pause. 'It's, it's this thing called Pilates, it's a form of exercise but not entirely, it's very popular right now, so it would be very competitive, but I love it, I've only done it a few times, so it's a bit mad, but, if there was nothing stopping me, if I could do whatever I wanted, I think I'd like to do a course in it.'

I wait for Andy to laugh at me. Instead he says, 'Pilates, I know about that. Sasha, my ex, used to teach it. She was always banging on about it being holistic. Good for body and soul blah blah, looking at how everything functions in relation to everything else. She was always trying to force me along to a class. I think it would be *great* for you!'

I hate it when people say that. I also think, if I had a penny for every time Andy said 'Sasha, my ex', I'd have at least 15p.

'Do you?'

'Yeah,' says Andy. 'I remember her talking about one guy, a rugby player, painfully shy, and she said Pilates totally changed him, made him feel good about himself. Something about making the method fit the person. I never tried it. I'm not an exercise person. Unless I'm doing it unconsciously it makes me feel like a loser. But, er, that's just me. And I loved sivananda. But you know, you get back to London, and all your mates laugh at you. No, sod it. Natalie, you've inspired me! You do your Pilates course, and I'll enrol in a sivananda class.'

Call me narrow-minded but I don't find this deal attractive. I'm just not forward thinking. I apologise.

'OK, great!'

Andy sticks out his hand and we shake on it. 'If that's what you know you want to do, Nat, go for it. Did you get a redundancy package?' His enthusiasm is a pleasure *and* a pressure. Usually, when someone expects something of me, I become paralysed with fear of failing them and inevitably do. Then again, I react exactly the same way when someone expects nothing of me. Best not to think about that.

'Yes,' I mutter, gazing out of the window at London's darkly glittering skyline. 'I could use some of that. We'll see. Maybe I'll make some calls.' I trust these banalities will dilute his interest and glance hopefully at his beer bottle to see if it's empty. It isn't. 'Do you, er, miss Sasha still?' I blurt, desperately. I wonder if this is a *faux pas* and if I should assume the crash position.

He seems unbothered. 'Funny you should ask,' he murmurs. 'I've been thinking about her this week.'

'Don't you normally?' I ask. Good grief! I think about ex-boyfriends for years after a relationship's demise – how they're doing, how they're doing in relation to me, wishing them well but not *too* well (I'm of the opinion that it doesn't do for exes to get above themselves). The other day I caught myself wondering about Saul, hoping he was happy in his work but observing a respectful mourning period of celibacy. Now that I don't have to endure the teeth-gritting irritations of his day-to-day presence and personality, I feel increasingly fond of him.

'No,' says Andy, 'not normally.' He stops, then adds, 'Hardly ever.' I nod. 'I don't see any point.' He stops again.

I say, 'I'm increasing your word ration from five to ten.'

He laughs. 'Dear Pot, Love Kettle.' Your sister says that too, I think. 'When she left me,' he adds suddenly, 'it was the biggest shock of my life. It was like, like, your *grandparents* divorcing.'

'Or your parents,' I say.

'Yeah!' cries Andy. 'Inconceivable! Er – God, sorry.'

'Don't worry,' I reply. 'I know what you mean.'

'When Sasha went, she was very civil about it, very cool. That was what hit me. She was there physically, but as she talked I realised she'd emotionally left the relationship a while back. She'd met some bloke, she didn't want to cheat on me – that would be the worst thing, she said, as if, so long as she didn't actually screw this geezer, she wasn't cheating on me. She wanted to end it *honourably*.'

He snorts.

'What did you do?'

'Nothing. She left, I cut off. I didn't want her name mentioned. I didn't want to think about her, see her, know about her. She thought – this was the most hilarious thing – she thought that one day we could be friends! Er, *why?* You make a choice, you face the consequences. You kick someone in the teeth, you don't get a hug. You can't have it all your own way. For me, it was: you walk out that door, have a nice life. My family were supportive but I didn't need it. I had to get away. Well, more than that. I didn't feel like *me* any more. That's what it felt like. I didn't feel comfortable. Or fine. Nothing felt right. My office wasn't exactly a place where you cry about girls. So I quit the job and ran. A quit and run.' Andy smiles weakly.

'But how could you *help* thinking about her?'

Andy looks into my eyes. 'It's possible to cut out an unpleasant feeling like a cancer,' he says. 'Isn't it?'

'Y – yes,' I stammer. I add quickly, 'So, why think about her now?'

Andy grimaces. 'I thought about her after that row with you, actually. When I stormed off to have a go at Simon. I *lost* it – I went mental. I was shaking, ready to beat the shit out of him, and then I saw myself in the car mirror – it freaked me out. I just thought, this is about *Sasha*. I mean, Babs and I are close, closer than we used to be – it's better now we're older. But it hit me – the way I felt, it wasn't all about Babs, a lot of it was about me and Sash. The thing with Simon brought it back, all this crap I thought was gone. I felt like I was being cheated on. I felt more like I was being cheated on than when I *was* being cheated on!' Andy shrugs.

'Siblings,' he sighs – in what a sharp PR would recognise as a 'bridging technique' – 'What can you do, eh? So, ah, how are you' – I *knew* it! – 'and Tony getting on? Is he still creating reasons to be annoyed with you?'

What the hell, I think, for the second time this evening and, probably, in my life. I tell Andy about the Secret Lovechild Furore.

'Oh yeah,' says Andy, as I nearly fall off my seat. 'I know about that.'

'You *do*?' I croak. 'Did – did Babs tell you?'

'No,' he replies. 'Tony did. Not about you telling your mum and redecorating the walls in mash,' he adds at my incredulous face. 'I didn't know about that bit. I'm impressed. I'd like to have seen that.' He winks at me. 'It's a bloke thing. But, yeah, Tony. He told me about his daughter, soon after it – she – happened.'

It takes a supreme effort to keep my jaw shut.

'To be honest,' Andy continues, 'I thought it was pathetic. Trying to keep a secret like that. I didn't think he'd manage it. He did, though, didn't he? Only Tony. Eleven years is pretty good going. Christ, he must have been *livid* with you. It must have been the first time ever he hasn't got his own way.'

I hear myself say, in a voice like squeezed lemons, 'It wouldn't surprise me.'

Andy smiles tightly. 'I'm sure.' I drain my peppermint tea – which is now freezing and tastes like spat-out toothpaste. 'It must be tough on your mum, the news about the kid,' declares Andy – who, I am convinced, suffers from a compulsion that a satirist once described as 'speaking your brain' – 'I'm sure she's thrilled and all, but to realise what she's missed, and that Tony kept it from her – that's got to smart. She worships him, doesn't she?'

'Yes,' I say. The word slides out in a hiss. 'Apart from this . . . lapse,' I say, to compensate, 'he's always been a good son. After Dad left.'

'After Dad left?' prompts Andy. Move over, Robert Kilroy-Silk!

'She relied on him.'

'What about you?'

I feel like a cow being poked with a cattle prod. 'What about me?' I mutter. 'She didn't rely on *me*. Why should she?'

'Why shouldn't she?'

'She had Tony!' I snap. 'I just lurked in the background and tried not to upset her or get upset. It upsets my mother to see me unhappy.' I look up from painstakingly dissecting a cigarette stub, to see Andy looking cross. 'What's wrong?' I blurt.

'Nothing *you've* done!' he snaps in a voice of Tunbridge Wellsian indignation. 'I can't believe it! I mean, no offence, but – *yes*, offence! Tony can relentlessly, remorselessly carve a long and distinguished career out of upsetting everyone – which he's done for as long as I've known him – but you aren't allowed to upset anyone, you have to keep smiling! I mean, how does *that* work? What if you *were* unhappy?'

I feel a squirliness in my stomach. 'Then,' I croak, 'builders would shout, "Cheer up love, it might never happen!"'

Andy makes like Queen Victoria staring down a court jester who's just cracked a mother-in-law gag.

'Seriously.'

'Oh,' I tease, trying to keep my tone light, 'you know me. I'm easygoing. If they were happy, I was happy. Mum and Tone, I mean. Not the builders.'

'Bollocks!' shouts Andy in such a loud voice that the slate-faced woman on the next table shuffles shut her copy of the *Guardian Against Fun* and bristles off. 'I've seen your airing cupboard – it's like you're looking for army promotion. You are *not* easygoing, Natalie, you're not. I know easygoing and you're not it.'

I shrink in my chair. He touches my hand, briefly – it's cold from the beer bottle – and says, 'Nor do you strike me as madly happy.'

I feel an adrenalin surge; it's as if I'm hanging off an electric fence. 'Andy, what do you want from me? Tears? A big embarrassing girly scene?'

Andy scowls. 'Yes. *Yes.* You should make a scene. Do what you want, stop worrying about what others think. Robbie said you were terrified to turn him down, as if it wasn't your right to turn down a prat with one eyebrow. The way you talk it's like being honest is a criminal offence. I've known you, on and off, for years, and yet I don't think I've ever seen the real you. I've seen the façade. And that's not what interests me.'

My eyes develop a fault and start to leak.

I swallow hard. 'You wouldn't like the real me, I assure you.'

Andy looks put out. 'I've worked on a farm and seen less bullshit.'

I've dodged bullets long enough. I'm tired now. I surrender. 'Andy,' I sigh. 'You're right. It was miserable, it was shit, it wasn't fucking fair, of course I was unhappy, jealous, whatever you want to call it – I'm not stupid.'

I plan to make a neat sarcastic little speech but the words gather their own momentum, until they're gushing out almost faster than I can say them.

'How would *you* feel, the constant implication that you

283

were not quite what she was hoping for, like it's all been a bit of a disaster ever since you turned seven, patiently *tolerated*, every time you expressed an opinion that was inappropriate, *un*feminine – feminine! – I hate that word, it disgusts me, it's wielded like a baseball bat – oh no, but "hate" – how, how *feisty* of me, what a slut, because anger is not what good girls do – only bad girls have opinions, speak out of line, as far as *Mother* is concerned, though yes, you're right, it was different for Tony – of course I resent Tony – he did whatever the fuck he wanted and it was all perfect, and I did nothing – nothing was expected of me – jobs, flats have to be found for me, food provided, oh yeah, lucky, privileged me, it's like living in a platinum jail. I hate *me* for being like this, useless, failure, ugly, hate hate hate – hating Tony! I adore Tony, I can see why she adores him, he's everything – perfectly gorgeous, clever, successful . . .' I tail off.

'Well,' murmurs Andy, who hasn't flinched. 'That needed to be said.'

I clench my teeth, to make them behave. 'Mm,' I say.

For no reason at all I remember the first time – aged thirteen – I wore make-up. I saw Tony on the bus home from school and he screeched, 'She's wearing *lipstick!*'

'He used to call me Miss Piggy,' I say – not to communicate this to Andy, but because I've just remembered.

Andy frowns. 'But Natalie, you can't take every comment to heart. It's as if you *want* to be a victim – you won't survive! Just because people say it, doesn't mean it's right. You need' – he draws breath and I sense that a gem of Backpacker's Tao is imminent – 'to have that inner sense of self that's unreachable. Anyway, brothers call sisters all sorts of shit. I used to call Babs "Alan".'

'Alan!' I am intrigued despite myself. 'Why *Alan*?'

'Because no twelve-year-old girl wants to be called "Alan".'

'I think I'd prefer "Alan" to "Miss Piggy",' I say.

'But Miss Piggy was very glamorous. For a pig.'

'That's not how Tony meant it,' I snap.

'You weren't fat, were you?' says Andy.

'No! I was skinny, but I ate a lot, I was always hungry, that's what he meant. But he did have a thing about fat people. When Dad left, Mum put on a lot of weight. I don't know if you remember.'

Andy wrinkles his nose. 'Sort of,' he says, and I think he's being tactful until he adds, 'But she's always been roundish, hasn't she?'

'Yeah,' I say, 'but at that point she wasn't round*ish*. She was round. Tony forbade her to come to his sports day. He said she embarrassed him, because all the other mothers were thin.'

'The little gobshite! Why didn't she give him a clip round the ear!'

'It would be like the Virgin Mary attacking Christ.'

'It must hurt to feel second best with your mum,' begins Andy, and it's like he's gouging snake poison from my skin with a penknife. 'But one thing you do have – I mean, according to Babs – that Tony doesn't: you have a great relationship with your dad. Don't you?' he falters, at my thunderous face. (He asked for the real me – pinch punch, sunshine.)

'Yes,' I say, 'until he fucked off to the other side of the world. I made – I make the best of it, we get on brilliantly. Now. I adore him. Obviously, more than he loves me, or he wouldn't have buggered off the day after I turned twelve.'

Andy depresses the corners of his mouth. 'Nat,' he whispers. 'What a sad thing to say. Parents are just *people*, and the thing is, the older they get the more they act like kids – of course he loved, loves you as much as you love him. He might have stopped loving your mum, but never you. Maybe he thought it would be bad for you, for him to stay and for them to be always arguing and unhappy. He had a right to live his life.'

'They weren't unhappy!' I snap. 'They never argued! They got on fine, until he left!'

285

'Natalie,' says Andy. 'Don't you think, if they were happy, he would have stayed? You don't leave a relationship for no reason. As I know. If there was this strange veto on rows and unhappiness – what a sound reason for leaving. Shit!' he blurts. 'All I meant was, there had to be good reasons he left, which were separate from how he felt about you – and Tony.'

'You don't do that to children,' I retort, hooking my feet around my chair legs to stop myself from spinning off into the ether like a deflating balloon.

'Oh Nat,' whispers Andy. 'Did you never say?'

'What do you think?' I say, through clenched teeth. 'Excuse me.'

I leave the table, the world spins as I do, but I make it to the Ladies. I want to scream and scream (nothing personal against Tate Modern's toilets) *GET ME OUT OF HERE* but I don't. I wash my hands first – my mother would be proud – then I lock myself in a cubicle, stoop over the toilet bowl, and stick my fingers down my throat. Jab, *jab*. It's violent, vile. Jab, jab. Again. Again, againagainagain. When every last gloop of the dark chocolate tart is up and out, I feel calmer. Not cleansed – I am more polluted than ever and I can feel a hard core of calories clinging stickily to my insides – but having done penance. I scrub my hands, splash water on my face, swill out my mouth. I walk back to Andy, my heart hammering in shock, my tears in suspension at the back of my throat, my hands only a little shaky. Disgusting and messy on the inside, but civilised and presentable on the out. And – no disrespect to Andy – isn't that what matters?

Chapter 33

I attempt a pleasant expression but something has changed. I can't quite fake it. My ever-ready smile is like a mean sheet of wrapping paper applied to a bulky object.

'Are you all right?' says Andy immediately. 'Did I say the wrong thing?'

'No,' I say. 'Not at all. It's been lovely. I'm just a bit tired, that's all.'

'Oh sure,' replies Andy, his smile uncertain. ' "Lovely." Well, do you want to go? I'll drop you home, if you like.'

'It's fine, it's fine,' I plead. 'I don't want to put you out, I'll get a cab.'

Andy shrugs and doesn't offer to drive me again.

I sit in the cab and my thoughts keep knocking into each other. The more I learn about myself, the worse I get. All that pap we're fed in women's magazines about self-awareness! I can barely believe the irresponsibility of these people. It's like prescribing vodka to insomniacs. Or alcoholics. How can it benefit me to realise I hate the people I love?

I swallow and wince. My throat feels like an open wound. Oh yes, my other disgrace. I want to evaporate. Where did *that* choice new habit come from? I can't help feel I'm setting evolution back. I'm sorry but I'm not sorry. There was a brief elation, a *respite*. The gift of blankness before the guilt and loathing swamped me again. I won't be sick again though. I am not a bulimic! Those people have no self-control! I'm an organised homicidal maniac sneering at her disorganised peers. And I'm about to accept work at the crime scene! At least at the deli I'll be under observation. I suppose it's less of a risk than being at home alone with a fridge.

I pay the driver without looking at him, run into my flat, bolt the door, keel into bed, and conk out.

A virgin day. I fling the duvet aside and determine that this morning of pale sun and sharp air heralds the start of a new improved me. No more aberrations. From now on I *am* the straight and narrow. I weigh a brown portion of Sultana Bran into a bowl, add a dollop of milk, and pat a scoop of Lavazza Qualita Rossa coffee into the filter compartment of my stovetop espresso pot (a moving-in present from Andy because he couldn't stand my cafetière and its 'piss-weak coffee'). Talking of whom. He's like a dog digging up a rose bed to unearth a skull.

I exhale a puff of air through my nose, and concentrate on spooning sweet soggy cereal into my mouth without gagging. From nowhere, a memory is triggered: Babs, me and Simon, haring down Brick Lane after a night at a comedy store with Frannie, Babs crying 'I'm starving!' and screeching to a halt by the all-night bakery, Simon wolfing a hot salt beef sandwich, Babs taking a mammoth bite out of it while driving and saying, 'Ik tuck to ga oof of gy outh!' *I* hadn't eaten a thing, of course, but now I remember the tingly smell of the hot salt beef, and the pure silly pleasure Babs felt in it sticking to the roof of her mouth.

I've despised and envied people who find pleasure in food, but today I just envy them. Aiming to join them is a bit of a stretch, but this weekend I will attempt to see food as my friend.

Despite this holy intention, I am drawn like a pin to a magnet to the ugliest aspects of last night. It's all very well being drawn to ugliness, as long as you can gaze on it from a softly padded distance. Car crashes, exploding bombs, child murders – dreadfully tragic, yes yes, but nonetheless ghoulishly riveting because someone else died, not you. As my mother once declared, 'When you hear about a plane crash you think, "Good, that's that out of the way," because these things don't tend to happen in clusters.' Alas, right now, I don't have that luxury. Metaphorically, I've had both legs blown off.

Still. Andy drove me to it. A man who (might I add, *surprisingly* for one so comprehensively travelled) doesn't know the meaning of the word 'boundary'. It's the one trait he shares with Tony. But I can't be too harsh. He so plainly wanted to help. He exhibited the scarily earnest air of the do-gooder. And while I know – after a long and illuminating chat with Kimberli Ann on my phone bill – that we try to exorcise the demons of others to placate our own, it's obvious Andy was bossy in the spirit of kindness. Furthermore, what he turfed up wasn't all bad. I can now take comfort in the fact Tony never called me 'Alan'.

I smile, partly because I've finished the dead-end pilgrimage that is breakfast, and partly because I imagine Babs's reaction aged twelve on being called Alan. A name that is surely hard to bear, even if you're male. Andy must be more courageous than I gave him credit for – as I recall, she had a ferocious right hook even then. I smile some more, then stop. In some ways, Andy doesn't know his sister as well as I do, or he wouldn't be blithely repeating Simon's cowardly logic. 'It's irrelevant' is the lousiest excuse I've heard since, 'If I wear one of those I can't feel anything.'

Babs deserves the whole truth. I'll ring her today. Not yet though, it's 10.25 a.m., they'll be buying sofas or planning the names of their children, or whatever it is married people do. I peel a yellow Post-It from its pack, write in capitals 'RING BABS, CONFESS' and stick it on the wall by the phone. There. For thirty seconds I am warm in a golden glow of piety. Then I remember they're in Prague and it fades. I'll just have to wait. OK. I'll call Jackie to accept her offer of work. On the sixth ring I realise that Mrs Edwards will *be* at work. I'm halfway to putting down the phone when a sleep-raddled voice husks, 'Hello?'

'Oh gosh, Andy, hi, it's me, Natalie! Sorry – I've woken you up, haven't I? Er, sorry about last night.'

'Why?'

'Oh look, doesn't matter, I'll phone back later – I was actually after your mum, to say yes to a job, and when does she want me to start, but I realise she's probably at the deli.'

'I can tell her-aaaaaaah!' he says, alarming me until I realise this is a yawn. 'Aa-aaah! 'scuse me, I'll be seeing her later today. And tomorrow. Waking up now – *ahak*! – sorry, frog in my throat!'

Normally I dislike being party to other people's bodily functions, or functionings. Frannie once went through a period, no pun intended, of talking compulsively and interminably about her periods. It was period this, period that, tired today (heavy period), violent headache (heavy period), vicious cramps (heavy period), virulent nausea (heavy period) – she's the only woman I know who has a regular period once a week and – call me a misogynist, in thrall to my mother, whatever – the incessant newsfeed off Frannie's Period Information Hotline ultimately rendered me nauseous myself.

However, frogs in throats I can just about tolerate, so long as the word 'phlegm' is kept out of it. Besides, when Andy says, 'frog in my throat' a resistant lump dissolves in my chest and I think, 'aaw!' 'Frog in my throat' is such a quaint little phrase, so formal, so resolutely uncool, that there's something innately vulnerable about a person who says it. I can't imagine, for instance, Vinnie Jones announcing a frog in his throat. He'd probably just spit.

'You know,' I say suddenly, 'if the parental home is closing in on you, you can always move back into my flat.'

The silence screams. I force myself to count my blessings.

290

I *could* have said, 'The glitterball in my spare bedroom has no one to glitter for.' (You'll never know.)

'Yeah? You sure?'

As the phrase 'I wouldn't say it if I didn't mean it' is, in my case, a grotesque fib, I restrict myself to 'Yes.'

'Er, how does tomorrow morning suit you?'

'Wow,' I murmur. 'The pressure must be on.'

'Well, Natalie,' says Andy in a gloating tone. 'You'll find out more about that on Monday at nine. Mum's on standby.'

'You think they'll want me to start that soon?' I squeak. 'I, I don't mind, it's just that Matt, my ex-boss, was going to give me some more work.'

'Oh right, yeah, of course, the bloke who came round last Monday. And we made the Pilates-Sivananda pact.' Damn you and your computerised memory, I think, as he continues, 'Look, Nat, it's cool. Do what you have to do and when you're ready give my parents a day's notice.'

'A day! Are you sure they won't mind?'

'What's to mind?' says Andy. 'Tomorrow, then. Back to Primrose Hill, land of little shops and poncy pubs. Thanks, Nat. I've still got my key, so don't hang about if you've got something on. Cheers! Bye.'

I replace the receiver and cover my mouth with both hands. Andy is coming to live with me again. How did *that* happen?

Dialling at high speed, I ring Matt at home, and ask him if he's ever done Sivananda yoga. He replies, 'Piss off! I'd rather drink ten pints and scratch my arse!'

Saturday stretches before me like a yawn. If you're not obsessed with food, what else *is* there? What bounces back is a phrase that Alex used in her Pilates class. 'Imagine your vertebrae as a string of pearls,' she told us. At the risk of sounding alarmingly sentimental if not borderline insane, it was an image that touched me (having never imagined my vertebrae in any other term than the plodding but

291

pragmatic 'my vertebrae'). While duly respectful of its importance as a body part, I never considered my backbone to be *gemstone* precious. I jump up and ferret through my bag for the gym schedule.

Three and a half hours later I am lying, jellified, on a blue mat, wondering how an exercise that is, according to Alex, 'ninety per cent lying down' can be so gruelling. Sitting up straight is a killer! Not that I'm complaining, but it is odd. I'll clock up ten miles on the treadmill and my feet will itch for greater challenges, but Pilates – which is, to all intents, a small step up from sprawling on a sofa eating crisps – wipes me out. I feel sedated. It is very rewarding.

'Oi, Sleeping Beauty. Do you want to go for that drink then?' says Alex, leaning over me, her wide smile white against her dark skin.

'If you've still got time,' I sigh. Alex rolls her eyes.

'I've got time,' she says. 'See you in the bar in five.'

I blush as I explain my mission because Alex has an unnerving way of giving you her full attention. She is not one of those people whose eyes are forever darting behind and beyond you, in case a more thrilling presence is at large (a habit I almost find reassuring) and she doesn't interrupt with 'right, yeah, sure,' to hustle along your yap so that *she* can talk. She sits and watches and listens and waits until you've said what you want to say. Most unusual.

'So, I'd just like to know a bit more. Before I do anything mad like spend my savings on a course,' I end (a tad self-consciously, as the one time I let slip to Babs that I had savings, she shrieked, 'You've got *savings?*' in a tone that suggested this was as bad as keeping a child on a chain in my hall cupboard).

But Alex nods. 'You're right, Natalie,' she replies. 'You have to know what you want for yourself before you can get it. *I* used to be a solicitor. I started this as a hobby.' Then she hits me with the bad news. It's not all poncing around on mats. A part-time course in Pilates can take two years. There are several thousand exercises to learn.

Anatomy, physiology, sports injuries, rehab techniques. A lot of ex-dancers go into it. It can be hard if you *don't* come from a dance background – you know about how the body works if you've come from dance, you can look at other bodies and assess them – she had to train for longer, so will I.

As if this isn't bad enough, there is further slog – 1,800 hours' training before you can take the exam. But I'm not put off, even when she states, 'Pilates appeals to a lot of people who hate exercise.' Then she says, 'It's about making the body work healthily rather than exercise for exercise's sake. It's customised to the individual. It tries to find a way to make the best of each person: you want them to go away feeling good about themselves.' I am nodding away happily, imagining myself as streamlined as a dolphin (without the fin), when she adds, 'It's about how you feel internally, rather than the external picture.'

At this, I stop nodding and wonder if I really *have* found what I'm after. We move on to personal chat, and Alex tells me about her background. Her mother is West Indian, her father is English, she has three sisters.

'I'd love to have sisters,' I sigh, but secretly I've started to feel uncomfortable. What is it with my friends, Babs, Alex, Andy? I have this creeping sense of being *got* at – they're all trying to change me, preaching the case for inner strength. But you can't spin flax into gold. I drive home, scowling. Pilates makes me feel taut on the outside and calm on the inside. But I have no interest in excavating my soul. Even though, I tell myself, that's not what she meant. Pilates is *not* psychoanalysis – it's lying on the floor with a bunch of geriatrics pretending to be Concorde taking off, all the better to stretch your lower back.

I walk in the door and see the yellow Post-It instructing me to RING BABS, CONFESS. 'Can't,' I say coldly to the note. 'She's non-contactable,' and scrunch it up. *But you've found something you love.* The voice in my head comes from nowhere, and I freeze. It's true. When something is perfect, I get an urge to spoil it. When I first joined the GLB, Matt and I would go to the pub at lunch and while I rejoiced in our friendship, my constant thought was: He's my boss! What if I chucked my drink over him? I realise I'm halfway to talking myself out of doing something I really want to do because I'm scared. In my bag is a number for a Pilates training course. I'll ring it on Monday.

I stamp around the flat straightening pictures on walls until I dare admit that while I don't like to be reminded of how ugly I feel inside, what actually unsettled me was Alex. She's so sorted, so capable, so at ease with herself. And, despite the Concordes, dolphins and pearls, I can't imagine ever being like that. As if to prove my point, I gorge on chocolate then throw it up.

Chapter 34

It occurred to me a while back that you can go for months and months without being insulted then speak to a relative and be resoundingly snubbed three times in the first minute. With this in mind, my mother is not the person I want to hear from at ten past ten on Sunday morning. The memory of yesterday hangs over me like a noose, and my aching spine has less in common with a string of pearls than with a rusty bike chain. I feel fragile and if my mother says anything less than complimentary I may fragment. At her worst, she is the human version of lemon-scented bleach. Her token nod towards petty sensibilities accentuates the toxic undertone.

'Mum. How are you?'

'Patronised!' ricochets the response. I gulp, and grope through my recent past for possible transgressions.

'Wh – why?'

'Yumminess, that's why!' snaps my mother.

I wait, and she waits too. I realise I've unwittingly engaged in a theatrical contract and my line – in the tradition of a doofus sidekick – is: 'Yumminess? What do you mean, "yumminess"?'

'I mean,' shrills my mother on cue, 'yumminess, as in "Slimwell's Whole Meal bread – All the delicious yumminess of brown malted wheat bread but a lot less calories!" The wretched stuff – advertised on every second page of *Lite Weight* magazine, until I felt morally obliged to buy a loaf. Morag at Weight Watchers said she swore by it. I might have known she was bluffing! Utterly ridiculous!

I'm not surprised each slice is only forty-five calories – each slice is mainly air! I had to eat eight slices to make the tiniest dent! How dare they? "Delicious yumminess!" It's outrageous, talking down to grown women, taking us for fools! I should have known. "A lot less calories" indeed! How's that? Not even a child's grasp of English grammar! I've a good mind to write and complain. They've even got a website! A website for a loaf of diet bread! They're lucky I don't own a computer, is all I'll say!'

I giggle. When my mother discards her alien shell and parties with the human race she can be quite likeable. Her beliefs are so dissimilar to mine – square nails, not ladylike; schprauncy car, no money in the bank; L-shaped sofas, common – that on the rare occasions she produces a thought I can relate to, I'm too lost for words to tell her I agree.

'That is quite a cheek,' I manage finally. 'How, er, how *is* the diet going?'

As the diet's been going for the best part of twenty-six years with no sign of abatement or indeed, waistline, this question is a formality. But I'm interested. It fascinates me, my mother's endless tussle with her weight, so much a part of who she is that her failure to lose more than two pounds in one week without gaining three the next is a warm, restful constant. While her lack of willpower irks me, I'm not sure I could stand her if she was thin. In fact, I feel it's a mother's duty to be a little plump (if they can't manage a large maternal bosom, it's the least they can do). Meanwhile, if *I* seem contrary, I'm nothing compared to her. My mother's double standards are such that she can talk happily about her own food fight and bewail mine at the same time.

That's a thought. I neatly divert the conversation with news of my imminent foray into the catering business.

'Jackie is going to give you a job?' she cries, her gratitude placing me as a Care in the Community case. 'What a lovely, charitable idea! What a kind gesture. She appreciated the thank-you note you sent her after Barbara's wedding. It's important to cultivate people, you see? Ah, well, I must call and thank her. She knew how anxious I was.'

I feel like a beaver trying to dam the Atlantic. Every road leads to a moan. I consider mentioning my Pilates idea but decide against it. If my mother knew I planned to plough my savings into 'a nonsense' – her preferred umbrella term, covering a host of unknowns including reflexology, homosexuality, Cubism, nouvelle cuisine, and the Montessori method – there'd be no stopping her. She likes me to keep 'something by'.

Six years ago my grandma left me a small sum in her will, and my mother nearly swooned when Jackie enquired what I might spend it on.

'I like-a to have something to show,' cried Mrs Edwards, as I quailed in my chair. 'To say-a, "this is what I got!" '

After Mrs Edwards left, my mother remarked, 'You do have something to show. Your bank statement!' Woo hoo! Fun on paper!

'Have you heard any more from Tara and Kelly?' I blurt. 'Have you thought any more about going out there?'

'Jackie thinks I should go,' replies my mother, as if she needed permission. 'I'll have to think about it.'

'*I* agree with Jackie,' I say, recalling my bitter rant at the art gallery and wanting to compensate. 'I think it would be lovely. You deserve a holiday.'

My mother sighs. 'We'll see,' she says, which – if my childhood memories serve me correctly – means No.

'But I thought you really wanted to see them.'

'Natalie, what we want in life and what we get are two very different things.'

I bite my lip. She may be right, although she often isn't. Years back, when Mr and Mrs Edwards were trying to think of a snappy name for their shop, my mother's inspired suggestion was 'Deli Belly'. When Andy and Tony finally hauled themselves off the floor, still gasping with laughter, Jackie took one look at my mother's hurt face and cried, 'Deli Belly . . . Deli Cirelli! Is a brilliant idea! *Brava,* Sheila!' While this idea was blatantly unconnected – Cirelli was Jackie's maiden name so it wasn't exactly a long haul of logic – my mother told everyone that she'd thought of 'Deli Cirelli'. She needs to feel useful, I think, because she doesn't.

This recollection enables me to say goodbye without crumpling. I stretch, wince, and wander into the bathroom. I am inspecting my head for pink patches – despite vitamin pills and feeding up, the dead hair still falls as steadily and silently as snow – when the doorbell trills.

My breath catches. I look like a scarecrow! I should have got up early to perform damage limitation on my hair and face. But forcing food back up is – if I may take a Pollyanna of a word in vain – holistically draining. Don't try it at home. I check the corners of my mouth for congealed spit, and race down the hall in three low lunging steps, like an athlete gearing up for the long jump. I'm wearing a flared corduroy skirt, knee-high boots and a huggy top. If I'd had time to reconsider, I'd have changed back into my usual camouflage of loose layers. (My mother once said that I dressed like a *millefeuille.*) My new look was inspired by chance. Yesterday, speeding home, I nearly crashed the car, thanks to a big flabby woman sauntering down the road in a miniskirt and crop top. Her soft white stomach bulged out of the gap between her clothes, and her large fleshy legs seemed to swell from her teeny little shoes. I was entranced. An elephant in cheeky red knickers. I saw and I couldn't compute. A bright smile, no apology. Her chins up, not in defiance but proudly. As if there was no controversy! This mountain of a woman dared to *be,* while I - a bat squeak – hid myself under the closest I could find in Next to a bodybag. From what?

I couldn't produce an answer that wasn't pathetic so, in spite of last night's toilet villainy, here I am, dressed to kill. (I may die of embarrassment.) I open the door.

'I'm back,' says Andy.

I notice his gaze flick over me. I fold my arms and look at him. My boots have heels, which makes us exactly the same height, a pet hate of mine, as I feel myself mutate into the Fifty Foot Woman. His hair is dirtier blond than ever, and his eyes – good grief – they really are chameleon eyes. I don't mean they're reptilian and lidless, I mean they seem to change colour according to what he's wearing. On Friday he wore a khaki shirt and I swear they were green. Today he's in a navy T-shirt, and they're bluish grey. The luck of some people!

'Problem?' asks Andy.

'Oh no, no,' I cry. 'Hello, come in.'

Although there *is* a problem. A problem that's been brewing ever since our brief corridor encounter was cut short. Despite the rudeness, despite the digging and the tartan dressing gown (for which there's no excuse, even though Babs once pardoned a bloke who wore slippers with 'He's not from London'). Despite the gallery of crimes this man committed in league with Tony, despite the kiss-and-run, despite his seven-year sulk in his black bedroom, despite his offensive attitude to food as celebratory, despite knowing that when he was ten he pinned down Babs and farted on her head, despite the overwhelming evidence stacked against him, I fancy the bloke rotten and it's getting worse.

Much worse. The way he's looking at me is best described by the legal term 'with intent'.

I shouldn't. What if—

The remainder of this query is muffled as I find myself hanging off Andy's neck, my mouth clamped to his like a barnacle to a boat. He's squeezing me to him so tightly, I couldn't let go even if I wanted to, and when he staggers into the hall, kicking the door shut behind him, my size seven feet trail along the floor. I would laugh but our kissing is so frenzied and ferocious I can barely breathe – I've no oxygen for luxuries like laughter.

299

Oh God, I think: bad news, what are you doing – he's not just delicious, he's – ugh, ick, *decent* – and if that doesn't put you off him, you are in serious trouble . . .

It doesn't. And I am. Andy isn't quite as decent as my mother imagines and neither – I discover – am I. What we do next is deliciously indecent, my pale blue hallway has never seen the like. (Chris, despite his allegiance to rock 'n' roll, could rarely bear to have sex anywhere but the bedroom. Saul could rarely bear to have sex anywhere.) Oh. Yes. This is real. I feel like an animal. I want him, I don't fucking care, the blood pulses red hot, and we're moving together, hard, harshly, gripping, grunting, his jeans at his knees, my knickers yanked to one side, my back pressed against the cool blue wall, this is, this is, I've never, it's not like me at all, but me, him, us, this – I love it, oh hang on, oh blimey, Oh, oh, *OH!*

We do it again, slower this time, in the cool dark of my shuttered lounge. Andy says my name over and over, and I feel like a pudgy green caterpillar turned into a butterfly.

Chapter 35

We lie tangled on my afghan rug, and Andy says, 'So will you still charge me rent?' I reply, 'Depends if you put out more than once a month,' and we kiss, giggling.

I realise I haven't chortled this much since Frannie burnt her chin on the steam off a pitta bread she was jabbing out of the toaster. Small niggles fly at me like insects and I swat them. I don't want any *fluids* staining my rug (Nat, dry cleaning is a wonderful invention). Andy, can you not balance that glass of water on the edge of the table, can you place it in the centre, otherwise we might accidentally jolt it and it will drop off (Nat, try to live with it, it'll be a test).

I try, and win. It's hard to care when you're this floppy. If a herd of buffalo charged through the flat, chipping my glass-topped table, I might just smile. Right now smiling is the most I'm capable of. My body is very gently buzzing and all I can think is, me and Andy. Nat and Andy. We, we . . . there is no way round it. We fucked. The feeling is incomparable. It really puts Prada in perspective. He is squashed up to me, his eyes shut, clasping my hand.

'I wasn't sure if you fancied me,' he murmurs suddenly. Neither was I, I think. 'But,' a smile cracks his lips, 'waiting for a sign from you. Christ, it was like waiting for Godot.'

'Well you weren't exactly blatant,' I complain. 'I wasn't sure about you either.'

I don't add that I'm not sure now. What happens next? What does this mean? Any port in a slight drizzle? I certainly feel very *snuggly* towards him. Maybe it's an evolutionary trick. I felt snuggly towards Chris when he made me ... you know ... but not like now. That was more gratitude, like he'd found my car keys. This is wonder and terror, fused. It's as if I've been promoted to the next level. Blissful, but there is further to fall.

Then Andy says in my ear, 'Let's have a bath,' and I stiffen. The shared bath is an evil invention, thought up by a misogynist. I suppose I could airbrush with candlelight.

'Yeah, okay,' I bleat, squirming out of his grasp and slipping on his T-shirt to delay the moment of truth.

I scurry from the dim safety of the lounge, my happiness diluted. It is no comfort that Andy appears to be at home with his nudity to the point of arrogance. He wanders whistling and naked down the hall with the blithe assurance of the fully clothed! My heart flutters, lust mingling with fear. He's like a Rodin – well, a slightly softened, wimpier Rodin – but I don't care. To me, he is perfect, I want to eat him up. I realise my mouth is ajar, and I shut it tight against my greed.

'Having a good look?' says Andy, with an insolent grin.

'No! Yes! Yes, all right, I'm looking at you, you gorgeous boy!'

'Boy? *Boy!* Natalie, I can't believe you! We've just done *it* - this is an egotistical disaster ...' He pretends to look crushed.

I fall into his hug, inhaling the warm scent of sex. It's intoxicating and I fight the urge to sniff like a bloodhound. Instead I say, 'So two –' I search for a dainty phrase and don't find one '– ah, orgasms from me aren't enough of a tribute? You want more, do you?' (I blush. I've never said 'orgasm' out loud in my life – except once in biology when, during a lesson on amoebas, I mispronounced the word 'organism'.)

'Yeah, I do Nat. I want more.' Various parts of my body twang. 'Take this ratty thing off,' he mutters. 'I want to *see* you.' He starts yanking at the T-shirt as we kiss.

'Wait a sec,' I say, struggling. 'Let me turn off the light, it's in my eyes.'

Andy tilts my chin so I'm forced to meet his gaze. 'Please, Nat,' he whispers. 'Let me see you.'

My desire turns to lead. I lift my arms listlessly, like a five-year-old, as he gently removes the T-shirt. I flinch as I see the distress in his eyes. For once, he doesn't seem to know what to say. He runs his hands from my shoulders down to my fingertips. He doesn't let go. The pink enchanted fairytale mood is tortured, killed, and hacked into a thousand pieces.

I pull away my hands and cover myself. 'I'm eating more,' I say defensively. Andy looks unconvinced. 'I wasn't eating much, I had a problem, but I'm eating more now, I promise,' I add, crouching, and groping for the T-shirt. Andy tweaks it out of my reach with his foot.

'There's more to it than that, Nat,' he replies gently.

I glance at the mirror and see myself. Next to him. I don't look well. I'm embarrassed. I can't think of what to say.

'Shall I run you a bath?' he asks suddenly. 'Give you some privacy.'

'No, don't bother, I'll run it,' I bleat.

Andy hesitates. Then he exclaims, 'You don't have to hold back. You can cry if you feel like it.'

I nearly laugh out loud. 'Don't patronise me,' I hiss. '*This* is my way of crying!' I rake my nails down my skinny chest. 'This!'

He snatches my hand away – the hot smarting beads of red smear – and snarls, 'Don't you ever do that to yourself! Ever! Jesus, Natalie!'

It's frightening to see a man so furious he's impervious to the comical effect of his willy wobbling. It's also frightening to realise your own rage is so deeply buried inside you, the only way to release it is to scratch yourself like a cat. 'Oh God,' I whisper, appalled. 'What have I done?' And then I do cry.

Andy dabs TCP on my wounds. I wail throughout. I thought thin was good! I thought it was good! 'And I, I've

303

started making myself si-i-ick,' I blub. Not the greatest line in the history of romance.

'Well then, you've got to stop,' snaps Andy. 'It's not necessary!' He looks horrified at his own gormlessness.

'Tell me something I don't know!' I say thickly through my tears. 'I think I'll have a bath now, if you don't mind.'

I feel marginally better, washed and dressed. I tiptoe into the kitchen. Andy has found some clothes and is sitting at the table reading the paper and eating a cheese sandwich. He smiles warily. 'How are you feeling?' he asks, wiping his mouth and dropping the sandwich as if the bread was green.

I grin weakly. 'Not bad,' I say, 'for a nutter.' I pause. 'You can eat in front of me, I won't faint. I'm even a bit hungry.'

'So you should be,' cries Andy gratefully. 'All that exercise!' We laugh, tinnily. We are less like two people who have gloriously bonked for the first *and* second time, than a pair of compulsive obsessives forced into germ-ridden proximity on the rush hour tube.

'If I make you a sandwich, will you eat it?' says Andy, wiping his hands on his jeans.

'Oh! Er, yes,' I squeak. Andy raises an eyebrow. 'Depending what's in it,' I add in a rush. Andy's eyebrow descends a fraction. 'No butter' – down a bit more – 'wafer-thin cheese but mainly tomato' – down – 'and has to be brown bread' – and rest.

I sit, while he makes me a tailored-to-psychosis sandwich. I tell myself this is progress. After all, the first step to defreaking arachnaphobes is to hand them a picture of a cute baby spider; the big-hairy-tarantula-fondling comes later. Maybe Andy should have drawn me a bap.

'Nat, you know I find you so attractive it's almost undignified.' I wait. I can feel the 'but'. 'But confidence is more attractive than fear.' Here we go! The Charter of *What's Wrong With You*. 'What I mean is, it's sexy when you ask for what you want. I wish I didn't have to force it out of you.'

I refuse to be lured by the sugar pill of 'It's sexy when you –'. Is my vanity *that* transparent? Anyway, we went over this in incy wincy detail forty billion times two days ago.

Andy places the sandwich before me, peeling it open like a sardine tin to prove the absence of butter. Then he leans on his elbows and watches me lift it to my lips. I take a teeny bite, chew forty times, then swallow.

'Andy!' I gasp. 'Can you not stare while I'm eating! You don't watch people like me eat! It makes it worse!'

'Sorry,' cries Andy. He stops. He rubs his nose. 'You won't ralph it up, will you?'

I put the sandwich down, cover my face with my hands, and start laughing. 'I don't even know anyone called Ralph,' I say. I laugh some more.

'What?'

'I – well,' I croak. 'I don't normally have cosy little chats about this.' It makes a change from the usual post-coital back-pedalling. Andy takes a small bite of his sandwich. 'Why . . . why do you think you do it? Not eat, or eat and, ah, throw it up?'

I don't answer for a long time. I want to get this right. 'It helps me block stuff. Sometimes,' I add, 'I hate myself. I feel thick and ugly.'

The way he asks, with real concern and zero embarrassment, makes it easier to speak. There is a sense of relief, each time I reply honestly. I can say what I feel without being condemned. This is a freedom I've rarely experienced with anyone, including Paws (canine king of the dirty look).

'Ugly?' repeats Andy, choking on sandwich. 'Nat. If you saw you how I see you, you'd see yourself so differently, I tell you.'

I can't speak.

He adds softly, 'You're so pretty. Although, you don't do yourself any favours when you're this pale and frail' – he blushes. 'You look better when you're healthier, so it's great you're eating more.' After a second he adds, 'I can see why you might have an inferiority complex if your mum favoured Tony. But I don't think you *hate* yourself.'

Now it's my turn to choke. Honestly, it's like being counselled by a steamroller.

'Really?' I say icily – thank you but *I'll* be the judge of whether I hate myself! – 'And how do you make that one out?'

'Well,' says Andy, beelining for the eye of the hurricane like George Clooney in *A Perfect Storm*. And look what happened to him. 'Well, Natalie, what stopped you going the one stage further? From doing a Lena Zavaroni? You obviously have some sense of self-preservation.' I bite my lip. Pass. 'I know you don't like me saying this,' he gabbles on, 'but I don't care. I think you're right. You're using food to block stuff. I think a lot of this is to do with resentment. Certain people pissed you off, but instead of saying so, you went on hunger strike.'

I snap, 'It's not that simple!'

'I know it's not that simple, I'm not a gibbon! You might not be wildly in love with yourself, but don't tell me you hate yourself when you get *this*' – he gestures at me – 'angry with people who diss you!'

I'm about to jam the last bit of sandwich into my mouth in defiance, when I realise what I'm doing and drop it on my plate. Using food to block stuff. Babs said pretty much the same thing, and I blocked that too. I can feel the mulch of bread and cheese in my stomach and at Andy's harsh words I itch to run to the bathroom and get rid of it. Using food to block stuff. God, but *why?* I've only yakked twice and already it feels like a compulsion. Using food to block stuff. From now on, I tell myself, it's not an option. 'Then . . . then, what should I do?' I'm paralysed. Using food to block stuff has been a flop of the highest order. The anger is still there underneath. It's just curdled.

Andy lifts his hands. 'What do I know? I've said what I think.'

I light a cigarette, although my hands are trembling so violently it takes me about a minute. I know what he thinks I should do. Although it's nothing to do with him and anyway, *I* know what I should do. It's doing it that's the great hulking problem with a glacé cherry (ten calories) on top.

Chapter 36

Tony has always enjoyed the practice of, as he calls it, 'a council house row' (a heartfelt disagreement that requires you to storm into the road and address a loved one at the decibel and pitch of a screech owl). I, however, favour the middle-class custom of feigned acquiescence while your opponent is present and ardent dispute under your breath the second they leave the room. So while I have unfinished business to discuss with my brother, my mother, and possibly my father, I ache for a less challenging task. Like, say, leaping from a plane without a parachute.

The trouble is, Tony has a black belt in intimidation. Taking issue with my father would be like smacking a puppy for chewing shoes. And criticising my mother would wound her irreparably, snipping the thread of our fragile bond for ever, and I don't think I could bear it. She takes even the mildest comment to heart. She once told me and Babs that ideally, men should be caught before they turned thirty as, 'Beyond that, they get set in their ways.'

Babs replied cheerfully, 'But Sheila, all the men I've ever met have been set in their ways since the age of six.' My mother went silent, and I knew she thought she was being dissed (although her actual phrasing might have differed).

I imagine saying, 'Oh Mum, about the last twenty-six years of mothering, can I have a word?' and feel ill. When I pick fault in any way I devastate her. She gets a My Angel is a Centrefold look on her face. I remember the mash incident and shudder. Never! Never again!

'Have you gone into a trance?' enquires Andy politely. I jump.

Andy gets up and shoves his plate into the sink. I eye it with suspicion but don't say anything. I recall that the morning after he made tomato bread soup I had to practically hose down the kitchen. Andy follows my gaze to the plate then gives *me* a look. It is similar to a look I frequently received from Babs when she was my lodger. Such as when I shouted down the hall, 'Did you just go to the toilet?' She'd stomped into the lounge, given me the look, and said, 'Yeah, why?'

Keen to reassure her, I replied, 'Good, because I heard a flush and I thought it might be the neighbour's toilet. I just can't stand the thought of being in my flat and hearing someone else's toilet.' Babs gave me the look again, and sang, 'Hello! Psycho!'

Andy doesn't actually sing, 'Hello! Psycho!' but it's as good as written across his forehead. He swishes on the cold tap, squirts about half a pint of washing up liquid on to the plate, and gives it a cursory rub. Then he sticks it in the draining rack.

'Better?' I show my teeth. 'You know,' he blurts suddenly, 'if you don't sort out the problem then you won't recover.'

I nod while trying simultaneously to convey the message that I want him to shut up. It doesn't work. He adds, 'I only say that because of what happened with Sasha.'

I stop mid-nod then start again. For some masochistic reason I want to hear this. 'Why?' I mouth, afraid that actual sound will derail his train of thought.

'I cut her off. I didn't want to hear her explanation. I didn't want to discuss it. To me, there was nothing to discuss. I thought if I acted like she didn't exist, she wouldn't exist in my head. It worked. For a while. But' – he looks at me and doesn't flinch – 'it's stopped working. I think about Sash a lot. Ringing her dad, asking for her number, getting in touch. Only thing stopping me is, she'll

309

be married to this bloke by now with five kids. I can't bring myself to do it. But I'll be honest, I can't get her out of my head. Shit. I'm sorry to land this one on you, Nat, especially after we—'

Why is it that some men aren't satisfied until they achieve wanker status in a woman's head?

'Don't be silly,' I interrupt, cranking what I hope is a faintly amused smile on to my face. 'Why should I mind? It's not as if our relationship' – I imbue this word with all the irony I can force upon it and, for the first time ever, quote Saul – 'was anything serious. We had a shag. It was fun, a one-off, and' – playful pause – 'You still have to pay me rent.'

Andy's eyes widen, his mouth shuts and he smiles. I see this smile and I know that he, like me, is in rapid retreat. He's bowing and scraping and twirling his hat as he does so, but only a whisker of self-control stops him turning tail and racing off as fast as his legs will carry him. Maybe he *is* still in love with the legendary Sasha. But it's not only that. I smell fear. I'll never forget Matt dismissing a cute contender with the words: 'No confidence, too much work.'

Men, gay or straight, there's little difference. They can't be bothered to build you up, and if they can there's probably something wrong with them.

I loll in my chair, body language set to *indifference*. But all the while I'm raging, what the hell did he do that for? Why even go to the trouble of getting his kit off? This morning he was talking about waiting for signs like a bloody shepherd on a hillside! Well, pluck out my heart and roast it on a spit, why don't you? This has all the makings of a pining situation, but to my surprise, a cold wedge of determination lodges in my head and forbids it. If he doesn't want me, then I don't want him either. This is the opposite of my usual response to rejection. It puzzles me.

'I'll have a shower then,' croaks Andy. He trudges out.

I frown. Why am I not upset? Another cigarette – yeah? give me cancer, you stupid little burning stick! – inspires thought. I click back through the day's events, and realise that Andy didn't see how unhealthy I was until *after* we had sex. What a lightweight. And that isn't a compliment. I smoke some more, and triumph again. I'm not upset, because if Andy and I had started seeing each other he'd have continued to bore me with Far Eastern wisdom until I agreed to confront my family. I had a narrow escape, ha ha. Then I hear Andy's shower rattling. I flinch involuntarily, but the pain is brief.

At times like this I reach for the running machine or, lately, the biscuit tin. But today, that cold wedge of determination forbids it. I'm reluctant to move in case it dissolves, leaving me to the mercy of my demons. They've not gone. That mad despotic impulse, to starve or stuff and vomit, still lurks. It's like a supersonic computer virus, it warps the hard drive and destroys the software. But its pull is weaker. I feel I can fight it. I'm bored with being ruled. It drains me, leaves me fit for nothing. I want to be rid of it. The most astonishing revelation is that when I think about what I said to Andy, one claim no longer rings true. 'I hate myself.' Suddenly I feel like a jaded actress, incapable of putting my all into the part. I'm sorry, darling, but it's just not *me*.

I shut myself in my bedroom to avoid the lodger and – after an hour of pretend-reading and not thinking about food – ring my father. Not to have it out with him, God no. I just want to hear his voice. And I want him to hear mine. After this mindwarp day I feel the urge to reconnect. I can only compare it to getting a nice haircut – you want to go out and test it on people. Infuriatingly, there's no reply. I leave a message, and strain my ears in the effort to eavesdrop on Andy, who is stamping around in the hall. Ouch, you. No, stop it. I hold my breath, but the flat is quiet. How could he? My heart is intact, no thanks to him. Maybe he's

thinking the same about me. No, sorry, *he* was the one
who—

Trrrg trrrg!

I snatch up the phone before Andy has a chance to pick
it up and embroil me in an embarrassing three-way
hellofest.

'Hello?'

'Poppet,' intones a cut-glass voice. 'Is that you?'

'Dad!' I cry. 'How are you?'

'Exceedingly well, my dear, exceedingly well.' Then, in a
hoarse whisper, he adds, 'Almost *too* well.'

'Oh!' I say, relishing his conspiratorial tone. 'Why's
that?'

'Kay Ay is very into soya, at present,' he replies glumly.
'Or *soy*, as they insist on calling it here. You know – "The
soy alternative to taste". I've just had spinach and soy
quiche for breakfast.'

I bite my lip in sympathy. When Dad lived in Hendon my
mother served him Frosties with full cream milk, followed
by fried eggs and baked beans on toast. 'It does sound
terribly good for you,' I say.

'Terribly good is a most accurate description.'

'And how's Kimberli Ann?'

'Thriving, my dear, thriving!' booms my father. 'It
would appear that soy suits her far better than it does me.'

'And her career?'

'Ah!' he sighs fondly. 'Kay Ay has some great ideas. She's
tinkering with her screenplay even as we speak.'

'Gosh,' I breathe. 'How glamorous.'

'Indeed,' says my father, in a neutral tone. 'And what of
your career, young lady?'

I cough, and update him. As ever, he is unperturbed.
'Pilates,' he declares. 'I know it well!'

'Really?' I say. 'Is Kimberli Ann' – I feel too shy to
abbreviate her to Kay Ay – 'into it?'

'No, no,' replies my father. 'Tantric yoga is her
penchant' – a flawless French accent caresses his Queen's

312

English in a brief kiss – 'just now. So how will you go about funding this new venture? I'd be only too delighted to loan you the money.'

I squeeze my eyes tight shut. 'Thanks, Dad,' I say. 'It's generous of you. But I think I'll be okay. I've got a bit saved up.'

'Exceedingly sensible! That's my girl!' he booms. 'Now, my dear, tell me. Are you still being very strict with your eating?'

My heart constricts. Malibu or no Malibu, there are some things in life my father will forever struggle to understand.

'I'm being less strict Dad,' I whisper.

'That's my poppet,' he says. 'Glad to hear it. Your mother was most concerned.'

'Have you, er, spoken to Mum recently then?' I squeak.

'I have, as it happens.'

'Did she, did she talk to you about visiting Tara and Kelly?' I ask.

'She did,' he replies. 'Heart set on it, by the sound of things.'

As I suspected. 'Do you, er, not approve still?'

'How could I not approve of my own granddaughter?' cries my father.

'Oh! Er, no it's just that the last time we spoke I thought you—'

'Not at all, not at all! I'm all for it! I think a trip Down Under to see the new rellies is a super idea!'

I bite my lip (again) to stop myself laughing at his ludicrous English. Not to mention his shameless hypocrisy. The new rellies, indeed. Last time we spoke he was on the point of suing them! A thought occurs. 'Will – ah, will you be contacting them, Dad?'

My father coughs. 'I don't think that would be altogether prudent at this juncture,' he murmurs. His tone implies that further enquiries on this topic are unwelcome. In the pause that follows, my heart beats wildly, and I think go on, Natalie, go on – *say* something. But it's like diving from a great height into a cold dark, shark-infested pool. Despising my weakness, I falter, 'So how was Mum when you spoke to her?'

'In fine spirits. As I said,' he retorts.

I wonder if I imagine the edge to his voice. I steel myself and blunder on. 'She misses you,' I bleat. I feel wobbly-chinned instantly.

'I find that hard to believe,' says my father briskly, 'after all this time!'

I blurt, 'So do I.'

There is a faint noise on the line then silence, as if Dad was about to speak but thought better of it. I hold my breath. When he does reply it's clear he knew precisely what I meant and chose to misunderstand me.

'A joke,' he says gravely. 'Forgive me. Living in LA, my sense of humour isn't what it was.'

I give up. I've got more chance of getting through to Russell Crowe's direct line. The frustration is acute and I don't trust myself to open my mouth. I am waiting dumbly for my father to put me out of my misery and end the call, when he says tersely, 'Natalie, thirteen years ago and last December 25th, I asked your mother to give me a second chance. She refused, both times.'

Chapter 37

As with certain 'live' television shows, my brain has an inbuilt time-lag between action and transmission. This sixty-second delay system means that when my father reveals he begged Mum to take him back twice and twice she told him to sling his hook, my mind fogs with dead air and the most coherent response I can muster is: *Oh*. It's a minute after I replace the receiver that the neurons jerk into motion and I start croaking, 'I don't get it.' I don't get it, I don't get it. Malibu, Hendon. Hendon, Malibu. No. I don't get it.

I need to sit down (I seem to be losing the use of my legs) but feel a moral obligation to remain standing. How can she *not* want him back? How can he *want* to come back? He wanted to come back. I could have had what I wanted, but she stopped him. My dad wants to come back! I fall back on to the bed with a plop. She must say yes before he changes his mind. Is she mad? I cannot for the life of me see why Dad would want to leave the gold car, the white house, the green palms, the yellow beach. Why voluntarily quit his privileged status as a 'Brit', the Beverly Hills practice, the celebrity tush, the Hollywood parties, the personal trainer, and the made-to-measure Kimberli Ann?

For Hendon! That dump! That dreary grey nonentity of a north London suburb, laden with lookalike semis and bearded orthodontists, neither here nor there nor anywhere, too far from town to matter, not far enough to be plush or leafy, its one concession to leisure a shabby little park strewn with glass bottles and plastic bags, and the huge Blockbusters its most glamorous feature. Is he mad? Every glimpse of the video shop would be a poignant reminder of what he'd sacrificed! Not just a pretty face – Kay Ay has some great ideas. I imagine her purring along the Pacific Coast Highway in her high and mighty black Lincoln Navigator, its number plate bearer of the legend, YIELD TO THE PRINCESS. What would the Princess think of yielding to my mother? My bollard-shaped mother, in her ever-present uniform of an apron – all that's left of her status as a housewife (an empty house, no longer a wife). My mother who has no first-look deals with any movie studios or television networks and drives a Metro. My mother who keeps abreast of others' self-enhancement – 'So I said to Susan, what *has* Melanie Griffith done to her mouth?' – but would no more think of renovating her own tired bosom than she'd think of piercing her tongue. Nothing my mother is or has ever done would inspire the Princess to respect her. My nostrils flare and, to my shame, I realise the Princess is not the only one.

I squirm for a while then get in the car and drive to Hendon.

My mother is, as ever, pleased to see me. She sits me down at the kitchen table and speeds to the fridge, shouting out its contents like a bingo caller: 'Chocolate! Yoghurt! Potato salad! Coronation chicken!'

I murmur, through clenched teeth, 'I already ate.' I look at her stiff hairdo (only she is last century enough to still get her hair *done*). The anger throbs.

'I've got a beautiful home-made vegetable lasagne in the freezer,' she adds pleadingly. 'I'll pop it in the oven if you like, it won't take very long to cook.'

I ignore her. Into my head pops a vision from years back: my mother hosting a dinner party alone. Dolloping out portions to all her thin, eating-concerned female guests, trying to get them to break their routine by politely insisting they should have more, you haven't eaten anything, on the premise that a woman on a diet couldn't really say she was.

It's nothing but spite. She doesn't care about me, she just wants me to be fatter than her. She wants me to sin, so she can feel pure. As I know from Tony, men aren't like that to other men. As I know – again from Tony – they'd be more likely to say, 'Look at you, you fat bastard.' Men have their own ways of being duplicitous, but right this second I envy their brutal candour. I am so used to pleasing others, to twisting myself in knots so as never to offend, that when my survival depends on talking plainly the words stick like toffee in my genteel craw. I don't know where to begin, but the war cry, 'Custard tart!' loosens my tongue.

'I said *no*!'

My mother wheels around from the fridge. 'I *beg* your pardon?' she gasps, in a tone that suggests she doesn't.

My insides liquefy with fear but I curl my toes and state firmly, 'I said no. I don't want any food.' – And, in a reckless surge, 'why don't you *listen* to me?'

My mother blinks. 'What are you so emotional about all of a sudden?' she replies. The taunting note in her voice affects me as water does a burning chip pan.

'You never listen to me!' I roar. 'You've never listened to me!'

'What are you talking about!' she splutters.

'You don't know what I want, you never have! You just want what *you* want, you don't care about me, and I'm sick of it!'

'I, I –' My mother looks like she's been hit in the face. 'Of course I care about what you want, dear, don't be silly!'

'I am not *silly*!' I scream. 'What's wrong with being emotional, what's wrong with it! I'm sick of not saying! You've never let me say what I think! I'm sick of being so fucking QUIE-E-E-E-E-E-E-T the whole time!' I screech the word 'quiet' so loudly that I give myself a sore throat. I proceed regardless: 'You won't let me be myself! Nothing I do is good enough for you! Tony's all you care about, you don't care about me, you never have, all you want to do is shovel food down my throat!'

'There's no need for language,' says my mother.

'Arruuh!' I shriek. 'You're still not LISTENIIIIIIIIIING TOOOO MEEEE!'

Her eyelids flutter shut and she cups her ears. The rage courses through me and makes me tingle. I'm suspended in the moment, too high on adrenalin for terror. I stumble towards speech – I'm fully prepared to bellow 'listen to me' again – but my mother gets there first.

'I'm very hurt that you think I don't care about you.'

My lips purse. 'No, *Mother*,' I hiss. 'Listen. You're not listening to me. You are not the one who is hurt. *I* am hurt. By you. Why don't you Get That?'

There is a long silence, during which my mother shuts the fridge door, walks to the table and sits down, opposite me. She's never hit me in her life so I don't understand why I want to flinch. 'Natalie,' she says, eventually. 'Please believe me when I say I never wanted to hurt you. That was the last thing I wanted.'

'Well, you did,' I say. 'And what's worse, you made me hide it!'

Now it's my mother's turn to flinch. 'The last thing a parent wants is for her children to suffer.'

'Yes, but you can't ignore it and hope it'll go away!'

My mother grimaces. 'When Dad left, I didn't want you to suffer. I don't know. Possibly I . . . I was too scared of your pain to allow it. When Dad left I tried to protect you. You and Tony. Especially Tony – because I could see that Tony was – was weaker.'

'Weaker?' I say incredulously.

'You're a tough young woman.'

I stare at her in disbelief. 'How can you *say* that?'

She shakes her head. 'I can't fight you any more, Natalie.

318

No one can. I want you to be happy. I don't know what to do any more.'

To my horror, she starts to cry.

'Mum,' I say, not daring to touch her. 'Mum, it's okay. Look. I'm going to be okay, I promise. I am, er, getting happy. We, we don't have to fight any more.'

She wipes her eyes showily on the corner of her apron, and immediately I feel I've been duped. I'm the one who's been done out of a two-parent family.

'Why wouldn't you take Dad back?' I growl.

My mother drops the apron corner. She says coldly, 'You make him sound like a faulty plug. It was over between Vincent and I. Once a cheat, always a cheat. I made the right decision.'

I clench my fists. 'Yes!' I cry. 'For *you!* What about me?'

'I *was* thinking of you!' booms my mother. 'What kind of an example would it have set if I'd taken him back? He called after he split up with the secretary! How *could* I take him back? What kind of an atmosphere would *that* have been for you and your brother to grow up in?'

'Better than the atmosphere I did grow up in,' I say bitterly.

'Natalie. We were *already* staying together for our children. It wasn't working. His affair was a by-product of our unhappiness, not a cause. I promise you that however, ah, unsatisfactory you feel your upbringing was, with your father around it would have been a great deal worse. I –' My mother's mouth twists, as if she's trying to pronounce a long word in a foreign language '– I'm not very good at relating to girls. I never have been. I never saw myself as a woman who would get divorced. It's been hard for me too. But. You must know. I love you. So much.'

When I hear this, I want to sink through the floor. But if anyone expects me to sob, 'I love you too, Mom!' and hug wetly, I'm afraid they'll be disappointed. I just sit, staring at my lap and blinking furiously. 'Right,' I mutter.

'Natalie,' says my mother. 'I've always thought, I was

brought up to think – perhaps wrongly – that if you can't say it, you can cook it.'

I look at her, and she looks at me. She whispers, 'I see it doesn't always work.'

Chapter 38

I drive home at ten to midnight with the stereo off. (Right now, Britney can teach me nothing.) I don't feel quite as glorious as I thought I'd feel. I *am* happy that I spoke the truth to her. Or, to be exact, screamed it. Yet, while it was cathartic – like relaxing after a long struggle – I am forced to realise that honesty is the selfish policy. Supposedly, I did the right thing and am now as cleansed and pure as a white towel fresh from a hot wash. But, much as I try to shrug it off, I feel a bit of a cad.

The thing is, you make assumptions about certain people for so long, they fossilise as fact in your head. Then you learn something unlikely or unexpected about those people which explains – if not excuses – their behaviour. All this time I've blamed my mother and now I discover that, in some ways, she did know best. So my triumph is muted. It reminds me of beating my father in a running race, aged six. I was proud and swaggery for one whole minute, until Tony revealed that Dad ran like an elderly tortoise on purpose.

But it's positive, I tell myself as I swing into my road, it *is* good. Our catfight was the bright shiny new start of a bright shiny new future filled with greater compassion, better understanding and fewer stodgy meals. Possibly yelling your head off isn't the adult way of working things out, but then again, I know very few adults who don't work things out by yelling their heads off. How else are you meant to work things out? Through lawyers? A mime show? Calm constructive rational discussion?! My first council house row. Tony would be delighted. And so would Babs.

Babs, I think, as I approach my front door, watch it swing open, and see her standing there.

'Barbarella!' I cry, bubbling with delight at the sight of her. I notice the dart of hurt on her face as she marches towards me – I'm afraid I haven't called her by this Highly Favoured nickname since before she met Simon. There's enough time for me to feel a flicker at her unsmiling expression, to think that Prague must be chilly at this time of year, judging from the cold windlashed look of her, to guess that something bad has happened to summon her to Primrose Hill at midnight – Andy? a cry for help? life meaningless without Sasha? – and then she says, 'You bitch', and hits me, hard and jarringly, on the face, and then I get it.

I gasp, and clutch my cheek, which burns – with shame or pain, I'm not sure which – and stutter, 'No, wait, I was going to tell you—'

Babs stares at me with intense dislike. 'Consider yourself lucky,' she says.

Having seen her floor a man who fondled her behind in a bar (he was dismissed with a swift uppercut to the jaw), I agree. I surreptitiously check with my tongue for loose teeth and taste the metallic tang of blood. Suddenly she grips my wrist in an eye-tingling pinch and drags me into my own home. I glance into the lounge, hoping, but Andy is nowhere to be seen. A few hours ago this would have pleased me, but now I pray for his presence like a farmer prays for rain. I don't dare ask where he is.

'He went to bed,' says Babs.

'Speak to him,' I plead. '*He*'ll tell you, he—'

'Isn't that so like you?' she sneers. 'Always passing the buck. Not this time.' She just about hurls me on to a kitchen chair. 'So tell me, Natalie, when exactly *did* you decide to make a move on my husband? Was it, ooh, when you saw me parade down the aisle in a big white

322

frothmonster dress and couldn't – and I know this is a radical idea – just *be* happy for me without wanting what *I* had? Or was it' – her tone acquires a lunatic singsong lilt – 'when, in the mad assumption that you were some kind of friend, I decided to trust you with the most painful problem I've ever encountered, even though it was private, even though it was the hardest thing I've ever had to admit, even though it shamed me to my fucking soul – *shame*, Natalie, that's something you don't understand – it tore me up, it still does, I feel like paper torn to tiny bits, and I tell you this, I tell you all of this, and oh yes, you make the right noises, you don't half come out with a lot of mealy-mouthed shite, and was it then, you thought, oh the man's seen sense, the time is ripe to have a pop? Because you never could understand it, could you? It never did make any sense to you, did it, that a babe like Simon could go for a fatzilla like myself, don't lie Natalie, I know what you think – no one else thinks of me that way, I'm fitter than you'll ever be – but I know what you think of me, you *abhor* that I'm a decent size, that I've got the brawn, that I don't play the little woman and I still get the man, you couldn't bear it, you had to prove to yourself – your inadequate empty self – that you could get *my* husband, that sick little ego boost meant more to you than sixteen years of friendship and my, my *life*.'

Despite the vehemence of this speech, Babs whispers it. It's like being very quietly sprayed in sewage. I stare at her, fearing another gush. 'Well?' she hisses. 'I'm right, aren't I?'

I'm desperate to contradict her. Yes, I wanted what she had – *not* Simon, for God's sake! – what I craved was unconditional love from another human being who I loved as much, but more than that, Babs, I craved your ability to love yourself, every bit of you, and the peace it brought.

I dig deep for courage. I'm such a stupid girl there's got to be a few scraps left down there.

Then I say, 'It's true that I, I felt – er – left out, that I felt *left* when you got married. And it's true that I feel more comfortable with you being' – I gulp – 'physically bigger than me.'

I pause, in case she feels the need to reach across the table and wallop me again. But she doesn't. She nods, coldly. I wince. I hate this. Hostility from Babs is forty thousand times worse than hostility from anyone else. To quote Princess Diana – not a frequent habit of mine – she is my rock. And being hit on the head by a rock is very upsetting.

'It's true, I already told you, I was jealous that you were, are, so in love, that you'd found the right man. The rest is wrong, though,' I blurt. 'Simon is, is, er, wonderful, but, er, he's not my type, but even if he was, I'd never, I wouldn't. I've got such respect for you Babs, what you do, who you are, and, and I've never thought that you were f-f-f- what you think I thought, you're Amazonian and it suits you. And yes I, I know it wouldn't suit me, but' – I am about to add that I see her as a real live Wonder Woman, with finer dress sense, of course. Thankfully she interrupts before I do so and earn myself another slap.

'You'd rather *die* than look like me,' she growls.

'Babs,' I whisper. 'I wouldn't betray you like this. I can't bear that you think I would. I hate that I've hurt you. Whatever Simon or Frannie told you, it, it, I promise, I swear, it isn't like they said.'

I stop, aware that I sound like a sneak and that Babs is cracking her knuckles. But I can't resist adding, 'When did she tell you?'

'She rang my mobile in Prague,' replies Babs curtly.

Foiled again. I'm so correct, so constrained by etiquette, that I refrain from calling my friend's mobile on her dirty weekend to confess my inadvertent mouth-wrestle with her husband because I feel it would be improper to shatter the romantic atmosphere with such a crude, indelicate blow. Frannie, however, barges right in there, trampling rose petals and convention beneath her flat hammer-toed feet, and is acclaimed as a heroine!

324

I bite my lip. 'And Simon?'

'He was *building up* to telling me when Frannie rang,' says Babs in a tone so acid it could pickle onions.

'But,' I splutter, 'Frannie saw what she wanted to see! Didn't Simon tell you what really happened?'

'You've got a nerve,' snarls Babs. 'I don't think you're in a position to be asking questions, do you? Yeah, Si tried to shoulder the blame, of course he bloody did, but I'm not stupid, Natalie – it takes two to snog in a bar, and Frannie saw what she saw, and I know *you*.'

Then you don't know me as well as you think you do. I may lack confidence, but I'm not . . . empty. I'm not a lost soul. There are certain crimes I wouldn't commit, even to satisfy my hungry ego, and stealing my best friend's fright of a man is one of them. I think all this, but don't have the guts to say it.

My last chance. 'But, Andy. Why don't you ask hi—'

Babs bangs her fist on the table. 'Why are you so determined to bring Andy into this?' she snaps. 'I don't want my family involved, I told you that! As far as he's concerned, I came round for a late night chat because that's what women do.'

I feel this is an undeserved slight on Andy and foolishly, it shows in my expression. Babs bristles. 'What's wrong, Natalie? My husband not enough for you? You want my brother too? I don't care what's gone on between you, put an end to it. I want him out of your flat, and out of your life. I don't give a toss what you tell him, just end it. As for working at the deli – in your dreams! You'll ring my mother and tell her you've changed your mind.'

'B – but –' I stutter.

I'd find it easier to share a bath with a piranha than to confront Babs, and my defence dries in my throat. I risk a glance at her from under my eyelashes. She's wearing a black polo neck sweater under a blue tracksuit and she looks like an undercover cop. All that's missing – thank God – is the gun. I sigh. I don't understand Babs, and I don't understand Andy. He knew Simon was going to confess this weekend. So when Babs banged on my door late Sunday night, he'd have needed a remarkably low IQ not to realise why. It would have been as plain as a boil on a chin – she'd either prised the harlot's identity out of that twit Simon, or Frannie had blabbed. Why didn't Andy speak up in my defence? He's not exactly renowned for keeping silent!

'Do it,' says Babs. With that, she stands up and stamps to the front door. I scurry behind her. Desperate, I cry, 'I only wanted to tell him off about how he was treating you! He came on to *me*—' I am about to add: But that kiss wasn't sexual, it was anger, resentment, and nine pints.

But Babs stops me with a second supersonic slap, which cracks and echoes like a gunshot. 'Enough,' she snarls, as I decide whether or not to faint with pain. 'Goodbye, Natalie. And may you get what you deserve.'

I stumble back into the kitchen, dazed. One door opens, another slams shut in your face. Does 'May you get what you deserve' count as a curse? I don't think it's the imperative. What should I do? Run round a church three times or will that double it? Actually, I want to run to the biscuit tin – only I polished off its entire contents in 0.02 seconds during last night's binge. I could drive to the petrol station. I glance at my car keys. No. No. No. You won't, Natalie, you won't. Just feel bad, *feel* the badness, don't try to convert it because you'll make it worse. I grip the underside of the chair, and the tears run down my face. For so long, such a fuss over coming second. Is this what victory feels like?

I think back through sixteen years of precious friendship and the ache is so searing it's as if Babs is dead. I want to bang down Andy's door and shake him awake. Will it be so hard to give up this man when he wasn't mine to begin with? *Ouch.* As for his sister, it doesn't seem real and I already feel her loss. Babs is the kindest, bravest, most generous person I've ever known. She's always been there for me. No one can replace her. As for me, I'm the opposite of Babs. I *am* selfish. It's incredible. To be so amenable and yet, at heart, so horribly horribly selfish. I sit, disconsolate, and rake through the ashes.

She always fought for me, and I let her. Babs is a fighter, in every sense. I remember when Matt first met her. He said, 'I admire you, Bar, but I think you're mad. When I see a fire I'm running out of the building. You're running into it!' My ex-friend, the hero. And she really was. Saving lives was the least of it. Two years it took, for her to be accepted into the Service. And then, her welcome speech from the Governor: 'Sleep with anyone and you're out.' The bullying. It took the guys on her watch three years to accept her.

Three years, and she didn't complain once. 'They don't perceive it as bullying,' she explained patiently to her dad, who wanted to go in there and sort them out. 'They think it's acceptable.' From the day she bowled up to her boss and said, 'Hello, I'm your new recruit,' and he snarled, 'You're not *my* fucking new recruit!' – not a squeak. She took it, as they say, like a man. Except she didn't have a nickname because no one would talk to her. They'd sit in the mess room, eat dinner and ignore her and she'd look at the table and say nothing. They'd play rounders in the yard and she'd study. Then she'd be pulled into the office and yelled at: 'You're not trying to be part of the watch!'

And then, an inferno. Babs and this guy called Dean, on the second floor, fighting the flames, Dean steps forward, the ground disappears and he's up to his waist in floor. Babs yanks him back. 'It was right where the fire had started, we didn't realise,' she said afterwards, playing it down. Dean wasn't exactly fulsome in his gratitude. And still there were jibes. 'Barbara will do your washing,' they told the new guy. 'She'll take it home and clean it for you.' The innocent approached her with his dirty kit and she told him where to go. She stuck it out until the most piggish offenders transferred or retired and the rest had to accept she was a five-star fire fighter. And the first thing she did? She invited me to the station.

She let me try on her kit – what with the boots and the breathing apparatus I could barely stand. 'This is the new lightweight gear,' she grinned. 'The old stuff weighed five stone.' She let me squirt the hose – I staggered backwards at the force of the jet. She let me sit in the fire engine and play with the siren. 'Press that button with your foot, Nat, okay, now set this switch – to *yelp* – that's wow wow wow wow! – or *2-tone* – that's ordinary old nee-nor nee-nor – or *wail* – that's my favourite, ooo-OOOOH ooo-OOOOH!' She let me slide down the pole. 'Try not to hold on with your hands, just your legs.' And she had the decency not to mention to the men on her watch that I was tarted up to within an inch of my life.

It's difficult to reconcile the gnashing fury of the last ten minutes with the benign glow of the last sixteen years. The tears keep falling and I don't bother to wipe them away. If you're ditched by a man, you can console yourself that he didn't really know or understand you, sex is sex, it wasn't personal. When it's your best friend, there is no denying that you've been judged, and condemned, on who you are. The pain is sharp like a knife. But pain I can deal with, that's not what's causing the tears. I'm crying because Babs deserved her happy ending and I helped botch it.

Chapter 39

I sleep like a baby. That is, I wake crying fifteen times in the night. I give up and get up at 6.37 a.m. I dress in black to suit my mood, and clank loudly and needlessly around the kitchen in order to wake Andy. Monday's a working day, he'll be grateful. Anyway, the layabout doesn't know it but he's moving house today. It'll be a joy to be rid of him. I'll be doing myself a favour as well as Babs. I will not be used, abused (pleasurable though it was) and tossed aside like a tissue. His problem is post-coital cowardice, spreading to general cowardice later in the day. He *knew* my friendship with Babs was at stake and what does he do? Stands aside to watch it burn!

'You can stop banging about now, I'm up,' says Andy, from somewhere behind me. I spin around from the sink so fast it takes a second for my body to catch up with my head. 'That was a mildly *Exorcist* moment,' he adds. For once in my life I'm in no mood for pleasantries.

'You knew what was going to happen yesterday,' I snap. 'Why didn't you stick up for me?'

'Hey, Baby Doll. I *did* stick up for you yesterday.'

I struggle to maintain composure in the face of monstrous cheek. 'Don't give me that,' I splutter. 'You know what I meant! You might like to know that Babs has dismissed me from her life of last night! You knew why she came round. Why didn't you say something? I might have known Simon would make a hash of it!' I stop, panting for breath.

Andy deletes his smirk. 'You're a big girl now, Nat,' he says coolly. 'You can fight your own battles.'

My mouth opens and shuts. 'I didn't, I wasn't asking you to, to fight my battles,' I bleat. 'I – oh God, just forget it.'

I drag out a chair and plonk myself in it. He's wearing a tatty old baseball shirt. While this is the antithesis of style, it suits him, and I don't even mean that as an insult. I can't look at him.

He sits down, and says, 'Nat.'

'What,' I reply, eyes still averted.

'Don't be a baby, tell me what she said.'

I light a cigarette and tell him, defiantly, keeping the whine out of my voice.

'You knew it was a risk,' he says, 'not telling her immediately. It's always going to sound five times worse coming from someone else. From Frannie, ten times.'

I nod.

'Maybe I should have talked to her,' he adds. 'But she didn't want me to. I could tell.'

I shake my head in a charitable manner. (Once I triumph my generosity knows no bounds.) 'No, you were right not to,' I say. 'You were right to keep out of it. I should have told her earlier, not delayed. It was my fault. I suppose I can't –' I pause. I needed a scapegoat. 'I can't believe that this is the end of our friendship, that's all. It's a hideous mess, it's spiralled. And—'

'And what?'

'Doesn't matter. Just a silly thing.'

'Go on,' he says.

'Well,' I blurt, 'I just remembered this time, Babs and I were at a party and the bathroom door didn't lock properly and so we guarded each other while we went to the loo and then we had this hour-long discussion about, about, if you were very beautiful, say, like Naomi Campbell, and someone burst in on you while you were on the toilet, would it be less embarrassing than if you were a normal person, and I just think' – with difficulty I stop my tone ascending to a wail – 'there are very few people in this world that you can have that kind of conversation with . . .'

330

I realise my dignity is halfway out the door. 'I told you it was silly,' I growl. 'You shouldn't have made me tell you.'

'I apologise.'

I cough, stub out my cigarette and light another. Andy raises an eyebrow. 'You're dedicated,' he observes, 'this early in the day.'

'Silk Cut Ultra,' I reply gloomily, indicating the packet. 'The non-smoker's cigarette.'

'Nat,' he says slowly, taking the cigarette from my lips and dragging on it – a move which should absolutely *not* be sexy but is – 'Ugh, God, yes, I've given up, it tastes foul. I'm sure you'll make it up eventually. She's in shock right now. It might take her a while.'

'Andy, she hates me,' I sigh. I stub out the cigarette. It's too distracting after where it's been.

'She hates you,' he replies, 'because she'd prefer to hate you than to hate Simon. If you were Babs, who would *you* want to believe was the bad guy? Your best mate or your husband? It's not a nice choice, but if I was her I'd go for the best mate.'

'Oh! Yes, yes you're right,' I cry, before remembering I don't want to owe Andy anything. 'But actually you're not right,' I add, 'because even if she does admit the truth to herself, even if Simon does clarify what went on *properly* instead of in a useless flop-haired unconvincing way, or I write to her, or' – I refuse to suggest that Andy might intervene – 'or Frannie's nose triples in length breaking all records, Babs will still resent me for being the conduit' – I stand by that word – 'of Simon's unfaithfulness.'

Andy blinks. 'Even if it takes a long time I still think she'll come round,' he says. 'Usually, she shouts her head off, gets it out of her system, and that's the end of it. If it isn't,' he adds, 'it's going to be very awkward, what with you and – ah—'

'Oh no,' I exclaim, snapping my fingers. 'That's another thing. She's banned me from the deli!'

'Right,' croaks Andy, 'right.' He coughs. He looks as if

he's just sat on a porcupine. I am preparing to announce his imminent change in living arrangements when he says, 'Natalie, there's something I was going to tell you.'

'What?'

'Yesterday. Do you remember when I said I couldn't stop thinking about my ex?'

'Vaguely,' I reply. Good grief. Why did I ever think I'd have trouble letting go of this fool?

'It was bad timing. It didn't come out right. I told you because I don't want to mess you around. You didn't let me finish. I'm not in love with Sasha any more. It's more about unanswered questions, about why she left me. I can't say why it still matters. But I wanted you to know what's going on. I've got to work through it. I was gutted when she left me and it's only now I've started to see how much. I don't want it to get in the way of, of what might happen with us. I don't know how you feel but I think you're lovely. We could have something. If you want.'

He looks at my stunned face and adds, 'Or not.'

Ten seconds later, Andy and I are frantically entwined on my bed, making passionate yet tender love, as the white organza curtains billow softly in the gentle spring breeze. Actually we're not. But hey, we could have been. My hand was in his and he was very lightly stroking the underside of my wrist. His fingers felt rough and scratchy on my skin, and made me shiver. He looked at me, and I recognised the tense look, that holding back of unsanctioned desire. I just wanted to melt into him. Oh, God, yes, take me, have me, all of me, I'm all yours.

But I didn't. Instead, I stammered, 'Can I think about it?'

He replied with a brisk, embarrassed nod. I stared longingly at his mouth for a short moment, replied in a high squeaky voice, 'Great. Thanks!' and ran to my room.

I heard the front door slam soon after. How could I evict him after that? I couldn't say it to his face and I wasn't about to write him a note. So I wandered, lacklustre, round the flat, forcing myself to tilt every picture frame askew. It made me itch but it wasn't enough. You blithering idiot, you should have said yes! I found myself gliding fridge-wards, dropping a succession of fourteen slices of bread in my Dualit, spreading each toasted square thickly with butter, and guzzling the lot.

Twenty seconds later I felt rotten and the toilet bowl beckoned but I shunned it. So what so what so what. I'm sick of pretending to rave about salad. I'd gain a pound. A pound! So what. Who'd notice, except me? Gaining a pound would be less psychologically damaging than selling my soul to the toilet. Anyhow, I promised Mum. I felt bloated and porcine but I stuck with it. *A minute on the lips, a lifetime on the hips!* Every oppressive slogan ever invented by the diet industry popped by to taunt me, but I wouldn't be baited. *Nothing tastes as good as being slim feels!* The size-16 bottom line was: my CV is fragile enough. I didn't wish to add bulimia to my dubious list of achievements.

We could have something. If you want.

I repeated Andy's offer over and over, using it as a charm against the toilet. Surely this was the pinnacle of romance? But sheepish though I felt – and I felt sheepish enough to say 'baa' – it worked. And while I couldn't resist straightening the tilted pictures, I still felt ridiculously proud of myself. There was a seed of warmth inside where before there was a cold cavern.

That said, it wasn't enough that he'd asked. Once it would have been but not any more. Denial is *so* last century. But his asking would have to do for now. I had a cute fantasy to call my own, and fantasies can be surprisingly sustaining – often more so than the real thing (during my teens, Tom Cruise and I shared many happy years together). Right this minute, the real thing would have been inappropriate. I wanted Andy but I also wanted to make it up to Babs. I'd do anything to make it up to her. I'm not about to start shagging on friendship's grave.

But there's more to it than that. I agree, every bit of me,

with Andy. I think we understand each other. We go together. Like jam and coleslaw, admittedly, but we do go together. Even if it means years ahead of shouting 'Don't stuff your socks down the side of the sofa', I know we could have something. It makes me tremble to think of what we could have – its potential feels *gothic* in scale. By which I don't mean spooky and sinister with me in a castle and him in a cloak, I mean the possibilities are so awesome I'm daunted. But I've spent too long living life as second best. I have to draw the line somewhere. And I recognise a severe case of Exgirlfrienditis when I see it.

So, much as I'd love to, I don't feel I can take Sasha's place until it's vacant.

Chapter 40

I foolishly hint to Matt of upheaval – so to speak – between lodger and landlady, and he starts planning his outfit ('This is the big one, I can feel it!'). I tell him it's a non-story as I've renounced men for, er, Lent, and he goes ballistic. What! What's going on? Don't I trust him as a friend? He doesn't dance the Nutcracker Prince for just anyone you know, he feels spurned. I explain that after an excitable weekend, I've called a halt on talking about myself. 'I've been jilted by Babs,' I add, breaking my resolution. My voice cracks. 'And this time it's official.' Matt invites himself round after work for a 'debriefing'.

I say if he's going to force himself upon me like this, we might as well be civilised. Would Mel and Bel like to come too, and I'll cook? I'd like to thank everyone for Friday's show. In that case, says Matt, don't cook. He'll bring some red booze and show up around seven. He'll see if the others are free, although I needn't think there's safety in numbers. Minutes later, Bel rings to say 'I'm there!' and Mel calls to tell me she's dancing tonight but she might pop round later. With Tony. I'm not wild about facing my brother, but then, I'm not wild about facing Andy. A friendly barricade could be just what I need.

When the doorbell shrills at 6.54, I'm surprised. Matt is never early ('It's suburban – I'll run round the block three times if I have to!'). I pull it open and find myself facing someone else I'm not wild about.

'Chris . . . pian!'

Chris, who judging from his bully-boy expression was

335

planning a verbal attack, turns poppy-red. Good thinking, Batman, I tell myself. I try to appear calm. Is *he* going to hit me too? Thank heaven Babs warmed me up. From the look of him, he's not too keen on his new army regulation hair. I'd better strike first.

'Your sister came round the other day. Henrietta,' I add. 'What a lovely, traditional name.'

Chris takes an uninvited step into my personal space. 'That stuff of yours *dissolved* my hair! I was the spit of Sherlock Holmes! I had to shave it all off! And now look at me! I look like a Nazi! You and your brother have near enough ruined me. I've got no band, no hair! I want you to know that I'm thinking of suing. I—'

'Oh my Lord, what *delicious* hair! You mustn't tell me! Michaeljohn? Toni & Guy? Nicky! It *was* Nicky, I know it, now don't be coy, I've *got* to have a feel, I insist, you *must* allow me – Ooh! Ooh yes, a forest of soft little pricks – a baby hedgehog! A shorn lamb! Oh, I'm in heaven, darling, in heaven – Natalia, who is this juicy biteable peach of a boy? He should be locked up!'

'Get off!' bawls Chris. 'Get your hands off me you, you freak! I don't even know you!'

I try to communicate my immense gratitude without laughing. Matt – having finished his virtuoso impression of a *Carry On* queen – clasps his hands to his chest and sucks in his cheeks to a perfect pout. Paws sniffs Chris's shoes with interest and cocks a leg.

'This is my friend Matt,' I say. 'He loves your new look.'

Matt simpers and extends a limp hand. 'I adore it! I'm *so* happy I came!'

Chris, who suspects this is a *double entendre*, shrinks away.

I bite back a giggle. 'Why don't you come in, Chris—'

'Forget it. You'll be hearing from my solicitor.'

Name anything it's possible to be scared of, and I'm scared of it. I hate trouble. I live in dread of stubbing someone's toe and being dragged to court by one of those

336

'Suffered An Injury That's Not Your Fault?' companies that advertise on TV and doing a ten-year prison sentence. But I find it hard to be scared of Chris. He's so terrified of Matt.

'Oh you big silly!' cries Engelbert. 'Come in and have a cup of char! You'll feel so much better!'

'Tony might be along later,' I add. 'But I wouldn't want you to feel intimidated.'

Chris glares at me. 'A dash of semi-skimmed. No sugar.

When I carry the tea and the red booze into the lounge, Chris is squeezed into the corner of the sofa, pale hands clenched between his legs like a shy virgin. Matt is just about on top of him. 'And so *I* said, "He's a member of the family, darling, he knows all about swagging!"' Matt laughs uproariously at this probably bogus punchline. Chris nods stiffly, then leaps up, clutching his mobile.

'I gotta make a call,' he bleats. 'Uh, no reception, I'll go outside.' He exits the flat at speed. Matt and I choke ourselves.

'I love you,' I tell him. 'I bloody love you!'

Matt blows a raspberry in the direction of the front door. 'I hate bullies. What a dick. I knew I should have vetted him! Well thank *heaven* I'm here to vet Andy! So – *vite*! Tell me, tell me all. Is he in? Please tell me he's in!'

I explain that there isn't going to *be* any Andy. And I explain why. I'm doing fine until I get to the bit where Babs stormed out. Then my chin starts to wobble. I can't believe she's gone for ever. It's as if a little piece of my heart has chipped off. I take a huge gulp of wine to douse the ache. It works, sort of. Matt looks at me and slaps his forehead. 'If ever there was a person who could be said to make a meal of things, it's you, Natalia.'

'That's very ironic,' I say. I think about this for another moment and snigger (we're two glasses in the red by now – I find most things funny after one).

'Allo! Anyone there? Yer door's open!'

'Belly!' we cry as one. I rush to greet her. Paws waddles to the door behind me.

'All right,' she grins, kissing the air. 'There's a geezer anging about yer front. Ee looks right fed up.'

'Most geezers who hang about my front look right fed up,' I say. We machine-gun laugh in each other's faces.

'Nice 'air. Oo is ee?'

'An ex. Come to exact retribution.'

'Why don't you see if he wants to come in, Bel?' adds Matt. 'His name's Crispian. He's a tad *dour*, but only because he's shy. Public school, you see. Not used to *ladies*.'

Belinda's eyes widen. 'I love a bit of posh,' she exclaims, and hurries out. Matt smirks into his wine glass. 'Poor Chris,' he sighs. 'The fun has only just begun. Ooh, has Bel been shopping?' By now, our inhibitions are marinated in alcohol, which allows us to start ruffling about Bel's carrier bag. 'Pop-Up Pirate!' cries Matt, lifting out a brightly-coloured box. 'What a sweet girl! She's bought us a game to play!'

I wrinkle my nose. 'Matt, it says "age four and over". I think it's more likely she's bought it for a niece or nephew.'

'Balls! Children are too young to appreciate these things. Anyway, one's mental age is all that counts.'

When Belinda and Chris return, Matt and I are immersed in our fifth round of Pop-Up Pirate. (It's a game that requires cunning and strategy. You take turns sticking red, blue, green, and yellow swords in Pop-Up Pirate's barrelly sides until one of you accidentally stabs him and his head pops up, and off. The score: 2-3 to me.)

'Blame him!' I squeak. 'He opened the box!'

'Oh, you know me – can't resist a red box,' purrs Matt, for Chris's benefit.

Bel, who is flushed with excitement, barely glances at it. 'So, so, carry on, Crispian,' she murmurs, 'you was sayin, at school, yeah, you ad *fags*, didja? To toast yer crumpets an all? And like, was it like, ow they say it is? Aw go on! This is amazin'!'

Chris looks as if he might burst into tears. It's a measure

of his agitation that when Andy walks in, he appears pleased to see him.

'The lovely Andreas!' squawks Matt who – correct me if I'm wrong – has met Andy once, for the duration of a minute.

Paws starts investigating Andy's shoes and wagging his tail.

Belinda checks out the newcomer as a possible toff and arrives at a happy conclusion.

The only person not awash with joy is me.

'Hi,' I say awkwardly.

'Hi,' he replies. He looks from me, to Chris, to me again, and scowls. Matt follows all this, waves a yellow Pop-Up Pirate sword in Chris's direction, and cries, 'Crispian returned to exact vengeance, Andrew. Apparently his long shaggy hair was his crowning glory – although personally I think this new butch style is *beyond* hot. Try telling him that! Anyway, it's all been terribly dramatic. Paws, get down – it's not like shaking hands! Oh, how sweet, you've brought a little friend!'

Robbie, who has just shuffled in clutching his bike paraphernalia (purple helmet, passenger helmet, scarf, leather gloves, leather jacket – everything bar the machine itself), rubs his eyes. He grins at me, then at Matt. 'Wotcha.'

Hastily, I introduce everyone. Chris nods at Robbie without coming over. Bel waves and smiles but doesn't move a toe away from Chris. Matt leaps up and kisses Robbie and Andy hello. Andy – patently gratified by the torturing of Chris – gives Matt a bear hug. When Andy glances at me, I allow myself a mini-smirk. So. I'm not the only one scared to face yesterday's bonk alone.

'Sit down, boys, sit down,' says Matt, patting the sofa. 'Natalia, we're nearly out of drink. Is there anything else?'

I stumble into the kitchen – which has turned wobbly – scrape around various cupboards, and return with a large tray of clinking bottles. 'Some of it might be out of date.'

'Jesus wept!' says Robbie, dropping his bike gear in a messy heap on my afghan rug. 'Where'd you *get* all this, this . . . shite?'

Matt lines up the treasure trove of booze. 'Martini Extra Dry, Beefeater Gin, Bailey's, Mezcal Lajita, Soviet – lord alive! – Soviet Strike Vodka, Smirnoff, Taylor's Port, Palwin's – good God, this is frightening – Palwin's no.11 – Andy, dear, save that face, it gets worse: Sang Thip Royal Thai Liquor, Jack Daniel's, Cointreau, Heering's Cherry Liqueur, one bottle of Miller Red Dog – Paws, look what she got for you! – and three bottles of Newton and Ridley. Mm. What a connoisseur!'

'I wouldn't mind trying the Royal Thai Liquor,' says Robbie, squinting at the label. 'It looks . . . interesting. Nat, have you got any ice?'

I fetch ice, glasses, Diet Coke and tonic water, and Matt plays mother. Chris grumpily accepts a Siberian vodka and tonic, Andy chooses death by Mezcal Lajita (Matt goes to the trouble of spearing the worm with a skewer and flicking it into his glass), Bel gets a half pint of Bailey's, Robbie stands by his Sang Thip, and I go for a large glass of cherry liqueur. 'Well, I'm having the Palwin's!' declares Matt bravely. He covers his head with one hand, cries, '*Baruch atah adonai!*', downs it in one, and submits to a choking frenzy.

'You sound like a cat coughing up a fur ball,' says Andy. He takes a swig of Mezcal.

Matt observes his agony with satisfaction. 'At least,' he replies, 'I don't look like one.'

'Yer all nutters,' declares Bel. 'I'm stickin' wiv me Irish Cream.'

'Oh no you're not, darling – and don't argue, I'm your boss – we're taking it in turns to taste everything. We're going to broaden our narrow, bigoted horizons. Aren't we, Crispian?'

Everyone looks at Chris, who is bright purple and clutching his throat. He nods dumbly and snaps two fingers at Matt to indicate assent. As Chris has been keeping a safe distance from Matt – rather like a shark circling a lawyer – I am intrigued by this thaw. So is Matt: he raises his eyebrows and twists the Soviet Strike bottle round to read the label. 'Thirty seven point five per cent proof,' he murmurs. 'The Russians certainly have struck. What *would* we do without the social lubricant of alcohol?'

'I'm sure you'd find another lubricant,' says Andy.

Matt pouts. 'Have a glass of Sang Thip, dear. That'll scrub out your mouth.'

I surrender to a giggle fit. All of a sudden I feel warm and floaty – the weekend's many horrors blur with my vision. I let Matt pour me a sweet comforting slosh of Palwin's. 'I wouldn't smoke *as* you drink it,' says Robbie. 'You're probably flammable. I think I'll try the Mezcal, although after you've tasted the amber nectar that is Sang Thip, everything else is an anti-climax.'

'*I* want to play Pop-Up Pirate,' exclaims Andy. 'Budge up, Natalie. And I want to be the blue sword. Matt, will you teach me?'

'Look out, Matt,' says Robbie. 'He's on the turn! Watch yer back!'

Matt crosses his legs. 'I don't think I *will* watch my back. It'll be a lovely surprise!' He squeezes my thigh. 'Natalie – we'll have to toss for him!'

Filthy pissed as I am, I recognise this comment as the great waddling oink of a *faux pas* that it is, and bare my teeth at Matt. He grins at me and sings, 'No one heard! Anyway, look at them, they couldn't care less!' Then he turns to Andy and says, 'Now, darling. You take your sword in your hand . . .'

Heart pounding, I glance at Robbie. He's clapped a hand over his bulging mouth, is shaking his head in horrified mirth, and holding out his glass to Bel. Chris is sitting on

341

the floor, tipping Heering's Cherry Liqueur down his throat. His gaze is fixed on the middle distance and he seems unaware of the red trickle dribbling down his chin. Bel oscillates between fetching His Lordship a tissue, and trying the Sang Thip. Matt is right: they couldn't care less. I sneak a glance at Andy. He's smiling. 'I'll be the green sword,' I say.

When the doorbell rings two hours later, Chris is snoring on the floor, bare-chested, occasionally whimpering in his sleep. Ditto Paws. Belinda is in the kitchen, singing *Diamonds Are Forever* at the top of her voice, and scrubbing the cherry liqueur stains off his Miu Miu tan leather jacket with Fairy Liquid and a Brillo pad. Robbie, Andy, Matt and myself are ensconced in, possibly, our fortieth game of Pop-Up Pirate. I feel a bit sick, so I've given Robbie power of attorney. A while back, Matt decided that whoever loses removes an item of clothing. This accounts for the fact that Robbie is in his pants. Andy is wearing green boxers, a T-shirt, and one sock. Matt is sporting a fake fur hat with earflaps, and black jeans. I took preventative action an hour ago, went to my wardrobe, and put on seven cardigans. I can't remember quite when Robbie decided we should play for money, and that he'd be Banker – 'That's banker with a "W",' said Andy – but I suppose it explains why I'm twenty quid worse off than I was thirty minutes ago.

'Somebody's at the door! Thank Christ for that!' bawls Andy, staggering to his feet. 'I don't know who the hell it is, but I thank them from the heart of my bottom!'

Matt looks at me, and laughs silently. *Oh please*, he mouths.

Vain, I mouth back. *What can you do?*

'I agree with Andy,' says Robbie, hopping about, trying to fit both legs in one trouser hole. 'If you ashk me, we've had mo-o-ore than enough of thingsh popping up, thank you verr mush, Matthew. And I sheem to have made shixshty quid.'

'Robert,' replies Matt, watching Robbie fall flat on his face. 'Try one leg at a time. Would you like some help?'

'You shtay right where you are, ta very much.'

'Why is it,' says Matt, 'that all straight men, even the mingers, think you fancy them?'

I shake my head. 'You tell me!'

'I'm a married woman,' adds Matt. 'And Robert, adorable as you are, you're not the *prettiest* boy in the playground.'

Robbie looks peeved. 'What!' he says, prodding his soft white belly. 'You mean, if I wash, if I wash gay – which I'm not, yeah? Yeah? Mate, Geez-aaa! Got that-ah? – you wouldn't want to have it off with me?'

'Robert,' says Matt solemnly. 'You're an absolute love, but you're' – his voice drops to a whisper – 'not my type.'

When Andy walks in with Mel and Tony, we are all crumpled on the sofa, sniggering like children.

'Oh NO!' shouts Mel, stamping her little foot. 'They've been having fun without us!'

'Mel, angel,' says Matt. 'You need to catch up, that's all. Have a sip of Sang Thip!'

Mel scampers across the room, then freezes as she catches sight of Robbie. Hastily, he does up his zip. Once again, I perform introductions, although a little less crisply than earlier.

'So this,' declares Matt, standing up, 'is the Tony I've heard so much about. Well, well.'

Tony glances at Matt with suspicion. 'Well, what?'

'Well, Anthony ... You're everything I thought you would be, if not more. Big Daddy Bear!'

Before Tony has time to deconstruct this, Mel cries, 'What's *he* doing here?' She points an accusing finger at the slumbering Chris.

'Yeah,' says Tony, frowning. 'What *is* he doing here? And why are you lot half-dressed?'

Mel, who is used to nudity, ignores him. 'I love your flat, Natalie,' she says. 'Can I look around?'

'Of course,' I say, as Matt cries, 'He's very growly, isn't he, Natalia? Do you think he wants a bowl of porridge?'

'Matt,' I mutter. 'Shh. Er, Mel, Tony, do you want a drink?'

Mel tucks her hair behind her ears, and does a mental tot-up of the men present. Her butterfly gaze settles on Andy. 'Who are you again?' she lisps.

'Andy.'

'Andy! Oh, OK. What drink shall I have, Andy? You live here, don't you? Will *you* show me round?'

Tony glances sharply at Andy. Andy doesn't notice.

'I don't know what you like to drink,' he replies. 'It's Nat's flat. I'm sure she'll show you round.' He smiles at Mel, but it doesn't reach his eyes. A crease of perplexity clouds her brow. She is used to men grasping the flirt-baton with both hands.

I feel a twinge of pity. '*I* think you should try the Soviet Strike, Mel,' I say.

Tony – whose mood has darkened from jet to pitch – pokes Chris in the leg with his foot. Chris jerks awake, squeezes his forehead and groans. He sees Tony and scrambles to a sitting position. 'You! I've got a bone to pick with you,' he croaks.

'Yeah? Then pick it.'

'You *encouraged* Blue Fiend to go with Piers, and they were in breach of contract—'

'Ah, what contract? Did they *have* a contract? I think not. Any other bones to pick? No? Good. Shut up.'

Chris stumbles to his feet. 'But . . . but . . . Where's my shirt?' he mumbles. 'My leather jacket?'

'There's your shirt,' I say meekly, pointing to a stained crumpled heap. 'I don't think Bel got around to washing it for y—'

'But I've done yer jacket!' crows Bel, bouncing in brandishing what looks like a chamois leather. 'It's a bit . . . it's a bit . . .'

'My jacket! It's fuckin ruined! You maniac! You . . .

that's six hundred and fifty pounds' worth of designer jacket! What have you ... my head hurts ... I'm out of here ... I should never have come ... you're all hatstand, the lot of you ...'

'Tell it to someone who cares,' says Andy.

'What's hatstand?' I squeak.

'I think it means "mad",' replies Andy. 'Crispian must have learned it off a *cockney*!'

'You *are* masterful, Tony,' coos Matt, as Chris runs for his life.

'You're not going to start on him, now, are you Matt?' asks Robbie.

'I was hours washin' that jacket!' cries Bel. 'Hours an hours! Aw sod it. I'm starvin' 'ungry, I'm goin' down the chipper.'

'You'll be lucky to find a fish 'n' chip shop around here, love!'

Bel ignores Robbie and veers unsteadily towards the door. My brother snags in her line of vision and she stops. 'You're Nat's brother, incha?'

'What's it to you?' snaps Tony.

'You know,' says Matt. 'You're really quite a grump.' I aim to kick Matt and miss.

'Stop that, Nat,' says Andy. 'You're the only person in this room who's scared of Tony. Oi, Big Daddy Bear, when did you get so tough?'

Mel giggles. 'He's not tough, he's the sweetest man alive! And no one's asked me how my dancing went.'

'That's because we know you were fab, darling.'

'I wasn't, I was terrible! My back hurt, my feet were killing me, it was agony. I was like a great big heffalump stomping about.'

'You were very light and polished,' soothes Tony. 'Though I didn't like the way that lech Oskar was looking at you.'

'Well,' remarks Matt. 'It *was Romeo and Juliet*.'

'I'm not talking to you!'

'Oh, get back in your box,' says Matt.

Five heads swivel in the direction of Tony. He looks stunned. 'Wha . . . Get back . . . ? You going to make me?'

Five heads swivel in the direction of Matt. 'Only if you insist.'

Tony laughs harshly. 'I'd like to see this! What you gonna do? Hit me with your handbag?'

Matt flutters his eyelashes in an expression of acute boredom.

Tony reddens. 'What? *What?* Come on then! You want to go outside?'

Minutes later, Tony discovers that homosexuals who hail from the roughest part of Exmouth are well practised in defending themselves – or, at least, this one is. Matt fells my brother with a single punch to the kidneys. And while he does spoil the effect with a little light weeping over his bruised knuckles, Andy and Robbie declare him the hero of the night. Secretly, I can't help agreeing with them.

Chapter 41

The phone rings at 10.39 a.m, shaking me from a booze-twitchy make-you-tireder sleep.

'You lazy girl.'

'Alex,' I rasp. 'You OK?' (My pounding head and lurching stomach agree that You OK? is more do-able than Good morning, how are you?)

'I'm really well thanks, Natalie, how are you?'

I lie.

'That's good. So what did you get up to at the weekend, anything nice?'

I suspect that my weekend doings are a little heavy duty for this newborn friendship, so I lie again.

'Sounds great! Now I've got something for you,' she says. Her voice is as loud as a drill. 'I spoke to my Pilates teacher, Robin, yesterday. I'm going to his studio later – I go there twice a week to teach – and I told him that you're a friend interested in training. He'd said he'd be happy to tell you about the course. If you're serious, Robin's your man. So if you're free, you can meet me at his studio at four. Otherwise I'm sure he'll chat to you over the phone another time.'

I croak, 'No, I'm free, I'll see you at four'. I roll into the kitchen and enter the appointment details in my enormous new business diary (which is about the size of the Domesday Book). Andy is out, and no wonder. We managed to do that very married thing of appearing great friends in public, while in private our relationship is tepid. I bite my lip, walk into the lounge, and blanch. It looks and

347

smells like a squat. The odours of basset hound and alcohol now clog my front room. Empty bottles litter every surface, and there is a congealed puddle of Heering's Cherry Liqueur on my pale polished hardwood floor. Multi-coloured plastic shards of Pop-Up Pirate – I think Andy accidentally trod on it – have been crunched into the rug. And my beautiful beige suede sofa looks *sticky*.

I rush to the kitchen for headache pills, but the cupboard is bare. 'The fresh air will do you good,' I say sarcastically, quoting my mother. It doesn't. I stumble to the chemist, whimpering. By the time I get home, I've developed the shakes. I squint at the phone, hoping for messages, but there are none. I press 1471. 'You were called today at 11.01,' says the BT woman maliciously. 'The caller with-held their number.'

Who could it be? Babs? No chance. Tony? Oh my *God*. I should think about hiring an armed guard. 11.01. Of course. A minute into my mother's first coffee break. But she always leaves a message; five to be certain. I don't want to call her. I think about roaring at her on Sunday night, and feel queasy. Queasier. I'd rather sweep the episode under the carpet, then glue the carpet to the floor. Before the infamous mash episode, I hadn't raised my voice to her in twenty-six years ('You were such a *good* baby! Not a peep out of you!'). What must she think of me?

I try to focus. This is why I never, ever get drunk on a Monday night. It makes the rest of the week too painful. *Think*, Natalie! Admittedly Mum didn't seem too trau-matised when I left. She waved me off from the door with, 'You'll have to think about what you want to do for your birthday.' My mother is to martyrdom what Texas is to oil. Ever since I can remember, she has celebrated my birthday by frogmarching me and Tony to Odettes – a smart restaurant in Primrose Hill – for a sumptuous dinner. I think she was suggesting that if I and my neuroses pre-ferred, she'd take us to the theatre instead. She is great at being understanding in an annoying way.

'Hello, Mum,' I say quickly, before I lose my nerve.

'Hello dear,' she exclaims. 'Nice to see you on Sunday, how are you?' She sounds on edge.

'Nice to see you too,' I echo disbelievingly, wondering if it's possible that I dreamt the weekend. 'I'm fine, thanks, how are you?'

'I'm well thank you, dear. I didn't want to bother you, that's why I didn't leave a message. I wanted to ask your advice, I didn't want to ask Tony. But it can wait, I know you're busy.'

I manage not to laugh. This is my mother trying hard. 'Now is fine,' I say.

'It is?' she replies anxiously. 'You're not working? What about the deli?'

'I am working. But not at this precise moment. And, er, not at the deli. Babs and I had a – an argument.'

'You did?' shrills my mother. 'What about? But this is your future!'

'Not really, Mum,' I say gently. 'It was only meant to be temporary.'

'Well there's always Eee –' She stops, and with difficulty, corrects herself. 'I suppose there are other options open to you,' she adds, as if reading from a barely decipherable script. 'So tell me' – her voice drops to a shocked hush – 'what happened with Barbara?'

'Nothing serious,' I lie. How long does it take these Stone Age headache pills to work? 'It'll be fine. Don't worry about the deli, and please don't say anything to Jackie. Anyway I've decided on a career change.' I take a breath and try to sound assured. 'I'm going to train to teach Pilates, which is a form of exercise, it strengthens mind and body and' – to placate my mother – 'even old, er, more mature people can do it. I'm going to use my redundancy money and do freelance work for Matt, and I'll keep on a lodger, so I won't starve, it'll be fine, it's a proper job, there's no need to worry.'

There is a long doom-filled silence.

'Who,' replies my mother, her voice tight as an overstretched elastic band, 'said anything about being worried?'

I am so gratified by her restraint – proof that she actually heard what I yelled at her the other night and modified her hysteria-gauge accordingly – it's not until I'm sitting in a small dingy reception room in Crouch End at 3.45, waiting for Alex, that I realise I didn't ask my mother what she wanted my advice on. I'll ring her the minute I get home. I write down this intention in my business diary, which looks pleasingly full as a result.

At 4.06 the prehistoric lift opposite my threadbare sofa clunks open and Alex appears. A tall shaven-headed hunk of a man with dark blue eyes and black eyelashes stands beside her. He's dressed in sweatpants, trainers, and a blotchy purple T-shirt. With no apparent effort, he has the grace and bearing of a god.

'Natalie, what a surprise,' says Alex with a grin. 'You're on time!'

Robin takes us to the coffee shop next door. From a purely anthropological viewpoint I can't take my eyes off him. After we've ordered a decaffeinated latte, a camomile tea, and a still mineral water (just call us the Crazy Gang), he says, 'So, Natalie. Why Pilates?'

I blush. 'Well, I' – I think, hang on, I'm *paying* aren't I? – 'Until recently I was in PR, and it wasn't very, er, karmic.'

As I'm unsure if 'karmic' is even a word, I add quickly, 'So now I'm freelance, but I've decided I want to do work I actually enjoy. I used to run a lot but my knees are starting to creak. Then I tried Pilates, Alex suggested it, and it was wonderful. It makes me feel calm and I never feel that. It's a total change from what I'm used to, but I'm addicted. I'd love to make a living from it. I hope,' I add hurriedly, 'that doesn't sound bad.'

'Not at all.' Robin's hands are gently expressive, rising and falling in emphasis as he talks. 'When someone tells me they want to train in Pilates, I need to know why. And yours are very good reasons.'

I feel inordinately pleased, as if the teacher has cried, 'Apples are my favourite!'

Robin smiles. 'Someone who wants to train with me,' he says, 'must come to the studio and work on their own body first. For a minimum of six months, twice a week. I don't like to compress that. The length of time is important. People should be allowed time to change.'

As someone who has always fought change with the determination of an ill-trained dog hanging on to a slipper, I nod and cry, 'Oh absolutely!'

'The training itself is a year long. For the practical part, you spend twelve hours a week in the studio with me. Each teacher has to develop his or her own way of thinking.'

Robin talks and, despite a low-boil sense of panic, I nod until my head feels loose. Five thousand pounds for the bogus privilege of my own way of thinking! I'll be learning about my own body, core stabilisation (whatever that may be), postural analysis and movement in relation to other people (*other* people? Yawn!), basics and remedial exercises, then traditional Pilates work in the studio, Pilates matwork and its benefits, then an apprenticeship and practical exams. We can start tomorrow.

Tomorrow?!

'Don't I have to er, audition to prove that I'm dedicated?'

'You've got six months of studio work before we decide whether to continue with the year of training,' replies Robin. 'That's enough of an audition, don't you think?'

'I don't mind exams,' I tell Alex after Robin exits the coffee shop with every eye – female and male – upon him. 'I can learn stuff by heart. It's the thinking for myself that scares me. I was taught to listen.'

Alex shakes her head. 'Natalie,' she says, 'you're not happy unless you've got something to worry about. One thing Pilates'll teach you is to let it ride. It gives you control but it's also about letting go. All Robin means is, eventually, you won't use the language he's used with clients, you'll use your own because it suits you better. You'll adapt the exercises to *your* way. And if you're nervous now, that's good, because it means you won't be arrogant, you'll be careful. That's important when you're dealing with people's fragilities. But,' she grins, 'steady on, girl, you've got a while yet.'

I nod gratefully, pop a few more headache pills, and set to work on changing the subject.

'You're right. It's just that I can't quite believe I'm about to do this. I *never* take risks, never! I'm not an impulsive person. But this feels right. It feels . . . this is a weird word to use, *healthy*. I'm excited but it's terrifying. So that's my excuse for being a wimp, how are things with you?'

Alex traces a finger round the rim of her cup. 'Not great.'

'Not great?' I gasp – I thought her life was wrapped in pink ribbons. 'Why not?'

She shrugs. 'Little things, Natalie.'

I can't restrain myself. 'Like what?'

Alex sighs. 'Last week,' she says, 'my car got broken into – window smashed, stereo nicked – the day after my insurance ran out. The hassle Natalie, you wouldn't believe. And then, this weekend, I visited a friend in Aldershot with my little sister. We were in this pub, and there were these guys, I think they were squaddies. That type of rough white guy. Like, they fancy you but they don't want to because of your skin colour. There was this one good-looking guy, and he was looking at me, and I saw the girl he was with say one word: "black". I said to my sister, "Come on, we're going." I'm telling you, Natalie, it's always a shock. I'm a middle class girl, I grew up in Islington, for God's sake! And then I get home, and my other sister, Louise, tells me my dog ate something in the park, vomited sixteen times during the night, she rushed

352

her to the vet, they did an op, and poor Miffy's stomach was full of bones, twigs, and bits of crab. She didn't tell me because "I know how you get about that creature." She's okay now poor thing, but I *warned* Louise that Miffy heads for bins at the first opportunity! It's her trademark! Andy, my ex – my ex-boyfriend – Andy called it Miffy's bin habit. Anyway, Natalie, I can't be dealing with it!' Alex looks at me. 'You asked. I told you.'

I nod. I feel ashamed about the racism, almost as if *I* am responsible, but I can't think of anything to say that isn't inadequate or patronising or both. I feel a twist of anger in my gut towards the ignorant woman in the pub, I want to smack her in the mouth but – to my shame – it's not the racism tale that's rendered me speechless. Eventually, I find my tongue.

'What a vile week you've had,' I croak. 'I'm so sorry.'

We stretch our lips over our teeth in mutual empathy. But my mind tumbles over itself and all the while I sit there stretchy-lipped I'm screaming mutely *what? what?* Miffy, I know about Miffy, and oh God, it can't be. Andy. There are a billion Andys. Am I going mad? How did this *happen?*

If Babs was here – well, if Babs was here this fiasco wouldn't have occurred in the first place, but – if Babs were here she'd say I had a frog on my tongue. And I can't hold it in any longer. 'Alex,' I blurt, 'this may sound like a stupid question but, is Alex your real name?'

She narrows her eyes. 'Not entirely stupid,' she replies teasingly. 'Obviously, Alex is short for Alexandra, but I only started calling myself Alex after the divorce. Fresh start and all that. I reverted to my maiden name too. My husband's surname was' – she giggles – 'Clench.'

I wait. It would be polite to giggle back but my giggle stock has been abruptly depleted.

'I guess,' she adds, 'I could have called myself Sandy or Sandra but they're too Olivia Newton-John.' She stops to take a sip of cold camomile tea.

'So, Alex,' I husk, knowing the answer but needing to hear it, 'what did you call yourself before the divorce?'

'Sasha,' she says. 'It's my favourite abbreviation of Alexandra!'

'Sasha,' I echo.

Chapter 42

While my general knowledge level has always been appallingly low (which I attribute to not being allowed to have a television in my bedroom) I've never thought of myself as stupid. I might have *said* I was stupid – as in, 'I left the lights on in my car, I'm so stupid' – but all women say they're stupid without meaning it. But now, I mean it. What an idiot, what a bloody twit. I've got the cognitive abilities of a roast pigeon. I'm Ricki Lake Guest Level stupid. I'm Who Wants To Be A Millionaire out on £100 stupid.

I feel depressed by how stupid I am – which disproves another long-held belief of mine – that only intelligent people get depressed because the stupid ones are too stupid to realise how stupid they are and get depressed about it.

Do I have any excuse? In my favour, I never met Alex when she was seeing Andy – a combination of having as little to do with him as possible, especially after the kiss, and Andy working in sunny Aldershot for the first year of his relationship with Alex, and then in the City. Not in my favour is that Helen Keller in a thick blindfold would have seen this coming.

I manage to thank Alex for introducing me to Robin and say that I'll be in touch. Then I drive home, muttering aloud. 'Now what? I don't bloody know! You stupid idiot! Hell-*oo*! McFly!' (This last is an old favourite of mine and Babs, gleaned from *Back to the Future*, when the class bully raps the hero's dad on the forehead to see if anyone's home. We call upon it in times of great stupidity.) By some miracle, having paid no attention to road signs and other drivers, I reach Primrose Hill alive. I loiter shiftily outside my own home until a woman leans her torso out of next door's bay window and enquires, 'Can I help you?'

'No,' I reply, outstaring her until she retreats.

I return to my car in case she emerges to attack me with a Le Creuset. I'm getting to be as rude as Tony. What the hell am I going to say to Andy? Should I say anything at all? He doesn't *have* to know I know her. But he'll find out. Alex rang the flat before, what if he'd answered? I could tell her the phone's been cut off and to ring me on my mobile. I just ... don't want them to meet. I'm scared. Although Alex, Sasha, whatever she calls herself, has never mentioned him. If she still loved him, surely she'd have said. If a woman fancies a man she'll crowbar his name into every conversation. But she never has.

But he's still mad about her, it's obvious. I don't want them to meet. Then, maybe, the iconic memory of her will fade. But how can it when – bugger bugger bugger – the Evil Ex has become my friend? Oh God, Andy thinks she's still married! When – in a hideous quirk of fate – the Evil Ex turns out to be a fairy godmother, a kind, generous woman who has repented of her ways (of her last-minute ditch and switch of husband at least)? It's so unfair. Evil Exes are meant to be full-fat evil. That way you know how to deal with them. You can hate with a clear conscience, you can wish them ill and hope the milk of life turns sour on them, safe in the knowledge they're Evil and that's what they deserve.

I *know* she'll fall for him again. The follow-your-heart thing led her to a dead end. Seeing Andy will be like slipping into her favourite scuffed trainers after a brief and painful fling with a flashy high-heeled pair of red patent shoes – the soothing comfort of familiarity will be irresistible! I have the feeling I get watching *Jaws*, when the men are in the little boat in the middle of the dark sea, drunk and singing, and it's cosy and fun, and the fantasist

356

in me hopes that in this version of the film the shark will decide he's not evolutionarily advanced enough to hold a grudge against a bunch of humans and he'll swim away and no one will get eaten. I watch, knowing the worst is a certainty, but still *faintly* believing I might have the one dud tape for those sensitive souls who can't face reality.

It's not going to happen. Alex will get Andy as surely as Jaws gets his man-sized dinner. Only stubbornness has kept them apart. But I want Andy. I want him, because he wants Alex. I want him, because I know Alex will want him. I want him because Babs doesn't want me to have him. I want him because I triple can't have him. But most of all I want him because I'm in love with him. Not because he's reserved for another woman, but because I love him. Out of all the men I could have and out of all those men I couldn't, I love *him*. I'd love him on a desert island, I'd love him under clinical conditions, I'd love him if no one in the world wanted him but me. I'd love him – and this is the real test – if my mother approved. And she would. I really love him.

I imagine a neat future, where Andy and I wake up together and live together and love together and cook together – I'll be healthy by then – and have sex twice a day (the national average is twice a week but we're better than that) and I own a Pilates studio because I'm good at what I do and I *feel* good, the ugly tug of badness has gone and . . . the dream scrapes greyly to a halt because reality is tapping on the window: Excuse me, but what happened to Alex? She's your friend. Her pal Robin taught you Pilates, your lives must have crossed at some point. Alex and Andy must have met, and what happened *then*? They've got to meet. I decide it's better to know the worst now, than to waste months in a fog of uncertain hope.

I sit in the car for ten more minutes trying to determine whether Andy is in before it occurs to me to look for his blue Vauxhall Astra. I scan the road and, oh yes, there it is, dissolving in its own rust, lowering the tone of the neighbourhood. I could, if I was brazen, march in – it is my own home, after all – and declare that I do want to 'have something' with him – sorry Babs, sorry Alex – and could we sign a contract (a billion pound penalty for transgression) to confirm that our exclusive relationship is, as from this moment, everlasting? I bite my lip, hard. After a good while spent biting, inspiration strikes. I'll call Robbie first.

I ruffle through my tatty old diary for his number – and it's a measure of how slack I've become that I haven't yet transferred all the details of friends and associates to my new business diary.

'*Chérie!*' exclaims Robbie, pronouncing it 'cherry'. 'What fun we had! You're still speaking to me. You must have liked my pants. Does this mean there's still hope?'

'It depends what you mean by hope, Robbie,' I say glumly. 'If you mean hope for the polar ice cap and me personally – no.'

'You know why I'm in love with you, Nat?' replies Robbie. 'You're weird. And I've got a baseball cap you can borrow. What's got you?'

I am about to blather out the pig's ear of a situation when something stops me. 'Nothing,' I bleat.

'Look, I –' Eek, what to say? 'Last night was fun but it was a bit of a mess, so I was thinking about having a dinner party. Well, more of a supper party, very informal, fewer people, that's why it's short notice, er, tonight depending on whether my guests can make it. You're one of them.'

What? Why did I say *that*? Supper party!? I hate eating under supervision. I will Robbie to have an unmissable appointment with his wide-screen television.

'I won't ask why the urgency. I'll just say yes and set the video.'

'Great, great,' I say, wilting. 'Well, look, it's er, six now, so let me invite the other guests and if you don't hear from me in the next twenty minutes I'll ah, see you at um, eight.'

'Fine by me.'

I bleep off, sense a shadow, and look up to see a huge face pressed against the car window. I'm about to scream then realise it's Andy. With as much dignity as I can manage (having just opened my mouth in a large red and white screaming shape), I whirr down the window.

'You've been sat in that car looking furtive for the last half hour,' he says. 'Either I'm interfering with police surveillance or you're avoiding me.'

'You're interfering.'

Andy gives me a look. 'So you've thought about my question and the answer is no.'

'Andy,' I blurt, 'are you free tonight?'

'Depends. If it involves Sang Thip or your brother, probably not. Why?'

'I'll tell you in a minute,' I whisper. 'Look. Go inside, I'll be in in a moment, I just have to make a call.'

His green eyes narrow, and my heart cracks right down the middle. 'Wait,' I stammer. 'I have thought about it. And,' I squeeze my hands into fists, 'the answer isn't no. But,' I add hastily as his face widens in a smile, 'I need a bit more time. I'm not playing games, but I'll know by the end of tonight. You'll understand.'

'I hope so,' says Andy, and stamps inside. I watch the door shut, sigh deeply and call my final guest. I feel like Hercule Poirot assembling suspects.

'Alex!' I shrill, when she picks up. 'Thank goodness! Where are you?'

'Natalie? Is that you? I'm on the bus – my car's in the garage. I'm on my way to teach a class. Do you want to come? I can squeeze you in if you want.'

'Oh no, no, I'd love to but I can't.' Why does this never happen to Hercule? 'But Alex, tell me, what time do you finish teaching?'

'Eight. Why?'

'Alex,' I say, forcing myself not to sound frantic. 'Please *please* would you come for dinner tonight? I know it's late notice, and it's a Tuesday night, and you'll be tired from

359

teaching, and you'll have to get a cab, but I've got a surprise for you, sort of to say thank you for everything you've done, and—'

'Yes, all right.'

'I know it's a detour for you but you'll see why when you come and—'

'Natalie, relax. Be calm! It's cool, I said yes!'

Another dilemma. Do I warn my love rival of the presence of the man we're fighting over? I manage to croak, 'Great. Just so you know, I'm inviting a few people.' I can't bring myself to be gender specific.

'Now you've done it,' I mutter, and plod inside. I can hear Andy crashing about his room. It sounds like he's shifting beer barrels. I rap on the door.

'Yeah?' he shouts.

I twist the doorknob but it's locked. And he calls *me* a baby!

'Andy, I'm cooking you and Robbie dinner,' I bellow through the keyhole. 'You and Robbie, and, a friend of mine. Robbie's coming round at eight and my friend, Alex, will be here about 8.30 or nine. So why don't you have a shower and get ready?'

There's a clack and the door's yanked open. 'You sound like my mum,' says Andy.

'Only because you're behaving like a teenager,' I growl, trying not to laugh. I think of Alex and succeed.

'What are you making? I just ate a salt beef sandwich.'

'Too bad,' I snap. 'You'll just have to force dinner down, er . . .'

Good question. What *am* I making? Whatever it is, I have an hour and a half to make it. That is, after I buy it. I look blindly around for inspiration and spy Andy's footwear. I don't believe this! He's from London!

'What?' he says, catching my stricken expression.

I pause. Trying to arrange other people's love lives is like being an infant school teacher without the perk of a zillion weeks' paid holiday. Can't adults do *anything* for

360

themselves? Will I have to force their mouths together?

'Andy,' I announce. 'If one thing stops me saying yes, it will be those foul offensive slippers. I'm sorry but even my grandad would have rejected them as being too dowdy for an eighty-year-old. They're even worse than your nasty tartan dressing gown. I hate them. I hate everything about them, I hate the way they curl up at the toes, I hate the cheap plastic soles, I hate the fuzzy grey material, I wish Paws had peed on them, and just please please promise me you won't wear them at the dinner table. I mean' – by now I'm spluttering – 'all you're missing is a pipe!'

I cringe in expectation of, I don't know what, tears? (Who knows how attached he is to those slippers, let alone the dressing gown?) What I do not expect is to be grasped by my shoulders and kissed, oh what a kiss, hard and soft, fierce and gentle, a deep sexy kiss that shivers through me, warming me to the bone, a kiss to cling to, a kiss that I could live off, feed off, no words but so much said in one long delicious lingering—

'I know what I'm going to cook,' I cry, springing out of the kiss with a rude popping sound. 'Linguine!'

Andy stands there, his eyelids heavy, his mouth still slightly open, his lips swollen, and a large obvious lump in his trousers. The slippers, I notice, are nowhere to be seen. Then I spy them, kicked off backwards on to the floor in his room. It takes every last grain of willpower not to launch myself back at him. I suck my lips, the taste of him. 'That,' I gulp, 'that was *cheating*.'

Andy clutches his hair. 'I'm going for that shower. Excuse me if I use all the cold water.'

I wait for the bathroom door to shut then run into the kitchen and spritz my face. I dig my nails into my palms to stop myself wailing. I want him. *Me*. I don't want Alex to have him. I don't care how nice she is or what she's done for me. It's too late, get a grip. I swallow the tears, and open the larder. No linguine, and an hour to go. My pulse is out of control. Any suggestions? Marks & Spencer's home cooking for fraudulent chefs still in denial to their pals? (who recognise the dark green flecks in the lettuce anyway)? It would be an honour, but they'll be shut by now. A takeaway? I couldn't, it's against my religion, if my mother wasn't alive she'd turn in her grave. My mother!

It would serve me right if she shouted my ear off and slammed down the phone ('And after Sunday's palaver, you have the nerve to ask me for food for your dinner party! If you think I'm going to give you so much as a baked bean after what you said! etc'). So when she picks up after one ring, I ask the favour haltingly, braced for a cool haughty rebuff. Moments later I replace the receiver with a sigh. What *was* I thinking? I faff about with knives and forks until there's a rap on the door. I open it to a long blast of sound:

'I've brought the vegetable lasagne there's enough for eight cover it in foil and stick it in the oven now on 200 it'll be ready in an hour now here's four pints of spinach soup stick it in the microwave on high it will be ready in no time and here's some cream to pour on it that's optional of course and here's an avocado salad it was already in the fridge I just chopped the avocado sprinkle lemon on it to stop it going black I brought a whole lemon and I thought you might not have bread so I've bought three olive breads and a block of unsalted butter and I'm going to Susan and Martin's tomorrow night so as luck would have it I'd made this chocolate mousse it's not a problem I'll just whip up another one tomorrow now it goes a treat with oranges so I've bought a bag of six and I thought you'd need something sweet to go with coffee so here's a fresh pack of Bendicks mints I knew you'd have the coffee I wasn't sure that you'd have the milk so here's a pint of semi-skimmed I thought you'd prefer it over the full cream now do you think that will be enough they won't go hungry?'

My mother dumps the industrial sized picnic basket on the side and smiles, a smile as wide and bright as a crescent moon. It shocks me because I realise how rarely she smiles.

'Thank you, Mum. Thank you. This is amazing. I'll tell everyone it was you. I feel embarrassed after what I said at the weekend.'

My mother busies herself unloading the picnic basket. 'That was different,' she says finally. 'I'd better get going. Who's coming to this dinner of yours?'

'Andy, and a couple of friends of his. He'd say hello except he's in the shower.'

'Well, I won't disturb him,' retorts my mother, as if I've suggested she pop her head round the bathroom door. 'Enjoy your evening.'

'Thank you. Hang on, I'll write you a cheque for all this.'

For the first time today my mother looks insulted. 'Not for food,' she cries. 'Never for food!'

My mother departs and I realise it's twenty to eight. I shove the lasagne in the oven and the soup in the microwave then speed to my room to get ready. Ready for what? Ready to play the martyr? No. Ready to *be* the martyr. I look at my face in the little mirror as I apply lipstick and I think, you know, this isn't a bad face. It could do with some padding, but it's not a bad face. I peer at myself until my breath fogs the mirror. I snap it shut. I am not looking forward to tonight. For so long, I've played at being the martyr – not eating, not loving, not living – but I realise that until now that's what I wanted, I *chose* to do it. Does that still count as martyrdom? I think not.

Offering Andy to Alex on a plate of lasagne is real martyrdom: for the first time ever I feel the burn and I don't like it one bit.

Chapter 43

Dot on eight Robbie raps on the door, clutching his large purple helmet in one hand and a bottle of champagne in the other.

We won't be needing *that,* I feel like saying. 'Hi,' I bleat instead. 'Thanks for coming. Champagne. You shouldn't have.'

Robbie leans forward for a kiss. 'Only the best for my favourite,' he murmurs. 'And now I know what you keep in your drinks cabinet, I didn't want to risk it. I didn't feel too clever this morning. You don't look too good either. How's the hair doing by the way?'

'The hair? Oh, my hair. Not too bad. I'm trying to be more healthy. It's still falling out but I think hair takes a while to catch up with the rest of you. And I don't wash it in the bath any more, so it can fall as much as it likes and I can't see the damage.'

'Good plan,' says Robbie. 'I like it! Mine's still going strong. As in, it's still going.'

I laugh. It's hard to panic with Robbie around. I want to confide about Alex but as I start to speak he grins, and I turn to see Andy emerging from his room with wet hair. I bite back a lustful whimper.

'All right Rob,' says Andy. 'Feeling butch enough in that biker's jacket?'

'It's a feeling you'll never know, Andrew,' retorts Robbie.

I smile tightly. Time's chopping on. I need an ally for the moment Alex walks through the door and all hell breaks loose and does the cha-cha-cha. I wonder how to distract Andy's attention while I confer with Robbie. Send him to purchase peanuts? Pretend I've misplaced the napkins? Then I think, oh for heaven's sake, and say, 'Andy, I need to talk to Robbie in the lounge for a second, can you check the oven for me?'

Andy trots obediently into the kitchen and Robbie meekly shadows me to the lounge.

I shut the door, lock it, remove the key, peer through the keyhole to check Andy isn't eavesdropping, and tell Robbie.

'Fuck!' he gasps, 'Oh fuck!'

Terror crawls over me in a thick slime. 'Robbie!' I screech under my breath. 'What do you mean, Oh fuck!? I did the right thing, didn't I? Tell me I did the right thing!'

Robbie drops heavily on to my suede sofa with what can only be described as a bang. I think he may have burst it. He wipes his hand over his face as if removing a sheen of sweat. 'I don't know, Natalie,' he mutters. 'Christ. I don't know what's going on with Andy right now, he hasn't been that keen to talk about it.'

'Well, he's talked about it with *me*,' I hiss. 'He's still in love with her. Speak quietly!'

Robbie lowers his voice to a wall-penetrating whisper. 'OK,' he says hoarsely. 'Here's what I think. If he'd wanted to get in touch, he would have, but—'

'Yes, but he thinks she's still with the other guy, he doesn't know it fell through!'

'Fair enough, but you can't just have him open the door to her with no warning! And what about Sasha? She ever mention wanting to get back in touch with *him*?'

I squirm. 'Andy said she'd wanted to stay friends. I can't remember, she might have said something wistful about her ex—'

'Whatever,' interrupts Robbie. 'We should tell him right now before she arrives, and if he doesn't want to know he can piss off to the pu—'

Drrrrrg! Robbie and I stare at each other in dismay and dive for the lounge door.

Clomp clomp!

'Locked!' I croak.

'Key!' shrieks Robbie.

'I'll get it!' roars Andy.

Clomp clomp!

'Wait!' I bawl.

'Stop!' screams Robbie.

'I've got it!' shouts Andy.

Click!

Silence.

Robbie and I freeze as we stand. We look like two contestants in a very miserable game of musical statues. Slowly, silently, Robbie hands me the key. We both strain our ears.

'Bloody hell! *Sash.*'

'Well, this isn't at all embarrassing.'

'Last time I saw you er . . . Haven't er, seen you around for a while.'

'You didn't want to see me around for a while, Andrew.'

'Can you blame me? So how is he?'

'Who?'

'Ah come on, Sasha! Whatsisface, Satchel, Shoulder Bag, the bloke you ran off with a month before our wedding, or don't you remember that little – *hiccup*?'

'Mitchell, Andy, his name was Mitchell. I wouldn't know how he is. We broke up.'

'Oh. Right. Well. I can't say I'm sorry.'

'Neither can I, Andy. It was a nightmare, as I'm sure you'll be pleased to know.'

'Why should it please me? It's nothing to do with me.'

'If it's nothing to do with you, why can't you say you're sorry that my marriage failed?'

'You . . . *married* Satchel?'

'Mitchell! Yes, Andy! I didn't leave you for a one-night stand!'

366

'So the white dress didn't go to waste.'

'There was none of that, if you must know. Just two witnesses in a registry office.'

'How incredibly *tasteful* of you, Sasha. That makes me feel so, much, better.'

'Why don't they just bonk on the floor and get it over with?' whispers Robbie.

'What do you mean?' I hiss. 'They're having a Godalmighty row! This isn't to do with sex, it's about, it's about – it's about, wait, now we've missed a bit! Shh!'

'Andy, don't give me that shit. You were the one who refused to discuss it. I *pleaded* to give you an explanation, you wouldn't have it.'

'And why do you think that was, Sasha? Any idea? Anything to do with the pain you caused me? I didn't know there *was* unhappiness like that.'

'Andy, all I'm saying is, don't play the guilt card on me now. I know I hurt you. But it was hard for me too. It was hard for me to do that to you. It devastated me to see how hurt you were.'

'You and your bleeding heart.'

'Oh God, Andy! What would you have preferred? That I went through with the wedding and started an affair when we got back from honeymoon?'

'No, actually, Sasha! Call me a head-in-the-clouds idealist but I'd have preferred that my *fiancée* had no fucking affair at all! With Rucksack, Clutchbag, or whoever!'

'I'm sorry.'

'What?'

'I said I'm sorry. Sorry for all of it. I am, Andy.'

'Yeah, well. You did what you had to do. It's done.'

'So, Andy.'

'Yeah?'

'What *are* you doing here?'

'Me? I live here. What are *you* doing here?'

'You *live* here! What, with Natalie?'

'How do *you* know Natalie?'

I can't stand it any longer. The storm is over and, if anything, I want to prevent the reunion hug. I rattle open the lock and burst into the hallway. 'Surprise,' I say weakly. Two faces stare at me accusingly. I glance at Robbie for back-up.

He chirps, 'Just call her Cilla!'

'Why didn't you tell me you knew Sash?' demands Andy. He sounds furious.

'Alex,' says Alex. 'I should have said. I don't call myself Sasha any more.'

'Exactly!' I blurt, 'I didn't know Alex *was* Sasha, she was my friend Alex, I only realised today and and' – I finish lamely – 'I thought it would be nice for you two to meet up again.'

'So let me get this straight,' says Alex curtly. 'You two are living together?'

Her implication is, if Andy and I are romantically involved, why would I invite his former fiancée round to be reacquainted? I might ask myself the same question. I feel reluctant to clarify the misunderstanding. Robbie has no such qualms.

'Not in *that* sense!' he pipes up. 'They're not saucing each other! He's just Natalie's lodger. Nat's a friend of Andy's sister Babs. There's nothing going on between Nat and Andy. He's free and single, darlin!'

I treat Robbie to a smile as sweet as sulphuric acid. So – I am gratified to note – does Andy.

'Robbie,' purrs Alex. 'What a pleasure to see you again after all this time.'

I can't tell if she's being sarcastic, but I pray she is.

'Natalie,' interrupts Andy in a cool voice. 'You still haven't explained how you know Sa— Alex.'

'From my gym,' I reply gruffly. 'Alex was the one who got me into Pilates.'

'Now I get it,' he sighs. 'So you thought—' He abandons this sentence, and starts a new one. 'And to think I once

368

wanted to be a psychologist. So. Are we going to eat or what? Do you *want* to stay, er, Alex?'

His tone softens and I feel the cold clutch of jealous rage. This wasn't the plan. When I say I wanted to test Andy, to see if he really was still in love with Sasha, I should have said that deep down I thought it was a controlled experiment. An hour ago he and I were kissing! We were having a *thing*. I thought I was safe. But incredibly, it looks as if my bluff has been called. I was wrong. I should have waited. Years of uncertainty would have been better than this.

'I wouldn't want to spoil the party,' drawls Alex, smiling at Andy from under her eyelashes.

I tense in annoyance. So you're leaving then? I say in my head. I try not to stare at her. The woman has an X-rated figure, thrown into relief by a bright turquoise open-neck shirt, cream bootleg trousers, and high chunk-heeled mules. I recognise raw sex appeal when I see it, and wish Babs – oh great, I've lost her too – was here with a fire extinguisher. I want those curves. For the first time in my life, I want curves. I feel like a pencil.

'Great,' I say, cranking my lips to a smile. 'Why don't you all go and sit in the lounge?'

I put one foot in front of the other and somehow make it to the hob without strangling any one of my guests. I am pouring the defrosted soup into a pan, when Robbie lollops in.

'That was hairy on and off!' he booms. 'But all credit to you, Nat, it's looking good! You did a nice job clearing up the front room an' all! They're drinking champagne. I thought I'd leave them alone for a sec – know what I mean?' I am fond of Robbie but it takes all my strength to refrain from tipping the soup-filled saucepan on to his balding head.

'Actually, Robbie,' I reply through my teeth. 'I think you might have made a mistake. They could start fighting again. It could turn nasty. You'd better get in there now.'

'But—'

'Go, Robbie!' I hiss, trying to sound like a senior official in the FBI. 'Go! go! go! go! go!'

Robbie gives me a stung, surprised glance over his shoulder as he hurries out. It reminds me of the look Paws gave Matt on being scolded for chewing up his Puppy Album. (Matt had brought it in one Christmas to show us – lots of photographs captioned 'Paws With His Squeaky Toy,' and 'Paws Eating A Peanut Butter Basset Biscuit.' It was cute, but I think Paws felt the pictures were degrading and took affirmative action.) I wrestle the soup bowls out of the cupboard and yell, 'Everyone! Dinner's ready!'

Robbie runs in – 'Sir! Yes, sir!' – and Andy and Alex shuffle in behind him looking moony-eyed. Or maybe I'm paranoid.

'Can I help?' offers Robbie.

'No. You've done enough, thanks.'

'Where shall I sit?' asks Alex.

'Wherever you like,' I say silkily. 'Next to Robbie.' I hurl everyone's soup into their bowls like a toddler throwing paint at a canvas. A green splash lands on Andy's shirt. 'Sorry, let me wipe it off,' I snarl, grabbing a smelly dishcloth and grinding in the stain.

'If you're not careful, Nat,' he murmurs, 'you're going to erase my nipple.'

I throw the dishcloth in the sink, and sit down. I realise that Andy has sat himself opposite Alex. The prime seductive position! *I* am facing Robbie.

'This soup is delicious, Natalie,' beams Alex. She has finished her champagne and is sipping red wine. I hope that it stains her teeth crimson. Red wine stains my teeth *and* my lips – whenever I drink it I end up looking like a pig in a blackberry bush.

'Good.'

We all embark on drinking our soup. I want to let off a social stink bomb, something like 'So was Mitchell better in bed than Andy?', but my rigid training won't let me.

Instead, Alex tells the boys what a natural I am at Pilates. She glances at me now and then, as if for approval. Andy and Robbie make encouraging noises, and I manage to crack my face. Despite this, you could cut the tension with a knife. Which is more than can be said for the lasagne (which, had I not cooked it to fossilisation, would have been delicious).

'Nat,' says Andy. 'I don't mean to be rude, but what did you use to bind the pasta? Concrete?'

I am fighting my tongue – which seems to have swollen to fill my mouth and prevent speech – when Alex chips in: 'Natalie, ignore him. He always says, "I don't mean to be rude" before coming out with the mother of all rudenesses. For some inexplicable reason he thinks it excuses him.' She smiles, and smoothes her hair, which is pulled back into a high sexy ponytail and doesn't need smoothing. Argh! It's a preening gesture!

'Oh really?' I tinkle, with a falsetto laugh. 'How funny!'

I cut into my lasagne like I'm stabbing it to death. I am blown away by her sheer nerve. Already she's acting like he's her property, her responsibility, her boyfriend, *apologising* for him. Seems like Alex has a low alcohol tolerance and a short memory. I dearly want to throw down my (blunt, useless) knife and run out bawling, but even at this moment of madness I'm aware that if I do I'll regret it, almost as much as I regret hosting this ludicrous dinner.

'Just leave it,' I say. 'I'll serve dessert.'

'Is that a threat?' enquires Robbie.

'That's funny,' I say again, stupidly. I hurl great dollops of brown mousse into three bowls, and plop a small dollop into the fourth.

'You know,' exclaims Andy, 'I believe that if you think something's funny, you don't *say,* "that's funny." You either laugh, smile or – you don't think it's funny.'

'So what are you saying?' growls Robbie. 'Nat's pretending she thinks I'm funny?'

'Robbie, mate,' sighs Andy. 'Do I have to spell it out?'

'No,' I blurt. 'No, you don't. Would you like an orange with your mousse?'

Robbie starts sniggering. 'I don't know why, but that sounds obscene!' I itch to slam Robbie's good-natured face into his mousse.

'This,' drools Alex, licking her spoon, 'is *unspeakably* good. It was sweet of you, Nat, to remember my New Year's resolution.'

She flutters her eyelashes in a parody of ecstasy and shivers. I sneak a look at Andy. He's watching her. Oh God, do men think women liking mousse is *sexy*? I've had enough. I spit in the face of protocol (it's either protocol or Alex) and light a cigarette. Fuck the Bendicks.

'Does anyone want coffee?' I ask, trying to sound friendly. Everyone reacts like 'coffee' is code for 'arsenic' or 'a game of charades'.

Robbie cries, 'Nah, not for me thanks, I'm still knackered after last night, what's the time, jeez, that late' – I glance in surprise at the clock which, if my nursery teacher was all she claimed to be, reads 9.37 – 'I'd better head off, but it was great, Nat, good to see you; see you, Andy, and *very* nice to see you again, Sasha, sorry, Alex – be seeing you.'

With that he kisses me, then Alex, briskly on the cheek, raises a hand to Andy, and disappears out of the front door.

Alex rises from her chair, stumbling slightly. 'I should get going too, Natalie. I'll call a cab.' She smiles. 'It's been a hell of an evening, doncha know!'

'Oh I do.'

She hugs me, tightly. I exert a feeble pressure in return. Andy hovers. I catch his eye and he smiles. I want to slap his face.

'Thanks,' she breathes into my ear. 'Thank you, Natalie.'

To a person with no understanding of the word

'subtext', Alex is thanking me for the rock-hard dinner. She pulls away and smiles into my eyes, a meaningful smile. There is no doubt she's telling me she wants him back. Oh God. If she weren't so bloody nice, this might be less of a wrench. If she wasn't a friend, at least I'd win the consolation prize of hating her. As it is, I resent her while resenting myself for my lack of grace. Thanks to Alex, I'm embarking on a career change, I'm making the new start I never thought I'd make.

Then again, thanks to Alex, the *other* new start I might have made has been gunned down Mafia-style: blam, blam, thank you ma'am.

But the truth is, even as I brood on this, a part of me hopes I'm a pessimist prone to insane exaggeration.

The part is speedily disappointed when Andy declares, 'You don't have to bother with a cab, Alex. I've only had one drink, and that was hours ago, I'll drive you.'

'Are you sure?' she asks bashfully. 'All the way to West London? You don't have to.'

'It's fine,' he says – as I scream in my head: One drink is still dangerous! 'Have none for the road!' – 'if you don't mind a Vauxhall Astra.'

'A Vauxhall Astra?' she laughs. 'You've changed your style.'

'I've changed a lot of things,' he replies, and grins at her. I might as well be a fly on the wall. Swat me, somebody, please.

Sadly no one does, which means that as the lovebirds flit into the night, I hear Alex giggle, 'You've forgotten, Andy. I never judge a man by his car.'

Chapter 44

Matt is unrepentant about his behaviour on Monday night. He says he was practically drowning in testosterone and it was his duty to be cabaret queen for the night; everyone expected it. He had fun with Andy and Robbie, and intimidated Chris. He also claims that Tony needed a lesson in humility. He says Mel wasn't offended, so why am I? I say Mel wasn't offended because she thought you were fighting over her. I'm not offended, Matt, I'm *concerned*. Cabaret queen, indeed. Killer queen, more like. Matt says, I did it for you.

'I knew that,' I manage, finally. My brain is milkshake, but I sense his frustration, and rush to make amends. 'I – I only wish *I'd* punched him. Thanks, Matt.'

'So you should be. Stephen was furious with me – getting into scraps, behaving like a lout.'

'He can talk!' I splutter. 'He's got two broken legs and a fractured hip from falling out of a window, pissed!'

'I did point that out to him. Anyway, let's not waste time – what about that gorgeous lodger of yours?'

'Well. There is news and – it's not *great*.' I yap it all out.

'Naughty Andy,' says Matt, practically panting with intrigue. 'He's just a boy who can't say no.' I want to reach down the phone and throttle him.

'But maybe he was just being polite. Maybe he—'

'Hold the front page!' cries Matt. 'Man Doesn't Want A Shag! He's Just Being Polite!' He laughs and adds, 'Sorry darling, they don't make 'em like that any more!'

I slump. I still have trouble accepting that even nice guys

374

carry the bastard gene which can be activated without warning. Even though Andy didn't return home last night (it's now 10.02 a.m. Wednesday) I continue to flail around for reasons to excuse his absence without condemning him. I can't believe that a man could swear undying like for a woman one day, and elope with another the next. How could he? Easily, it would seem. I now know there's no such thing as a safe bet. Yes, I set them up. But all I wanted to do was lay a ghost. I didn't expect *him* to lay it. I thought if I tidied up the loose ends, I could happily proceed with my future. I blame myself, but I blame him too. He could have rung. Surely he owes me that much?

Maybe the engine fell off the Astra and the AA said it would take days to fix so Alex suggested he sleep on the sofa? Maybe they stayed up all night talking until Andy fell asleep on the sofa? Maybe Alex realised she still loved him but he realised he didn't love her and said so and then she got upset so Andy stayed out of pity but slept on the sofa?

What if there *is* no sofa? Why didn't Andy ring? Maybe he was on his way home and had a minor accident and is in hospital? I don't want to think about whether I'd prefer Andy to have a minor accident than sex with Alex.

'Do you think he could have had an accident?'

'Oh *no*,' replies Matt. 'Andy seems like a sensible boy. I'm sure he used a condom.'

When I put the phone down I'm a squeak away from storming to the fridge and plundering the remains of the chocolate mousse. I feel angry and full of spite and I want to self-destruct the old way. I rip open the larder door and the box of Bendicks winks at me. Go on, you know you want to. I imagine tearing off the cellophane, fumbling open the lid, pulling out those fat chunky little chocolates, the creamy fondant, stickily thick, that irresistibly gunky *mouth-feel*. I reach out and take the box. Dull the pain. I pick and scratch at the wrapping.

I throw it in the bin. As I'm not above retrieving food from the bin (my complaint turns you schizoid – part drug fiend, part alleycat – a hard habit to break) I tip the remnants of the mousse and lasagne on top of the Bendicks as a safeguard. I want to scrape out the lasagne dish, lick the mousse spoon, eat, eat, eat, everything, anything, including my Kiehl's Milk Honey and Almond Scrub, just cram it in – so I swish on the hot tap, dump it all hastily in the sink, and I'm safe. I refuse to replace Andy with an after-dinner mint – he may be a tart but give the man some credit.

It's tempting, though. My blood roars loud in my ears. The urge to binge and vomit – not, on paper, the most alluring prospect – is like a pact with the devil. I know it's the worst possible thing I could do, but ache to do it regardless. It's like any compulsion, I suppose. It becomes your best friend, when you were under the impression that it was merely a passing acquaintance. You ignore the undercurrent of wretchedness, you shove the 'no no no' to the back of your mind, and submit. You're spellbound. You don't give a stuff about later, you are embroiled in stuffing yourself *now*. I suppose I might have had the odd lapse I haven't told you about. You get a few precious seconds of relief post-yak.

I'm sorry. It's crazy trying to explain my peculiarities to normal people. I don't mean to sound patronising (actually, that's a lie, I feel like a crack addict consoling someone who smoked a cigar, once) but maybe you get a similar high buying a sinfully expensive handbag when your overdraft is at break point. There comes a moment where you physically cannot stop yourself. Your entire existence is geared towards this handbag, your soul is screaming out for it. You'd risk your home, your reputation, you'd lose your job, go to debtor's prison for this handbag, yeah, yeah, whatever, keep talking, just swipe the card, sweetheart, hand over the m*****f***ing – *purrrrr* – baaaaag!

That monomaniacal madness, that stripped-of-dignity desperation is a millionth of what the act of bulimia feels like. When you're happy, you could resist a roomful of bags, marzipan, crack, whatever. But when you're low, your demons find you. Rejecting temptation then - that's the test. So far, I've failed fatly. Yet today, something stops me – me. I realise that I don't want to be a loser twice over. I will not. I steel myself by pretending I'm being filmed by a hidden camera. One doesn't lapse in front of people. After Andy left, viewers would have seen me tidy up to the tune of Tina Turner. Quite right, Tina – love *is* a second hand emotion.

They would have seen me spray, scrub and sanitise the flat, until the lingering scent of Alex's perfume – Chanel No.5, could she *be* any more annoying? – was eliminated. But again, to viewers it would have seemed normal. They might have seen me stare into the fridge once or twice or forty times, but that could be explained away as boredom. As could the frenzied glances at the clock. And what of the channel-hopping till 2 a.m in full make-up? One likes to look one's best for, er, oneself. As for the intermittent pillow-punching, I could be an amateur lightweight boxer. Or possessor of a very hard pillow. I even ate a prescription breakfast this morning (they probably thought the milk was sour, they weren't to know I was hallucinating about pancakes). I'm not going to ruin my public's impression of me by morphing into a psycho. No, indeed.

'Where *are* you, you miserable sodding BASTARD?!' I screech, slamming both fists down on the table. 'I bloody haaaaaaaaate you, you ARSEHOLE!' And you've ruined my television debut, I add silently, scowling for the camera's benefit. I try not to feel bad about it. My Tourette's outburst wasn't ideal but, I tell myself, as breakdowns go, it could have been a *lot* worse.

I should start work but I'm too ruffled. I'll ring my mother. She'll be itching to know if everyone enjoyed her lasagne and – were it not for our council house fracas – she'd have rung me at dawn to find out. So I call the surgery, endure a three-day grilling on the appetite of each guest (I tell her what she wants to know: yes, they all had seconds, no, there wasn't a scrap left, yes, everyone cleared their plate, no, it was the perfect consistency, yes, I remembered the Bendicks) then ask the question I keep forgetting to ask.

'Mum,' I say shyly. 'You wanted to ask my advice about something.'

'So I did.'

I wait.

'Mum? You still there?'

'Wait!' she hisses in a hammy whisper. 'Susan's loitering by the Rolodex!' There is a pause, during which I assume my mother gives Susan a look to indicate her cover is blown, then: 'Natalie. I've made a decision. I'm going to Australia.'

'Mum! That's great news! When did you decide? When are you going? Do Tara and Kelly know?'

'I made up my mind on Sunday night. I booked the flights first thing yesterday. It's all settled. Of *course* Tara and Kelly know, dear. You don't descend on people without warning! I haven't told Tony yet. I'll get around to it, I haven't had a moment. I'm leaving a fortnight today, and staying for three weeks. If I'm going all that way and for that price I might as well make the most of it. Kelly invited me to stay at her house – apparently she's got a lovely little townhouse in an area called Paddington, she's lived there for years and years – but, well, I said I'd book into a hotel for the first week and we'll see how we go.'

'Mum, well done,' I exclaim, wondering if there are further revelations in the pipeline. Purple hair extensions? Stop-off in Ibiza? A dolphin ankle tattoo?

'However,' adds my mother, 'there is a small fly in the ointment. Your father.'

378

'Dad?'

My mother sighs, as if this is a dim response. 'That was what I wanted to talk to you about. I had words with your father on Sunday, after I spoke to you. And I suspect he'd like to come too. He would *love* to meet his granddaughter. I know your father. Even if he has refashioned himself into a Julio Iglesias-Bertie Wooster hybrid.'

'Mu-um,' I say reprovingly.

'So. The question is, should I invite him? Or should I let the silly old sod stew in his own lo-fat juice?'

'Mother!' I gasp. 'I think . . . I think it would be the right thing to invite him. If' – I gulp – 'you think Kimberli Ann would let him go.'

'Natalie,' replies my mother, 'I was married to that man for sixteen years. And I'd bet my bottom dollar, as I suppose they say in California, that little Miss Silly Knickers is *not* head honcho in that relationship. Even if she thinks she is. Your father makes all the right noises but he'll do as he likes. The only thing stopping him from hopping on a plane to Sydney is his pride. He won't come unless I invite him. And I'm not sure he deserves to be invited.'

I suck in my cheeks and bite gently on the flesh. I want to yell, 'Invite him!' but I know that my father is not the only one who does as he likes. Also, I realise that I've been fighting the wrong battles for too long. I tell her I'm flattered to be consulted but I feel the decision isn't mine to make. Irksomely, my mother doesn't appreciate the ethical piety of my response and ends the call abruptly. Or maybe Susan was loitering by the Rolodex again.

I try to concentrate on my latest commission but am distracted by the urgent need to, eg, check my teeth for abnormalities, remember the names of everyone in my junior school fourth year class, find my snowman eggcup. I am appalled at this drop-off in drive. Once I'd have set my alarm for seven, been at my desk by 8.30 – having sped to the gym for a ten-mile run – determined to make every minute a success. As it is, the last time I faced the

StairMaster was three days ago and every step was heavy hell. My heart felt like an overdone steak inside my chest. This is me, who used to flit through aerobic boot camp six days out of seven! Pilates is tiring but not skinnifying. Why don't I care? Well, I *do* care but not to that somewhat crucial degree of doing something about it.

Talking of which. I must ring Robin, confirm my Pilates appointment for 5 p.m., and write a large cheque. Although my mother has sanctioned my decision to roll my future to a cliff-edge, I now have another worry to chew on: signing up with Alex's contact means tangling in her love life. But I suppose, one way or another, I'm already tangled in it. I'm her friend. I don't suppose I will be for much longer, once she knows about our tussle over Andy. Then it suddenly occurs to me that Alex might not *know* about the tussle.

Why should Andy tell her? She's bound to ask if there was anything between us – she's a woman. But he could lie about me having an unrequited crush and she'd believe him. Babs would be thrilled they're back together and delighted to back up his story.

I bash out a press release, hitting the keys so hard I nearly snap a finger. I consider ringing Mel, to ask after my brother's ego and see if he's been told about the Australia visit. I'm betting Mum won't 'get around' to telling him until she's standing in line at the Qantas check-in desk. It's weak of me not to ring Tony direct, but recent debates have kicked up a pile of grievances. I'm trying to come to terms with the realisation that I resent him. Also, despite Monday night and the discovery that he fights like a girl, I'm still scared of him. He has a lot to answer for, but I don't dare ask him the questions.

Knowing Mel will be in rehearsal, I take the coward's option and leave a message on her mobile. I check the clock, again: 2.25 and still no Andy. I sniff, wipe my nose on the back of my hand, and feel tragic. 'It's not fair!' I bleat, at the empty kitchen.

I drum my fingers. I'm sure Andy didn't lock his door. Maybe he keeps a diary. I take the first step towards damnation, the phone shrills, and I jump. I snatch it up, guilty yet grateful.

'Hello?' I say, in my best throaty purr.

'Natalie? You sound poorly.'

The second blast this week from boyfriend past.

'Hello, Saul,' I say, quickly adjusting my tone to unisex. 'What an unexpected ple—, what an – this is unexpected!'

We have a six-minute conversation which lasts for hours. I'm still yawning when I get to Pilates. I stare round the studio in dismay.

'I know it *looks* like a torture chamber,' says Robin. 'That's because it is!'

I smile, politely. I didn't expect there to be other people wafting about, but there are. A tanned bleach-haired girl with a pierced belly button, sparingly dressed in Nike's finest. A solid horsy woman in a loose T-shirt and baggy leggings. A nondescript man in a tracksuit. They are all stretched on various types of rack, their legs or arms attached to pulleys, and moving slowly back and forth. My instinct tells me to run for my life. As ever, I ignore it. I fill in the form Robin hands me and await his verdict. He beams and his eyes crinkle.

'PR*rrrr*,' he says. 'Lots of hunching over a desk, I imagine. I think today we'll work on the upper body, we'll concentrate on opening your chest.'

Grateful as I am to have a man concentrate on my chest, I feel drawn to apologise. 'I know I stoop, I know my posture's not that good. People are always telling me to stand up straight.'

'Are they?' says Robin, arching an eyebrow. 'Bossy old farts. Tell them to mind their own business!'

I laugh, and my shoulders unhunch. This is the last time, for a while, that I'm allowed to relax. I never knew that lying on my back could be such punishing work. Actually, I tell a lie. And speaking of Saul, we're meeting up later. On the phone, after ploughing through endless civilities – how I'd been, how he'd been, how my mother had been, how my work had been, how his work had been, how our respective cars had been (no enquiries after the health of Chris's car, however) – Saul got to the point. I still had his favourite tie, the Tweetie Pie one, and his signed copy of *Stalingrad*.

If I'm not otherwise engaged (only Saul could reduce me to the level of a public convenience in the course of courtesy) might I consider joining him for a light supper some time this week? I could return his possessions and we could catch up – kill two birds with one stone. I wanted to reply: How about we do our bit for bird protection and I post your possessions instead?

Then I thought, be fair. He's a lovely man and you cheated on him. And the truth is, your main gripe against him was his weight. He had a beer tyre (it was more than a belly – it went all the way round) and he didn't even drink beer. You've moved on. Anyway it would be fun, no, it would be *kind* to see Saul again. So we're meeting outside the studio at 6.40. I lie on my back on what looks like a skinny four-poster pinched off a dominatrix, grip the poles behind my head, and lift my legs to what Robin calls 'a tabletop position'. He orders me to, 'Tense your stomach, and drop your legs to one side.' I misunderstand and flop open my legs like a spaniel wanting its tummy tickled. Or worse.

'Keep your knees jammed together,' says Robin, ignoring this fine *Carry On* moment. I cringe. 'Here, squeeze on this cushion. Good, now try and lift your legs using only your stomach muscles. Slowly, relax the neck. Good. And to the other side. Nice. Don't arch your back . . .'

Robin is patient, especially when I have trouble with a lower back exercise. (I'm supposed to lie on my stomach, rest on my elbows, contract my 'corset muscles' and rise up like a 'swan'. My back feels like an old wooden ruler being bent against a desk and my swan emerges as a slug.)

382

'It annoys me,' I pant from my undignified position, 'that I can't do it!'

'Natalie,' murmurs Robin. 'Have you ever met any masters of martial arts?'

'No,' I say crossly.

'They're all about ninety years old.'

When I apologise for being useless because I can't peel up one vertebra at a time, he enquires, 'So Natalie, if I came to you for a lesson in PR, would you be furious if I couldn't do it immediately?'

'Probably.'

What I like most about Robin is that he knows how to tell people off. I'm on my back – surprise! – bending and stretching my legs to manoeuvre myself back and forth along a sprung trolley-like arrangement, and trying to breath correctly. There is a correct and incorrect way of breathing and Robin has even more rules than Alex. I'd assumed the incorrect way was to hold your breath until you suffocate. But no. It's lifting your ribs. 'Natalie,' says Robin sweetly, 'if you don't stop lifting your ribcage, I'm going to take a picture and put it in a book of how not to do Pilates.'

As a person with the sensitivity of an alarm system in *Mission Impossible* I tend not to cope well with being told off. But Robin tells me off so beautifully, the rebuke bounces. I marvel at this, as I dress in the changing room. Is it my imagination or are my clothes starting to pinch? I'd freak except it's hard to panic when your muscles feel like foam. I tug at my jumper and dab on lipstick, to show Saul that I haven't let myself go. Goodness knows what kind of a state that cake fiend will be in. Oh well. A few hours out of my life. I wish he were Andy.

I shake off the wish. Not even a call to say thanks for the lasagne. Stuff him. I'm doing all right. Look at me, gliding around a Pilates studio while the rest of the world works. I'm living on the edge! This is *my* thing and I'm doing it for me, without caring what other people think. I bounce back into the studio to write a cheque and make my next appointment. Now is a moment of triumph and I won't let Andy spoil it. Nothing can spoil it.

'Alex will be along in a minute,' says Robin. 'She booked in specially.'

The moment is spoiled, and five seconds later I'm yomping down the stairs three at a time. If Saul's late I'll kill him. I don't want to see Alex, please don't let me see her, be here Saul, I don't want to see her. I tiptoe the final stair and peek round the corner. The lobby is empty, apart from a sleek young man in a sharp suit and a crew cut, his elegant nose buried in a copy of *Dangerous Sports Monthly*. No Alex, no Saul. I check my watch. Six-forty. How unlike Saul not to be punctual. I sigh, and the sleek young man looks up. I do a spasm of a double take.

'Blimey,' I croak. 'You've changed a bit!'

'Do you think so?' says Saul. 'Fancy that!' He smirks, showing born-again cheekbones. Fancy that indeed.

I attempt a breezy smile, and reply, 'Yes, I've never seen you with your hair short like that. I didn't realise accountants were allowed such short haircuts.' I don't mention his astonishing weight loss – all the blubber melted and replaced by muscle – I don't need to. My impression of a San Francisco aftershock was more than adequate.

'Yes, well,' chortles Saul. 'I've had a few strange looks in the office, I can tell you!'

I join in the chortle but I'm furious. How *dare* he do this to me? I know what this is. The most juvenile trick in the relationship book! Wanting his tie and his *Stalingrad* indeed! The new model Saul doesn't give two hoots about ties and tomes! He's all into (groovy click of the fingers here) calypso shirts and *Men's Health*. I've walked into a trap! He's here to parade his pecs. To taunt me with his digitally remastered personality. To make me realise what a fool I was to cheat on him. And, may I say, it's half working.

'Well, where shall we go?' I say briskly.

Saul rakes a hand through his shorn hair and my jaw yields to gravity. He's wearing a chunky silver ring on his thumb – his *thumb* – like a garage DJ! Where did he learn that? He's been watching late night television!

I know that it's normal to swear revenge on a faithless ex. To picture scenes in which the fickle one watches, alone and dejected, as you laugh in the arms of someone better looking. I know it's normal*ish* to stick pins in the private parts of a Barbie or Ken. But only Saul would see the bluster through to the bitter end.

'I took the liberty of reserving us a table next door,' he replies. 'I looked it up in *Time Out*.' Ah yes, the Bible of the unspontaneous.

'Would you mind terribly if we go somewhere a bit further away?'

Saul frowns. 'But, Natalie. I've *booked* it.' He makes it sound as if he's carved our names on the best table.

'Right, fine, whatever.' Saul hasn't changed a bit. 'Let's just g—'

The door flies open. 'Natalie! So glad I caught you! Robin said you'd be here till half six.'

'Alex,' I choke, as Saul looks on, bug-eyed. 'Hi. This is my er, friend, Saul.'

'Your friend Saul,' twinkles Alex. 'Hello, Saul.'

'Pleased to meet you, Alex.'

They shake hands and I watch, with gritted teeth. She doesn't know. Andy hasn't told her. Alex turns to me and I force a smile. So much for our fab new friendship. I *know* they slept together last night. This is awful.

'Sorry I haven't rung to thank you for last night but I hoped I'd catch you here. Saul' – she beams at him – 'let me tell you. You've got a good woman here! Hang on to her!' I laugh miserably. So does Saul. 'Natalie,' adds Alex. 'Are you off now?'

'Yes, unfortunately,' I simper, at exactly the same time Saul simpers. 'But only next door. Not the greasy spoon – the *bar-café*.'

'Excellent. Can I barge in on you for a second when I've done? I won't be interrupting anything?'

'No!' cry Saul and I together.

'*She's* rather attractive,' breathes Saul, scurrying to keep up with me as I sweep into the bar. 'Is she, er, on the market?'

'She's not a Texas longhorn, Saul, and no, you're twenty-four hours too late,' I mutter, as the waiter leads us to a showcase table at the window. *We* must be rather attractive.

'I think,' begins Saul with a chuckle, 'she presumed we were a cou—'

'Yes, she did.' I soften my voice as a fiendish plan occurs. I squeeze Saul brutally on the arm and say, 'You know – if a man is in a relationship it makes him irresistible to other women.'

'Oh, it goes without saying.'

His tone is pleasingly thoughtful. I remove my hand from his arm and spend the next forty-five minutes treading conversational water, while keeping an eye out for Alex. Saul does the same. At 7.35 she puts us out of our misery. Saul makes a big palaver – leaping up, offering his chair, fetching the menu. She orders an orange juice and lets him fuss.

'Ah Natalie,' she murmurs, as Saul gives the waiter detailed instructions as to the precise strength of his Bloody Mary. 'That was so special of you. You know what I'm talking about.' She touches my arm. I nod. She isn't referring to the lasagne. 'I would have called Andy eventually,' she adds. 'But. The way we left it, the atmosphere between us didn't encourage me to pick up the phone. So thank you.'

'Pleasure,' I bleat.

'He should be here any minute,' she adds, glancing at her watch. 'After fourteen months we've got a lot to catch up on.'

I knew it. I excuse myself and walk to the Ladies, where

I peer into the mirror, re-perfect my lipstick and practise narrowing my eyes. Let my heart crust over!

When Andy saunters into the bar five minutes later, I'm ready for him.

Chapter 45

Apart from Saul, the men I've known are not time sensitive. Aged nineteen, I invited a guy round for dinner and he only rang to re-confirm two hours before he was due. So, because I liked him and was hurt by his slack attitude, I pretended I'd forgotten our date and was busy. When I told Babs, she was furious and ordered me to ring him back and say I'd made a mistake. She couldn't understand why I would judge a man's behaviour by *my* standards. Men simply weren't *up* to being judged by my standards. I keep forgetting this.

'Saul,' I say, playfully ruffling his hair.

'Natalie, please be careful. That style is very hard to maintain!'

'Sorry,' I add, wiping the gel off my hands and on to my trousers. 'All I was going to say is, Andy, you have my chair, I'll sit on Saulie's lap. OK, babe?'

On the pretext of stroking the base of Saul's neck, I poke him hard between the shoulder blades.

Saul makes a face like a soldier who's just been shot in the back. Then, mid death throe, he gets it and croaks, 'Certainly, er, darling. Come and perch on your Uncle Saul!'

I want to glare at Saul for turning our *Romeo and Juliet* into a farce about incest, but I sense Andy's gaze drilling into my skull. Instead I mutter that I've run out of fags and escape to the cigarette machine. I can tell Andy wants me to make eye contact – he's emitting a beseeching aura – but I refuse to acknowledge him or it. When he greeted me with a kiss on the cheek, I sat as still and cold as a marble statue. If he wanted to communicate he should have picked up the phone. I shove the coins into the slot with venom.

'Natalie,' says a tense voice in my ear, 'what's going on?'

I yank my fag packet out of its tray and whirl around. 'What's going on?' I splutter, trying not to quake. 'You tell *me!*'

Andy looks me up and down like the worst sort of shop assistant. 'I *was* going to tell you,' he snarls. 'But fuck it, I won't bother.'

We scowl at each other, bristling. I itch to slap his face, but frankly, I don't want to give him the satisfaction.

'Don't then,' I hear myself say. 'Like I give a damn.' I stare at him, and will myself to speak. I want him to understand me. I want him to know the truth, whatever the consequences. Speak, says my head. How? says my heart. The reason I'm acting so cool, I say silently, is I love you, and I'm petrified that you don't love me. I'm trying to hurt you, because I'm hurt. This situation is my fault. I should have used words, instead I played games. I made you guess. And you misunderstood. I hate you for choosing Alex but, if anything, *I* drove you to her. I was too timid to tell you outright and, by risking nothing, I've risked everything. I stare at Andy, helplessly. Years of not speaking take their toll.

I blurt, 'I presume you'll be moving out. Again.'

'Tomorrow morning,' he replies rudely, and stalks off.

When I gather the strength to walk back to our window seat only Saul remains. He is fiddling dejectedly with his silver thumb ring and staring out into the street. He looks like a mutant manikin from the Harrods menswear department. He isn't pleased to see me.

'Natalie, wherever did you get to?' he asks. 'Andy returned from the lavatory highly perturbed about something or other – what, I can't imagine. He said he had to leave, and Alex said she'd grab a lift. It was all rather abrupt. I thought you said that women were attracted to men who weren't on the market.' Saul's expression is indignant and – as he does when discomfited – he pulls at his left earlobe, repeatedly. Once this would have irritated me beyond belief but now it makes me feel protective towards him.

'Yes,' I say. 'And I'm sorry to say that Alex is attracted to Andy.'

Saul's shoulders slump. 'So what will we do now?' he asks plaintively.

'Well,' I reply – in a kindly, platonic tone so there's no misunderstanding – 'you're welcome to come back to mine for a coffee.'

Saul perks up. 'That's very kind of you, Natalie.' He fiddles some more with the silver ring, then adds – teasing me for past sins – 'As long as it isn't Nescafé.'

The next morning, I wake to find my head has turned to dough. I've slept but not rested. I slouch into the kitchen and, to my displeasure, see two coffee cups unwashed and abandoned on the table. I lurch towards them – *Exterminate!* – then stop. Can't you leave the washing up? I drop two slices of bread in the toaster, dot them with Marmite – I'm still not reconciled to butter – and mechanically chew it all down. I also pour a small glass of orange juice and a monster coffee. I forbid lunatic thought. Yes, yes, of course I'm twitching to eat the whole loaf but why should I? I didn't speak but nor did he. And that makes him a schmuck.

I take a leaf of A4 out of my printer, write out AND THAT MAKES HIM A SCHMUCK in big bold black capitals, and stick it to the wall above my desk. Then I scan the press release I wrote yesterday, and refine it. Now for the second press release, about the GLBallet's forthcoming *Alice in Wonderland*. I read through Matt's notes and realise that Mel hasn't returned my call and I actually need to speak to her, as she's one of the principals cast as Alice. I could put words into her mouth, as I know what she'll say

('I want to ecthpreth my inner life on thtage'), but it seems like betrayal, so I won't.

I call her mobile again. No answer. I'd like to get this done today. I consider calling Tony to gain access to his girlfriend. I'm scared of him, I'm angry with him. He's just angry with me. I want to call him and be friends. I miss his approval. I need him to like me. My hand creeps towards the phone. Why am *I* always the peace broker? Why can't *he* make the first move? I know he expects me to give in, I always have. And what about Babs? Does *she* expect me to give in? Or doesn't she care? Maybe she never wants to hear from me again. I grit my teeth and place the phone in the furthest corner of my desk (as it's still in easy reach this is a symbolic gesture). I'm not giving in this time. This time I'm going to tough it out.

The doorbell shrills, a long bone-jangling blast. The noise is almost a trademark and for a moment I believe it *is* Tony. Until I remember who I'm expecting. I breathe deep – my ribcage lifts about a metre – set my face to neutral, and open the door. My social instincts urge me to say, hello, but I crush them. Andy strides in without looking at me. A tube of mascara wasted. I shut the door quietly and try to rally strength. Come on, you spoke to Mum. You confronted her. After all those passive years. You *can* do it. And it made a difference. Yes, perhaps, but that particular memory makes me feel sick. The fear – it drained me. I can't repeat it. You can. Speak, Natalie, tell him. There's still a chance.

'Can you please ensure the room is left tidy?' I say coldly. 'Last time you left it in a state.'

Andy gives no indication that he's heard me. He drags a scuffed leather holdall into the middle of the floor, roughly yanks drawers from their slots and shakes their entire contents into the case. *I* wouldn't mind being manhandled by him, I think. Instantly, I think of my mother who said something once that shocked me rigid. (I was a prim nine years old. She was listening to Barry Manilow sing *I wanna do it with you*, and she suddenly blurted, '*I* wouldn't mind doing it with him!') I gaze at Andy and try to think cool thoughts, but each one sizzles.

I slyly check his neck for lovebites. If I could, I'd rip off his shirt to check his back for scratch marks. And take a DNA sample from under his fingernails, to be thorough. Andy isn't what you'd call a hunk but he has a beautiful solidity about him. He isn't plastercast handsome either but to me – I realise gloomily – his looks are perfect. The trust fund is now a lust fund. I retreat to the kitchen. It strikes me that there is no one in the world I want to tell this to but Babs.

Moments later he walks in. 'Where's the dustpan and brush?'

'Behind the door,' I retort, my face as po as I can get it.

I swivel in my seat, as my desk faces the window. Andy gives me the sort of nod that Marie Antoinette might have given a peasant. Then he drones, 'And that makes him a schmuck.' For one horrific second I think he's read my mind. That's the least of it, pal! I'm almost relieved to realise he's read the big bold black capitals on the sheet of paper. I snatch it off the wall.

'I bet you think this song is about you,' I say.

'And you're telling me it's not?'

The blood roars in my head – eek, it's a fight or flight situation! Slowly I turn my whole self round to face him (not because I want to – I have a crick in my neck). The truth is I would quite happily argue with him till doomsday, just so long as he remains in my kitchen. I raise my eyes to his and I'm shocked to see the anger there. It's not a game. I grope for a searing phrase to shrivel his arrogance, but he's not even looking at me. I trace his gaze to the coffee cups and— Oh. A chunky silver ring placed neatly equidistant – possibly with a ruler – between them.

What. Andy thinks I— With Saul? Oh *really!*

I forget that, in my attempts to drill for jealousy, this is precisely the myth I've been promoting. We snarl, unfortunately in chorus, 'You're pathetic.'

Andy trumps me by adding, 'Clean your own sodding room, you little cow!'

In fight or flight terms, I'm airborne and halfway to Jamaica, but this remark brings me skidding back to land with clenched fists. 'You've got a nerve,' I shriek, 'pulling a strop on *me*. After what you've done, you you you cheap tart!'

'Tart!?' bellows Andy. 'Takes one to know one!' His face is taut with rage as he hurtles out of the kitchen. 'And I tell you what' – he roars, thundering down the hall – 'that Saul bloke looks even more of a prick than Chris!' – thundering back up the hall, lugging the suitcase – 'And you bloody deserve each other!' – wrenching open the front door so wide and fast it bounces on its hinges – 'You're even more of a psycho than your nut of a brother!'

Boom.

No way. I heave the door open and scream at the top of my lungs, 'I wanted to get you out of a rut, I didn't mean you to shag her!'

Andy pauses by his wreck of an Astra and tilts his head as if he's heard a small bird tweeting. He waves a hand irritably, as you would to swat a fly – a bored dismissive gesture. Then he hurls the suitcase into the boot (the car sags), and speeds towards the dead end. The army of parked Land Rovers make turning tight and I gasp as he hurtles towards them. To my annoyance, and relief, he performs a sharp, screechy handbrake turn – the Astra spins on its haunches – and roars off, in a cloud of dirty grey smoke.

'*The Professionals* come to Primrose Hill,' I say, wasting my wit on next door's cat.

Then I shut the door quietly, run to my room, fling myself on the bed and burst into tears. Brilliant, Nat, you really told him how you felt. Your eloquence is breathtaking. You really cleared up all misunderstandings, you, you, you – *mute!* I wail for three full minutes, decide

393

I'm too distraught to be lying down, and stand up. I hobble into the bathroom and wipe the dirty rivulets of mascara off my face. My eyelids are already puffy. My cheeks look puffy too. Can crying make your cheeks go puffy? I pinch my cheek. Then I lift up my jumper and pinch my waist.

If you can pinch more than an inch. I suppose women are lucky 'millimetre' doesn't rhyme with 'pinch'. I take off my shoes and step on the scales. I peer down at the verdict and whimper weakly. I've piled on another two pounds! I'm the tabloid cliché of a sad old cow! I must go for a run. Cut back. Yesterday. At that stupid café. I ate chips. Me, chips! This is tantamount to the Chief Rabbi eating a cheese and ham sandwich. With pork scratchings on the side. Off Claudia Schiffer's stomach. On Yom Kippur. While driving. On the wrong side of the road.

I don't know how it happened. (I'm sure the Chief Rabbi would say the same.) Maybe it was Andy's inadvertent look of pity. Or something Babs said sank in at last. Maybe it was talking to my mother. Or watching Alex eat mousse. Or doing Pilates. Being away from Mel. Maybe I realised that there was no *need* to be bone-thin. Not any more. It's as if someone gave me permission to eat, and I can't stop. Everything I ever denied myself, I'm eating. The guilt is not enough to stop me. Even the self-loathing is half-arsed. I'm bored of using my body to speak my pain. If only I could learn to use my voice instead.

I lift up my jumper again, and stand back from the mirror. I prod my stomach. Fatter. Softer? And my bosom (I can't bring myself to say 'breasts' or 'tits' – too sensual, too raunchy, I prefer the safe Victorian alternative). I press my arms inward to squeeze a cleavage. Wow. I look almost, almost *womanly*. I step closer to the mirror, and lift a lock of fringe to inspect for damage. Tiny wisps of new hair, growing underneath. I pull on a few. They feel hardy. Rooted. I graze a hand across my collarbone. It's still knobbly but not so . . . distressing. I straighten my jumper, tear my gaze from the mirror, and return to my desk.

'Oh, well,' I sigh. 'Back to work.' I try to put all thoughts of Andy and food out of my head. The only way I can do this is by putting Tina Turner on the CD at top volume. My other bright idea is to light a scented candle. I've never particularly liked scented candles, they remind me of my mother's obsession with air fresheners – the need to choke nature from the room and replace it with stifling artificiality. But this is a posh candle, purporting to smell of 'Rain Forest'. I lit it on my first day of liberty from the GLBallet. Babs bought it for me, as a thank-you for sending her to a Kensington spa for a Thai yoga massage. It was her twenty-sixth birthday present, and she loved it.

'Would *I* like it, do you think?' I asked, after listening to her rave.

She paused. 'They don't half yank you around, Nat. This way, that way, cranking your legs open and shut like a pair of bellows. At one point I said to the bloke – a young geezer, in his twenties – I said, "I'm telling you now, I won't be held responsible if I let one off"—'

I interrupted. 'You *actually* said that to him? You actually said it?'

'Well, what was I going to do?' she cried. 'Fart in his face with no warning? It was only fair!'

'I can't believe you did that!' I squeaked. 'I'm mortified.'

'Nat,' she grinned, 'he'd been a masseur for ten years. He's witnessed more than a few farts!'

I shuddered. 'Still. I'm horrified.'

'Ye-es,' she sighed. 'That's why I can't recommend it to you, Nat. If you accidentally did a fart, even a small non-toxic one, the loss of face would be so great you'd have to kill yourself. And him. It would be the only honourable recourse.'

I put my head in my hands and laugh, a half-hysterical laugh that could turn soggy at any time. Pilates isn't entirely fart-free. How will I feel when students start farting at me? Good Lord, I'd better get some practice in. The phone rings. Listlessly, I pick up the receiver. Thanks to the whirlwind exit of romance from my life, the telephone – that magical purveyor of thrills and glorious opportunity – is reduced to a humdrum business tool.

'Hello?' I say, dully.

'Is that,' replies a voice, meek but unmistakable, 'by any chance my old friend Nat?'

Chapter 46

I rehearse in the bath for moments like these. I could have said 'No.' And put the phone down. Or sneered, 'You and your brother – are you taking it in turns?' Because it *was* like watching two little figures on a weather vane, the forecast veering from sunny to stormy, to sunny again, each figure sliding out to scold or soothe me, scold, soothe, one after the other. But when she rang I was reeling from the very obvious effects of not speaking. I wasn't about to sacrifice another soul mate to silence. I was just glad to have my friend back and I had the excellent sense to say so. She didn't call me her *best* friend, but it no longer mattered.

'It might be me,' I say gruffly, jiggling in my seat.

'This is Babs,' she adds, still in the same deferential whisper, 'ringing to say I'm a complete pillock and I understand if you don't want anything to do with me ever again.'

'*Ba-abs*,' I beam. 'You have no idea how much I've missed you. You're not a pillock at all, you are my very great friend, and I'm thrilled to hear from you. Where are you?'

'At home, feeling ashamed of myself. I'm a friend-beater.'

'Babs, I understand that slap. So don't be ashamed. I was –' I search for words dramatic enough to express my stupidity, dig about, retrieve something from a long evening with Saul watching *Hamlet*, '– a rash intruding fool.'

'I don't 'ave your book learnin', Miss Miller!' replies Babs. 'Hey. Andy told me about Sasha.'

'As I said,' I add hastily, 'Yes, actually he just er, came by to get his stuff.'

'I think it's amazing!' cries Babs. 'It was so kind of you.'

'I think so. So, er . . .'

'I had another talk with Si. I take back, um, quite a lot of my accusations. I'm sorry, Nat. It was all too much. Everything'd got on top of me. Except my husband. Oh hush my mouth!'

'How is Simon?' I ask. I also want to know when she last spoke to Andy. Not in the last five minutes, I suspect.

'He's good, thanks. He's all right. I believe we are *progressing*.' She says this last bit in a silly posh voice in case I should imagine she's taking herself seriously. 'So Nat, what are you up to right now?'

'Me? Oh, er, working.'

'Of course you are! Sorry, why didn't you say? I'll let you get back.'

'Nonononononono, it's okay, I didn't mean it like that. Do you want to come round?'

'What, now?'

'Well, not if you're bu—'

'Don't be daft, I'm on me four-day break – I'm knackered, we had a fire yesterday, it was a shock to the system! – I've been training, now I'm sat in front of the box eating teacakes and popping bubble wrap.'

I feel a twinge. *I* should have been training. Not the bulk-you-up training that Babs does (circuits, weights, cycling, running). *My* kind of training: Running. Running. Running. Running.

I sidestep the irritation, and say, 'Teacakes?'

'Mini-marshmallows, covered in milk chocolate, biscuit base, peel the chocolate off first?'

'I didn't think they made those any more,' I breathe, impressed. 'I used to love them!'

'You have to know where to look,' replies Babs happily.

'And I'm a pro. I'll bring some – I'll just bring myself, shall I? But are you *sure* I'm not disturbing your work? I know what you're like, you'll say it's fine, and all the while you'll be fretting about how to make up the time, and will it put out your gym schedule and—'

'Babs,' I say sternly. 'Priorities, please. I'll put the kettle on.'

I jump up to clean the flat, but it's already squeaky. Except for the coffee cups. My fingers start to itch. But I leave the cups – Babs will be so proud – and try to do a little work. But, what with the good and bad stuff squiddled up like spaghetti, there's insufficient space in my head. Andy *said* she would forgive me – good – I earn a gold star for match-making him and Alex – good, bad – she must assume I asked him to leave – good – when in fact he left of his own huffy accord – bad – she hated the idea of me and Andy – bad – although now I'm no longer Bitch Number One, maybe she won't mind me getting jiggy with her brother – *great*.

But then. I've got more chance of getting jiggy with the Archbishop of Canterbury. I feel gloom at the thought (no offence to the Archbishop). Forget him! (Andy, that is). When the doorbell rings, I'm there. After a short, self-conscious head-bobble, we hug. I'm so happy you're my friend again, I say in my head, I'm so so happy. It translates as, 'Good to see you, Barbarella.' Which isn't *terrible*. Babs pushes me away.

'Natalie!' she gasps, one big grin. 'Looking good!'

I run a hand through my hair, tug at my jumper sleeves, and mumble my thanks at the floor. Compliments embarrass me. Then again, Babs only gives a compliment if she means it. Equally, if you look a fright she's happy – as I'm only too aware – to say so.

'Seriously,' she continues, as I scurry into the kitchen, 'you look, you look . . . I don't know what it is, you look less *shrivelled*. I mean—'

'Thank you very much.' Babs frantically rakes her hair forward until it hides her face.

'Come out of there,' I order. 'I know what you meant.' She flicks her hair back, hangs her head, and says, 'The stuff I said on Sunday.'

I turn from the cupboard. 'Babs. Don't. I deserved it. I'll be totally honest. When you got engaged it was the biggest shock – the second biggest shock of my life. I didn't want to lose you. When Dad left . . . it's muddied everything since. I know it's ridiculous. I know things change, *obviously*, I didn't want them to. To me, change means loss when often it just means . . . change. I suppose barging into the Pitcher & Piano to sort out your marriage made me feel necessary. And Simon was . . .' I decide to be charitable – 'vulnerable. I caused you a lot of misery and I apologise.'

'Nat,' Babs says. 'Things do change. But, you know, deep down, you'll always be my best friend.'

My heart curls like old paper. I want to clutch my stomach, and groan from my soul. I pour the kettle instead. 'Yeah,' I reply. 'You too.'

Babs clears her throat. 'You know,' she exclaims, dragging out a chair screechingly, with zero regard for those in the basement flat. '*You've* changed. I don't just mean how you look.'

'Do you think I'm looking thin on top?'

'Well, Nat, you were never Dolly Parton but at least if you're small people don't classify you as "mumsy", and you're still too thin but you seem to be—'

'No, Babs, that's very sweet of you but I was talking about my hair.'

'Your hair? Oh! Er, no. You've got a fine head of hair, from where I'm standing. Or sitting. Why shouldn't you have?'

'It's been shedding. You don't think it looks sparse or – unstable?'

'No, Nat. As hair goes, it looks reasonably sane. You eejit. So what happened?'

I jerk guiltily. 'What do you mean?'

Babs tilts her chair on to two legs, and I bite back my

reflex response ('don't tilt!'). 'I mean,' she says, 'what's happened to you all of a sudden? The place is' – she nods at the two stained coffee cups on the gleaming table – 'a filth pit. And you seem more . . . sure of yourself. I'm not knocking it.'

'Do you think?' I reply, pleased. 'I'm training myself to be a bit less tense. Gosh, I—'

'I take it back,' grins Babs. 'You haven't changed at all. You still say "gosh".' She adds, 'Does this mean you're going to ask if I want a yoghurt with my tea?'

I make a face like I'm trapped in a wind tunnel. 'Did I really ever ask you that? I'm sorry. I *was* going to say did you want a biscuit?'

'You did, and I do. What sort?'

'Plain chocolate digestives?'

'Mm. OK. Although, for future reference, I prefer the milk chocolate sort.'

'Yes,' I say. 'So do I.' Babs looks intrigued. 'That's why I got these.'

'*Right,*' she says slowly, as one might say to a child who's too old to insist on his invisible friend. 'Although, I'll say it – I'm impressed you got them in the first place.'

I squirm. Even at my worst I always bought biscuits. Only I never ate them. I'd squirrel them away at the top of the larder in the tin box. They were there to urge on other people, or for me to stare at or sniff. Like a parent sniffing the clothes of a dead child. How did I get like that?

'I lost control,' I say teasingly. 'As prescribed. I went mad in the shop.'

Babs nods. 'I'm impressed. I'm not messing about. I really am. So whose' – tap tap tap – 'is this man-sized silver ring? Um, are you, er, back with Chris?'

'Oh no!' I cry, 'I'd forgotten about him. No, it's Saul's, if you can believe that.'

'*Saul's?*' she yells. 'What! Why haven't you told me?'

'You and I haven't been speaking,' I remind her. 'And it's not what you think. I did not have sex with that man. He

401

decided to get in touch to teach me a lesson, show off his hot new body, honed and toned, starting from the day we broke up. In fact, now I come to think of it, he must have run straight from the Oxo Tower to the gym, and stayed there.'

Babs looks stunned. 'Saul? God, that's so sly! Still – shows how much he cared. You *are* telling me the truth, though? You didn't fall for it, did you?'

'It's okay. It didn't work. Because the hot new body remains attached to Saul's personality.'

'Poor Saul,' purrs Babs. 'So how is the young fogey? God, that's another thing I feel bad about. Urging you to stick with Bowcock.'

I glance at her, surprised. 'Did you, did you *know* you were doing it?'

Babs dunks her digestive in her tea (my toes curl instinctively – once she performed an independent laboratory experiment to discover how many milk chocolate digestives you can drown in a standard tea before it turns into a semi-solid poor man's tiramisu. Conclusion: ten and a half). Then she says, 'Not until I thought about it. I sort of realised that it mattered a bit *too* much to me that you stayed with sensible Saul. I think it had something to do with feeling defensive about getting married. It's difficult when you're the first. Sorry,' she adds.

'Forget it. How is it with Si, really? You don't have to tell me if it's private.'

She waves this notion away, smiles – acknowledging *something* – and says, 'It's getting better. Slowly. It's not great. No one tells you, marriage is different. Even if you've been living together, which we weren't, it's emotionally, psychologically different. I know that sounds like a crock, but it is. The adjustment is huge. Not for me so much – I know what I want, I always have, I've never been that bothered with what other people think – but Si is, he's less confident in himself, in his decisions. He's still – and I'd say this to his face – *young* in that sense. He admits it. Which is progress in itself. It's funny, Nat. You think you're getting on great, you think you can talk about everything, you think your relationship is solid, you're feeling pretty smug, and then – this *gulf* opens, you realise there's this huge rotting problem which you've both expertly ignored to the extent that you no longer really believe it's there. And then, out of the blue, you're both of you, standing on the brink. You try and approach the problem but you can't – every time you tiptoe towards discussion, try and keep it little, it blows up big, it's like taking a match to an oil refinery. It's the most frightening thing, Nat. It makes you feel so helpless. It's the worst feeling. I'm not used to it.'

'How,' I say haltingly, 'does Simon feel? Does he know what he's done to you? Is he serious about making it work?'

Babs forces a smile and her eyes crinkle. 'He know's what he's done, and he is sorry. I know he loves me. He's trying. It's still hard for him. I think he's got to get used to it, to see that I'm not stopping him from doing *much*. He's still his own person, he can do a lot of what he likes. All that shit is drummed in until they believe it – "the nagging wife". It feeds the fear of men like Si, till they interpret every word you say – including "pass the salt" – as nagging. And the losers in his office – who haven't matured beyond twelve and think that having any feeling for a woman other than "phwoar" is, hilariously enough, "gay" – they goad him with it, they make it worse. I know what they're like. I used to work with them! It's like school.'

'Have you said this to Simon?'

'I gave him earache. I've tried to say that if *they* were happy with themselves, they wouldn't care what Si does, they'd accept it. It's just that because they're so weak, a choice of lifestyle that's different to theirs is a threat to them, it forces them to question their sad, loserish lives. That's why they're so vicious about him getting hitched.

They're scared. I've tried to make him see that they have the problem, not him.'

'And does he?'

'Half. He's taken it on board. But he insists they're happy. With their drug problems, drink problems, personality disorders, et cetera.' Babs manages a feeble grin. Then she adds, 'But I did say one thing that seemed to hit.'

'Oh?'

'I lost patience. I just said, "Look, it's not the *law*. You don't have to be married to me. No one's making you. You don't have to be here, it's your choice. You chose to be with me because we are – *were* good together." I think he thought I was about to leave him. It made him sit up.'

'Oh God!' I gasp. 'You wouldn't. Stuff like this takes ages to sort out, Babs. Ages. And he *is* young. It's so hard, so tough, but give it a chance. He wasn't, he hasn't been . . . ah?'

Babs shakes her head. 'He says not. I believe him. No, you're right. I was only trying to make him not take me for granted and it sort of worked. It's stressful though, trying to mend a fraying relationship, because you don't know when or how it's going to end. Whether all this grief will be worth it.'

'It will be, Babs. You have to have endless patience, that's all. You have to keep making the effort, even if you do want to bash his head in with a saucepan.'

'Don't give me ideas.' She frowns, and says, 'I keep thinking, I'm just married! I should be swinging from the Chinese lantern! I should be wearing his dick out! I should be flying home to bubbling pots of chilli con carne, cooked by his loving hand! Not sitting tense and huddled on one arm of the sofa, him on the other arm, the pair of us stiff and apart like bookends, him hard-faced, me on the edge of hysteria, with my fists clenched to stop myself screaming and slamming out the house. You know, we didn't even do it on our wedding night. Si was too drunk.'

'Babs,' I say, ' "should" is like "*nagging wife*". It's a term of oppression. You don't know what other people's relationships are like. Yes, of course all newly-weds present smiley faces to the outside world. It's what the outside world expects. They bow to the pressure. They're hardly going to say, "Actually, we didn't have sex on our wedding night, we were too tired," because to those who don't know any better, that looks like failure. When it's probably normal. Common. There *is* no normal. Most "shoulds" are media hype. There to sell newspapers and magazines. And I should know, I'm a PR, sweetie.'

Babs reaches across and squeezes my hand. 'You're a good friend,' she says, 'is what you are.'

Chapter 47

Time slows or hurries according to venue. In church, synagogue or mosque, it dawdles, stretching minutes into months. In the kitchen with friends, great chunks of the stuff go missing.

'It's 2.35,' gasps Babs. 'We've been gassing for three hours! Do you mind? Do you want to get back to work?'

I shake my head, to free up some of the guilt. Coffee breaks are essential; I wouldn't want to overdo it, and get ME. (ME is a terror of mine – I'm sure I have it at least twice a week.) 'No, no,' I cry. 'It's brilliant to see you, stay for as long as you want. Are you hungry?'

'Ish. Do you want another coffee?'

'Yeah, OK. There's stuff in the fridge, Babs, have a look.' *Brrt brrt!* 'Oh, let me get that.'

I hurry to the phone, while Babs hangs off the fridge door like a teenager.

'Hiya!'

'You sound cheerful,' says my mother accusingly.

'I know. I can barely believe it myself. Babs is here. We're having a chat.'

'That's nice, dear,' she replies in a monotone. 'I hope she's not distracting you from work. You've got to be prudent now you're not properly employed. How is she? Taking care of herself? I do worry about Barbara, of course I don't say anything to Jackie, but it's not really a job for a woman. I'm not being old-fashioned, Natalie, it's a matter of brute strength—'

'Mum,' I say, as kindly as I can – while booting the

kitchen door shut with my foot – 'Babs might not be as strong as the men but she's strong enough. She's had to pass exactly the same tests. If anything she's *better* than the men, she's had more to prove.'

My mother – who'd insist the sky was green if she was in the mood – makes a noise not a million miles from a grunt.

'Are you OK? Is something the matter?'

'Nothing *you* need bother yourself about,' she retorts. 'I asked your father if he wanted to come to Australia' – a gesture requiring her to swallow about a litre of pride. He must have turned her down – 'And the wretch of a man said "Yes"!'

'But Mum – that's grea- well that's not *awful* news. It'll be nice to, er, know someone. It won't be too bad.'

'I've told him he'll have to stay in a separate hotel. Otherwise Lord knows what poor Kimberli Ann will think.'

As my mother has never, in eight years, betrayed the smallest concern for what Kimberli Ann might think (indeed, has questioned whether Kimberli Ann thinks), I suspect this rush of anxiety on Kimberli Ann's behalf masks a desire to punish my father for his presence.

'I did ask Kelly if she thought it would be too much, to have him along too, and you won't believe what she said.'

'What did she say?'

'"No worries!" I didn't think Australians actually *said* that! I didn't think *Neighbours* was true to life! I'm the one who made contact, and now he's muscling in! And Kelly told me to pack my "swimmers", my "sunnies" and my "thongs" – I was speechless! I didn't know what she was talking about, but I do know what thongs are, and I most certainly will not be packing any. I didn't know what to say, so I said, "I see", and left it at that—'

'Mum,' I say quickly, 'I think a thong in Australia means flip-flop. I don't think she was asking you to pack your G-strings.'

'Oh. Oh. *Oh.* I see. Well, I don't own flip-flops either.

And now I've read up on Australia, good heavens, it's a minefield! I'm surprised it's inhabited. It's teeming with poisonous creatures, I'll be lucky to survive the trip. If I'm not eaten by sharks, or bitten by a redback spider, I'll be stung to death by a box jellyfish. If you're stung by a box jellyfish you're dead in seconds. It sounds so uncivilised! And Susan said friends of theirs went and they saw a snake and the heat was *choking*.'

'Mum, it'll be fine. They probably saw a snake on television. And I doubt there are box jellyfish in the Hyatt Regency. And it will be lovely to see sun, you haven't had a holiday in – in sixteen years. You've been so looking forward to this, don't let Dad spoil things. He'll be fine. Look, why don't we talk later?'

'And I can't reach Tony,' whines my mother, who is on a roll. 'I don't know *where* he's disappeared to, he could be dead for all I know.'

'There are no box jellyfish in Camden. He's probably in meetings, Mum.'

'Natalie, I can't talk to you when you're like this. Just go back to Barbara. We'll speak when you can spare me a minute without being juvenile.'

Pank!

I return to the kitchen, teeth clenched. They unclench only slightly when I see that Babs has transferred all the food in the fridge to the table, and is waiting patiently for me to say 'start'.

'Start.'

She wrinkles her nose. 'Brown bread, tomatoes, lettuce, and cottage cheese. So Nat, tell me, what does cottage cheese bring to the party?'

'It's very good for you.'

Babs sighs in the direction of the tub. 'It's gotta be. What's up? I'm joking. Cottage cheese rocks!'

I smile grimly, and hand her the Pringles I've stashed in the top cupboard (she mimes fainting with joy). Then I tell her about Australia.

Babs nods all the way through then claps her hands, creating a sonic boom. 'I've just had a brilliant idea. *You* should go!'

'Me?' I cough on a crisp.

'Yes, you!'

'I can't!'

'Why not?'

'Well, I've got work to do.'

'Yes, well. The deli. That's *so* urgent.'

'Oh! That's back on? No, the other stuff. The PR stuff. And the Pilates! That's urgent!'

'Says who?'

'But I've started. I've paid for the first six months.'

'So? You're getting private tuition, aren't you?'

'Yes but . . .'

'So if you take time off you won't fall behind the class.'

'No, but Robin—'

'You could take three months out and pick up where you left off.'

'Three months?' – I laugh – 'Where did you get that from? Mum's only going for three weeks!'

'So? You could stay on, travel, see Australia. It's a big place, love.'

'What? By *myself*?'

'Why not?'

'But it would be highly dangerous!'

'Oh, get off! Not unless you're stupid. You'll make loads of friends – all the other backpackers.'

I stifle an involuntary shudder. Backpackers! And me, one of them!

'Don't you want to meet your niece?' adds Babs slyly.

'Yes.'

'And see your dad?'

'Might do.'

'So?'

I sigh. 'It seems so, so . . .'

'Exciting? Adventurous? Spontaneous?'

'Yes, but—'

'Frivolous? Unnecessary? Reckless?'

'Exactly.' I'm nodding, grateful she understands, and then I look at her, and realise she doesn't.

'Nat,' she says. 'I urge you to think about it. You didn't take a year off, you missed out, girl. All the time I've known you, you've never cut yourself some slack. This would be such a treat for you. You'd love it. You'd have the time of your life. Ah Nat, imagine it. You deserve a break. That's what life's for. It's not about working yourself to the bone, always being careful, sticking to every boring pointless rule in the boring pointless rulebook.'

'I'm not working myself to the bone,' I say sulkily. 'I've put on four pounds. And what about the cost?'

'Fuck the cost!' shouts Babs. 'Get an overdraft or a fourth credit card like everyone else!'

'But—'

'Nat,' sighs Babs. 'I'm sorry, but I parked next to you, and yours is the *only* car in the street with the glove compartment left open and empty, like the police advise, to deter thieves from breaking in to nick your stereo. You can't even watch *The Breakfast Club* because you start fretting about everyone's careers. Now I'm afraid that's not normal. You need to chill out.'

'Well, I—'

'Tara and Kelly live in Sydney, right?'

'Yes.'

'Which part?'

'Um,' I wrinkle my nose, trying to remember what my mother told me. 'Paddington?'

'Padd-ing-ton!' Babs smirks.

'What? What's wrong with it?'

'Nothing. Couldn't be better! Paddington is cool. Nice cafés and great clothes shopping. It's in the middle of everything *and* it's just down the road from Bondi. It'll be interesting to see what your mother makes of Paddington.'

'Why?' I say, suspiciously.

'It's a place where anything goes,' says Babs, head bent in concentration over the crumbs on her plate. 'It's got the San Francisco vibe. It's very trendy, very arty, and it's a big gay area. It's got the Albury, the best-known gay pub in the city, it has drag shows every night. It's fantastic. It's a pity you didn't go earlier, you would have caught the Mardi Gras, your mum would have loved that, it's a real family event, all the families watching the gay couples on their floats in tight pants—'

'You're doing this on purpose, aren't you?'

'Doing what?' shrills Babs, wide-eyed.

'Trying to make it impossible for me *not* to go.'

'Not at all,' she says primly. 'I'm merely acting as tourist information.'

'Blackmailing me into feeling obliged to escort my mother.'

'What?'

'To stop her unleashing her Hendon personality on the Paddington Ozzies.'

'How can you *say* that?'

'It's a big thing. I'll have to think about it.'

Babs returns to scrutinising her plate, but to no avail as her grin is so wide it reaches her ears.

When Babs finally leaves, it's 4.30, and she only goes because Simon calls to ask if she wants to see a film tonight.

'See. He *is* trying,' I say, and she smiles.

'He probably means on Channel Five.'

After she's gone, I wash up – the protest coffee cups included ('in the sink with you, you've had your fifteen minutes') – taking ages over each cup. I find washing up therapeutic in small doses, though I know it's treason to admit it. Babs and I discussed everything except Andy, who I suppose is now taboo. Beyond her initial comment, Babs didn't mention him so nor did I. The old fears pound heavy in my chest. He could vanish from my life. Even if they *are* interested, men are lazy. The ones you'd sell your mother for (well, my mother) are hopeless at keeping in touch. What hope is there if you shun their interest to death?

I champ my teeth hard together. Australia. Why shouldn't I go? An adventure. I've never had one of those (apart from when someone sold my Visa card number to a gang who went on a spree with it in Hong Kong). I've always needed to know what I'm doing before I do it. I like routine – it makes me feel safe. But I suppose there *is* no safe. I once thought if you got married, you were safe. I'm as bad as my mother.

My mother.

It would be easier for everyone if I was there to smooth the way. But I won't go because Babs thinks I should. Or for my mother. If I do go I'll go for me. I won't go to get away from Andy. I refuse to be a love refugee – I haven't got the right clothes, and Frannie would be cock-a-hoop – apologies, but that word is perfect for her – if she knew. Andy will not affect my decision. He made his choice (and I helped him make it) and that's the end of it. I wouldn't want a man who wears slippers anyway. And didn't he use the word 'wally' once? What a wally.

My heart thuds dully like an old plastic football hitting concrete. Nothing to do with him. Australia. I could do it. I bet Robin would condone it as spiritually beneficial or whatever. And I could avoid Alex without seeming unfriendly. I know that's weak. But I'm just not big enough to feel warm towards her yet – although I'm small enough to fake it – and I'd prefer to dodge the dilemma, until I am (by which time I'll have made it to Toys Я Us and Ken will double for a pincushion). Maybe I should backpack around Oz like a human turtle for three months. I arrive at the thought that nothing is stopping me, when I realise this isn't true.

Tony.

Tony will kill me. He'll scoop out my innards and roast them in a pot. He will hate me if I go to Australia. He doesn't want us to add Tara and Kelly to the family. It'll be bad enough when he finds out Mum is going. Worse when he finds out Dad's going. Dad, meeting his daughter! When Dad left, Tony punished him. He ensured that Dad got no pleasure out of being his dad by declining to have anything to do with him. (Although, if you know Tony, whether this *is* punishment is questionable.) But Tara is a loophole. Luckily for Dad, Tony's refusal to speak to him precludes Tony telling him what he thinks of this move. But he'll tell *me*.

I fiddle with my hair. Now that there's a large Tony-shaped hurdle between me and Australia, I definitely want to go. I'd love to go. Attack is the best form of defence. I should ring Tony. I've never attacked in my life. The most I've attacked is a Caesar salad, only to be defeated by the creamy dressing. What if he rang Mum back and already knows? I'd better check. And I should ask her if she wants me to come too before I book. My mother will always be a stickler for etiquette.

'But Natalie, are you sure you can spare the time?' is her immediate response.

'Probably,' I mumble, deflating. (I would have preferred, 'Jubilation, I never thought you'd ask!' but sadly, it wasn't to be.)

'That's the trouble with not being properly employed,' she sighs. 'If you take a break you lose money hand over fist.'

I ignore the barbs – hard when there's about twelve of them jabbing into your behind – and hurl one of my own.

'Well, it's not as if I'm earning much anyway.' But I'm not as harsh as I could be. I decide to reveal the three-month plan later.

'I hope there are seats left on the flight. You've left it so late. Australia's remarkably popular.'

'I'm sure there will be other flights. But Mum, I don't *have* to come. I won't come if you don't want me to.'

'Nonsense, dear, I didn't say that, it would be a pleasure to have you along. Tara and Kelly will be delighted, I'm

413

sure. You can share my hotel room. Although it does mean inconveniencing the travel agent. They like to have notice, but' – *sigh* - 'it can't be helped, you weren't to know.'

I weather the deluge of guilt, tell myself she's undergoing a momentary lapse brought on by stress, and say, 'Mum. I know you like to have your space . . .'

'Some people don't have any choice!'

'Yes, and it's a kind offer, but I don't think it would be fair on you. Or me,' I mutter, after a sharp prod from my conscience. 'Why don't I see what else is available, or' – I wheel out a favourite phrase of hers – 'reasonably priced?'

'Natalie, I can quite understand you not wanting to share with your mother, it's not a problem, I'm used to being all alone. I wouldn't want to put you out' – long-suffering pause – 'I think your father should pay for you.'

'Sorry?'

'He'll pay.'

'But—'

'I'll see if *Leading Hotels of The World* has anything in Sydney.'

'But—'

'It's the least that man can do!'

'Mum—'

'Speak softly, dear, I'm getting a migraine.'

As 'a migraine' is code for 'my own way', I concede defeat on this topic and try another. 'Mum, have you spoken to Tony yet?'

'No, I haven't and if he carries on like this, he won't know we're going until we've gone. I've stocked up the freezer for him. I suppose he could let himself in and take it, the BMW has a fair-sized boot, but—'

'Mum. Don't worry. I'll find out where he is.'

'I don't see how you can. That secretary of his is like a bull mastiff. And he never answers his mobile. I don't feel it's right to leave a message in this instance.'

The silence that follows is thick with disgruntlement, so I say, 'I'll find him.'

I say goodbye, and text Tony with a short message:
Dear Tony, I'm pregnant by Chris Pomeroy
But I'm too much of a coward to send it. I delete, and
start again.
Dear Tony, I'm texting you from intensive care
I scrap that, and start again.
*Dear Tony, Mum, Dad, and I are going to see Tara and
Kelly in Australia, love Natalie. PS. It's all booked!*
Then I sit on my hands and quake until the phone rings.

Chapter 48

I know politicians are hard-boiled egomaniacs, and that being a politician is a clever way of getting your Habsburg chin in the paper, but I still find their career choice hard to comprehend. It takes a special kind of egomaniac to, day after day, stand up and address a roomful of people who then laugh and jeer openly at what they've said. How hurtful is *that*? And wouldn't you be crushed? I couldn't cope – not even if I had a pack of self-esteem counsellors passing me jolly notes from the back benches. I'd drag myself home every night snivelling 'nobody likes me!'

My problem is, I like to be liked. By everyone. Starting from the paper boy and postman to – more ambitiously – my ex-boyfriends and relatives. It's a tough ambition to achieve. You have to bend yourself a lot of different ways. And even then, there's no guarantee. I was once walking to the tube station from work, some distance behind Miranda Morgan, a dancer in the *corps de ballet*. I *saw* her notice me, pretend she hadn't, and hurry ahead. Even though I happened to think Miranda was the most dull, shallow, intellectually vacant creature I'd ever met, I'd always been sweet to her and I was stung. She didn't like me either! The nerve! Obviously I had *my* reasons, but what were *hers!?*

Happily, I have improved. In the last few months I've started to risk not being liked. Thank goodness, the postman and the paper boy are still my biggest fans, but Crispian Pomeroy most definitely isn't. He was the first bend in my learning curve. The more I tried to please him, the less he respected me, so there was no incentive. Which made it easier to incite his dislike – a terrifying but exhilarating experience, and quite different from the sleepy blunders that endangered my relationships with Matt and Babs. As for the head to head with my mother, that was like jumping out of a burning building and hoping someone will catch you.

Escaping with some minor cuts and bruises gave me strength, I think. I saw that if I never challenged people, they'd assume I felt there was nothing to challenge. I suppose I owe my mother that acknowledgment, at least. The rows I've had with Andy are different. That man irritated me in a manner quite unique. It's hard to hold back when someone needles you as he did. He also had an alarming habit of shouting out his emotions as they occurred, like a football commentator. He drove me to express myself, and my annoyances, because otherwise I'd be standing there dumb as a post while he yelled at me. Yet, at the crucial moment, I still held back. Ultimately, my training got the better of me. It's a warning that, despite making progress, I'd be no match for my big brother. He's all I'll never be – sleek, smooth, and so full of confidence he leaves a glittering trail of the stuff behind him, like a dolphin dancing through the sea at night, trailing phosphorescence. When Tony favours you, little else matters. You're a cat basking in sunshine after a chicken dinner. His patronage is so selective, you are blessed. The phrase I keep thinking of is 'he shines his light upon you', and I'm sure it's from a prayer – which might seem a little *overexcited* (as my mother would say) – but that's what it's like. Equally, when he chooses not to bless, favour, and illuminate you, it's hell.

I pick up the receiver and say hello.

'What the fuck is this about?'

'Hi, Tony,' I squeak. 'I hope you're feeling better after Monday and your kidneys aren't too bruised. I— I, just thought you'd, ah, like to know. Mum couldn't get through to you.'

'You're not going.'

'But' – vowing to book my ticket the second I get off the phone – 'it's booked.'

'Are you deaf?'

'No, but I thought—'

'Did I ask what you thought?'

'No, but—'

'Tell me what you're not going to do.'

'Tony, I—'

'Did you hear me?'

I'm silent. It's like trying to reason with a cat.

After a knee-trembling pause, Tony speaks again, and this time his voice is a low hiss. 'Get this. What I did in my year off was my business. It was nothing to do with this family. The woman and I came to an understanding about the kid. The end. She goes back to her life, I go back to mine. No *shit*. No fucking *bother*. Everyone's *happy*. Until you open your big mouth, and the whole bloody world gets involved. It's not what I want, Natalie. I don't want this. Do you understand me' – his tone is incredulous – 'or are you too stupid?'

'No,' I reply miserably. 'I mean yes. Yes. No.'

'So,' he says softly. 'Tell me what you're not going to do.'

'I'm not going to go to Australia,' I whisper.

He cuts me off.

I stare at the receiver in disbelief. The rage boils, froths, and explodes.

'It's YOUR kid!' I scream at the phone, 'It's *your* daughter, you stupid pillock! What's wrong with you, you moron, you should be PLEASED! We're going because of *you!*'

I fan my hand in front of my face, and catch my breath. I want to snatch up the phone and tell it all to Babs in one long wail. My finger is on the speed-dial button when it strikes me that Simon will have got home in the last half hour and maybe now is not a good time to ring. I cross my arms. She's

418

got enough problems. She doesn't need to be wrenched from a romantic opportunity by my spat with Tony.

'What a foul man!' I say aloud and indignantly. 'Foul, foul, foul.' I repeat this until I feel a bit better. Then I purse my lips. And I text the foul man again.

It's your kid. It's your daughter, you stupid pillock. What's wrong with you, you moron, you should be pleased. We're going because of you. (It doesn't look so bad without exclamation marks, so I send it.)

I chew my hair and my fingernails – I would chew my toenails too but I can't reach them – but the phone doesn't ring. Keep calm, I tell myself, it's classic powerplay. He'll call in a minute. I sit like this for a quarter of an hour and then the doorbell trills.

Drrrrrrrrrrrrrrrrggggggggggggggg

It isn't Andy.

My brother doesn't grab me by the scruff of the neck but he looks as if he wants to. I open the door an inch and, using his torso as a battering ram, he sails in. I'm all but crushed between the door and the wall.

'I said, you're not fucking going!' he screams. 'What's wrong with you, you stupid fat tart!'

I think he's slightly upset. I gingerly edge myself out from behind the door.

'I—'

'Shut up!' he roars. I can't help noticing that his ears are bright red with rage. It makes him look silly, and I wonder if he knows this – it could matter in meetings. My brain shakes itself like a wet dog, and the insult hits me with a splat. Stupid. Fat. Tart.

'What did you call me?'

'You heard,' he snarls.

'No, Tony,' I exclaim. 'You—'

'Shut up,' he murmurs, in the way an executioner might murmur 'sorry' before chopping off a head.

'No, you shut up,' I murmur. (It was a good tactic, *I'm* not proud.)

419

Amazingly, it works. Tony blinks and splutters, 'What?'

'I am not stupid, I am not fat, and I am not a tart, Tony.' I prod him in the solar plexus three times; once for stupid, twice for fat, three times for tart. He coughs, gasps and stares. 'I'm tired of you, Tony,' I say, hoping he can't hear my heart banging against my ribcage. 'I'm tired of your attitude—'

'The mouse that roared,' he says scornfully, rubbing his neck. 'You sound like my fucking headmistress.'

'. . . towards me, Babs, Mum, towards all women, in fact. You're pathetic. You think it makes you look big but it doesn't. Everyone thinks you're a misogynist prat.'

'What is it *really*, Natalie? You on the blob?'

'That, Tony,' I spit, 'is exactly what I'm talking about.'

'I don't know *what* you're talking about, darlin'.' Tony seems to be considering another tack because he's stopped bellowing.

'Yes, you do.' Suddenly, the coolness is no longer a front. I feel as if I'm facing him through a shield of ice.

'Floozie,' sighs my brother, 'calm down.'

'You,' I reply, 'are the one who's out of control – shouting and screaming like a baby with wind.' (I choose to forget the solar plexus attack.) I smile and add, 'I'm going to Australia, and so is Mum and so is Dad, and no one is asking your permission, we're just informing you of the fact.'

'I don't want you to go,' says Tony through his teeth. 'And I don't want *him* sliming around *my* daughter.'

'Your daughter! You haven't seen your daughter since she was born! You've got no say who slimes – who sees her! And this pointless ignoring of Dad! Have you noticed you've modelled your fatherhood on his? You're only spiting yourself. No one else.'

Tony starts. 'Not true,' he says. So quietly the words are barely there. 'Not true,' he repeats, louder. 'It *kills* him that I won't see him.' He scowls, turning fifteen for a second. 'And that pleases me.'

420

I shrug. 'Fine. Just be prepared for the fact that in ten years' time your daughter might be saying the same about you. We'll all be off in Sydney having a laugh' – while this phrase is not notably applicable to my mother I use artistic licence in the name of my cause – 'with Kelly and Tara, and you'll—'

'That fat bitch.' But the way he says it is almost mechanical. As if his mind is busy elsewhere.

'Tony,' I exclaim. 'You're obsessed with people being fat. Even if they aren't. You were always on at me when we were growing up, even though I had the figure of a car aerial. And Mum. Giving everyone else *your* complex. You really should see someone about that. What is it? Were you a fat kid? Were you teased at school for being fat? I should get out the old photo albums and—'

'Natalie,' snaps my brother. 'Yap yap yap. Do what you fucking like. But if you go to Australia, that's it. You won't be seeing me again.'

'Is that a promise?' I say wearily. 'Get out.'

He turns at the door. 'Never, *ever* tell me who I'm like.'

By the time I work out who he means, he's revving up the Beamer. I watch him go and wonder if it's worth it.

Damn, I think, two minutes later. I've got to warn Mum.

'You *told* him?' she gasps. 'I thought you were finding him! You didn't say you'd tell him! What did he say?'

I give her the uncensored version.

'Oh, Natalie!' she cries, and I can't deduce if she's disappointed in me or angry with me or both. I brace myself for the rebuke. I've upset him, I've interfered, I've driven him away, why couldn't I keep quiet? 'Oh, Natalie,' she sighs again, and her voice brims with regret. 'He's a difficult boy. But he has to learn.'

When I put the phone down I'm choked. I'm not sure – because that's all she says – but I *think* she's on my side.

I decide to go for a run. There's too much grog in my head, running will clear it. And to be honest, despite preaching to my brother, I'm still not comfortable being heavier. If I'm going to put on weight, I'll have to keep going to the gym in order to feel smug. I mean, fit. The bigger me needs wearing in, like new shoes. The other reason I decide to go for a run is that if I stay in the house I might stuff myself with stale biscuits. I feel low about the showdown with Tony.

I check the class schedule before setting off for the gym – I don't want to see Alex. Happily, there's no Pilates tonight nor any sign of her. I bound towards the Stair-Master like an old friend, and try to run with good posture – hard when you want to slump and curl with exhaustion. After five weak staggery minutes, during which I feel horribly self-conscious, my posture being that of a galley slave – I give up and switch off the machine. Oh my *God*. I can't run any more. My heart is a cold little pebble, sat there for show. I walk out and drive home depressed.

I can hear the phone shrilling as I go to unlock the door. Instantly, my fingers become potatoes and I drop the keys and finally clatter in to silence. Whoever it was hasn't left a message. I press 1471, don't recognise the number, decide this is in my favour, and dial it.

'Natalie? Is that you?' The bundled-up Eskimo sounds snuffly. 'That's a coincidence. I just called you.'

'Mel,' I say, in surprise. Has Tony asked her to ring? To try and persuade me against Australia? Not his style. Tony doesn't employ heavies, he is the heavy. Anyhow, no one could ever call Mel 'heavy'. 'I rang you the other day,' I say finally, 'about *Alice in Wonderland*. Although it might be a bit late now . . .'

Sniff

'I was writing the press release and as you're one of the Alices, I thought . . .'

Sob

'Mel? Mel! What is it? Are you okay? I'm sure it's not too late, I'm sure we can still squeeze in your quote—'

blu-uhuhuhuhuuurr

'Mel! Oh no, what, sorry, please, what is it?'

422

With a great shuddering gasp, Mel stops crying and manages to spit a few words out. All I can understand is 'mithing periodth' and 'danthing ith my life' and 'parmethan thauth'.

Parmesan sauce? 'Pardon?'

'They said I had a severely low bodyweight and there was all this stuff I have to eat and it was fattening things like pints of semi-skimmed milk – *pints* of milk – and p-p-p-parmesan sauce . . .'

She's the queen of drama queens but this *über*-hysteria is exceptional. I am starting to feel terrified. 'Mel,' I say. 'I'm so sorry, but I don't know what you're talking about.'

'Nobody knows yet, not even Tony. I thought *you'd* know what to tell him.'

'About what?'

With much prompting, it emerges that last week Mel slipped in the shower and hurt her back. She barely knocked it but the pain was so inordinately excruciating, her flatmate called an ambulance. The X-ray found a vertebral fracture. A bone scan confirmed low bone mineral density, which doctors agreed contributed to the fracture. The fact it fractured so easily showed the loss of bone mineral density had reached a certain stage. Mel has starved herself into osteoporosis. The specialist told her, 'I can only speculate that constant high impact work will significantly increase the risk of a second fracture.'

So Mel will not be dancing *Alice in Wonderland*. She may not be dancing again.

Chapter 49

Mel's anguish still reverberates in my head two days later. At one point she'd cried, 'Oh, Natalie! Bad things happen to good people!' It was like she'd reached her little hand into my ribcage and squeezed my heart till it bled. I feel shaken. Mel is regarded as silly. She has a naïve gigglish way about her which undermines her talent. People pet her and patronise her and I have too. You pat her on the head, call her sweet, and chuckle quietly over her baby-doll lisp. But osteoporosis turns her into a serious person. That's *awful*.

Guilt and shame don't stop me from eating a calcium-rich breakfast of muesli with semi-skimmed milk and a low-fat strawberry yoghurt with a chopped up dried fig mixed in with it, and freshly squeezed orange juice not from concentrate. I hope she'll be okay – you never know (as one always says when the worst is a definite and you can't quite summon the gall to say: It'll be fine). Poor Mel. I've called to see how she is twice, but she hasn't got back to me. I know she was upset that I didn't want to help her break the news to Tony. 'Break' the news! She's the one with the fractured back, what's she fretting about *him* for?

I suggested that she shouldn't treat Tony like a delicate plant. She said what if he stopped liking her when she put on weight. I told her, partly to comfort her but mainly because I meant it, 'I've never seen my brother in love, until he met you.' (I was about to announce it was love at first sight, but thought better of it.) 'I swear it, Mel, you're the love of his life. He worships you. He's never been like this with anyone. Ever. And I don't think there's anything you can do to change that.'

Meanwhile – and maybe this is also because of Mel – I've booked my flight. I'm leaving on a jet plane (with my mother, which slightly soils the glamour of it) in three weeks. It's an open ticket, so I can fly back when I want to. I'm salivating at the thought of white sand and turquoise sea but I can't quite bring myself to buy a rucksack. I called Robin yesterday to ask permission before I paid the travel agent. I said if he objected I'd just pop over for a fortnight, and the three-month trip wasn't my idea, but everyone kept threatening that it would be 'An Experience', though if he thought it would be wrong to interrupt my training—

'Natalie,' he said. 'I don't usually encourage my students to go travelling directly after they start the course. You have to put in six hundred hours' work to qualify, so if you want to teach before the age of a hundred and five, you need to stick with it. I need to know that you're committed. ('Oh I am, I am, I won't do this if you say no!') OK. But the time has to be right. There's no point in me forcing you if you need to be doing something else. And I think you need to do this. I'll make an exception and we'll treat these first few weeks as *pre*-training. I'd prefer to start afresh when you're back. Shall we book a session now?'

I gibbered with gratitude in the face of such goodwill. Even if I was a little taken aback at being regarded as a special needs student. Whatever, I'm going to the studio at 4.30 tomorrow. I'd have liked to have gone today, but today is a squash. I've got to write a short piece for Matt's theatrical friend. I've got to nip into the deli so Mrs Edwards can show me how to make a cappuccino and use the meat-slicer. I'm having my hair cut. I've got to ring the bank to organise an overdraft (the work is generating a trickle of income, whereas the gallivanting is haemorrhaging money from my account at a fatal rate). And Babs and Simon have asked me round for dinner tonight, so I want to buy them a present. Considering the state of Simon the last time we met, I feel champagne or alcohol of any kind would be inappropriate. Babs told me not to bring anything, but I'd like to. I was touched, and shocked when she asked – we've never *formally* invited each other anywhere, so grown up. I blurted, 'Don't feel you have to invite me!'

The second I said it, I felt ungracious. Thankfully, she took it the way it was meant and retorted, 'Don't feel you have to come!'

'I'd love to,' I said hastily, biting back the inappropriate questions on the tip of my tongue (but won't it be awkward with Simon? won't we all be thinking about the bar attack? does Babs *mind* having an elephant in her living room?).

'If you're worried about Si, for God's sake don't be,' declared Babs airily, as I squirmed and pulled elaborate 'please no' faces at the phone. 'He was very keen to have you round, to make a new start and all that. He's promised not to make a lunge at you over the canapés!'

'Blimey, Babs!' I spluttered, amazed at her capacity for the unattractive truth. She's not afraid to take the elephant by the horns, as it were.

'Oh, I know,' she replied with mock-disgust, 'Canapés. Don't tell anyone.'

I was desperate to ask if Andy would be there. 'So is anyone else coming?'

'Just one other person,' crooned Babs.

'Anyone I know?' I said, trying to sound tinkly and unconcerned.

'It'll be a surprise,' she sang. 'The clue is, I thought it was about time you two kissed and made up. See you eightish.'

That means *yes!*

I speed to my hairdresser – who is based in Hendon but whose soul is forever Soho. Stuart is the kind of gay man that Matt would call 'a poof'. His first word to me was 'Sign?' When I said I didn't know what time I was born he made me ring my mother. She didn't remember, so he ordered me to find out and tell him the next time I came in. 'Mercury rising,' he lisped as he clipped. Stuart has the *air* of being interested but it's mortifyingly clear that everything I say bores him. I have to beg him three times to cut my hair short, because he doesn't want to and sulks. We compromise on a 'Beatles crop'. Retro chic though this sounds, it looks remarkably similar to the bowl haircuts my mother cursed me with aged six.

'Elfin!' sighs Stuart.

'Lovely,' I warble, bravely.

On the way home I manage to impulse-buy Babs and Simon a seventies-style phone the *exact* colour of Heinz Cream of Tomato Soup without looking the shop assistant in the eye once. I feel shy and vulnerable without my long hair. Lighter, bouncier, and possibly – oh dear – elfin. But I'm not ready for it to be assessed by shop assistants. I skid-park outside my front door, carefully place the orange phone on the kitchen table – I have a hunch Babs will love that phone, it's so screamingly 999 – and race to the bathroom. A blonde elf blinks at me. I jut out my chin. What will Andy think? The message is: 'I've got you out of my hair.' I hope he's read enough women's magazines to get it.

I picture his face. I've been strict so far, but I can't resist. I open the door of the spare room and pad in. It's so silent. The glitterball hangs greyly over the bare mattress. There's a sad feel to it, like a fairground in the rain. I sniff, and smell dead air. It's just a cold empty room. I pull open the wardrobe. The metal hangers clink. I drop to my hands and knees and squint under the bed. Hang about, there *is* something. It's so far under I can't reach it. I grab a broom from the kitchen and poke it out the other side of the bed. I scramble over the mattress to see what it is. A slipper! A dowdy fuzzy grey plastic-heeled slipper! Size eleven. Wahay, that figures. I grin, recall our last shouting match, and the grin fades.

Oh. I have *not* got him out of my hair. If he and Alex are

at dinner tonight it's going to be very tough. But you'll get through it, madam, you'll put a face on. For a moment I think of a cousin of my mother's who disgraced herself – according to my mother – by refusing to attend the christening of her best friend's son, because she couldn't have children herself. She asked them to excuse her as it was too painful. This was years back, but at the time my mother behaved as if *she* was the best friend. 'Selfish!' Ought to 'rise above it!' *I* privately disagreed. It was a decision palpably made in therapy, but I felt for the cousin. Forced to celebrate what she couldn't have.

But babies are different to men (true). I'll be there tonight, if I have to keep my smile in place with a coat hanger. I sit at my desk, tap-tap-tap out a press release – £150, *ching!* – and wonder. Freelance PR and making cappuccinos isn't a bad life but I won't be a millionaire by thirty. What *will* I be? All the best ideas are gone already. A friend of Simon's has a nifty sideline in 'Driveways of the Rich and Famous', tootling Japanese tourists around Totteridge in his car. Another is working on 'Houdini, the Musical' as we speak. In five years' time though, I could be teaching Pilates in my own studio. Five years' time. My own studio. Well, I could convert the spare room if necessary. While I know happiness can't buy you money, the thought of it makes me smile.

I'm still fantasising as I drive to the deli. Jackie said that 5.30 would be best, as it's quiet around then. I keep touching my hair – it *ends* at the nape of my neck! – to check it isn't a dream. That's one habit to shed before I reach my destination. I park round the corner, and check in the mirror in case I've got carrot stuck in my teeth and am a hygiene hazard. I used to drive Babs mad asking her if I had anything stuck in my teeth. 'Yes,' she'd reply. 'A large prawn.'

But today my teeth are clear. I look presentable. It will be fun to work with Mr and Mrs Edwards, when I get used to it. They squabble and flirt and are quite shockingly still in love. I watched *Addams Family Values,* and was reminded of their relationship.

Mrs Edwards engulfs me in a mammoth hug and says, '*Ciao, bella!*' I feel the soft squash of her breasts against me. Mr Edwards, who is sitting at a table in deep discussion with a man with a pencil moustache, waves at me. There are two empty espresso cups on the counter, and the place is hot with the rich aroma of ground coffee. And there's a peeling bluish poster of the Tower of Pisa on the wall. I grin like an idiot. This is *so* continental!

'You wanna a cappuccino?' says Jackie, peering at me. 'A sandwich? Parma ham? Salami? So different from the English one, much more tasty!'

'I'd like a black coffee,' I say shyly. 'I won't have a sandwich, though, thank you – I'm going to Babs for dinner.'

Jackie wrinkles her nose and says, 'You better have a sandwich!'

I giggle. 'Don't you think the food will be nice tonight, then?' This is a sly question as I know it's going to start her off on her favourite topic. It's bad of me but I like listening to her talk.

'Her cooking is medium quality! People here, they eat so much shit! The junky food! They don't wanna cook! Barbara, she don't wanna cook! The pizza, Domino's Pizza, packed on the weekend, dey so lazy! The English, all the week, they don't wanna ave de alf an hour for cooking! Food in Italy, the taste is better than here! All this stuff' – she indicates the shelves – 'for me is common, for you, special! Dis is a small choice! If you go in a deli in Italy, is double sized!'

All this is said as she constructs a giant sandwich. She places it before me and watches me as I eat. I have to stretch my jaw perpendicular like a snake's. I try to smile reassuringly between mouthfuls (more for my benefit than Jackie's, as all unscheduled food has to be accounted for and each mouthful sticks until I rationalise that I didn't have lunch, so this can be it). Once the maths is done, I start to taste it. And while this is undeniably, deliciously, a non-British sandwich – in size, attitude, and flavour – a worrying thought occurs.

'What if customers ask me to recommend something and I don't know what it is?' I mumble.

'Slowly, slowly, you taste everything,' she replies.

'But there's about a hundred different salamis and cheeses here!' I squeak.

'*Buongiorno, signora!*' cries Mrs Edwards as a large pale woman waddles into the deli, with an eye on the tiramisus. She winks at me and rushes to serve her. I struggle on with my sandwich and watch as the queue grows. Mrs Edwards greets each customer as if they were a dear friend and I watch as their tense office faces relax into smiles. Her husband is still talking to Moustache Man, who Mrs Edwards identifies for me as a rep. I look at the clock. I can't stay for too much longer, I've got to get ready for tonight. I'm feeling full and edgy and wondering if I could hide the rest of the sandwich in my pocket so as not to offend Jackie, when I hear a voice say, 'Hiya Mum. I'll load the car up then come and help if you want.'

I freeze in my chair, head low, sandwich to lip. Good grief, what's *he* doing here? I look wildly at the deli door, as the nearest escape route. He must have sneaked in through the back! But I'm not ready. Only my hair! I'm bare of face and scruffy of dress, and I've got about a pound of salami stuck in my teeth. This will ruin the impact of later! I hastily wipe the crumbs from my chin. I'm hidden by the counter, but I can't cower behind it like a frightened animal. I rise slowly to my feet, as Jackie announces my presence, gestures to Andy to teach me how to make a cappuccino, and to show me what's what.

'Hello,' I say.

Andy gawks. 'Ringo,' he declares, eventually. 'Best drummer in the world!'

My hands fly to my hair. I can't scowl in case Jackie sees

me. I duck under the counter, and think of the nastiest thing I can say in front of her.

'You left one of your lovely stylish slippers in the spare room,' I purr. 'I'll bring it along tonight, I'm sure you don't feel whole without it.'

'What's tonight?'

'Oh!' I exclaim. 'Aren't you invited?'

'I don't know what you're talking about, so obviously not.'

Great. Now he knows I've been thinking about him.

Wordlessly, Andy hands me an apron, and starts yanking and clanking at the coffee machine. I say, 'Babs and Simon have invited me for dinner.'

'You and that plank?'

'Who?'

'*Who?* You know. Silver ring boy.'

'Saul?' I squeak in genuine surprise. 'What's he got to do with anything?' I think back to the performance I staged at the bar-café, and squirm. 'Saul,' I say firmly, 'is very much an ex. I've seen the guy once in the last two months, we had a nice civilised chat over the kitchen table, thank you, good bye, have a nice life.' I pause. 'There is,' I add, 'only one plank I've had anything to do with in the last couple of weeks.'

Andy shrugs, and clanks at the coffee machine harder than ever. 'The coffee goes in here, smooth it over, clicks in there, flick the switch, da da da, cup under here, milk in the jug, swirl it, slowly, froth froth froth, pour it on, bit of chocolate, there you go. Easy. You try it.' He smiles in a not altogether unfriendly way.

I try it and burn my little finger on a hot bit of machine. 'Ouch,' I say crossly.

'Run it under the tap,' says Andy, gesturing loosely in the direction of the sink.

'No,' I growl, wanting to. I hate men who sulk and sulk and then – when they feel they've leached every atom of joy from you – cheer up. I *said* it! I spoke out. I dropped him a

431

hint as big as a brick! And what do I get in return? As Bruce Willis would say, dick! (mind you, I should be so lucky). Nothing. Fine. All right.

'So how's lovergirl?' I add, glaring at him.

'Lovergirl?'

'Don't give me that!' I cry. 'Don't give me that,' I repeat in a whisper, as Mrs Edwards glances over her shoulder. 'Alex!' I hiss. 'You know! Sasha! Gorgeous kind witty clever bloody perfect Betty Boop Sasha-Alex! The woman you're living with! Ring any bells?'

To my annoyance Andy starts laughing. He sees my expression and quickly stops. 'I'm living by myself, in my old flat in Pimlico, and have been since last Wednesday,' he growls. 'I was going to tell you what was going on with Alex in the café, but you're so *feckin* impatient you couldn't wait. You were off with Plank before I got a chance.'

'I wasn't "off" with him!' I shrill, as my pulse goes bonkers. '*You* were off! I was waiting to hear from you all morning!'

'All morning is nothing!' Andy splutters.

'You've spent too long lolling around hostels smoking pot!' I snap. 'I'm on London time!'

'You should get out more,' murmurs Andy, shaking his head.

I say in a small voice, 'What did you think I'd think, when you left with her that night?'

Andy, to his credit, looks ashamed of himself. 'I'm sorry,' he sighs. 'I didn't think. I know what it looked like with Alex. I was confused that night. When I saw her, after all that time, I did think, what do I do? But Natalie, I swear, nothing happened. She didn't want it to, and neither did I.'

I thin my lips. Andy glares at me. 'Jesus, Natalie, I'm not an animal! I can keep it in my trousers! I am capable of exerting rational thought and a bit of self-control! Not *all* men think with their schlongs twentyfour-seven! Some of us even have brains in our heads!'

'All right, OK, I didn't say anything,' I mutter. 'Anyway, animals don't wear trousers. Calm down.' I try not to grin.

Andy continues in a quieter voice. 'Sash is still in bits about her marriage breaking up. She was pretty pissed that night, she wanted someone to cry on. It was four hours of Mitchell this, Mitchell that. How he hurt her, how I hurt her. We stayed up all night, going through a lot of the old stuff. It was good, for both of us. There was no smoochy stuff. Ask Alex, if you don't believe me. And anyway—' He stops, and looks at me.

I feel dizzy, so I look at the floor.

'I *am* getting out more,' I murmur. 'I'm going to Australia in three weeks. Travelling.'

'Oh,' says Andy. 'Oh. Right. Good for you.' He pauses. 'Well. These are the meats. That's parma ham, prosciutto alle bonce, prosciutto cotto, speck, bresaola, mortadella, coppa di parma, pancetta coppata, pancetta affumicata, salami milano, salame fiocco, salame felino, salame aglio, salame ventrilina, salame finocchiona, carnevale sausage, spianata calabrese, chorizo, and golosa sausage, and these are the cheeses; pecorino romano—'

'Andy,' I say softly, 'this is very nice of you but I can read the labels myself. I need to know what everything tastes like so I can tell customers, but there's no point starting now. I've got to be at Babs's in an hour, and I've got to go home and change. Thanks for' – I waggle my charred finger – 'showing me how to make a cappuccino. Bye then.'

I turn away and say goodbye to Mrs Edwards, who forces me to take a box of cantuccini con gocce di cioccolato (crisp chocolate cookies) for the dinner party tonight, 'At least you have a nice biscuit with the espresso!' I thank her, I glance again at Andy, and walk out.

'You've plumped out in the face!' says Frannie, giving me the fright of my life as I stand on Babs's doorstep in a trance. Frances Crump – in 'I'm Ugly So There!' Mother Hubbard shoes and no lipstick (apparently Roman prostitutes wore it

433

to indicate they'd perform fellatio) – is the most disagreeable sight I've seen in a while. But her bristling presence doesn't bother me. I'm too wrapped up in thinking about Andy. I want to kiss him or hit him, I can't decide. Probably hit him. 'And anyway,' he said, '*And anyway*.'

Why couldn't he finish his sentence? I as good as told him he had an exclusive. I finally managed to use my mouth for its true purpose (to eat my sandwich, speak my mind) and he goes quiet on me! The biggest yap on the block, and suddenly he's inarticulate! I broke the habit of a lifetime. I expected results. As for Alex – I've been so mean to her, although mainly in my head. Such a lovely woman! I'll ring her tomorrow. Maybe we can meet for a drink some time. I feel very charitable towards Alex.

'I *needed* to plump out in the face,' I tell Frannie, smilingly. 'Whereas your face looks more like a Hallowe'en pumpkin every time I see it. Do the babies start crying on sight? The doctors must save hours of manpower in smacked bottoms.'

When Babs flings open the door to welcome in her guests, one of them is standing there, pale with rage, while the other beams ear to ear like a demented pixie. I mean, elf.

'Nat,' breathes Babs. 'Your hair looks great. Look at this! It's so sophisticated! When did you do it? Frannie, doesn't it suit her?'

'As much as a pudding basin haircut suits anyone.'

'It looks sensational, Natalie,' sighs Babs.

'Thanks,' I grin, not even caring about being called 'sophisticated'. (It makes me feel like a nine-year old having her frock praised by adults at a party.) 'This is for you and Simon.'

As Babs coos over the Bagpuss wrapping paper, Simon hovers in the background, twiddling his wedding ring.

'Hi, Natalie,' he mumbles, shaking my hand and leaning forward to bestow a kiss on the air. 'Good to see you. Frannie, how are you?'

'Worked to the bone,' lies Frannie.

'Can I get you a drink?' blurts Simon, clawing desperately at social convention.

'This is *excellent!*' shrieks Babs. 'My parents used to have one of these except bog green! Si! Look what she got us!'

Simon regards the orange phone in bemusement. Then his mouth twists into a grin and he says, 'A fine choice.'

Frannie, whose gift is a cactus, says nothing. Babs hustles everyone into the warmly lit lounge (plump russet sofas, sheepskin rugs, orange arc lamps), forces great goblets of red wine into our hands, and the silence melts like ice. Simon does the cooking and, to my surprise, the food is delicious. It's a relatively new experience, thinking of food as 'delicious'.

'I was in the deli before and your mum didn't have high hopes,' I say to Babs, forking a small heap of wild mushroom salad into my mouth, 'but Simon is talented.'

'Aw he is, isn't he?' beams Babs, stroking her husband's arm. 'He's been practising, he used to be awful. I'm useless, I've always relied on men to cook for me. Men and my mum, and the guys on the watch.'

'I like men who cook,' says Frannie, whose plate is already stripped. 'Although the kitchen remains largely the woman's domain. Every female has one foot straddling the cooker whether she likes it or not.'

'It sounds rather kinky,' I say. Frannie shoots me a death look.

'I enjoy cooking,' says Simon. 'It relaxes me. And Babs is so appreciative. What was it I made that you really liked? Risotto with lentils and sausages?'

'Mm,' says Babs. She grins. '*Risotto con lenticchie e salamini.* Si's been swotting up on Northern Italian cookery in a bid to impress my mother. I've told him it'll never work and to concentrate on impressing me. So what was she on about before? She didn't tell you the Christmas pudding story again, did she?' (When Jackie Cirelli first came to England she bought what she described as 'a horrible pudding' in Harrods. 'I don' know what dis is, exactly,' she scolded her husband-to-be, who worked at the food counter, 'but I tried with it, and then I put it in da bin.' He found her honesty, and her huge brown eyes, endearing and offered to take her out for a pudding-free dinner . . .)

'No,' I say. 'She might have got on to it, but the shop was busy and –'

'I can't believe you're eating,' says Frannie, resting her elbow on the table and jabbing her knife at me. 'I should take a picture.'

'Frannie,' says Babs. 'Fourth helping?' She nods at me to continue.

'And so she had to serve the customers. So –' I fantasise that saying his name will summon him like a genie '– so Andy, your brother,' I explain helpfully 'came by to collect something, and your Mum made him show me how to make a cappuccino.'

'Don't tell me,' murmurs Simon. 'You burnt your finger on that blasted machine.'

'*Yes!*' I cry, never so pleased to have burnt a finger in my life. Simon and Babs smile at each other and laugh. 'But it wasn't Andy's fault,' I add quickly, lest anyone should think I'm apportioning blame. 'I mean' – I feel my face turning as red as the wine – 'it was very sweet of him to show me, he was in a rush and I, I, I . . . he left one of his slippers in my flat, did I tell you, I nearly brought it along!' I realise I'm talking rubbish and stammer to a halt, under the collective gaze.

Babs sucks in her cheeks, and places her fork on her plate. For a second I think she's going to shout at me. But she doesn't. She looks at me through her eyelashes and smiles.

'Well, I do declare,' she drawls. 'That big ole brother of mine is a true gentleman!'

Frannie looks from me to Babs, appalled. 'You don't

mean Natalie's got her sights set on *Andy*?' she barks, eyes bulging in pique. 'My God, there'll be no men left for the rest of us!'

'I was under the impression you were fine on your own,' I mutter to my plate.

'We all want to find love, Natalie!' snaps Frannie, as if love is something that can be yanked out from behind the dresser drawer if only you pull hard enough.

Everyone nods meekly, but later, when Frannie is in the loo, Simon addresses me and Babs in a timid whisper: 'Natalie,' he says. 'I know we've had our, er, differences. But if it's going to be you or Frannie – *please*, I beg you, don't let it be her.'

Chapter 50

All love is conditional on something. It's just establishing
what conditions you're prepared to accept being loved on.
That makes it sound easy but it's not. When you want to
be loved by someone and want to *keep* being loved by
someone, you can find yourself accepting terms that, in an
ideal world with no sharp edges, you wouldn't stand for.
There was a point when I'd say yes to anything even if,
deep down, I didn't agree with it. But I'm a lot fussier than
I was and, what's more, I'm not nearly so coy about
making it known. I find it cuts down on bother.

This might be why I haven't contacted Tony, and why
Mum and I might feasibly last twenty-four hours in an
airborne tin, squashed up like a pair of battery hens,
without needling each other to death. This might be why I
haven't returned Andy's calls. It's been two and a half
weeks since Babs's dinner and he's rung five times. He also
turned up in my front garden last Friday at 2 a.m., singing
a drunken solo – a travesty of Tom Jones's *It's Not
Unusual* – while Robbie staggered around on the pavement
with a traffic cone on his head. I'm not saying it wasn't
persuasively cute but I'm harder than that. I'm certainly
harder than Robbie bawling, 'I'm so bloody bored of his
moping aw Natalieeee please!'

This might sound nuts, but I'm very busy with visas and
mini-sewing-kits and water purification tablets (well, *I*
don't know what the water's like in Australia), so right
now a relationship is not convenient. Not yet. It's not easy,
re-training to be normal. I still think about the calorific

value of everything I eat. There's still guilt, worry, twitching. I can't imagine that I'll ever feel wholly comfortable around cake. And forgoing the manic exercise in favour of a more holistic – I'll never like that word – pursuit sucks up gallons of willpower. But I'm making slow progress and I want to reach a certain point without a placebo. If I can be fine without Andy, *then* I can be fine with him. I need to be sure that my mental health doesn't depend on someone else. Not my father, mother, brother, Babs, or Andy (although if all five were wiped out in an earthquake, I suppose it might have some bearing).

I feel quite calm about it. This may have something to do with Pilates – the boost I got from acquiring the ability to bend over an imaginary beach ball without squashing it cannot be underplayed – or it may relate to the fact that I now know that Andy didn't lie to me about his ex. I guess I knew it in the deli. Anyhow, I asked Alex straight out. I suggested we go for a drink, relayed the entire story, and to my surprise, she said she already knew. Andy had told her everything after the café debacle. I asked if she minded, and she laughed and said, 'Would it make a difference if I did?'

Actually, it makes no difference. Nor does the fact that Babs isn't going to shoot me for trespass. (She's said nothing on the subject since the dinner, and I'm assuming she's decided to keep out of it.) Right now, I want to sort myself out at my own pace, and see what he does meanwhile. As well as untangling the food/ body/ mind/ weirdo issues, I need to know that Andy wants me *first* - that I'm not a fallback because he's over Alex. Then I'll know what *I* want.

'You want to get yourself some new kit,' says Babs. 'If I see you in that dreary pink top one more time I'm going to rip it off you and cut it up. Get yourself into town and burn plastic. Nothing shapeless or baggy, though, or it's going back.'

439

'But,' I plead, 'I've already spent about a hundred pounds on knickers.'

'What sort of knickers?'

'Your average ladies' knicker, Barbara.'

'What! Common-or-garden pants?'

'Babs, this isn't *Debbie Does Dallas* – I'm going travelling, it's just so I don't have to do washing every day.'

'Natalie, it isn't *Nuns on the Run* either. Anyway, I'm talking about your leaving do. Do me a favour and go and score yourself some nice lingerie. Nice knicks are good for the soul. And some new shoes. Tarty ones. If you can't find anything down the road, go to Selfridges. And a dress. A dress that stops traffic. People won't start arriving till nine. It's only 3 p.m., you've got ages, now go on, go!'

I put down the phone and check my list again. Crisps, got; carrots, got; dips, got; nuts, got; orange juice, got; alcohol, got; more alcohol, got; extra alcohol, got; reserve alcohol, got. What else do people need? Should I get extra toilet paper? I don't know why I let Babs talk me into having an I'm Off party. The last 'celebration' I hosted was my flat-warming – a disaster seared deep into my ego. No one turned up till 10.40, and the first guests to arrive were an ex-boyfriend and his new girlfriend. My mother had advised me not to move in the furniture until afterwards – consequently, there was a vast and humiliating excess of space per person.

I hope I've learned from the trauma. Tonight's ordeal – sorry, party – will be restricted to the kitchen and lounge so however measly the attendance, I'll achieve a deceptively high concentration of guests – no one can thin it out by sneaking off to the bedrooms, both of which will be locked. Also, last time I was picky. This time I've invited everyone I've ever met, including my enemies. I've practically handed out flyers on the street. I've also invited the neighbours so they can't moan about the noise. I'm considering paying an escort agency to send people *en masse*. Or borrowing the cardboard Stallone from the video shop. My mother, Susan, and Martin the Raconteur are on standby.

I decide to stop fretting and go shopping instead.

Why am I going to Kensington? It's the other side of London. And what am I doing paying for a pair of pink snakeskin mules? And tell me how can a pair of sugar-spun knickers cost fifty quid? And I should know by now that if it isn't navy it doesn't suit me. What made me hand over good money for a sheer purple top with ruffle trim and only *two* pieces of string where the buttons should be? Of course it looked good in the shop, they tilt the mirror so far back, Roseanne Barr would look like a waif. The stark reality of your own mirror is a different, fatter matter. I scramble into the top, yank on my black trousers – *Christ* they're tight! – and dangle a foot in the mules. I bite my lip. I feel as heavy as a bus. But I look like a real woman.

I take everything off and lay it lovingly on the bed. Then I leap in the shower, wash my hair, wiggle into my new extortionate knickers and high concept bra, scrub my teeth, spend a good five minutes coaxing my new short hair into an elfin shape (it wants to go from elfin to goblin), and a further ten on make-up (I can't ever spend longer than that – I run out of features to emphasise and find my hand creeping towards novelty stuff like 'gold hair mascara'). I don't want to think about other people getting ready right now, I don't want to tempt fate. Babs and Si are definites. Matt *said* he'd come – I told him Paws was welcome, he could even bring friends from puppy school, anything to make the place look busy. And Saul. Well, that's five of us, plus dog, six.

At 8.15, I take off the purple top and put on an old navy one. I feel too exposed in sheer purple, I might as well attend stark naked. Should I start putting out dips? Are garlic dips the key to a good party? I fear not. I arrange the alcohol nicely on the table instead. Music. Elvis is safe. No one would dare object. But the shocking truth is, I'm not an Elvis fan. I like *him*, I don't like his music. And I've met far too many people (Saul, although I'm naming no names) who fake an Elvis obsession as a populist cloak for their sad unpopulist personalities. I dig through my CD collection and put on Burt Bacharach instead.

I've just scraped the garlic dip into a bowl, then back into its plastic pot because I don't want to come across as chi-chi (whatever that is, but I suspect that garlic dip in pottery bowls is it), when the doorbell goes. Thank god now I can start drinking! I pull open the door and—

'I think there's been an error, what is *that*?' booms Babs, whose hair is resplendent in a chic flyaway style – think Louis the Sun King meets Salon Selectives.

'Hi,' grins Simon, very establishment in a blue quilted puffa jacket. 'Thought we'd get here on time, make the joint look, er, jumping.'

'It's a navy jumper,' I say weakly.

'Yes yes,' she sighs impatiently. 'And where's the *real* top you bought this afternoon?'

'This is it.'

'Nee-nor nee-nor, it's the fibber police! I repeat – where is the real top you bought this afternoon?'

'In my room,' I reply in a small voice. 'How did you know?'

'Because I know you,' she says, frogmarching me to the end of the corridor.

'Help yourself to garlic dip!' I squeak at Simon.

'Will do,' he shouts back.

'Please wear the purple,' cries Babs, when she sees it, crumpled on the bed. 'I implore you to wear the purple. It's stunning, I love it, it's so *riaowww!*' (She makes a noise identical to the noise next door's cat made when I accidentally trod on his tail.)

I sigh heavily, throw off the navy, and pull on the purple. 'You can see my bra through it,' I say grumpily.

'Hardly,' scoffs Babs. 'Anyhow it's an exhibitionist bra, it wants to be seen. And it's your party. It's your prerogative to dress how you want.'

'How *you* want, more like,' I mutter, doing up the strings.

'Doorbell!' trills Babs, unnecessarily. 'It could be Mark and Ben off the watch, I lured them here with the promise of ballerinas. And Si's invited a few of the less cretinous guys from his work. Oh, perfect. Very bling-bling, darling! It *so* shows off your figure!'

I scurry down the hall, flustered. Until five minutes ago I didn't know I *had* a figure. It's great to be told I look 'bling-bling' (I'm presuming bling-bling means something nice rather than a dog's dinner), but I still feel like I've ransacked an adult's dressing-up box. I yank open the door, to see Mel standing there with two soloists (she'd never fraternise with the foot soldiers) and three burly men who look like they can't believe their luck.

'We followed this lot,' grins one.

'These men are firemen!' exclaims Mel. 'We met them outside the station. I mean the tube station, not the fire station.' She giggles and tilts her head like a robin, and I come close to witnessing three grown men swoon. 'Tony isn't coming, he refused to, and I can't stamp my foot in case I jar my back. Natalie, you've got all big, I like your top though!'

I decide to leave this last comment unscrambled.

'How *is* your back?' I say, as they all troop in. I didn't expect Tony to come but it still hurts.

'It's awful,' she murmurs. 'The pain has been horrible. I've had to take it easy, I hate taking it easy! I feel like a big fat frump, I cried all day yesterday. Then I stopped because I didn't want to go to your party with puffy eyes. This is the first day I've felt okay about walking about. I decided to get a cab here with Clara, and we arranged to meet Isabelle at the station and pick her up. And she was talking to the firemen and then they jumped in too, Clara and Isabelle sat on their laps. I sat in the front because of my back.'

I'm about to ask her what she wants to drink, but one of the fire fighters beats me to it.

'Red wine, please, Mark,' she lisps sweetly.

'I've got soya milk if you prefer,' I whisper. 'It's good for, for er, bones.'

'Yes, but it tastes foul. Alcohol tastes nicer and it's a good anaesthetic,' replies Mel. 'Have you got a straight-backed chair, Natalie, to support my back?'

I rush to get her one. 'So, you must have told work, and Tony about your –' I hunt about for a euphemism but can't think of one '– osteoporosis.'

Mel nods, and says sadly, 'I've got sick leave.' Suddenly her cheeks dimple. 'But when I told Tony he was so sweet!' she cries. 'So, so sweet, your brother is the sweetest man I've ever met! He cried a bit when I told him, although he tried to hide it, and when I told him they said to put on weight he said the important thing was that I was healthy, and if that meant putting on weight I had to do it, and I'd always be the most beautiful woman in the world to him, whatever I weighed. I don't think I'd love him any more if *he* got fat, but it was lovely of him to say that, wasn't it?'

I hear this and the whoosh of relief just about knocks me flat. Because as certain as I was that his love wouldn't shrink as Mel grew, I could have been wrong. (It has been known.)

'What did I tell you, Mel?' I sigh, as Mark hands her a glass and crouches at her feet like a giant puppy. 'He'll stick like glue.' For a second I feel something between envy and awe. With no effort, Mel has unblocked a seemingly endless flow of love from my brother. I can't help think that it would be nice if a trickle could be diverted to his thirsting family. I say casually, 'I don't suppose Tony's said anything about me, has he?'

'Oh yes,' chirps Mel. 'He says he's furious with you because you're going to Sydney. I told him to stop being a silly billy but I think he wants to sulk at home for a bit longer. I think he's still cross that Matt beat him in a fight. Ooh, thank you, Marky Mark!'

444

I bite my lip. 'Mel,' I say. 'I might ring him. Do you think I should ring him?'

Mel looks startled, shocked even, that I would ask *her* opinion. And then she blushes with pleasure. She even tilts her head to help herself think. Finally, she lisps gravely, 'No. I don't think you should. I think' – and her voice trembles with the weight of responsibility – 'that Tony will call you before you go. I don't think he liked it when you told him off. But I think, in a way, he did like it. That's what I think.'

'Thank you, Mel,' I say. 'That's good advice.' She blushes again.

I feel a warm hand on my shoulder, and spin around. 'Alex!' I gasp. 'Hi! Thank you *so* much for coming!' I feel ashamed of myself just looking at her. She smiles warmly at someone behind me, my heart leaps, and I turn. 'Robin!' I croak. 'I'm so pleased you're here.'

'You sound terribly disappointed,' he purrs, kissing my cheek.

'Not at all!' No wonder I couldn't even make it into my junior school's Christmas pantomime. 'What would you like to drink?' I say hastily, 'I've got cranberry juice, orange juice, mineral water—'

'Lager?'

'Of course! Alex?'

'White wine spritzer, if – Barbara!' she exclaims. It's the first time I've seen Alex look flustered. 'How *are* you? God, it's been a while! I hear you got married, congratulations, you know I saw Andy last week, don't you? It was good to see him again, I missed him, er, as a friend, I have to say I . . .'

Grateful for a legitimate mission, I allow myself to be swept into the corridor. The doorbell rings on cue. Matt looks mischievous. He, Paws, and a tall handsome guy on crutches, are standing on my doorstep flanked by two chunky men. Men who wear rugby shirts but don't actually play rugby. Each with a big ruddy baby face, a

B&H cigarette stuck between stubby fingers, and a six-pack of Stella. Both are machoing it up for some reason.

'Ex-public-school boys,' murmurs Matt, kissing me on the mouth. 'They protest too much. Natalie, you look divine, I knew getting away from me would agree with you. This is Stephen – professional layabout and your theatrical source of employment.'

'Stephen, *hi!* At last! I've heard so much about you! Thank you for giving me work! Hello, you two must be, er, Simon's colleagues?'

'The pleasure's mine,' says Stephen gallantly, as Simon's colleagues grunt and shuffle in. Happily, I don't recognise them from the nightmare evening in the bar. Unhappily, I can't think of a word to say to either of them beyond 'hello'. So I'm grateful when Simon appears behind me like a homing pigeon – prompting a loud flurry of greetings ('Todger! My man!' that sort of thing) – and ushers the two goons towards the booze mountain.

'Mel's here,' I tell Matt. 'With Isabelle and Clara.'

'Poor love,' he says. 'Did she tell you? She was always on the route to destruction, that one.'

'Shall I bring them over?' I say, anxious that Matt and Stephen are entertained.

'Natalie, relax!' replies Matt. 'I'll get a drink down my neck first, and so will Fen. Trust me, Fen, it's a good idea. And Paws would appreciate some spring water. He's teetotal.'

'Volvic okay, Paws?'

Matt makes a face. 'He prefers Evian. Stop flapping, you're too easy to tease. We'll be fine. Mingle, darling, mingle! And where's *your* drink?'

Matt pours me a large white wine, and I don't mingle because Stephen and I get into a chat about theatre. With my extensive knowledge of theatre, this has the potential to be a very short chat. So I'm happy to let Stephen talk (in fact I'm delighted: a guest, at my party, talking – this is perfect). The last play he PR'd was superb, very witty, with

446

a marvellous cast. But they'd got in a cheesecake Hollywood actor – 'B-list is putting it kindly' – to star – 'put bums on seats' – and he'd ruined it – 'a plank of wood, centre stage' – and the rest of the cast were rabid – 'it demeaned their art'—

I'm so enjoying our conversation that I stop running to the doorbell every time it rings. Belinda trots in with cries of 'I swear I saw Jude Law comin aht the pub!' and the biggest Gucci handbag I've ever seen – it might even be a suitcase on a strap. An intensively tanned man with spiky hair and a good-natured grin trundles adoringly in her wake. I see Frannie arrive with a sour face (it sours further as she sees the place is packed with people who seem dangerously close to enjoying themselves).

Saul saunters in at *11.38* – this is a man who accords a cinema programme the same degree of punctuality as a wedding ceremony, insisting on being seated, with a bag of Maltesers and a can of Pepsi (purchased in advance from the newsagent in protest against Warner Village prices and smuggled in under his raincoat) *before* the advertisements start. And he arrives at my party at 11.38! Still, at least he came. (Chris left a terse message on my answer machine saying would I please never contact him again.) And then, twenty minutes later, I spot an FBI jacket.

I'm talking to Babs at the time. 'How long has Robbie been here?' I say, lighting a cigarette.

'You do give yourself away with those. He said hello to *me* about two hours ago. He probably meant to say hi but' – she nods at Frannie who has all but planted a stake in his personal space – 'got waylaid.'

I feel my mouth drying up. 'Did he come by himself?'

'Why do you ask?'

I glance at Robbie. He sees me looking, and pulls a rude face. But I'm the *host!*

'Do you, ah, think he might be annoyed with me?'

'What about?'

'Nothing. Doesn't matter.'

'So,' she grins, swigging from a can. 'Looking forward to Sydney? How do you think your parents will get on?'

'Badly,' I sigh, 'and well. It entirely depends on who's in the room at the time.'

'And do you think Tony will have a last-minute change of heart and hop on a plane?'

'Er, no,' I say.

'You never know. He might!'

'Babs, you know he won't,' I growl. 'Mel says he's still furious. He'd do anything for her, even sit through *Swan Lake*, but he still wouldn't come here tonight. I'm not too upset though. Mel seems to be confident that he'll ring me in the end. Which is a big step for mankind, don't you think?'

Drrrrrrrrrrrrrrrggggggggggggggggg!

'Sounds familiar,' mutters Babs.

I sashay (involuntary in pink snakeskin) to the door, and heave it open.

And there he is.

'This time,' he says, 'I'm not going away.'

I gaze at him and my throat does its usual trick of seizing up. I take a deep restorative breath – from what I *think* Alex calls my jurassic abdominals, but I'll have to check – and say, 'I wasn't going to ask you to.'

He blinks.

'In fact,' I add, 'I was expecting you earlier.'

He shoves his hands into his pockets and replies, 'I thought I'd wait till midnight. I thought if things didn't work out I could turn into a pumpkin.'

'The *coach* turned into a pumpkin,' I say. 'Get your food facts right.'

He laughs. 'You look fantastic,' he adds. 'I hardly recognised you.'

'Thank you. That's the nicest compliment I've received since Mel arrived.'

'What I mean is' – he nods at me, shyly – 'you look a million times better. Happier, and stronger. Really. Like you're looking after yourself. Like you could rule the world. Maybe I *should* go away again, if this is how you do without me.'

I grab his hand, and the words flow. 'Not so fast, schweetheart. I've been straightening myself out. I want to be well. It's quite a long boring haul. I thought I'd spare you some of it.'

Andy smooths his thumb over my palm, pressing it into the flesh. 'I don't want to be spared anything,' he says, stroking my skin. 'There's nothing you can do that will put me off you.'

'What about if I wander about the flat eating Nutella straight from the jar?'

He gives me a reproving look. 'Natalie,' he says. 'Nutella is *meant* to be eaten straight from the jar. Eating it with bread is plainly ridiculous.'

I smile. 'I am a lot better. But, I lapse. And, yesterday' – a perverse part of me wants to shock him with the grim, unladylike truth – 'I'd eaten like a well person all day, and then I did the Nutella thing and I walked into the bathroom and saw myself – no make-up, wearing pyjamas, spoon in hand – and I thought, is there any woman, alone in the house, who takes a big scoop of Nutella from the jar, looks in the mirror, and loves herself for it? There wasn't *loathing*. But it wasn't a great feeling. I wanted to, you know' – I force myself to speak – 'be sick. I wasn't. I don't do that any more. I was proud of that. But Andy, it's a very low-grade kind of pride.'

I look into his eyes, challenging. He hasn't stopped massaging my palm. He replies, 'Nat. Forget the Nutella, forget the mirror, forget other women. The real question is, do you love yourself? If you enjoyed shooting ocelots for their fur, or smacking babies, then you'd have a reason to doubt yourself – your empathy for other living things. But this is about your empathy for you – it's about you accepting you. Unless you're hurting someone, pride or shame shouldn't apply.' Andy clears his throat. 'Once,' he adds, 'in college, I woke up hungover, groped for the pint glass of water by my bed, and drank it, except – and remember the toilet was down the hall – it turned out not to be *water*. Not my finest hour. But, I promise you, I'm still a nice bloke.'

He lifts my right hand and gently waggles each finger in turn. 'This,' he says, 'is a special hand. It belongs to someone precious. But she was sloppy. She didn't read the manufacturer's instructions properly. She ditched the batteries. And it took her a while to see that she wasn't working and that she'd better take more care. And though it was a big yawn, paying attention to the small print, that's what she did. And' – his voice dips to a whisper – 'now, she's working beautifully.'

I banish the tears to the back of my throat. We look at each other for a long while. 'You know,' he murmurs. 'My hygiene habits have improved since college. I'm 99 per cent sure you won't catch anything.'

I giggle. 'Hey, Prince Charming,' I say. 'You know all the best lines. There's a really revolting slipper in your old bedroom. Let's go and see if it fits.'

Read on for a taste of
Anna Maxted's wonderful new novel
Behaving Like Adults

See back page on how to order your copy

Chapter 1

Modern women don't believe in love. Believing in love carries roughly the same stigma as wearing court shoes. It's as old-fashioned as going on a diet (as opposed to a detox). It suggests you have no sense of irony and you like Meg Ryan films. A modern woman cannot accept that Father Christmas is a fraud *and* persist in believing that one sunny day her dark handsome destiny will appear in a puff of Fahrenheit and haul her off to Happy Ever After.

I know all that and yet, I *do* believe in love. I apologise. But I can't help it. I presume it's a genetic blip which might also account for my dress sense. (Too pink.)

I just like stuff to be nice. That's even worse. If you wish to maintain even a shred of credibility, you have to be cynical and keep your mouth in a hard straight line even when you find something funny. I'm not stupid. I do know the world is cruel. But I always like to hope that it isn't. I test my *ahhhh!* count. You proceed through the day, listing every occasion you're prompted to think Ahhhh! You can't cheat and hire a puppy to peep out of a basket. Often, my total is horrific.

When I started the dating agency, Rachel crowed that *now* I'd see what people were really like. I wouldn't believe the lies they told to get laid! She said this as if I were either a nun, or a social retard who believed – despite living in a densely populated part of the planet for twenty-nine years – that seduction was about honing in on the obvious and blurting it. Whereas I'm well aware that if *that* were the case, the human race would have fizzled out in the Iron Age when Wilma stared at Fred and said, 'That's quite a small flintstone you've got there'. Sometimes, I think my friends confuse optimism with idiocy.

Of course unpleasant characters applied. When you launch a dating agency, even if you specify as we did that Girl Meets Boy was for the 'young and funky' (which no doubt deterred everyone in both of those categories), you invite weirdos to your door. It's Open Day for Oddballs. It's the Marilyn Manson Fan Club Parents Evening. But overall – despite the nutters, nerds, squares, sociopaths, oafs, halfwits, dummies, brutes, airheads and deviants gracing our files – the Ahhhh! count was immense.

Partly to distinguish ourselves from the Christians with an interest in ornithology brigade, and partly to discern if anyone out there possessed an SOH (a GSOH is a luxury), we asked silly questions on the application form. Even Nige – who'd only agreed to help out because he was between acting jobs and is nosy – agreed that the hoi-polloi were far wittier than he'd given them credit for. I particularly warmed to the twenty-seven-year-old man who replied to 'Do you have any talents?' with 'Probably not'.

Girl Meets Boy began as a business, but the people who used it fast melted my heart to a soft sticky caramel.

Also, towards the end of the great fiancé fiasco (*not* before in case you were wondering), it did occur to me that *I* might find someone. Don't mix business with pleasure? I thought it was a phrase made up by killjoys to stop you smiling at work. I was trying to enjoy what I'd achieved. I'd achieved *so* much, said everyone, I should be *so* proud. Oh, absolutely. I'd made sacrifices, but not whole lambs, more the odd chop. I should be happy.

When I'm told I should be happy, I start trying to measure it with a ruler.

Everything is a test. Rachel rings to say that the cab dropped her outside her flat whereupon she bade farewell to a loud luxurious fart, then turned and saw her neighbour padding up the path behind her. We howl with laughter, yes, but *is* that happy? The cat sits on my lap, her purr rumbles through me, and I sigh – that's happy, surely? I visit the arthouse cinema because I hate Warner Village (Village? It's not a village!) and I feel comforted by the fact they sell wholegrain flapjacks – even though I wouldn't eat one for a bet – and I *watch* myself do this, and I think, that woman, she's smiling, but is she happy?

Self-interrogation is dangerous. Your inner voice pronounces the obvious, 'You don't realise you're happy till it's gone', as if it's your fault for not keeping an eye out, thus making you feel worse than you do already. But you're not to blame. Mostly, happiness doesn't just drop from you like an apple from a tree. It trickles away silently, evaporating over the months and years, until one day, you feel a strange hollowness inside and you glance around and it hits you – despite all you own, your great, glorious success, you have nothing.

The good – and therefore unreported – news is that you can find it again. It might be a bit of a trek. If you haven't the least idea of your destination, the journey takes a little longer. But I'm your non-court shoe wearing proof. Rachel was right. I *did* discover what people were really like. And yet, after everything that happened, I got happy again. I still believe in love. As I said, I can only apologise. And explain.

When Nige suggested a party, to celebrate the success of Girl Meets Boy, I did wonder.

I had done well, creating a company from scratch and making it pay. Although, any old pinhead can *create* a company. They make it foolproof at Companies House – for around eighty pounds they hand you over a shrink-wrap company. All you, the pinhead, have to do is provide the names of the board of directors and their share allocation. I was the director, with seventy shares, and – in a selfless act – my younger sister Claudia was secretary, with thirty. (This was in lieu of pay, for the first month. Nige, however, preferred to resist bribes – that way, he said, he didn't feel 'obligated'.)

Another twenty quid to Companies House, and I could name my baby, Girl Meets Boy. Then, the most important part of any business plan, I found a good accountant. And that, give or take a bit of fuss, was it. My accountant did the bore's share of the paperwork, instructing me what I owed the taxman each month via apologetic email. This allowed me to devote myself to my real interest: making Girl Meets Boy a hit.

My strategy was unscientific. I hoped that if I ensured people had fun, and I shelled out for advertising, financial success would follow. And, after seven months, it did.

So did I really want to tempt fate and host a party? People *might* have fun, but it wasn't guaranteed. And you have to be pretty pleased with yourself to host a party. The subtext is, 'I'm *so* interesting, I think you should all come to my home and bring wine'. And parties are like cakes. They can fall flat for no apparent reason. Also, if you care the least bit about whether your guests are enjoying themselves, you are bound to have a stressed, hassled, fun-free time.

Nige, the arch manipulator, saw me hesitate and cried, 'Oh, go on! Everyone will have so much fun!'

I looked at his beseeching face and said, 'Let's do it.'

That's my weakness. I like other people. They interest me. There's hardly anyone you can't learn something from, even if it is, 'Check in the mirror, front *and* behind, before you go out'. Nige wanted cool and exclusive, but I thought we should do the bash Elton John style, invite the world, every member of Girl Meets Boy included. I felt protective towards them, as if they were my kids. Most of them I was fond of. When people trust you, it's hard not to like them. Even the annoying ones. This party would be a way of saying thanks.

My only problem was Nick. My ex-fiancé. Our

relationship was over, except he hadn't moved out. He was still waiting for his friend Manjit's girlfriend to clear out her spare room (an excuse so poor I wanted to huddle it in a blanket). The truth was, he wanted me back. I was past being flattered. Nick stayed fixed at that stage of emotional development where you yowl for whichever toy is removed from your grasp. I ended it too amicably for my own good. I feel sheepish about this. I think it's far worse for the Ender than the Endee. Especially an Endee as charming and wily as Nick. He'd guilt-trip me into inviting him to the Girl Meets Boy party, then worry me like a fox, all night.

Because of this, I wasn't overjoyed about going on my own. Normally, I wouldn't fret about it. If there's one thing I don't need a man for, it's to attend a party. They're a hindrance, every time. But this was different. I wasn't in the right frame of mind to be fighting off Nick the entire evening. I needed a safety barrier. Also, there was something about attending a party for Girl Meets Boy without a partner that bothered me. It felt too puritan. If *I* saw me there, alone, I'd be suspicious. Like meeting a baker who wasn't fat.

As Party Night loomed, Claudia tried to encourage me to pick a man off the pile. 'Come *on*, Holly,' she said, poking the morning's stack of letters with polished fingernails. 'It'll be like Cinderella in reverse. Just ring one up, and explain who you are. They'll be thrilled. A date with the boss of Girl Meets Yob. Plucked from obscurity to attend your grand ball. The token date. It's the kind of thing that gives blokes a kick. Or – or! or! or! How about this – you could ask Stuart again!'

I choked. Despite my devious plan of skimming off the single cream for myself, after time spent thinking about it, I'd gone off the idea. I felt *maternal* towards these men. Even the thirty-eight year olds. Thus, it would not have been healthy to shag them. Plus, I'd had one bad experience, which I'm unwilling to share because it was such a disaster. However, as I've just let slip the disaster's name, I might as well tell you, if only so you see what I was dealing with.

A month before, the PA of a solicitor named Stuart Marshall had emailed us, asking for an application form on his behalf. I sent it to her, but couldn't resist adding, 'Does he make you forge his Christmas cards too?' She replied, 'That's the least of it.'

Two days later, Stuart's details were delivered – by courier – to our office. Stuart's rapacious misuse of company resources gave him an air of benign familiarity. Despite never having set eyes on the guy, I felt I knew him. Claudia was half in love with Stuart already. She fell on that envelope like it was a fifty pound note.

Nige tweaked Stuart's photograph from her grasp. He arched an eyebrow, drawled, 'Whiff of the Channel Five Newsreader', and spun it through the air to me. Well. Possibly. Groomed like a racehorse. In blue Speedos. A lot of our clients do that – send us a snap that has more in common with *Readers' Wives*. Nige finds it 'sad and grotesque', but I tend to find it more *ahhhh* than *aaaagh*. It's only because they want to be accepted. They want to find someone. They're desperate to prove that they're good enough.

I understand that. It maddens me when I tell someone what I do and they sneer. We're biologically programmed to seek out nurturing relationships and yet, somehow, there are people who assume the attitude that this pursuit is *trite*. I tell them that those unable to empathise or forge rewarding bonds with others start by pulling the wings off bluebottles and end up breaking into people's homes and dismembering entire families. It usually shuts them up. So. I was more sympathetic to Stuart than Nige was. Even when Claudia stuck her feet on the desk and started to dissect Stuart's vision of the perfect woman.

'Jesus Christ, listen to this. ' "She should have a healthy zest for life" – as opposed to an unhealthy apathy – "she should be secure in herself and her choices" – blimey, he sounds like *you*, Nige!' (Claudia once overheard Nige telling a fellow thesp that he 'admired Brad Pitt's choices'. Unbelievably, Nige wasn't refering to Gwyneth or Jennifer, but to the genius decisions Brad made when acting a character. Quite rightly, she's never let him forget it.)

'"Not needy, but looking to share her passion and vitality," – what an arse! – "ambitious, but probably already sorted careerwise, able to maintain a balance between work and play, prepared to make quality time for her partner and friends, interests of her own but would share a love of good food, wine, company and exercise. She would enjoy long walks or runs along the beach" – sorry, but who *alive* doesn't enjoy a long sodding walk along the beach? – "and would enjoy riding high when I fly my plane" – good God, is he for real? What does that mean? Is it some sort of filthy pun? I bet it's not his, I bet he hires it.'

'He probably means his toy plane,' suggested Nige. 'He runs round the garden holding it above his head, he wants his perfect woman to watch from the upstairs window.'

Agreed, Stuart did sound a little – no, a *lot* – much, but I was intrigued. That superlative sense of self-entitlement always starts me wondering about the mother. Not the father, you'll note. Just the mother. I blame her. What a sexist. Shocking. 'Go on, Claw.'

Claudia grinned. '"She should ideally be at least 5 foot 7 but no taller than 5 foot 9, physically very active" – well, we all know what *that* means! – "have blonde hair" – no! surprise me! – "and be aged between 24 and 29. I would hope she has at least one relationship of respectable length behind her and has lived with a former partner. She should live in Zones 1 or 2" – unbloodybelievable – "however, ideally, she would not have any baggage (i.e. children or be divorced.) She would be a female version of me." Wow. Holly, you've *got* to go out with him!'

I'd tipped back on my chair to listen, and I nearly fell off it. 'What? I'm nothing like that woman! No one is! And you know what I'm like about flying. I panic if the pilot has a weak chin. Anyway. Why *me*? What have *I* done?'

I looked beseechingly around our cramped little office – paper everywhere, it seemed to grow from the walls and breed on the floor – hoping for Nige's support. When he pursed his lips, I knew I wasn't going to get it.

'It's what you haven't done,' he said. 'You need to take action, Holly. Show Nick that it's over. I know you're still fond of each other, but it's not wise, him still lurking round the house. You need him to witness that you've moved on to better things. Claw is right. Stuart is just the pissing contest that Nick needs. You needn't tell Stuart who you are. I'll ring him, tell him Girl Meets Yob is giving him a free, er, trial. If we deem an applicant to be, ah, a *VIP*, we don't put them straight into a speed dating session. We assign them what we call a "free-range" date with an elite *counterpart* that's unsupervised and can last as long as they wish. How's that sound?'

'Like bullshit,' I said.

Claw started banging her fists on the desk, shouting 'Yes, yes, yes!'

While I am old enough not to be intimidated by two people disagreeing with me, I am also wise enough to know when to save my breath. 'I'll think about it,' I lied. Well, *I* thought I was lying, but my mind had other ideas. It danced around Stuart the whole day. I want to make this clear, I wasn't *attracted* to Stuart – I'm not an insane sado-masochist who doesn't know Hitler's CV when she sees it – but Nige was right.

I *was* still fond of Nick, dangerously fond. We'd gone out for five years, most of which were good, great even. And then, we'd coasted. We were two parallel lines, always close but never together. Occasionally, we'd have a passionate row, during which many promises would be made. But not kept. Nick admitted that he didn't know how to make an effort in a relationship. I was his first, as he put it, Big One. Incidentally, when I say 'effort', I don't mean he didn't send enough roses or stud the walls with little love notes (although he didn't). I mean he didn't talk much, wash enough or seem to take particular pleasure in my company. Don't do me any favours.

But, if I had to pinpoint the single factor that drove me to Stuart, it was the Febreze. As Claudia and Nige hummed about me, murmuring, 'Go *on*, Holly, oh *please*, it'll be *fun*, etc', I thought of Nick, too lazy to shower, spraying his stinky feet with Febreze ('Safely eliminates odours on fabrics and kills the bacteria that cause them'). And then a ripple of hard-done-by billowed airily through me and I thought, 'Ah, why not? What harm can it do?'

How long have you got?

Chapter 2

I thought I was good at reading people. Is there anyone in the world who *doesn't* think they're good at reading people? I shouldn't have trusted myself. My judgment had already proved faulty with Nick. Why did I presume to know Stuart? The truth is, I'd painted my life into a corner. Instead of freeing me, every choice I'd made hemmed me in. It's a pity to regret, but I did. I needed an escape. And if you're dying in a desert, you'll see hope in air and dust.

I refuse though, to begin with Stuart. He'd love that, if I began with him. The best way to gall people who wish you ill is not to give them space in your head. There's a great put down in *Casablanca*, where Peter Lorre says to Humphrey Bogart, 'You despise me, don't you?' He replies, 'Well, if I gave it any thought I probably would.' I think that's funny. So, I'll start with me and Nick. Five years ago, when I met Nick, he was helping a duck.

I was driving through one of the quainter parts of London and I saw this duck waddling along the pavement. A thin young man with a cigarette hanging out his mouth sauntered behind at a respectful distance from madam's tailfeathers, ushering her away from the road. Everyone was ignoring them. Londoners are good at this. We can ignore *anything*. That disappoints me. I get a kick when I say hello to the ticket guy at my tube stop, and he says, 'All right, darlin',' and gives me a high five. It turns my city into a village.

Anyhow, I got the urge to offer the man and the duck a lift. I decided there was no way this guy was a lunatic, as he was helping a duck. So I swerved across the traffic and buzzed down my window. 'Excuse me,' I said, launching into one of the silliest sentences I've ever spoken, 'do you and the duck need a lift anywhere?' Then it struck me that the duck might be his pet. He could be taking her for a walk, and I'd just busybodied in there. In the smarter parts of town you can act like a complete nut and get away with it, so long as you own the matching bag.

So I was grateful when the man took the cigarette out of his mouth and smiled. 'It's very kind of you,' he said, 'but I think being in a Golf might scare her. I wouldn't want her getting in, you know, a flap.' He giggled at this bad joke, which made me smile, he then looked at me again. 'But you could always leave the car and help me get her back to the pond.' I parked on a double yellow, and together we directed Jemima towards her pond. We got as far as the Chinese restaurant when, very sensibly, she decided to fly the rest of the way. We returned to a parking ticket.

'You might as well make the most of it,' said Nick. 'Do you want to get an ice cream?'

Our relationship was not about being adult. Some couples race to become less liberal clones of their parents. Nick's best pal Manjit chose Bo, a woman who clamps down on fun like it's illegal. When Nick showed Manjit a new purchase – a shirt with a design of a cat, a cockerel, a donkey, a bird and a beaver on its back, plus the beautifully embroidered words, 'pussy, cock, ass, tit, beaver' – Manjit said mournfully, 'I wouldn't be allowed that.' Same when he saw the two electric love hearts dangling from the Golf's rear-view mirror. *Tacky*.

I felt sorry for Manjit, although privately I wondered what Bo could actually *do* to him if he bought a shirt like Nick's. Tear it off his back? Ignore him for a month? Refuse to leave the house with him? Stop hauling him to classical concerts and her school reunions? Manjit, buy the shirt. (He didn't, so I could only presume that in some way, he enjoyed the childish relief of relinquishing free will, one of the few advantages of shacking up with a dictator.)

Maybe Nick and I weren't so different after all. We gave each other permission to behave like babies. On the face of it, that was good. In any romantic movie, the universal code for 'these people are meant to be together' is a shot of the guy sitting opposite the girl in a diner gazing at her adoringly, as she stuffs down a burger, talks nonsense with her mouth open, oozing gunk, her cheeks bulging with bun, mustard dribbling down her chin – i.e., the precise opposite of how a woman eats on a date. The point is: it's okay to act like you're five, you are officially in paradise.

With Nick I acted more like I was five than when I *was* five. I was quite a serious kid. It took me until I met Nick to realise I'd passed up on half my childhood. Nick would say, 'Remember the episode of *Fawlty Towers* when Basil attacks the Mini?' and I'd blush and say, 'No.' He'd recall the time he bet Manjit that he could eat three tins of golden syrup, won the bet, but alas, puffed up and spent three days in hospital. Or when he and Manjit went exploring on their bikes and found a dead bullet by the stream. High on good citizenship, they'd sped it to the local police station, where officers had to practically stuff their hands in their mouths to keep from laughing.

To me, this was idyllic, a marvellous adventure tale, *Tom Sawyer* meets *The Secret Garden*. My upbringing was fine, nothing wrong with it. Just a little more cautious, conservative. Our TV was black and white, toaster-sized and kept in a cupboard. I was a bookworm. Whereas Nick lived the dream, I read about it. My parents are wonderful people, old-fashioned in their innocence, never expecting much. The first time we went on holiday to Portugal, I remember my father blinking in pleasure because the hotel had a pool. My mother looked cowed at her good fortune. It hurt me to see it in their eyes, *what have we done to deserve this?*

While they were keen to give us – me, Claudia and our

big sister Isabella – whatever we wanted, it never occurred to them that we could want more than we were given. Which was, books. Visits to stately homes. Museum trips. Two thousand piece jigsaws of English country gardens. Love. My parents never wanted more than they were given. My mother would have bitten off her tongue before she complained about anything. Her old friend Leila once gave her a cotton tissue-holder for Christmas. It must have cost 5p. A garage wouldn't dare give it you free with your petrol. Mum had bought Leila a painting by a local artist she admired.

It was painful to see my mother wriggle to excuse Leila. She didn't give a damn about the meanness; it was the lack of respect that got her. 'Well,' she said, 'money's tight for Leila. And you know Leila, she's a batty old thing.' Even though we both knew that 'batty' didn't cut it. Unless you're clinically insane, you know Tissue Holder As Gift is unacceptable. But I kept quiet. It's easier to forgive than to confront. If you've been slapped in the face, you don't need people saying, 'Gosh, you've been slapped in the face'. 'Why didn't she just give you a pooh wrapped up in a hankerchief?' cried Nick.

Yea, behold the miracle. My parents adored Nick. He could say, do anything, cheeky as you like; they were in awe, treated him like a prince. That meant a lot. I'm uncool, parental approval matters to me. In fact, *any* parental approval matters to me, probably to the extent of weirdness. Once, Nick and I saw a brilliant new band play their first big gig, and the frontman kept saying, in a croak of disbelief, 'This is incredible for us, thank you so much for coming.' All I could think was, 'His parents must be so proud.' That's my first thought, every time I see talented people on stage, 'Their parents must be so proud'. (My second thought is, I wish *I* could do that.)

The mindset, I suppose, of a woman resisting adulthood. I fell in love with Nick *and* his parents. I cherished the fact that he came from a glamorous family. His mother and

465

father, Lavinia and Michael Mortimer, were a revelation. Rich, sparkly, magical, mysterious, like the parents in *Peter Pan*. They travelled endlessly, collecting art. They campaigned for their favourite charities. They owned a villa in Italy, which they'd renovated from ruin a decade before Umbria became fashionable. They both spoke fluent Italian. I was so bedazzled, the first time I went there, that when Nick's mother offered me a dish of olives I went blind with fright. I reached for the brightest item on the plate, and she said kindly, 'No dear, that's a lemon.'

Nick's parents indulged him, like we all did. He entertained us. The first two years of our relationship I had a blast. I'd never been naughty – I was content, I hadn't felt the need. But it was liberating, to play. I thought it wild that I had a boyfriend whose job was to dress as Mr Elephant at children's parties. It endeared me that his small Islington flat was a shrine to grime, and that when his mother visited she would sigh, in her silvery voice, 'Oh *Nick*.' I didn't comment. If my man chose to live on hygiene's edge, I wouldn't interfere. I was proud of not trying to change him. So very modern of me. Nick and I spent a great many months in his king-sized bed screwing, drinking vodka, or both. Only twice was I bitten by a flea.

We bought a candyfloss maker from the Shopping Channel and ate pink candyfloss for breakfast. We got drunk and ran along the road swapping people's doormats and then, because I felt bad about it, we ran along the road swapping them back. We bought twenty squirty bottles of chocolate sauce and had a food fight in the garden until we and the grass were brown. I was thinking to myself, 'This is what couples do in films.' Then Nick stood up and said, 'I don't like this. It's like we're covered in pooh.'

I thought I was a secure person till I met Nick. Then I saw what it was to be heart and soul at peace with yourself. I do believe that people treat you as you present yourself, and Nick presented as a gift from God. Luck followed him around like a puppy. Nick's parents owned a big white boat, and Nick blew it up.

He'd filled it with fuel after a day on the river, turned on the ignition and *BANG!* The wooden deck splintered under his feet, flames shooting high everywhere. He grabbed my hand, and we jumped into the Thames. The boat sank. Or, as Nick told his father on the phone, 'Was lying low in the water.' A pipe had come loose and fuel had slopped into the engine. The firefighters said we *could* have had fifty foot flames. We were lucky it didn't explode. Lucky Nick.

It was his idea to buy a house together.

I was flattered. I don't mean that in a gee, lil ole me kind of way. I mean that I loved Nick so fiercely I wanted to eat him up. If I could have crawled inside his skin, I would have. I could almost understand the cannibalistic lust of Jeffrey Dahmer, my desire was so violent – some nights I'd sob aloud because one day we'd die and then what would I do if we weren't together for eternity? He felt the same about me. 'I worship you,' he said. 'Marry me.'

We found a house and bought it with less thought than some people buy a newspaper. (Islington flats, even small dirty ones, scrub up well and sell for silly money. Even my *non*-Islington flat, bought four years earlier when property was affordable, had in those four years earned more than I had.)

It was a riot, flying by the seat of our pants, cheating death. When you live apart, and meet for the good times, you can pretty much edit out the worst bits of yourself. The cold slap of joint property ownership put an end to *that*. Often, Nick would lie in bed till midday. He ignored bills, claiming an allergy to paperwork. He left a trail of crap behind him like a snail. I'd considered myself easy-going. Now, to my embarrassment, I found I wasn't.

'Let Nick face the consequences of his actions,' bossed my sister Isabella, a psychologist. 'If he doesn't water the plants, let them die. He'll learn.'

467

I didn't let the plants die. You don't nurture something, then let it die. Anyhow, I knew they'd die and he wouldn't notice. I consoled myself that Isabella counselled couples on how to argue effectively – be specific in your complaint, employ the pronoun 'I' not 'you', keep your voice calm and level – but when I enquired how *she* argued effectively with her husband Frank, she replied, 'I scream at him.'

I screamed at Nick. What next, cutting out recipes? Before I'd been proud that I didn't want to change him. Now I did, I discovered that I couldn't.

It hit me with a shock, that Nick wasn't playing hard before he embarked on forty years of working hard. This was *it*, for him. He'd continue to live like a student till he was sixty-five. There was no grand plan, no passion to make a success of his life. His idea of making a success of his life was to live in the moment, be happy. But, I thought, you need *things* to be happy. We didn't set a date for the wedding.

I was ambitious. I wasn't going to end up like my parents – meek, humble, grateful for crumbs. Nick, it struck me, *was* like them in that he accepted whatever happened to him. His fatality bordered on Australian. He had an end of the rainbow approach to finances. He was pleased for me to earn the cash. My career became a sanctuary. At the office I could blank out the rage that pulsed through me when my metal hairpins jabbed my scalp because Nick had absent-mindedly picked off their smooth plastic ends. Because he refused to behave even the teeniest bit like an adult, *I* was forced to grow up and I resented it.

I was an imposter. Do adults think, 'This book I'm reading matches my pyjamas'? Blush when a shop assistant calls them 'Madam'? Feel heartless when trading in their rusty old car for a new shiny one? Fold a black and white checked dishcloth onto the cat's head and proclaim her Yasser Alleycat? Eat all the chocolate off a KitKat first? Lie on the floor and wish they lived on the ceiling? Stroke their childhood toy (not that Fluffy is real, but just in *case*)? Jab

468

a knife into the toaster while it's still on? No? Well then. I was an adult at work, taking care of others, but I refused to be that at home. Inside, I was still a little girl. Because you're not truly grown up until you're what, fifty?

Our relationship dropped sheer off a cliff. I kept more and more of me to myself. Nick didn't offer to make me a coffee, so why should I leave him any cherries? He never wrote down my phone messages, so why should I tell him he was missing *Larry Sanders*? I was a hypocrite. I had endless goodwill for the world and none for Nick. I'd watch the RSPCA's TV appeal and phone them £500 to repent for the human race. Same for the NSPCC, guilt by association. But I'd spit and boil when Nick begged a fiver. So much for our eternal love. It couldn't survive a broken dishwasher.

Yet, when I thought about ending our engagement, I felt panicked, sodden with dread, my insides heavier than I could carry. But then I didn't want to be fifty-eight, married, miserable and marooned, looking back on a shadow of a life. Girl Meets Boy was a joy for me, but I needed something separate, outside it. I didn't blame Nick wholesale. He hadn't changed, I had. He was the love of my life. But he was also, undeniably, the catalyst that turned me into a person I didn't much like.

I told him it was over on what must have been the prettiest night of the summer. A fat moon lay low, heavy and golden, in the sky. Earlier, the setting sun had tinted the streets and houses pink. I chose to take all this as a cosmic sign: it's not the end of the world. But, fuck, it felt like it.

To read more, buy the brand new book by Anna Maxted

Behaving Like Adults £6.99 (recommended retail price)

Available at WH Smiths and all good bookshops

Or by ordering direct on 01624 677237

www.randomhouse.co.uk